The Tokyo Diversion

The David Knight Series
Book 2

Tony Ollivier

Reviews

"A globetrotting espionage adrenaline rush that hooks from start to finish."
— **Robert Dugoni, International & NY Times Bestselling Author of the Tracy Crosswhite Series**

"Ollivier delivers again with non-stop action and high stakes."
— **Eileen Cook, Author of *You Owe Me a Murder***

"...if you think for a second that a dancer can't be the lead character in a spy thriller, you've just been proven, dead wrong."
— **Jeff Messick, Author of *Knights of the Shield* and the *Mage Hunter Series***

"The Tokyo Diversion is a deep study of relationships among trusted allies and corporate greed run amok, something that's pertinent in today's world. It's a fun, roller-coaster thrill ride that will have you checking your pulse rate multiple times before you reach the exciting conclusion. Once you get there, you'll immediately be craving more."
— **Benny Sims, Award winning Author of *Code Gray* and *Mile Marker Zero***

"The Tokyo Diversion is a Ludlumesque thriller for the modern age. When a young girl's blood holds the key to curing cancer, only ballet dancer David Knight can save her from the nefarious plans of software billionaires. In this sequel to The Amsterdam Deception, David heads to Tokyo to battle billionaires and their yakuza friends."

— **DC Palter, author of *To Kill a Unicorn: a Silicon Valley Mystery***

Jack Remick and Robert Ray

The Tokyo Diversion

Chapter One

"A girl in trouble is a temporary thing"
- Romeo Void

Kabukicho, Shinjuku, Tokyo

YUMI HATTORI PRESSED her hand against the narrow window of her Kabukicho accommodation, the gold charms on her bracelet tinkling against the frame. Her favourite, the ballet dancer in a full pirouette, caught the light from her room. She sighed, remembering a love of dance that felt three lifetimes ago. Touching her forehead to the glass, she watched hundreds of neon signs twinkle through the drizzle advertising bars, cafes, massages, and short-term hotels. The most infamous red-light district in Japan, Kabukicho's many tiny alleys filled with hidden staircases and doors promised anonymity. She had hoped to remain invisible for a long time.

She was wrong.

The men looking for her would be outside on the street, in a doorway, or at a corner. Under umbrellas. Probably a team of three. One near the door. The other two hanging close.

Just like the last time.

Like predators, the men wanted her to run so they could drive her into a narrow alley. At first, she hadn't known better. Young, naive, and trusting; the men said they just wanted to talk. She was pregnant and sick thanks to a love affair that got carried away. Maybe if she had accepted her lover's offer, she wouldn't be in this situation.

They brought her to a man who told her he would pay for her time. He flashed lots of yen, and she thought because they'd taken her to a clinic of sorts, he had a medical fetish. She expected to be asked to dress up as a nurse or doctor. Instead, she was the patient. The other two stood like sentinels outside the tiny room, while inside the first man drew blood. He performed it expertly, wrapping a band around her arm to make her veins pop before using a needle and tube to extract several vials of blood. The man paid in real bills and wanted to see her every day.

Each interaction was the same; he'd draw a few vials of blood and then give her money. Each prick of the needle made her hate herself for ever agreeing to it. Then they wanted her to stay the night. When she realized their ultimate intent, she almost didn't get away. She didn't dwell on what might have happened if she hadn't.

They thought she was just another faceless Japanese bar girl. She had few friends and virtually no relatives. Her mother died when she turned ten. Her father didn't exist. A series of aunts provided a futon, a place to sleep, and some food; nothing more. When she was old enough, she left the last aunt without saying goodbye. A pattern in her life she realized much later.

She shook her head at the thought and just accepted what it was. *Shouganai* in Japanese meant 'it can't be helped.' She had escaped the men with everything intact.

Months later, with the help of an old friend, she found a woman that would take the baby. Adoption agencies were almost unheard of in Japan and foster care wasn't a good option. Most Japanese didn't want to raise children that weren't their own. However, the woman said she knew a husband and wife that would take the child, no questions asked. She said the family was middle class and would be good parents. Yumi wanted the child to have a better life than she did.

The baby had been sleeping when she gave her away. She remembered the tears that welled up inside her, but the image of her baby growing up with a better life than hers allowed her to go through with it.

The image of the baby's father surfaced again; she hadn't thought about him for a long time. Something that couldn't be helped. She shook her head to push all the memories away. She had to escape and didn't need any distractions.

She pulled off the fake gold earrings, followed by the silver wig and the stilettos, before squeezing out of her shiny blue tube dress. As a hostess in several tiny bars in Osaka, Kyoto, and now Tokyo, she listened to sad stories from junior salary men wanting a beautiful woman to pay attention to them. She did what they paid her for and in return, she kept in shape, helped by exercise, careful eating, and her lucky genetics. She occasionally moonlighted with select customers that could afford her higher rates.

As a hostess, she needed celebrity-level elegance. She spent money on makeup and, once a month, splurged on a haircut.

Tonight, like a few times before in the last dozen years, she abandoned her carefully curated persona without hesitation.

Yumi pulled on jeans, sneakers, a white sweatshirt embossed with the English word "Addiction" in capital letters, and a matching gold-rimmed baseball cap with a long ponytail of black hair hanging out the back. The disguise was important, but transformation mattered more. For her escape, she chose big rimless glasses and pushed the look of a rich and spoiled fan girl. Even though she was almost thirty-five, she still looked like she was in her twenties.

The Mama-san had said men came to the club and asked for her by name. Her real name. She said they came back three nights in a row and described intimate physical characteristics, including a tattoo only Yumi knew about. She asked the Mama-san if the men were yakuza, and she said she wasn't sure.

Yumi had been running for a long time and for a while she felt safe, as if the men had stopped looking. But they hadn't.

They wanted her blood.

She overheard a conversation during the testing when they thought she was sleeping. Her blood was the key and a white man required it; no, needed it, like some kind of vampire.

Well, he wasn't going to get it.

After mentally saying goodbye to the room, she rushed out the door with a small backpack, wallet, phone, and a passport with her picture and someone else's name. Her money wasn't available until morning. She didn't trust banks; they needed too much personal information. Instead, she had an account at Tokyo Personal Deposit—a private facility that required only money to rent a box. Access was via an RFID card provided by the company. In the morning, she'd empty her safe deposit box, and hop on the Narita Express to the airport. Once there, she'd convert to euros and US dollars and take the first flight out. Maybe to Hawaii or even Canada. São Paulo had a big Japanese population—if they were looking for her, she didn't want to be an easy target. She had skills in many areas and would have no trouble blending in wherever she landed.

At the bottom of the stairs leading up to her tiny room, she stood inside the open door to the street and watched. The drizzle continued, and the neon reflected off the shiny stone sidewalk. Kabukicho swarmed with overworked salarymen looking for love, sex, or any kind of distraction as long as it finished before the trains stopped. She waited until a group of laughing adults, all looking just over twenty, walked past the door. She merged into their stream, and her change of clothes made her look like a clone of the other women.

Behind her wide glasses, she thought casual thoughts and kept a karaoke-girl smile. Transformation, not disguise. Her appearance could change, yet if she walked nervously, they'd catch her. An article she once read said victims had a particular gait. She imagined singing with this group and pushed out the fear of abduction. Instead, she visualized that she didn't have a care in the world.

After about fifteen minutes of winding her way through the cramped streets with this group and then others, she reached the Shinjuku train station as hordes of people streamed through the wide hallways. No one gave her a second look, although she felt herself being watched. Her face hurt from her perpetual smile.

On the Yamanote Line platform, the train rumbled into the station, stopped, and doors opened, spilling drunk men and perpetually thin women trying not to make eye contact onto the platform.

Behind her, near the wall, she noticed two salary men keeping to themselves. Not raucous like the others. Quiet. Stoic even. They wore the same uniform: black suits, white shirts, and dark ties. Except they were larger and heavier than the skinny ones that only ate ramen for dinner. Well-dressed and looked like third-generation criminals. Crime in Japan had gotten muddled over the last twenty years. Government legislation targeted organized crime, but that didn't stop the crime from happening. Crime was crime; just the players and their affiliations had shifted.

The two men had either followed her to the station or the people looking for her had used a bigger crew. More men meant more money and bigger stakes in whatever game they played. They would think she'd be an easy pickup. Shadow her on the subway until she jumped off. Then, as they bumped into her, one of them would jab her with a needle and lights out.

With her smile intact, she sidled up to a younger man wearing leather pants with a girl dressed like her on his arm. Yumi grabbed his free arm and laughed. "Nice to see you again!"

He squinted through his red-rimmed eyes and smiled. The eye-candy on his other arm was tipsy, too. Good. No need for any kind of rational thought from either of them.

She pulled Leather Pants' arm, and he followed like a trained donkey. The girl trailed without argument. As she entered the train, the two men pushed off the wall and jumped towards the closing doors, making it inside just as the doors closed.

Leather Pants had a momentary lapse into reality. "Do I know you?"

"Yes. Last week at the club." Yumi flashed another big smile.

Leather Pants nodded and frowned slightly as if he tried to make sense of what she told him. Last week. Club. Girl. Last week.

After five minutes, the train pulled into Harajuku Station and the doors slid open with clusters of people exiting first before others entered. She kept smiling at Leather Pants, relaxed as if she waited for the train to continue. As the doors started closing, she squeezed through the almost shut doors to the platform. The two thugs didn't react quick enough and the big one pounded the door as the train pulled out of the station.

Gotcha. She wasn't paranoid, after all. The complex Tokyo subway and train system hopefully would prevent thugs at every station. However, she didn't want to be exposed on the street longer than needed.

She hustled down the stairs and out to the street. After pulling the yen and credit cards she filched from Leather Pants, she dropped the empty wallet behind the garbage can. His credit cards would provide her some invisibility, as he wouldn't notice the wallet gone until morning.

A yellow Tokyo taxi waited on the street. She raised her hand, and the passenger door in the back seat opened as if by magic. Japan was full of these incongruities. Old men paid prostitutes to dress up like schoolgirls, and white-gloved taxi drivers always opened the door for their customers.

Twenty minutes later, she entered a room in a tiny love hotel in Dogenzaka. The love hotel hill area had a cluster of small and quirky hotels, each with its own theme and colours. Yumi went deeper into the area to choose one that looked rundown from the outside, but she knew the inside would be acceptable. Plus, she didn't need to talk to anyone as a touch screen and tap credit card machine were all she needed to book the room. She selected overnight as the length and the best-looking suite they had. Leather Pants' credit card worked fine. In the morning, she'd take a taxi to her bank and grab her money to disappear where the white man would never find her.

She hoped.

Chapter Two

Yorkville, Toronto

DAVID KNIGHT WOKE DRENCHED in sweat beside a woman he didn't know. Candy or Candice. Possibly Catherine. He had paid little attention when she picked him up.

He laid his head back on the silk pillows as the dampness evaporated in the cool air. Crumpled linen sheets lay on the bed and floor. He and the girl had engaged in some heavy gymnastics, and she didn't seem to have minded messing up the room.

The dream came every night, and he remembered little of it.

Other than the terror.

Candace or Candy or possibly Catherine rolled over, her breasts pointing towards the ceiling. She had approached him at a club on Toronto's Adelaide Street. He'd been standing at the bar, noticing everything. Where the exits were and the size and capability of the bouncers. He noticed her across the room and watched as she sidled up to him, wearing expensive shoes and a more expensive dress. He wore a dark t-shirt, black jeans, and a well-worn pair of Converse sneakers. The dark room hid the shoe's imperfections but he didn't think she was looking at him for his fashion choices. She smiled as she drew the tip of her right finger down his chest while holding a big martini in her other hand. She talked about her job and smelled as good as she looked.

He told her he was a dancer. She said dancers were paupers, and she was a patron of the arts. She glanced at his shoes and smiled. She offered to buy him a drink, and he nodded to the bartender. A Scotch. Neat. Short glass. He picked the glass up, swirled it around, and touched his lips to the edge. Tasting would kick in his alcohol allergy, but he could sniff all he wanted.

A year ago, he wouldn't have been in the bar or allowed a random woman to pick him up. He had just become an apprentice dancer with the National Ballet of Canada and never stepped out of line, but then everything changed. On his first tour with the company in Amsterdam, he had been abducted and implanted with memories of a dead spy. Over the next couple of weeks, he was chased, attacked, and almost killed several times. When he returned to Toronto, with the help of a US government agent he didn't like, he did his best to forget what had happened.

However, the implant left him with the echoes of another person, like craving the heady fumes from a glass of whiskey or his vigilance being turned all the way up.

Her black sleeveless mini-dress showed her gym-toned arms and the rest of her beautiful body. She took care of herself. He knew her matching patent leather pumps were thousand-dollar Jimmy Choos. That meant she had money. She hadn't introduced him to her friends at the corner of the bar, but he noticed a glance and a smile when she closed the deal with him. The women both smiled back in approval. She was smart not to hook up without having another person provide some oversight to her decision.

He had waited for her to finish her drink and take his hand. He followed her out of the club, and they took an Uber back to her place.

She lived in a nice place. Granite counters and stainless-steel appliances. West Elm furniture and a few tasteful sculptures. The condo felt like it was all her and not somebody else. Not like his. Not even close. He lived in a basement suite, sharing the dungeon with another dancer in a shitty part of town. The girl had money and he had none. She said something about working in the financial sector. Trading stocks. US,

Canadian, Euros. He had faked interest. Once they had arrived at her condo, all the talking stopped. She kicked off the shoes, and the dress fell to the floor.

That was two hours ago. Time to go.

She rolled over again and mumbled something without waking up. He pulled a sheet off the floor and covered her naked body.

Rising out of the bed, he dressed. Two condom wrappers lay beside the bed. If she wanted to, she could find him. Even though Toronto had a sizeable dancer community, he could be found easily. However, he didn't expect to see her again.

He tugged on his shoes and let himself out. A quick trip in a mirrored elevator down to the lobby and then out the front of her swanky Yorkville condo. The door locked behind him.

She'd had more to drink than just that martini. Probably a weekly ritual. He drank cranberry juice and soda and kept the scotch for the aroma. In the morning, he'd be sweating out the extra sugar in a ballet class while she nursed a hangover.

At 1:00 a.m., Toronto was a different place. Calm for a few hours with only the occasional ambulance racing somewhere. He appreciated the stillness and the privacy as he walked south through the blocks of Canada's rich and almost famous. He considered taking a cab, except he knew his meager cash had to hold out a couple more days until payday. Plus, a walk would clear his head.

He thought about the dream again. Pinpoints of light and how heavy he felt when he woke. His final memory was not being able to move as if he was submerged in concrete.

Always the same. He pushed and pushed and broke free of whatever held him down, and then he woke. Usually drenched in sweat.

He gleaned no meaning from it. He tried to pull back the curtains and didn't get anywhere. The dream was a sharp-toothed invisible monster. He could make up a story about his life or career choices, except no explanation ever rang true.

Maybe the dream wasn't a dream and instead another memory that wasn't his. Something told him not to poke at it.

As he crossed Bloor Street, heading south on a sidewalk, a solitary hot dog vendor stood with a line of club-goers waiting for a tube of meat in a bun. Japanese twist. Wasabi and Kobe beef. Late-night exercise always made him hungry, and he knew he might have a fiver somewhere. He pulled out his wallet and stared at a couple of fifties and a wad of twenties, plus the single five. Three hundred dollars.

Shit. The girl must have slipped the bills inside before the gymnastics began.

For services rendered. He grimaced, and a deep ache filled his stomach. He should be mad or at least indignant, but he wasn't. Had she gotten the wrong impression? Or perhaps the mistake was all on him. He thought about returning to her condo and giving the money back until he realized the only cash in his wallet was from her. Instead, he turned to the hot dog vendor and ordered one with everything, paying for it with a crisp twenty. A small note was stuck to one of the bills. "For new shoes." She had noticed, after all. He made himself a promise on his next paycheck he'd invest in a nice pair. Maybe Tom Ford or even splurge for Gucci.

As he waited for the hot dog, he checked his email on his phone. Some random spam for the dance world and a few audition emails from other dance companies. Stuttgart, NY City Ballet, and San Francisco. Dancers moved around as they grew in their careers. Some followed choreographers, and some wished to live abroad. However, David preferred to stay in Toronto, but the last time he'd thought about it was over a year ago.

Now he wasn't so sure.

He read a job posting for a Canadian ballet teacher to teach in the US. The same one showed up every few weeks and he just deleted it. The rumour was a couple of teachers applied but didn't get anywhere. He was too young to move from performing to teaching, anyway. The hot dog guy handed him the tube steak, and he stuffed the phone into his back pocket.

The first bite was extra delicious. It might have been the Kobe beef or that he used the money he'd received for his performance with the woman. *All the world is a stage,* went through his head. Maybe the payment was justified.

Everyone performs for someone.

He wiped his fingers with a single napkin served by the vendor and dropped it in a bin before continuing his walk home.

A few minutes later, a wide wooden door to a strip joint flew open as he walked past. Two bouncers pushed a fat guy and a skinny guy in expensive suits out onto the street. They looked like stockbrokers. The fat one sported a large gold watch that looked like a Rolex. The skinny guy had no watch but had a half-eaten burger in his hand.

Why was a guy with a $15,000 wristwatch causing a problem at a strip club?

"Assholes, we weren't doing anything!" the big guy said.

"No touching the dancers. We warned you once. Two strikes and you are out. Go home."

"This is a strip joint. What else are we supposed to do?"

The bouncers ignored them, walked back inside, and pulled the door shut. David chuckled before turning and continuing his walk. Money apparently wasn't an indicator of intelligence. The show was over.

"Hey you, asshole! Are you laughing at us?"

David continued. Without thinking, he squeezed his hands into fists. But his usual anger never appeared.

"Asshole in the T-shirt. I'm talking to you!"

He stopped. A burning sensation started down at his toes and moved up. *Just walk away*, he told himself. Something hit his back. The hamburger the skinny guy carried now lay in a lump on the sidewalk.

"Hey! That's right. I'm talking to you. You were laughing at us, shit-for-brains, weren't you?"

The big guy gestured at him, his fine wool jacket open and his gut hanging over his pants. Brooks Brothers suit. Two thousand dollars, probably. The guy had money for sure and maybe still thought he was the star player on the football team.

He half-expected the spy's memories to slide into his consciousness and take over, kicking ass and not taking names. He even remembered the voice coming through him like a spirit had possessed him. In some ways, it had.

Yet, as he waited for the familiar feeling, nothing happened. Maybe the other guy was on permanent vacation. Or the two drunk idiots were not a threat. David wanted no part of James Bond's memories, anyway.

He could outrun these jerks but he didn't want to. Two drunk assholes were threatening him. One threw a burger at him. Big deal. His life wasn't in danger. His only worry was that the guy's awful breath could knock out a moose.

"You guys are having a lousy night. Why make it worse for everyone else?"

The fat man moved closer. His thick arms stretched the fabric of his jacket. Twenty years ago, he could probably do a sit-up. Not anymore.

From the side street, a woman appeared and tried hailing a cab. She didn't make eye contact.

"Billy boy, that's the slut that had us thrown out!" The fat man pointed at the woman. She started walking away.

Where were those bouncers? David thought.

"Hey, baby? Come and party with us!" The man's attention moved from David as he started walking towards her.

David stepped between the big man and the woman. "You need to back away."

"And what are you going to do?" the man said and launched a thick punch towards David's head. David ducked and grabbed the man's arm and pulled down hard. Already off-balance, the man fell face-first onto the sidewalk.

The skinny guy screamed at David before swinging with both hands at once. David stepped to the left and swept his leg under the second man, crashing him to the sidewalk.

Two dickheads in suits. Rich dickheads, more than likely. He looked down at the fat man. The crystal on his Rolex had cracked from smacking the concrete. Too bad. So sad.

A yellow cab pulled up, and the woman opened the door. She turned to David and smiled. "Want a ride?"

"No thanks. I'm walking."

"Thanks for your help. Come and see me sometime. Ask for Nina."

The taxi sped away. David looked down at the heap of men. Both were dazed, a little bloodied, but not dead. The police patrolled downtown Toronto religiously, so a car and hopefully a paddy wagon would show up in a few minutes.

Not his problem.

He walked down Church Street and then to Jarvis, still heading south. He was buzzing from the adrenaline and realized he didn't feel any pain. Last year, after he seized control of his body from the memories, he was overcome with incredible pain almost to the point of blacking out. After this almost-a-fight with two drunks, he felt nothing. Not even a slight headache. He had reacted to the threat and took appropriate action. Maybe the over-the-top memories were gone. The echoes of the other man left him with confidence where he had little before and anger where he should have none.

This was a good thing. He wanted to be David without the extra super-spy flavoring.

Or did he?

He thought and acted differently after the incident. He knew the other dancers whispered about him.

When he returned to Toronto, he felt the anger. Low level, but always present. He thought at first it might be PTSD from the incident. Even his close friend Frederic Razour—or as his friends called him, Razor—had told him he didn't like the new level-five-edgy David. Except for what Razor took for edge, David experienced as vigilance. On the subway, on a bus, and even just walking, he observed everything. Sounds. Movement. Smells. Everything registered in his brain like a security camera.

Then Razor left the ballet company and moved far away.

Without Razor's presence to help him moderate his own anger, the other dancers grew distant and his temper increased. Maybe that's what attracted that girl and the others to him. Some kind of animal pheromone thing. Alpha male and all that.

The ballet company had sent him to a shrink who diagnosed him with PTSD. Although he didn't believe it, he agreed with the label to appease the artistic director.

Some days, the anger helped. Like tonight. Candy or Candice or possibly Catherine came on to him and ignored better-dressed men with probably more money in their wallets. She wanted David and David only. No action on his part. He stood at the bar and waited. Sometimes a testosterone overdose worked to his benefit.

Physically, he danced better. His reflexes were sharper. His timing was exact.

Yet, no matter what he tried or what he did, the echo of someone else's life sat behind the veil. He felt the adrenaline dissipate as his body relaxed, but vigilance stayed high. He felt always ready to attack, even with no imminent danger.

All dressed up and no place to go. Except to his shitty apartment to get some sleep for another day.

Chapter Three

Queens Quay, Toronto

"Back at 2 p.m. for rehearsal," the ballet mistress said.

The room exploded in applause, and then a few dancers rushed out of the dance studio with bags whipped over their shoulders. Most talked and smiled with others before sauntering out to the hallway. A few glanced toward David, but most walked away as if he wasn't there. He had gotten used to feeling like an invisible troll to the rest of the company. No sneering or whispers, either. Just general apathy.

For the first few months after returning from Amsterdam, the troupe had been overjoyed in his and Razor's return. However, Razor soon became sullen and withdrawn because of problems with his injuries at the hand of a contract killer. David had tried to help his best friend, attending his doctor's appointments with him for the concussion he'd received and sitting patiently, watching as his friend went through hours of rehabilitation, until he finally realized the source of Razor's depression.

Razor couldn't dance anymore. The concussion had thrown off his balance and timing for a role he'd trained his entire life for. A few weeks later, Razor stopped returning David's texts and moved out of his apartment, leaving the ballet and Canada behind to teach English somewhere in Asia.

He never said goodbye.

After a couple of months, another dancer sent Razor's new number to David. A weird area code. He tucked it away on his phone and never called his old friend. David blamed himself for Razor's injury, even though he had no control over anything that happened to them in Amsterdam.

David stood in the center of the studio and practiced a sequence of steps from one of his variations. He wanted to work on his turns and fine-tune a short progression before the afternoon's rehearsal.

The remaining dancers grabbed their water bottles and hiked their dance bags over a shoulder before walking out of the studio. An older man stood just outside the door, leaning hard on a cane. A shiny gold bracelet hung on his thin wrist. After the dancers left, he hobbled into the room. Some men used a cane as a fashion accessory, but this man used it to keep standing.

"David," Fitz said.

He hadn't seen Asher Fitzsimmons since just after Amsterdam. The ex-pat Brit and former spy master looked older and frailer than he would have expected. He had first met Fitz when the memories of his dead friend had been forcibly implanted in David's head.

"The leg giving you trouble?"

"The leg, the hip, the knee, the foot. I prefer the cane to the wheelchair my surgeon has tried to force upon me. It also gives me a weapon if I get in a tight spot." He eased himself down on a chair near the door and winced.

"I suspect it would be hard to force you to do anything. What's with the new jewelry?" He pointed to the gold bracelet on Fitz's wrist.

"Part style and part protection. I will tell you more about it sometime."

The pianist, a middle-aged woman with poofy hair, jammed her music into a leather bag and left the studio without glancing at either man.

"Why don't the other dancers like you?"

"Why would you say that?"

"I'm old, not blind. No one looked your way when they left. If I didn't know better, I'd suggest the group seems afraid of you. Have you always had this effect on people?"

"No."

"Maybe because you aren't the same person you were before the incident in Amsterdam."

"Incident? You make it sound like a traffic accident."

"Forgive me. Your abduction, the implant, your escape, and the chase you led us on across Europe."

"During which crazy people tried to kill me."

"Many times, as I remember."

David took a long swallow from his water bottle. "Yet you stood by and let a mad scientist inject me with whatever brain goop they had lying around."

"I've apologized before, and I've worked to make amends. So has Westlake."

David grabbed a sweatshirt from the floor and pulled it over his head. "Yes, you both have. For a situation I should have never been involved in."

"I agree. If your friend Razor hadn't taken drugs of his own volition earlier that night, I might be talking with him today instead of you."

Fitz was right, but that didn't make David feel any better. He looked back into the old man's eyes and saw some empathy towards him. First time he'd seen that.

"And how are you doing now?" Fitz asked.

"I'm angry."

Fitz grinned like the Cheshire cat. "I've gathered that. There are so many things to be angry about. Global warming, the war on drugs, male pattern baldness. Anything, in particular, bothering you?"

David looked off into the corner of the room as if he had forgotten something. "Nothing and everything. I'm upset when I ride the subway, then pissed when the girl in front of me at the coffee shop can't decide between a scone and a muffin, and I'm mad when a dancer can't get the steps."

Fitz looked around the studio. A polished ballet barre jutted out from tall mirrors running along one wall. "When we were in Paris, what did you tell me you wanted?"

"To get my life back."

"Didn't you?"

He nodded. "It's not the life I had. Something changed, and I don't know what it is."

Fitz touched the top of his cane. David wondered if a knife was hidden inside. "Westlake contacted me," Fitz said.

"When?"

"Recently."

"What did he want?"

"Your help."

"My spying days are over."

"He said you told him that. He wants the memory technology."

"He has it already."

"I pointed that out to him. He said there's a piece missing."

"What?"

"You. You are the only one that was successful. Westlake can't tell why. He asked me to convince you to let them run some tests."

"That's funny. I didn't volunteer. Where's the test facility at? Guantanamo Bay?"

Fitz laughed. "I don't think so. However, there's good reason to tread carefully with any government."

"Westlake took some blood samples before they let me return to Canada."

"Yes, he told me. They need more and a few other things to continue testing."

David swung his knapsack over his shoulder. Something pulled at him. Was he worried or did he trust him? A year ago, this man put his life in danger to save David's, even though he had been complicit in helping a billionaire inject him with the memories of a dead spy. Trust or distrust had many levels. He wasn't sure which level this old man was on.

"Let's go somewhere and talk more. If you help me out of this chair, I will buy you lunch," Fitz said.

The June sun streamed into the streets of downtown Toronto as David walked down the sidewalk with the old man. Fitz talked about the restaurants he'd visited in New York and Paris. David wondered why since Fitz rarely liked small talk.

"I've always treated lunch as the day's most important meal." He raised his hand and pointed, "And here's our destination. I've been eager to return."

They arrived at a historic office building with a boutique optical store taking up most of the front. A man in a suit opened the door and smiled at Fitz. David seemed invisible. The man opened a tiny elevator that only had room for four people.

"Where are we going?" David asked. "I don't have much time before I need to be back for rehearsal."

Fitz just smiled and said, "Patience. We will get you back in time. I promise."

The elevator rose to the top floor and opened to a large restaurant with a high ceiling and suspended chandeliers with bright linens on the tables. The place was packed, and a gaggle of men and women in sharp uniforms rushed around the room, serving drinks and carrying plates piled with steak, chicken, and various salads. Every customer had some kind of drink in front of them. Wine, beer, or a short glass full of ice and liquid. David suspected it wasn't water.

"Monsieur Fitz! I'm delighted you've arrived. As you requested, we have a table at the back of the room." The maître d' smiled at David and looked him up and down, as if he was making sure David was a person. "Excuse me, sir. Jackets are required in the restaurant." David frowned, and the man continued with a bigger smile. "Don't worry, Monsieur, I have something that will fit you." He disappeared into the cloakroom and returned with a dark blue blazer. "Try this on," the man said. David laughed to himself that he needed to be formal to eat a sandwich.

He tried slipping his arms into the sleeves and said, "I need a bigger one." The man nodded and pulled another one from the cloakroom. Although male dancers were muscular, David had increased his gym time last year. Trying on the jacket showed him he'd put on more muscle than he realized. The larger jacket fit better.

The maître d' smiled and said, "Much better! Let me show you both to your table."

Minutes later, the two sat at a table in the back at Fitz's request. A smiling woman with inky hair appeared and draped a cloth napkin over their laps. David sat against the wall. Fitz's cane leaned up against the empty chair. With the service they were getting, he felt like he was visiting royalty. He didn't even own a suit jacket.

"Can I order just a sandwich, or am I required to eat a full suckling pig?" David asked.

"I'm sure they could accommodate either request," Fitz said.

A short, black-haired server deposited two pastrami sandwiches on the table, each with a long pickle perched on top.

"Best pastrami outside of New York," Fitz said. "I pre-ordered because of your schedule. I assumed you liked them because Brooks once said his love of these things might kill him."

"He was wrong," David said. In Amsterdam, the implanted memories force David to re-live Jonathan Brooks' untimely murder, and it had nothing to do with food.

"Yes, he was. But it might have if he'd given it a chance."

David chuckled. The old man had a dry sense of humor. He started feeling at ease for the first time in months. "You've been here before?"

"Occasionally. This restaurant has been in Toronto since before you were born." Fitz grabbed the sandwich with both hands and bit into it. He didn't elaborate further. Fitz was cryptic as ever. After another bite, he said, "I viewed the rehearsal yesterday. What are you preparing for?"

David didn't know how Fitz got approval to watch and how he didn't notice the old man, but he wasn't going to ask. He stared at his sandwich and pushed the pickle off the top. He wasn't as hungry as he thought. "Detroit. In three weeks. A two-night performance and home. Nice, safe, and quick."

"Do you expect any trouble with the border?"

"No. Westlake fixed everything."

"That's a relief, I'm sure, now with all the extra levels of security crossing the border."

David nodded. The USA continued ramping up control in and out of the country with enhanced passports and tighter computer systems. Westlake assured him he'd have no issue traveling back and forth.

As he nibbled at the sandwich, David surveyed the room. A tall man and woman in blue jackets were ushered to a table by the same maître d'. The two of them looked too synchronized to be here for just a business lunch. He thought something else might be going on. Surveillance? He took another bite of his sandwich. Maybe he was overreacting.

He heard a loud booming sound from across the restaurant. The same one from last night. A fat man with a gut overhanging his belt, dressed in an expensive white suit, appeared. A bandage covered the side of his face where the sidewalk had smacked him. A silver watch on his wrist instead of the cracked Rolex.

Fitz squinted at the man as David scowled. "A friend of yours?" Fitz said.

"No."

Walking behind the fat man was a young and beautiful girl with a big smile and a Gucci purse over her arm. The maître d' led them to an intimate corner while the girl snuggled in beside him. She could have been his daughter, which would justify the affection, but the man stared at her like she was his next meal.

A few minutes later, a server brought a large glass filled with liquid and ice for him and a small glass of wine for the woman. The fat man took a long swallow and gestured to the server for a second. David noticed another man in a dark suit sitting by himself at a table between the man and the door. Jet black hair greased back. A small untouched salad sat in front of him. He looked Eastern European. *Bodyguard perhaps?* David thought.

"I had a run-in with the guy in the white suit last night."

"Interesting. During the ballet?" Fitz asked.

"After a ballet of sorts. He was drunk and took a swing at me as I walked past him on the street. I stepped out of the way, and he tripped."

Fitz sipped from the glass the server brought him. "As you can imagine, this restaurant isn't on Yelp. It's members-only access for those with money or connections. I'd expect that man has both. If he's who I think he is, he could purchase this building with his pocket change."

"He's got security," David said.

Fitz nodded.

"Money can buy happiness is what you are telling me."

"That's the magic equation and the root of many of the world's problems."

David's hunger evaporated. The irony of watching this man who had no more consequence of his actions than a large band-aid on his face grated on him. He needed a distraction. He pushed his anger down and looked around the restaurant. "Are you traveling with anyone today?"

"No," Fitz said. "What are you noticing? Jonathan had a better eye than me."

"That surprises me," David said.

Fitz shrugged. "I was management. He was labor."

David laughed. "I suspected as much." Another couple joined the man and woman in blue. When they sat down, the four of them toasted and then ordered. Smiles all around. No danger.

Crisis averted.

"Are any memories surfacing?"

He shook his head. "No. Nothing specific. Just other things."

"Like what?"

David turned towards Fitz to distract from the fat man. "I'm vigilant all the time."

"How so?"

"I see and remember everything. What people are wearing. The license plate on the GM Tahoe parked a block away. The color of the man's tie that left as we walked in. The fat man's security detail has a Russian watch on his wrist."

"Some kind of Vostok, I suspect," Fitz said.

"I thought the same thing." He sipped his water. "I didn't know the name of the timepiece until today."

Fitz pushed back on his chair and said. "I see everything also. Everyone in the business does, or at least the good ones. Vigilance keeps you alive. We trained for it. It either becomes second nature or it doesn't. If it doesn't, you don't last long."

The server whistled by and refilled their water glasses before bouncing to the next table.

"Since you have some time before your next performance, I wonder if you might do an old man a favor."

"What kind?" David asked. A favor for an old man might mean bringing back a bottle of duty-free scotch. He suspected Fitz wanted something else. "I thought our favors were paid up. You saved my life, and then I saved yours."

"Let me put it to you this way. I have a minor job I need your help with. Better than average compensation, and it won't interfere with your performance. I suspect you could use the money."

David wondered if Fitz kept tabs on his bank account or if he just knew dancers were paid shit.

"I can't. The rehearsals are grueling for Detroit, and we've also started preparing for our fall performance."

"I need one day of your time, tops, plus a travel day. A quick in and out as it were."

David heard voices raised, and the hair stood on the back of his neck. He ignored it and focused on Fitz.

"What kind of job?" He sipped his water as his mouth had gone dry, like an automatic response to something out of whack. "Any guns, hookers, knives, or gigantic men with bulletproof vests?"

"No. Nothing like that."

Fitz had a twinkle in his eye. "I just need you to interview for a job."

David frowned. A noise from the other part of the restaurant had increased, and he turned to look. The fat man bellowed at his tall and skinny waiter like a bleating calf.

"This steak is tough and overcooked. I ordered it blue rare!" The fat man gestured at the server that looked not much younger than David. The server looked terrified as the fat man became more belligerent. Maybe David caused the man's overreaction by slamming his face into the sidewalk last night, or maybe he was always like that.

The server leaned in and said something in a lower voice until the fat man said, "That's not good enough! I want to talk to Marcel."

David suspected Marcel was the owner or at least manager of the place. The server shrunk back as the fat man continued to berate him. The man's glass was empty. Who knew how many drinks he'd had before he arrived?

David pushed his chair back from the table and stood up before he realized what was happening. He buttoned the restaurant-supplied jacket, walked to the table, and took the fat man's plate from the server. "Excuse me, sir. I understand you have an issue with this steak?"

The fat man's eyes focused on David, as if something wasn't quite right with this picture. He had been so drunk the night before, he probably didn't remember what David even looked like.

"I told that boy I ordered the steak blue rare, and he had the nerve to argue with me about it. I—"

David swiveled to the server. "Is that right?" His other hand upended the plate full of a steak and all its juices, a baked potato filled with butter, and a single lettuce leaf, all over the front of the fat man's white suit. The fat man started hollering and David said, "I'm so sorry, sir. Let me get something."

He walked back to Fitz's table, took off the jacket, and draped it over his chair. "I'm going to pass on the opportunity. I'm having too much fun here." He didn't let Fitz respond before making his way to the stairs leading down to the street. As he pushed open the door, he chuckled as the fat man's security tried in vain to clean the steak and fixings from the front of his jacket. The rest of the staff hovered around trying to help but couldn't. The man was beyond help.

Karma is a bitch, David thought. *You never know when she might rear her beautiful head.*

David strolled down Yonge Street to clear his head. Something inside him said nothing was ever simple with Fitz and neither were his operations. Too bad; he could have used the money. Yet he worried that accepting Fitz's offer was a slippery slope in the wrong direction.

As the summer sun glared off the office tower, he realized his emotions were jumbled. He had trained as a dancer. He enjoyed an enviable position in the best dance company in Canada. Other than the occasional tryst with women, his life was all about dance until he'd been thrust into the spy life a year ago and it had almost killed him.

Still, something didn't sit right, like walking with a tiny stone in his shoe. He didn't know what it was.

The company rehearsed in a studio at the new National Ballet Headquarters on Queens Quay, close to the Toronto waterfront. Wonderful in the summer and cold as hell in the winter. He walked under the expressway, his bag hanging over his shoulder and his stomach glad he only ate part of the sandwich.

His cell phone buzzed and the text read, "Rent overdue. Need it today or I find another roommate."

Shit. He'd forgotten. The ill-gotten money from the woman last night would cover what he owed. He shared an apartment with a guy he barely knew and he'd been living there for about four months. He didn't really know what his roommate did. The guy was asleep when David arrived home late and was gone in the morning before he awoke. Almost a perfect situation, except the place was close to the bottom of the barrel as far as rental accommodations go. He texted back that he'd leave the cash on the kitchen table tonight.

He needed to find a better place.

A few minutes later, he reached the doors of the new National Ballet of Canada Center on Queen Quay West. He checked his phone, and he was early for the rehearsal. He filled up his water bottle and entered the studio. Several dancers stood on the sidelines, warming up for another grueling afternoon. As he dropped his bag and stepped through some more complex steps before the class started, the ballet mistress ran up to him and gave him a note.

"She wants to see you before class."

"She who?" David asked.

"Jo."

David snatched the paper, turned, and left the room. This wasn't good. Josephine Patton, or Jo to the dancers, was the current Artistic Director. And he adored her. She'd risen from the ranks years ago to become a principal dancer, and then had been promoted into leadership for the ballet.

Nearly fifty, beautiful, and graceful, she was almost a second mother to him, as many times as he needed one.

However, getting a note before rehearsal was unusual. She booked regular one-on-one meetings with the dancers on a bi-monthly basis to check in and provide reassurance of their ability and hard work. He'd had his meeting only a few weeks ago. He shouldn't be on her schedule for at least another month.

As he left the studio, he felt the other dancers' eyes on him. Silent. No expression. *Shit.* Fitz was right. The others hated him, or at least feared him, even though he danced better than before Amsterdam happened, including the soloists. Or maybe that was his ego talking.

He climbed up the stairs to the executive floor when Jo came walking up dressed in summer slacks and a matching sweater, her hair pulled back in a ponytail. White Nike runners and short socks. She might as well be doing a Sandra Dee impression.

"David! I just finished my lunch. Do you want anything?"

David smiled, but before he said anything, she continued, "We had a lovely automatic coffee machine recently installed, but no one has tried it out. Want to be the first?"

"I'm fine, thanks. Just finished lunch."

Her smile warmed his heart, more than he thought it would. He could use a little mother's love and care even if it were simulated. Just then, she put her arm over his shoulders and squeezed him. "I haven't seen you since our last meeting, other than watching you run into class and run out again. Everything okay?"

She'd helped to convince him to visit a psychiatrist after he returned. He appreciated her concern but didn't need it. The shrink was an older guy that wore a suit and had the irritating demeanor of a lifelong smoker that regretted his decision to quit. David had agreed to continue to see him, and eventually David enjoyed talking to an older man about life. Yet, he never talked about what was really bothering him; the doctor wouldn't have believed him anyway. Instead, David regurgitated the official story of him being mugged and escaping with a case of amnesia.

Josephine walked into her office and sat down in her office chair. Headshots of dancers covered her desk like wallpaper. "I'm picking who's going on the website this coming season. Not a simple task."

David dropped his bag and stared at the pictures until he thumbed one out from underneath the rest and placed it in the middle. "Decision's done!"

She smirked. "Nice try." She moved the picture to the side with a smile. "We will look at this next year."

David frowned. "What do you mean?"

"Please sit down. We need to talk."

He sat in the chair in front of her desk, and she continued, "I understand it's a little unusual for me to call you here before a rehearsal..." She stopped talking for a second. David could see her struggling with the next words. "I'm sorry, David. I've decided to make some changes, both for the good of the company and for you."

David frowned. He hadn't expected this. "What do you mean? Have I done something wrong? I've been working extra hard on my roles."

"Working hard has never been your problem. Whatever happened to you last year has affected you and is impacting the company."

"How so?"

"David. I'm not sure how to put this."

"I'm scaring the other dancers."

She leaned forward in her chair. "There's some fear and trepidation, yes. I've decided to put you on a hiatus. At least for a little while. Six months to begin with. You can go on short-term disability and then the insurance company can evaluate you for long term if it comes to that."

David's shoulders slumped and shook his head. He wasn't angry at her or the company; instead, he wanted to kill the man responsible for injecting him with the memories of a dead man permeating his psyche.

"I've already been in touch with the insurance company. We think a program for people that have experienced trauma would be appropriate. The stress of day-to-day life would be gone, and you could just focus on getting yourself back."

David sat in silence, staring at the posters of principal dancers from the company. He managed to say, "I understand," before grabbing his bag and walking out of her office without looking back. He knew she was protecting the troupe. And he knew the mental health of the dancers was key to a great performance. If he was the loose cog in the wheel, he needed to be replaced. The harmony of the team was the most important thing.

That thought didn't help much.

The afternoon sun had peeked out from behind the clouds and warmed the entire downtown. David left the building and walked into Queen Quay, a boutique shopping mall on the waterfront. He threaded his way through the stores to the water's edge and found an isolated park bench. He put his sunglasses on and let the warmth of the sun purify his soul.

Emotions bounced around his head. Confusion, anger, rage, and then finally after some time had passed, he relaxed. For the last year, his body and mind hadn't fit together. Like two different coloured socks. He had put it down to the trauma diagnosed by the doctor because of his European-not-a-vacation trip. Underneath, something else was going on.

He hadn't jelled with the company since he returned. His operating method had changed. For most of life, nothing had really bothered him. He'd run into some issues with his dad, as most sons did. His mother had died when he was too young to remember, and his father raised him as best as he could. At the ballet school, other students recounted almost unimaginable drama about the smallest things. That wasn't him. Before Europe, nothing really upset him. Post abduction, post implant, post spy game, everything bugged him.

As he walked back into Queens Quay, he texted Fitz. "Changed my mind. I'm in. Send me when and where, and it's a deal."

Chapter Four

Seattle

THE PACIFIC NORTHWEST sun was like no other. Shiny and sharp and without the humidity of New York or the dehydration of Las Vegas. David had considered applying for a job in Vancouver after ballet school, however, for a Canadian and a dancer, Toronto was the centre of the universe. Vancouver sported West Coast weather with Canadian sensibilities and a high as hell cost of living. Nothing a dancer could afford. Toronto prices weren't much better.

Seattle was neither. It wasn't Toronto, and it wasn't Vancouver. It was San Francisco-like, with more damn bridges.

David arrived in Seattle on Friday evening. They scheduled his interview for Monday morning. He had two full days to prepare, except he didn't know what he was preparing for.

Fitz didn't tell him the name of the company or the position he was interviewing for. He promised no religious nuts or guns during the operation. What could go wrong? *Lots*, David thought, *Lots*.

Fitz wanted David to interview for a job, and while inside the company, install some specialized tech. Fitz said the entire operation was *legal-ish*. A quick in and out. He suggested it would be faster than some of David's one-night stands.

On the plane, David paid for the in-flight internet and researched corporate espionage cases that included shampoo companies digging through their competitors' trash to steal formulas and Chinese nationals trying to swipe secrets from Apple; all examples not pointing to anything altruistic, just greed.

If someone were paying Fitz to steal corporate information, why couldn't they bribe a minimum-wage janitor instead? Fitz said that was a no-go and didn't explain further. David needed the money anyway. As the plane landed, he felt the same butterflies as just before a performance. Anticipation with a lot at stake if he screwed up. He missed that feeling.

He met Fitz in his hotel room and started preparing for the operation. Fitz said David initially would be vetted by a Human Resources recruiter and if he survived that meeting, they'd move David to other employees and finally to the hiring manager. Fitz coached him to appear charming and capable at first, and then as the interviews continued during the day, to act gruff and insensitive. The goal was to have enough interviews to place the surveillance devices around the building and be off-putting enough to not get the job.

"How gruff do you want me?"

"Just be yourself and the interview will take care of itself."

David laughed. He knew he'd been a challenge for the last few months and didn't realize it could be an asset this time.

During the meetings, he would install surveillance devices the size of a large grain of sand. Fitz suggested under a chair or on the side of a table; anywhere close to the interviewer's computer they would use during the meeting.

Fitz had used David's real name and credentials, which struck him as odd. Hard to hide the fact he was a dancer. Too public, and the National Ballet of Canada liked to brand their performances with the dancers. A search would bring up his picture on the ballet company's website. Fitz wouldn't tell him what he was interviewing for until he arrived in Seattle.

Once he agreed to Fitz's request, much of his anger evaporated. He joked with the cabby on the way to the airport and with other passengers on the plane. Fitz provided half the payment upfront. He'd make more in one day than three months in the ballet. That suited him fine.

He moved through US immigration at the Toronto airport with no issues. Westlake had come through. No stopping, searching, or questioning by a humorless immigration officer. As he boarded the plane, the entire event felt oddly familiar, like pulling on an old pair of jeans for the first time. The implant turned déjà vu into an extreme sport.

David looked out of Fitz's hotel room towards Pike Place Market and the ocean. Lake Ontario was nice in the summer, yet nothing matched a view of Puget Sound and the Pacific Northwest. Fitz sat in a chair with his cane leaned up against the wall.

"I'd like to go over a few things," Fitz said.

"Me too. I still don't understand why you couldn't tell me the name of the company and the job I am interviewing for."

Fitz reached into his bag, withdrew a folder, and handed it to him. "You are interviewing at Sagasu Cyber Security, known as SCS. In Japanese, Sagasu means 'to search'. They are one of the world's largest security software companies."

David sat in a chair by the window and reviewed the documents. There wasn't much. "Who's paying us for this little operation? I'm assuming it's another corporate asshole like Reynolds." Richard Reynolds was the billionaire owner of a tech company that just about killed him and Fitz a year ago.

"No. Not at all like Reynolds. However, every corporation has some similarities."

"Like what? Large and mostly greedy?"

Fitz nodded his head. "Maximum shareholder value and profits drive most of the behavior. Sociopathic leadership like Reynolds drives outcomes that aren't legal. Most companies don't intentionally break laws. However, many bend them as far as they can."

"Who is paying the bill this time?"

The old man said nothing for a few seconds. David wondered if he trusted him or not. He expected Fitz's trust issues had kept him alive all these years. Fitz grabbed his cell phone and sent a text.

"You've paid your dues, so to speak, so you deserve to know." Fitz pushed himself up to standing with his cane and went over to the door. "Who would be interested in the secrets of a top technology company?"

"Another technology company?"

"But who would care if SCS sells software to the Russians or the Chinese?"

"What kind of software?"

"Encryption software. More precisely, software that can decode information that shouldn't be able to be decrypted. A universal unlock key."

As a Gen-Z, David grew up as a digital native and never lived in a time without computers. However, he had only played video games and used social media. After the incident, he noticed he followed technology news more closely with an interest in information security, probably more than any other ballet dancer would.

Yet, he'd never heard of SCS.

There was only one organization that would care if SCS was selling technology illegally. David narrowed his gaze at Fitz and instantly felt set up. "Did Westlake put you up to this?"

The hotel room door opened and US government lackey, Arthur Westlake entered the room, his wonky eye not tracking correctly. Westlake wore a blue suit, blue tie, and white shirt. He looked like a banker about to sell you a mortgage. He carried a thin briefcase in one hand. David had never known what part of the government he worked for, but the CIA was a likely candidate.

"Speak of the devil and the devil appears," Fitz said.

"Good afternoon, all. I'm glad that David has agreed to help us out with our little problem," Westlake said.

David stared at Westlake but said nothing. Instead, he turned to Fitz. "I wish you had told me in Toronto."

"Would you have turned me down?" Fitz looked him in the eyes. "Look at you. You are happy. Almost giddy. Do you think that's just because you've traveled three time zones?"

He didn't want to talk to Westlake. The spook had been complicit in the spy's memories that were pumped into David's head. While David was being hunted by rich psychopaths, Westlake sat back and observed. Like a behavioral scientist watching a rat trying to escape a cage.

As he looked at Pike Place Market again, he felt a flush of anger as he considered his options. One option was how to leave gracefully without killing either man.

"David. I expect you are angry. I would be too if our places were reversed," Westlake said.

He turned and fought the urge to stick his finger in the face or the eye of the government agent. "You don't know how angry I actually am. I just lost my job because of anger caused by the fucking procedure that you could have stopped before it happened."

Fitz looked at David and said, "Son, this is my fault. I told Westlake that you would be willing to participate once you learned about the operation. I didn't know you were going to lose your job and didn't realize how deeply the anger was affecting your life."

"That's just it. I hate that I'm angry, but I know I'm better than I was. I'm sharper and more exact in my dancing. My confidence is over the top, but the other dancers are afraid of me. And the incident didn't just affect me—Razor got injured because of me and now he can't dance." He turned to Westlake and said, "All because you observed me like I was some lab animal and didn't intervene." David's heart pounded and he wanted to punch Westlake in the mouth, except that wouldn't help, no matter how much he wanted to.

"David," Westlake said. "I apologize. I knew what Reynolds was planning, and I let him. I didn't anticipate the consequences the experiment would generate. For that, I'm truly sorry. I'm hoping that, in some small way, that the money for this operation will give you some time to get yourself together. I'd like to help if I could."

David squinted at Westlake and couldn't tell if he was serious, but something told him the old guy felt at least some remorse for what happened. Maybe that would have to do. And although he hated it, he had to agree with Fitz; the anticipation of the work had lifted the cloud he'd been under.

David sat back down in the chair. "Tell me everything about this company and what you want me to do. If I agree to do it, I want no more surprises."

Westlake extracted a folder from his case and handed it to him. "The technology revolution coupled with global terrorism has put the US government in a tough position. The free market is a noble concept unless the market produces something that can damage the country or its citizens. After what happened with Reynolds, my leadership wanted to try a different strategy. SCS is one that's been marked for closer inspection."

"I don't need Brook's memories to tell me that the CIA, FBI, and NSA have all kinds of resources to investigate companies like this. Why are you hiring an old man with a cane and a broke ballet dancer for help? And if it's a US company, shouldn't the FBI be on point?" David asked.

"Two good questions. The CIA is involved because of the international nature of the threat. That's why I'm here. Second, we've been trying to monitor SCS for a few months and noticed an unusual job posting."

"You didn't answer my question."

"You are correct. What kind of role do you think you are interviewing for?"

David realized Fitz still hadn't told him. "Office intern perhaps?"

"You are interviewing to teach ballet to a group of SCS employees. As the CIA doesn't have a stable of dance teachers in our employ, we believe you are the best person to get an inside view of the firm."

David remembered the email he'd gotten last week. A US company hiring a Canadian dance teacher. The email showed up every few weeks and he just deleted it. The email conveniently left out anything about the company or why they wanted a dance teacher.

"I've seen emails from a US company recruiting for Canadian dance teachers. I expect every dancer in Toronto did. I'd heard a few applied but didn't get anywhere. Is this the same company or is teaching dance this year's corporate yoga?"

"Same company we think. The company's founder is a bit of a recluse with some unorthodox ideas—ideas that have pushed him into the technology stratosphere, so to speak. SCS hires mostly Japanese landed immigrants or Japanese nationals with H1B visas. They appear to balance the workforce makeup carefully to not trigger any US labor laws. The founder also doesn't travel by car. He flies by helicopter from his house on Lake Washington to downtown Seattle," Westlake said.

"What's his name?"

"Nolan Spencer."

Spencer sounded familiar. The Spencer Scholarship. Awarded out of Seattle. A new scholarship that's well funded and much sought after by any ballet company in North America. "Same Spencer that funds a dance scholarship every year to attend schools like the National Ballet School in Toronto or the New York City Ballet School?"

"Yes. From what we can tell, he's not attended any award presentations. This is the only scholarship his company gives. You would think he'd be at least interested in the results."

"Any family?"

"There's a reference to a daughter but no current information."

"What does the corporation do exactly?"

Fitz said, "They develop and sell software that no one has ever heard of and leads the world in computer security and analytics. They are a private company that does no PR or interviews. No mainstream business articles. Publicly, their goals are modest. Behind closed doors, the rumor is Spencer drives the employees hard."

"We want to monitor the situation and take appropriate action before we find any hints of wrongdoings. Gathering intelligence is the first step," Westlake said.

"Anything else?" David asked.

"No. And that's the problem. Look, we are in a tight spot here. I'm prepared to double the agreed-upon rate." He looked at Fitz and said, "For both of you."

David reviewed the document Westlake provided. Nothing more than a couple of thin business articles talking about the software and speculations about the company. "I'll do it. Except at the first sign of anything off the rails, I'm bailing."

"That's all I can ask," Westlake said.

Fitz said, "One last thing David, he's also interested if you've..."

Westlake cut him off. "A year ago, because of the procedure, many of Brook's capabilities surfaced in you and saved your life. Skills that took Brooks several years to acquire. I am curious if you've noticed anything else appearing either accidentally or during times of stress."

"None. No new ninja skills. Everything kind of evaporated. All I'm left with is his attitude and anger."

"Probably mad at letting himself get killed," Fitz said. "He wasn't generally an 'angry' man. Pragmatic, yes. Always angry? No."

David thought about last year. He wasn't lying. No new skills appeared that he recognized.

"Still," Westlake continued, "After this little operation is over, I'd like to run some more tests. Our scientists suspect there's something in your genetic makeup that kept you alive during the implant."

"That's not going to happen."

"Why not? I'm not asking for a vivisection. Just some blood tests."

"I gave blood a year ago so you could clear my name of all charges in Europe and the US."

"And didn't I do that? Did you have any trouble clearing the border yesterday?"

David shook his head. "No. Everything was fine."

"And it should be unless you get yourself into some new kinds of trouble. Look, I'm just asking for a few more vials of blood."

"I said no. I don't want to be a template to create more of your implanted spies. I don't wish that on anyone."

"We've decided that angle is a dead end anyway. Too unpredictable. However, we believe implanting a language might make more sense if it was possible. Imagine learning Arabic or Japanese as easy as getting a flu shot."

David shook his head. "I'm not convinced. The memories and the pain are gone. That's all I'm concerned about. I just want to be David."

Fitz looked at David and smiled. "Yes. You've told me that before."

He considered saying more and decided it wasn't the right time.

"Tell you what. If this goes as easily as you say and we receive all the money, I will consider it. For an extra charge, of course." David said.

"That's all I ask," Westlake said with a smile on his face.

Monday morning and David sipped coffee in a china cup across from his destination. New building. Tallest in Seattle. Fresh asphalt and concrete encircled the area. Workers clad in blue coveralls scrubbed the sidewalks while others searched the ground for any bits of garbage or litter. Disneyland-level cleaning protocol.

Over the weekend, Fitz gave David an accelerated course in tradecraft. He even went through the trouble of having the hotel deliver a whiteboard for diagrams. David felt as if he was in grade 10 and there was an exam approaching. However, Fitz meticulously covered covert techniques and how to use dead drops, secure communication protocols, and counterintelligence tricks like dry cleaning to expose a tail. He occasionally let slip his own history and David learned about the old man's involvement with the fall of the Berlin wall and the Vietnam war. If pressed for more information, Fitz would deftly change the subject. Many of the tricks sounded familiar, but David couldn't tell if they were holdovers from the memory implant or plot devices from James Bond films he watched with his dad when he was growing up.

At the end of the extended lesson, Fitz took a serious tone. "I can't stress enough; if the operation is compromised, don't try to make it up as you go. I've done these kinds of operations my entire career, and if something can screw up, it will. We manage the risks. Backup plans and following procedures are critical. You need to adhere to them to the letter. Understand?"

Fitz's face looked the sternest David had ever seen it since Amsterdam. The old Brit walked through the plans again, including the nightly meetings, daily communication by secure text only, and hotel room logistics. Most would require David's limited involvement, but the when-shit-hit-the-fan procedure was extremely detailed, Fitz made David repeat it back a few times until it was second nature. Finally, when the old man was satisfied, he let David leave.

Later, and alone, David researched what he could about SCS. Record high profits allowed them to build a structure taller than the Space Needle and the seventy-six-story Columbia Tower. Built with lots of glass and steel in such a way to reflect the sunlight in some kind of energy-saving thing, the tower stood near the end of the hill, looming over the harbor.

The coffee burned in his stomach as his vigilance ramped up. He twirled the big ring on his left hand and felt the hardness against his thumb to ground himself in the now. He couldn't stop himself from watching people entering the building, so he went with it. Any information helped; he never knew what observations would be useful.

He counted the bodies. Ninety-five percent Japanese. Men entering wore their hair cropped close. The women were opposite, with their hair kept long and straight. The ratio of men to women seemed balanced if you thought an entire Japanese workforce in downtown Seattle wasn't unusual.

Two of Seattle's homeless skirted the traffic and the sidewalk cleaners, planting themselves near the entrance with empty cups outstretched in their hands. A man and a woman, both white, and looked like they'd seen better days. Tattoos covered their bare arms. David read that panhandlers typically scored near minimum wage in coins in most major cities. He wondered how they'd do with such a culturally similar workforce. With everything going digital, did they accept Apple Pay?

Security guards at the front had disappeared. Perhaps they were doing a sweep around the building or a shift change. The panhandlers waited for a clear path. Not too dumb, so far.

The two appeared polite and smiled at each passerby. However, as David guessed might happen, none of the Japanese workers entering the offices gave them a second look. A few stepped to the right, as if a few feet of distance would help.

David whispered into his coffee, "There's something happening." The hidden earpiece would transmit to Fitz.

A black SUV pulled up to the entrance in a no-parking zone. A middle-aged white man in a black suit and coiffed dark brown hair emerged from the back door. A younger Japanese man with a briefcase jumped out from the other side and ran around the car to the older man. Boss and assistant. *Employees or selling something?* The first man looked different from the other employees. White, confident, and self-important. Still no security guards. The younger man swiveled his head back and forth, looking for something. They stood near the SUV and waited.

Then things went a little off the rails.

The two street-people turned, and David saw a glimmer of recognition in them towards the white man. Maybe it was the fancy car and expensive suit. With their smiles turned on high, they walked towards their targets, positioning themselves as blockers to the main entrance. Both stuck out their cups and mouthed something David couldn't decipher.

The white man stepped back and wrinkled his face in disgust while screaming something at them. David was sure it wasn't a good morning. The assistant reacted and crowded in front of them to let the older man pass. The white guy looked angry at someone that made seven dollars an hour panhandling to his thousands.

Being rich meant you rarely had to subject yourself to the unwashed. Not today, however. Maybe David would get the chance to up-end a steak and trimmings over this guy too.

He swallowed the last of his coffee and said, "I'm going to take a closer look" and watched the missing security guards appear and escort the panhandlers off the property.

As he crossed the road, one of the guards walked back to the entrance. He was white, blond, good-looking, and not Japanese.

David came up to the man and said, "I saw what happened, and I'm curious. Do the street people harass employees a lot here?" The guard glanced at David's suit and tie that Fitz had acquired and must have decided he belonged to the corporate club.

The guard leaned in and said, "Every damn day, we have to run them off. And the police don't do jack." He didn't seem much older than David and had a high school linebacker vibe to him. Maybe post-high school didn't agree with him.

"It looked like they tried to scam the wrong people."

"You got that right. Mr. Moore hates these guys with a passion. He arrived a few minutes earlier than normal, otherwise, we'd have made sure he wasn't bothered."

"Mr. Moore?"

"Yeah. Nick Moore. He runs the place."

Chapter Five

Nick Moore entered his office, and his assistant pulled a sheaf of papers out of the briefcase and organized them on the desk. He needed a coffee, but really wanted a drink. Almost too late for the first one and too early for the other. The coffee would have to do.

Within thirty seconds of entering his office, a short Japanese woman on the other side of thirty bowed at the door, placed a steaming cup with a lid at the edge of the desk, and left. Moore didn't acknowledge the delivery or her.

"Sir, I apologize for what happened. I will instruct security so it won't happen again," the assistant said.

Moore stared at the assistant for a beat and said, "See to it," before taking the lid off the coffee and taking a sip. The assistant bowed and left the office, closing the door behind him. Moore pressed a button on his desk, and the clear glass walls of his office frosted immediately.

With the folder in one hand and the coffee in the other, he leaned back and stared out the windows of the seventy-second floor. In the distance, the Olympic Mountains gave a stunning backdrop to Puget Sound. He'd chosen his view from the initial plans and suggested strongly to the architect how he wanted his office oriented.

Nicholas Moore was the son of a Boston police officer and had the good fortune to share a university dorm room with a thin brainiac named Nolan Spencer. Spencer was the smartest guy he'd ever met. A few years later, after he'd spent time in the Army and in the newly formed Cyber Command, Spencer contacted him after returning to the US from Japan under circumstances Spencer only said were 'difficult.' He asked Moore to run his new software company funded by a Japanese investor. Spencer wrote the software while Moore created a profitable business using every harsh business tactic and policy he'd learned in school, the army, and on the streets of Boston. Moore and Spencer created a money machine, yet over the years, Spencer had become more eccentric and thankfully left Moore to run the business as he saw fit.

And Moore did, creating a roaring success through the strength of Spencer's software and his take-no-prisoners approach to selling and licensing the product. However, Spencer's behavior had reached a critical point and created a problem that put SCS at risk.

As he leaned back and read the first page from the folder, he swore under his breath. A more immediate problem stared at him from the paper. A customer wanting to "get tough" with SCS's terms and conditions for licensing their software. *Good luck with that,* Moore thought.

He dialed Jacob Mori, his deal maker, and told him to come into his office. A buff Japanese man with a white shirt, no tie, and a Jason Statham haircut appeared two minutes later. He looked like he had just stepped from the pages of Japanese Vogue. Moore knew he was trustworthy, loyal, and ruthless. In more things than just a business deal.

"Our friends to the south wish to renegotiate our terms and their payment."

"What did you tell them?"

"I want to tell them to go fuck themselves," Moore said.

Jacob nodded his head like he had that written on his business card. "I will make them see their tactical error."

"Tactical error?" Moore said.

"In thinking they have any leverage."

Moore smiled. "Your special talent."

"Mind if I borrow the jet for a couple of days? I get better results in person rather than a phone call."

"Absolutely," Moore said. Jacob's title was the chief deal maker.

However, deal whisperer or ass-kicker would be better, as he whispers to the client that he'd kick their ass if they don't sign. Jacob had never lost a deal. SCS sold software that no other vendor could supply. Many tried and failed and he used Jacob as a blunt instrument to remind them.

Now that he knew the problem was handled, Moore felt some of his stress evaporate. "Once you are back, I've got some other work that's a little more delicate than perhaps what you are used to."

"I'm interested to hear more. What's the problem?"

"Who's the problem is the right question," Moore said.

Jacob raised his eyebrows and nodded. Moore didn't need to say anything else.

Chapter Six

DAVID ENTERED through the big doors and walked to the reception desk. Holding true to the lack of information about the company, a subdued SCS logo hanging on the main wall was the only signage. Once he gave his name, a rotund Japanese security guard instructed him to stare into a tiny eye-level camera on a stand and handed him a tablet and a plastic pencil to sign in. The guard presented him with a red ID badge with his fresh image laminated on the card a minute later.

"Take third elevator," the guard said in accented English. However, a waist-high piece of thick glass embedded into the wall blocked his way. As he walked up to it, nothing happened. He waved his hand with still no response. Behind him, the guard yelled and motioned to touch the card to a small panel on the wall. Once he followed the guard's instructions, the glass slid back, and a single elevator door opened. He gave the guard a thumbs up.

No turning back.

The door closed, and he saw no buttons to press. Just stainless steel on all sides and an LED floor number. A red button for emergencies. Nothing else. He touched his finger to the Fitz supplied earpiece and heard nothing back; the signal didn't make it past the lobby. He was really on his own, but that wasn't unusual. *All in a day's work,* he thought. After a rapid rise, the number twenty showed on an LED read-out, and the door opened.

A petite woman stood waiting for him. Her long black hair was pulled tight into a ponytail, and her hands were crossed in front.

"Mr. Knight?"

He nodded and stuck out his hand. She didn't respond.

"We limit physical contact inside the building. Touch spreads disease, so we don't shake hands. I understand how a foreigner would think that's strange."

David said nothing . Her comment about him being a foreigner seemed out of place, even if he was Canadian.

"Please follow me," she said.

The no handshake rule was odd. He suspected it might not be the last thing.

"My name is Marisa, Mr. Knight." She didn't supply her last name. "I will guide you through the interview process."

"Call me David."

She smiled again as though she would never use his first name. "Please, through here." She waved her hand, and the double glass doors slid open. Lots of Star Trek doors here.

She led him into an enormous conference room with floor-to-ceiling windows gazing out to Puget Sound. A few pieces of art hung on the walls. He'd done his homework geography-wise. Across the water, Bainbridge Island watched the city while the Olympic Mountains kept a watch over the Pacific Ocean. A lone ferry boat headed towards the island from downtown.

Another woman in a white lab coat with a small tray sat at the table. Her hair was pulled back into a ponytail. David's eyebrows rose. She looked like a doctor or a nurse.

"Mr. Knight, it's customary for SCS to test all applicants for drug use prior to the first interview." Marisa smiled like she was asking him to fill out a form.

The last time someone jabbed a needle into his arm, it didn't go well. He didn't move. The nurse smiled and motioned him to sit down.

"I don't do drugs, and I'm allergic to alcohol," David said.

"I understand that. I'm sorry you weren't notified before you arrived this morning." She kept smiling and didn't offer another option.

Fitz and Westlake expected him to make it through the day and install several devices. He couldn't complete his mission if he didn't get to the first interview. He shrugged his shoulders, rolled up his sleeve, and sat down.

The nurse's eyebrows rose as she wrapped a rubber tube around his bicep and swabbed the veins on his forearm. He gritted his teeth as she drove the needle into his arm, except he felt almost nothing. David looked away as she filled up a couple of vials. He wouldn't tell Westlake; he'd insist on his own pint from David's arm.

"All done!" the nurse said. She took his hand lightly and pressed his finger to a tiny piece of cotton over the top of the tiny wound. Her fingers were delicate. A sense of déjà vu came over him, yet no real memory of a similar event surfaced. She gathered up the vials and her tray and disappeared out the door.

Marisa offered him water and nothing else. He was about to ask for coffee but thought against it. She also didn't mention anything more about the blood test. Instead, he searched for something to say that wouldn't get him ejected before the first interview. "Your office has a very Zen feel to it."

She screwed up her face as if David had misused the term or passed gas.

"Zen is a form of Buddhism with the monks endorsing rigorous meditation and intuition. Is that what you mean?"

"No. I meant your office furnishings are minimalist."

"Yes, they are." He was glad she let his comment slide. Precision seemed to be everywhere in the company. Much different from how he judged corporate life. His view of a corporation was limited to the movies where the people worked like drones in tiny cubicles. He didn't understand why anyone would subject themselves to that. However, he earned a living by dancing on a stage and wearing tights. Today, he was supplementing his income by installing surveillance equipment without being caught.

"Tell me, Mr. Knight, why do you want to work here?"

"In truth, I'm not sure. I've never worked in a place like this."

"Isn't a ballet company a large organization that works together for a common goal?"

"Yes. But the no handshaking rule is a little odd."

"Not so strange in Japan."

"This is Seattle."

"Mr. Spencer has adopted many Japanese business practices as he considers them efficient and productive."

"I've noticed." He looked past her and stared at a piece of art behind her. *Impressionism*, he thought. "You do pose a good question. I have one for you. Why should I work here?"

She sat back in her chair and crossed her hands. She seemed caught off guard.

"We are the number one security software company in the world."

"I understand that."

"We get over a thousand qualified applicants for each job we advertise."

He nodded. "I'm a performer. I'm still trying to wrap my head around teaching dance to office workers."

She half-smiled. He couldn't tell if she was amused or pissed off. Fitz told him to be himself, which was more or less a charming asshole. He aimed to get to the next interview, and he hoped he hadn't pushed too far.

"Mr. Spencer is a patron of the arts, particularly dance. He funds an award every year."

"I know." David nodded. "His award helps many dancers go to ballet school that couldn't afford it."

"And you wouldn't be teaching office workers."

"Who then?"

"You would give a class every morning to a group of former dancers that respect and want the precision of ballet in their daily lives." She replied.

"What about the afternoon?"

"We can discuss this after the first interview." She looked down at her tablet and said. "Please wait a moment. I will be back." She stood up, and he watched her lithe body walk and disappear through the automatic doors. She moved with the same grace as most dancers he knew.

He wondered what Fitz had gotten him into.

After several minutes, he walked out of the conference room and discovered a small kitchen area tucked into a hidden corner. A high-tech espresso machine sat on the counter. After a few seconds of staring at it, the device said, "Select your coffee. Short or long?"

Wasn't technology incredible?

"Long with cream."

"Cream is not available. Please select your coffee. Short or long?"

"Why is cream not available?"

"Cream is against corporate policy," the machine said.

Interesting. First germaphobia, and now lactophobia. David suddenly felt better at being clandestine in this company of weirdness.

"Long, please."

"Your coffee will be ready in thirty seconds."

A paper cup slid into the space, and thirty seconds later, steaming black liquid filled the cup. If he made it to tomorrow, he might bring his own cream.

The coffee was strong and dark with a slightly bitter aftertaste. Like the company, unusual but not unpleasant. He'd review his next Starbucks order.

While sipping the drink, he stared out a sizeable west-facing window opposite the conference room. The view of the Olympic Mountains was stunning. He suddenly got why people liked the west coast. Rain in the winter instead of snow and a summer that spared the crushing humidity that roasted New York and Toronto this time of year.

Back in the conference room, he examined the large art pieces hanging on the walls. A small bar code adorned each frame at the lower right corner. No information on the artist or name of the piece. Just a code.

After meeting Fitz and Westlake, David researched what he could about Spencer. He'd investigate Moore later today. Company culture, like dance culture, is formed at the top. Assholes in charge created assholes lower down.

Except Spencer seemed like a ghost. The available information wasn't much use. A Wikipedia article pegged him as a bona-fide billionaire. The company had appeared from nowhere and delivered revolutionary security software to companies wanting the best protection from hackers or bad actors looking for a way inside. Apple had initially licensed SCS's software for all their computers, including the iPhone and iPad. The company and Spencer's fortune grew from there. Few pictures of the founder. Mostly old ones. Rumours spread of Spencer being reclusive and afraid of illness. Kind of like if Howard Hughes and Steve Jobs had a love child.

A large LED clock hung at the top of one wall. A similar clock decorated the front reception. Time: Hours, Minutes, Seconds. Seconds apparently counted with this guy.

9:57:10. David's second interview was scheduled for 10:00 a.m. At that point, his real challenge kicked in.

The conference doors slid open a minute later, and Marisa walked in with her tablet in hand. She looked at his drink and smiled.

"It will be my pleasure to take you to your next meeting. You may bring your coffee with you. Follow me, please."

David sat in the hard chair and twirled the ring on his left hand back and forth. His grounding ritual wasn't helping. The chilled air from the ceiling evaporated most of the sweat on his scalp. He'd finished his coffee, and the extra caffeine jolt wasn't helping his anxiety. However, being nervous in a job interview was expected.

He touched his thumb to the bottom of his ring, and the tiny bead on the bottom felt sharp and out of place. He had to push the ring onto a flat surface near or on the computer screen. Easy, except that a tall, cadaverous man sat in the way.

"Mr. Knight. Your resume is very impressive. Why do you want to work here?" The man spoke with perfectly pronounced English. David thought about the man's history. Native Japanese speakers had to work hard to lose their accents. Well-pronounced English didn't just happen. A Japanese dancer once told him that many English syllables don't exist in Japanese. A 'V' sound was problematic. Vancouver gets pronounced '*Bancober*.' This man got the syllables right.

As per Fitz's guidance, he lied on his resume and included teaching dance classes part-time. "Precision," David said. "I'm attracted to teach here because SCS values precision." He hoped his last interview hadn't been recorded, transcribed, and transmitted to the interviewer while traveling two floors on an elevator. He wanted to change his answers to fit the operation.

The man nodded, "Please explain."

"Your founder spoke publicly about his obsession with precision. Everything I've seen so far reinforced his comments. It seems all the rumours are true."

"Ah yes. The famous interviews." The man looked at his computer and typed something. "What rumours are you speaking about?"

David glanced back at the computer screen. The bottom edge would be a perfect location for the surveillance device. If not, Westlake said under the table would work as well.

"From the security guard to the CEO, the culture and the company prides itself on its attention to detail. Even though I'm not technical, I'd guess that writing security software requires a specific level of focus, or the bad guys win."

"Isn't a ballet company a precise organization?"

The interviewer's desk looked high-end. Manufactured wood. Probably expensive. The colour and size fit the room exactly. Custom made, possibly.

"Classical ballet is precise. Many of the dancers aren't. Too many egos and too much vanity. I'm a dancer at heart, and teaching dance helps me hone my precision on the stage."

"When do you intend to stop dancing?"

"In another ten or fifteen years. Baryshnikov still dances, and he's over sixty."

"Your resume says you've danced for many years."

"Since I was six."

"Do you think you'd miss performing on stage?"

The man was asking insightful questions about a dancer's career plans. David wondered how many of the questions were pre-written.

"I'm looking out for my future. A dancer's career starts to wane at thirty. I don't want to wait to come up with a plan." David chuckled at his insight. He realized that he'd never had this conversation with anyone, and it rang true.

The man nodded again.

"May I ask you a question?"

"Please, go ahead."

"Isn't it unusual for a corporation to teach ballet to employees?"

"Yes, it is."

"I understand the attraction of yoga or even Pilates in a stressful corporate environment. Ballet seems a non-intuitive choice."

"You spoke about precision. That's why Mr. Spencer has requested a daily ballet class for interested employees. He believes it will improve employee morale and well-being."

David let the man continue while he focused on something else. Fitz warned of extensive video surveillance inside the building. He needed to install the bead on the computer. Preferably on the bottom edge to remain invisible.

The man turned the conversation into company values and overall employee welfare as David ran through scenarios that might work. The irony of a dancer installing surveillance devices inside the leading security software company wasn't lost on him.

As the man spoke, he wondered why the government wanted to bug them. With all the company's rules, breaking the law would be the last thing they would be guilty of. Maybe supplying coffee cream without a license. Nothing else looked probable.

David touched the bottom of the ring again. Fitz had explained that he would need to press the bottom of the ring against the back of the computer, and the thin membrane would rupture, spilling a tiny amount of fast-acting glue to the surface. Two seconds later, he could withdraw his finger, and the bug would be in place and invisible. Energy came from the ambient heat in the room or the computer's heat. The bug should remain hidden unless they regularly scanned the rooms with specialized equipment.

He only needed to install one. Westlake had placed two more on his ring as a backup.

The computer faced a window looking over downtown Seattle. He stood abruptly and walked over to the window. "I'm concerned about one thing, however."

The man raised his eyebrows as if a candidate had never stood before in an interview. No one probably had. However, Fitz had said to be himself.

"What's that?"

"Ballet takes commitment. Look at this building being built over there." He pointed to a giant pit off 8th avenue. "My father worked in construction all his life and always talked about the commitment necessary to build a building." His father had indeed worked in construction and never said anything like that to him.

The man stood up and peered in the pit's direction.

"As a builder, a supervisor, or a worker, you can't be timid. Ballet is like that. To get to a level of precision, the company and the staff need to be committed, or nothing will happen. Is SCS serious about dance, or is it just the flavour of the month?"

As the man squinted slightly and was about to produce an answer David didn't care about, he touched the ring to the bottom of the screen and pushed. He counted one, two, and three to himself and then pulled his hand away. The tiny bead was gone from the ring. He breathed a small sigh of relief.

He'd successfully installed the first bug.

"The founder is serious, and therefore the company is serious," the man said.

Chapter Seven

Fitz watched David enter the shiny SCS building from a Starbucks. The operation should be easy, except they rarely were. Unexpected complications always cropped up. As a famous German strategist once said, 'no battle plan survives contact with the enemy' or in other words, hope for the best and plan for the worst. Westlake provided the tech and believed an outside vantage point would give the best range for the miniature microphone hidden inside David's left ear. He listened to David's comments as he sipped his coffee. Westlake said the microphone should provide an acceptable range through standard concrete and steel construction. However, he'd discovered the SCS architects had dictated some unusual materials during construction. He'd hoped the tech would work and the signal wouldn't degrade.

He listened to David's conversation with a security guard about the altercation outside and heard the name "Moore." The man in a suit must be Nicholas Moore. COO and CFO of the company. White and middle-aged. And until a couple of days ago, was all the information that he or Westlake could find.

After Westlake came up empty-handed with more intel, Fitz turned to another source. He didn't know who or where they were except, they referred to themselves as 'The Hardy Boys'—a reference to a 1960s teenage detective series. For all he cared, the architects could be a set of cyber-gifted twelve-year-old female cheerleaders. Either way, they always over-delivered on his requests.

An old Russian he trusted made the introduction to their unique services. He said, "Make your contact. Ask your questions and pay their bill upfront. It will surprise you at their thoroughness."

And he was. And the more times he used them, the better and faster they responded. A couple of weeks ago, Fitz asked for intelligence about SCS and its employees. He pre-paid the hefty bill. He'd pass the charge on to Westlake once the operation was over.

Besides an offhanded remark on the materials used in the construction of the new building, The Hardy Boys provided a treasure trove of useful information. Nicholas Moore, the COO and CFO, was Spencer's closest and maybe only friend. They'd met at university, and after, Moore did a stint in the Army's Cyber Command. Spencer returned from Japan and asked Moore to run the company as Spencer wrote the software.

Moore took his army training and ran the business like a military operation. Any detail about the company, product, or operations was on a need-to-know basis. No outsiders and no public leaks of information. As COO, he directly controlled large business deals and always played hardball. SCS's unique software landed some big initial customers, and others followed. However, based on Fitz's observations, Moore's overreaction to the panhandlers indicated he was under stress or perhaps was just an asshole.

Fitz replayed Moore's reaction. Extreme stress results from problems at home, work, or both. Fitz checked the Hardy Boys' research; Moore wasn't married and had no children. The company was all he had.

Some people take the half-empty approach or the never-enough view of their world. Yet, by the type of car he arrived in and the assistant that blocked the beggars, Nick Moore had worked hard to enjoy the fruits of his position. A one-percenter that wanted a hundred and twenty percent. Not unlike most other corporate executives.

Yet even with Moore's limited public persona, Nolan Spencer was the real mystery man. A Howard-Hughes-level recluse with hopefully better nail care. During Fitz's initial recon, he had watched a helicopter leave the top of the SCS building every day at the same time and return precisely thirty minutes later. One day, he waited on the other side of the 520 highway and tracked the helicopter to a spot on the edge of Lake Washington. Spencer's house. Close to his billionaire buddy Bill Gates. Perhaps they traded recipes or chefs on weekends.

Fitz searched Bellevue's public real estate records and traced the helicopter to a plot of land owned by Himitsu Corporation. *Himitsu* was the Japanese word for secret. He asked the Hardy Boys to check, and they replied in fifteen minutes. Himitsu Corporation was a shell company owned by Spencer.

The expensive commute pointed to all kinds of narcissistic issues. Entitlement, sociopathy, and the-law-doesn't-apply-to-me level of grandeur. Seattle's traffic grew year after year; downtown from Lake Washington would add thirty minutes to a commute in rush hour. Hard to justify a helicopter for thirty minutes.

Spencer's and SCS's philanthropic endeavours were minuscule. He funded a dance scholarship, and then a few months ago, SCS advertised in Canada for the dance teacher position. Fitz knew David had gotten the emails.

The details of SCS proved as elusive as information on the founders. The Hardy Boys reported Spencer had written some groundbreaking software while working in Japan and convinced some Japanese investors to fund the company to build and market unique security software and hardware.

Fitz had read up on the finer points of computer security. For many years, computers had needed protection from rogue programs and ransomware via antivirus software, yet intrusions around the world kept increasing. Security breaches into systems were daily or hourly events, and corporations needed help. Spencer's hardware and software gave companies the equivalent of barbed wire and guards with guns protecting their information. And apparently, his competitors hadn't caught up to producing a similar product.

A lucrative endeavour, Fitz thought as he drank an espresso out of the tiny cup in a cafe in the shadow of a building built from the extreme profits of their specialized software.

But something wasn't right. Spencer shunned media interviews.

The company had a limited sales force with no turnover in staffing. Once engineers were hired, they stayed. There were no firings or layoffs and very stringent hiring procedures. The last picture of Spencer was taken five years ago. There were wild rumours on the chat boards about Spencer replacing himself with a robot or being an alien. One thing was for sure: Spencer was the head of a big, boring company that had cornered the market on security, making him and others rich. Rich enough for the company to afford its own helicopter.

And that made the government nervous. At least that was Westlake's story.

Fitz thought back to a lunch meeting with the government agent in Manhattan. Westlake had said, "We can't go after them. SCS is a good corporate citizen, but our intel is weak. They are like our own version of Cold War Russia. No one knows what's going on. We need to find out."

"Can't the government get a warrant to look?" Fitz asked.

"Only if we have evidence of wrongdoing. They are scrupulously clean with a vast army of lawyers. Their money and assets are legally owned and kept offshore. A shell company owns the building. Personally, Spencer pays all his taxes and doesn't take tax loopholes. His company pays its fair share. They invest in other Washington companies through the Spencer Foundation without a board of directors. All of the money came from Japanese investors. Spencer is the CEO and Nick Moore is his CFO and COO. His company has the largest Japanese-speaking workforce in the USA. However, as far as we know, he has minimal staff in Japan."

"Sounds positively evil. I see why the government wants to go after what appears to be almost a model corporate citizen," Fitz said.

"At one time, Enron and Lehman Brothers were model companies. We don't want another meltdown with a company that holds all the keys to the kingdom. Everything might be fine. However, we won't take that chance. We need some covert intelligence to make our own assessment."

"If there was some impropriety, how would it affect the country?" Fitz asked.

"Spencer's software manages the security on most cloud servers in the USA and close to sixty percent of the rest of the world. SCS protects your privacy and makes it easy to hide the fact you're surfing porn on your computer. What would happen if someone else got those keys? What would happen if Spencer was dealing with China or the Russians, offering to sell them your credit cards or just your social security number? It would jeopardize you and everyone else. If done on a large enough scale, we'd be screwed completely. So, I'm here with a hat-in-hand and asking for your help."

Westlake asking for help caused Fitz to make a face like he'd swallowed a bug. "Why? How would an old fossil, that walks with a cane, could be useful?" Fitz pointed to his walking stick leaning up against the wall beside the table. He still hadn't accepted his need to use it.

"I left out one thing."

"Which is?"

"Spencer is a patron of the arts. Ballet in particular. And SCS is recruiting for a dance teacher."

Fitz knew exactly one ballet dancer. Now he understood why Westlake wanted to meet.

"Are you suggesting young David could help?"

Westlake nodded. "I'm convinced he's the only one that could."

"He's a bit touchy about the US government and you in particular, allowing Reynolds to use him as a guinea pig to test the implant. I rather think he'd chew his arm off before helping you."

Westlake smiled. "Yes. He made that apparent when I cleared all his charges and got him back into Canada. He said he wanted no further contact. However, I'm told he's having some challenges in his personal and professional life. The compensation for the operation would go a long way to help him continue his recovery."

"By putting him into another operation? You have a strange view of recovery."

"We aren't asking very much of him. A quick bit of reconnaissance, with no danger other than some jet lag. I'd like to run some more tests too, but we can talk about that after."

Fitz raised his eyebrows at the 'no danger' comment. There were always risks. The worst ones were the kind you didn't expect. "Let me think about it and I will get back to you."

The memory of his conversation with Westlake faded and Fitz swallowed the last of his Starbucks espresso. He'd ordered only one shot to tide him over until David completed his mission.

As he expected, David's audio dropped once he was deep in the building. Westlake's bug, however, was small and untraceable. Different technology, Westlake told him. Powered by the ambient temperature of the room. No battery to worry about.

As of right now, David was also untraceable and on his own—not unlike being thrust into the Amsterdam winter with another man's memories bouncing around in his head.

Over the last year, Fitz had developed a fondness for David. The boy was strong-willed with an edge of sardonic humour—not unlike the man whose memories the boy had carried for a short time. However, since Toronto, Fitz saw a foreboding in him. Fitz knew David's life had been turned upside down, but there was something else. He wasn't sure if David even knew what it was.

Chapter Eight

DAVID HAD two more interviews in other parts of the building. Both interviewers were male and spoke English with only a trace of an accent. And best of all, he installed the last surveillance beads with no trouble.

Marisa retrieved him from the interview and ushered him into the elevator that rocketed upwards and stopped. The doors opened to a large, mirrored room with a polished wooden floor with expansive windows on one side that looked out at downtown Seattle.

"This is our new studio," Marisa said.

David whistled. Most studios were in lower sub-basement walk-downs. A few more profitable companies had studios on the ground level, but he'd never seen such a grand room. They had installed a professional vinyl dance floor, along with a ballet barre running against a mirrored wall. A grand piano faced out from a corner.

"We have been looking forward to this for some time."

"What?"

"Ballet classes in the building. Mr. Spencer built this tower to allow for flexible workspaces and re-configurable walls to handle the situations that we couldn't predict."

"When did you decide to include dance in your wellness program?"

"Mr. Spencer has always been a patron of the arts."

"I think this room wins the award for the best view of any studio ever constructed."

"I would agree with you."

"Have you had other teachers?"

"No. You would be the first."

David looked back at the studio and the view. Words he'd heard somewhere resonated in his head: *if something is too good to be true, it probably is.*

"What kind of schedule do you expect?"

"Besides two classes daily at 10:00 a.m. and 1:00 p.m., you will also teach a private class to an employee's daughter."

"Do you mean in the evening?"

"No. 3:30 p.m. every day."

"Isn't she in school?"

"Her time is flexible."

"What am I teaching?"

"You need to teach the full syllabus of the Royal Academy of Dance. I understand that's the syllabi taught at the National Ballet School."

"It is. Usually, privates are for coaching before an exam or a performance."

"This is a special situation. You've been interviewed and vetted. You must agree to the terms of the position if we make you an offer."

David walked to the edge of the glass and looked down at the street below. He felt a little like Alice before she stepped into the rabbit hole. "There are other teachers who are more qualified. Why do you want me?"

"You fit Mr. Spencer's requirements. You are..." she was about to say something and stopped herself. "You have danced all your life and graduated with honors from National Ballet School in Canada and are a strong dancer. The 'one to watch,' Toronto dance critics said."

"What is the compensation?"

"Your pay grade will be calibrated against the equivalent pay scale to our software engineers. The average starting salary for an engineer is one hundred and seventy-five thousand US dollars plus bonus and benefits. We also provide a ten-thousand-dollar signing bonus the day you start."

David inhaled slowly and tried to calm his racing pulse at the dollar figure. That kind of money would give him more freedom than he could imagine. Even if he lived in the US full time, a dancer's average income hovered around $40,000 annually, with no bonus and few benefits other than blisters and sore muscles.

When Fitz talked about the operation, his job was to enter the building, plant some surveillance equipment during the interview process, and then get the hell out of there.

Now he wasn't so sure he wanted to leave.

"I'm interested. One last question."

Marisa smiled for the first time. "Just one?"

"How many other dance teachers did you interview?"

"You are the third. As I said, SCS is very selective in our hiring process." She opened the door to the studio and walked into the middle of the room and turned towards him. "There is one last part of the interview. We'd like you to teach a class to a group of employees."

David frowned. "Teaching a class usually isn't something that just happens with no preparation."

Just then, six women walked into the studio in leotards, pink tights, and dance slippers. All Japanese. Typical for any ballet studio, however, he hadn't expected to see them on the 75th floor of a software company.

"I don't have a pianist."

Marisa touched a button on her tablet. "I will play for you."

"Have you played for a ballet class before?"

"I've played for the Tokyo and Osaka National Ballet daily classes."

David smiled. "Yes, of course you have."

"I apologize for the suddenness of this. At SCS, we like to surprise people during the interview to assess how they handle pressure."

"I can see that."

"Anything else you need before we start the demonstration?"

"No. Please take your seat." He directed her to her piano. "What level are these women?"

"Excuse me?" she asked.

"Are they experienced dancers, or do they just look the part?"

"All the women are classically trained."

David nodded and felt sweat build up under his arms. He removed his jacket and was glad he wore a black t-shirt to cover his anxiety.

He should have bailed at that point, thanked the nice lady for the interviews, and said he wasn't interested. Westlake was paying him a lot of money for a couple of days of work and the money would finance auditioning for a role at another company. New York City ballet came to mind, or he could return to Europe and audition for the Stuttgart or the Frankfurt Ballet.

Instead, he ran his hand through his hair and smiled at the group of women. He was out of work. This could be a good stopping point—at least for a little while. No harm in teaching a ballet class, was there?

"Good morning. I'm Mr. Knight. Please take your places at the barre."

The dancers nodded and took their places against the wall, one arm holding lightly onto the wooden barre.

He said to Marisa, "A slow 2/4 please, for a warm-up."

Chapter Nine

Lake Washington, Bellevue

MARISA ASKED him to return the next day at the same time for one more interview. That night he debriefed with Fitz and Westlake what he'd discovered at SCS and shared everything he remembered. As Westlake peppered him with questions, he realized his memory had become more acute, and he could recall more detail than ever.

"A hold-over skill from the implant, perhaps?" Westlake liked to fish for confirmation the spy's skills were still somehow in his head.

"More like muscle memory, I expect. When I learn a particular performance piece, my body, instead of my brain, remembers."

Westlake tried to glare at him with his wonky eye but failed. Still, David wondered if there were any skills he hadn't touched. None that he could tell.

However, both men seemed happy at the day's outcome. Westlake added a couple more beads on his ring to install if he found a suitable location.

"More the better, of course—if the opportunity presents itself."

He shook his head. "Depends on who else I'm going to interview with; Marisa never said."

"Any other observations?" Fitz asked.

"Company policies are a bit weird. There's a no-handshake rule, and it's against policy to provide cream with coffee."

"Positively barbaric!" Fitz said. The old man smiled for the first time in a while, maybe because David had made progress.

Westlake added, "But that does point to the eccentricity of its founder. Howard Hughes went the other way. Once, he had his staff store three hundred and fifty gallons of ice cream because he liked the flavor."

The next day, as a light summer rain filtered through the gray Seattle sky, David entered the building with more spring in his step than the day before. He made sure he grabbed a latte at the shop across the road, something he wouldn't get once he was in the building. Yesterday's panhandlers weren't around.

Once inside the front entrance, a short, wide man in a suit approached him.

"Mr. Knight?" he asked in a thick accent.

"I am."

"My name is Yoshi."

"Like the video game character?"

The man narrowed his eyebrows. "I am here to escort you to your meeting. Please follow me." Immediately, David's fists squeezed shut, and his legs tensed. The harder he fought his body's reaction, the harder he struggled to stay calm.

Yoshi looked at him and frowned. "Are you feeling okay, Mr. Knight?"

David managed a breath and said, "Yes. I was told there would be more interviews today."

Yoshi said, "I understand."

The big man didn't provide an answer. Instead, he turned and walked a few steps through the foyer and nodded for him to follow. David had no choice but to move forward. He took two deep breaths and felt his anxiety drop enough to continue forward.

Yoshi wore military-style close-cropped hair. The wool on his suit jacket strained against his body. David saw muscle where an untrained eye might think the man was overweight. Linebacker-style in a compact package. He didn't look like he was from the HR department; this man looked and smelled military.

David followed as Yoshi walked past the primary set of elevators and through a security door. He still did not know where he was going. Had they discovered his ruse and were taking him somewhere to beat his ass? However, if Yoshi planned to push him down an elevator shaft, he should be in front, not behind.

The series of hallways grew progressively more industrial. He took a closer look at his escort. He guessed, based on the fit of the man's jacket, he carried nothing underneath. His sheer size would negate the need for a gun.

Yoshi stopped in front of an open elevator door. "In here, please." He extended his hand.

"Doumo," the Japanese word slipped out of his mouth. Doumo meant *thanks*, and he didn't know that until he said it. Curious. Maybe he saw an anime show as a kid and learned the word unconsciously. No other words came to mind.

Yoshi raised an eyebrow before following inside and touching his thumb to a small black panel. No floor numbers like the main elevators. The door closed, and the acceleration tickled his stomach for about a minute until it slowed and stopped. He swallowed and cleared his ears. What floor were they on?

The elevator opened into a glass-covered area with a free vista toward Puget Sound. The mountains sparkled in the background. To the south, he saw planes taking off at SeaTac airport. In front of him was a helicopter. Executive grade. Painted flat black.

Didn't Fitz say that Spencer used a helicopter to get to work?

"Please follow."

"Where are we going?"

"Ten minutes only." David stayed in the elevator. Yoshi turned and leaned in slightly. "Do you have fear?"

YES, his inside voice screamed. "I wasn't told I was leaving the building via the roof."

"My apologies. Please follow."

'No' wasn't a word that Yoshi understood. Instead, David followed him towards the helicopter as a fast wind blew across the landing pad.

The rain had stopped, and they were the only ones on the roof. A thinner man with headphones sat in the pilot's seat. Just the three of them. Yoshi didn't ask him for his cell phone. He hoped Fitz was tracking his GPS if someone had to find his body.

The engine caught, and the quad blade started rotating. He fastened his seat belt, and Yoshi squeezed his bulk beside him before passing him a pair of thick headphones. "These will help," he said.

After a few more minutes, the engine whine rose, and the helicopter took off before taking a slow turn to the east and accelerating. Yoshi never smiled; as they lifted off, he held up five fingers on one hand and two on the other.

Seven minutes.

Alarm bells rang in David's head like church on Sunday. His mind heard that Yoshi was taking him to another interview, yet his body reacted like the big man planned to throw him out of the helicopter mid-trip. A tragic accident for a prospective employee. The company wishes to offer condolences to the family of the dancer.

Yoshi's bulk kept him squeezed tight against the door. He kept imagining that Yoshi would reach over, pull the door open and, in a quick motion, unlock the seat belt and push David into the water below. He'd die either from the fall or by drowning. No way he could stop him from doing it. No weapon or room to maneuver.

David's mind fought the fight impulse by looking out the window and taking slow, shallow breaths. *This is crazy,* he told himself. He repeated to himself; *I've got nothing to worry about.* Yoshi leaned his head against the headrest and closed his eyes.

Maybe David would live to the end of the interview after all.

As they crossed the I-5 highway and then over Capitol Hill, the sprawling University of Washington sat to the north and Lake Washington to the east. A large clump of tall office buildings appeared in the distance. *Bellevue,* he thought. The longer the helicopter flew, the less danger he felt.

Where were they taking him, and why did they need a helicopter? Fitz hadn't prepared him for any of this.

David knew that Bill Gates famously owned a behemoth mansion on the lake below them. Maybe Gates wanted a dance teacher of his own. You know how billionaires are.

The helicopter continued a few minutes to the south and then slowed, dropping over a line of trees onto a hidden, well-manicured helipad. After the blades had stopped, Yoshi and David stepped onto a bark-covered trail leading up to a small hill.

He followed Yoshi until they reached an extra-large West Coast house with wooden beams and lots of glass cut into the rocky hillside. Yoshi circled them around the back to a hidden doorway encircled with blue lights. Yoshi washed and disinfected his hands in a small sink beside the door and directed David to do the same.

"The ultraviolet light kills germs," he said, pointing to the door frame.

His escort pushed an ID card to a small black square, and the door clicked open, leading them into a small entry area. At the top of a wooden staircase, a tall, thin, and very white man with gray hair stood waiting. He wore loafers, tan slacks, and a button-down blue cotton shirt. His hair wasn't just gray; it was almost pure white, like someone in their 70s. However, he seemed under fifty.

Nolan Spencer.

He waved them upstairs. "You must be David. Sorry about all the cloak and dagger as a way of getting you over here. As you can imagine, I'm a little crazy about my security and privacy." David extended his hand, but Spencer kept his arms to his side. Yoshi shook his head.

"Sorry, I forgot," David said. "No handshakes." From what Westlake had said, David stood in front of one of the wealthiest men in North America after being flown to his house in a private helicopter. Was his comment about security showing he knew David deployed the devices inside his company?

"Call me Nolan."

"Okay. Nolan." David frowned and said, "Thanks for the helicopter tour and everything, but there must be a mistake. I interviewed for a job yesterday in your company."

"Yes. To become our resident dance teacher."

"Do you fly all your prospective employees over here?"

He chuckled. "No. Never. You are one of the first outside of my security team I've invited here."

"Why am I here then?"

"Because of Leia." He pointed to a thin girl standing in the middle of what looked like a dance studio on the south side of the main hallway. She faced the window and didn't look in his direction.

"My daughter. Leia is short for Ophelia."

David stared at the girl. She looked younger than fourteen and older than ten. Perhaps twelve. A skinny twelve. She stood in dark leggings and a tank top, swaying to invisible music. He didn't see any earbuds. She swayed and then twirled in a tight, almost pirouette before continuing to sway. She wore a tiny Hello Kitty backpack large enough to hold a chocolate bar.

She reminded him of someone. Maybe she looked like one of the younger kids from his ballet school.

"I want you to teach her. Or at least try to teach her," Spencer said.

"Ballet?"

Spencer nodded.

"I don't have any experience teaching kids. I'm sure there are some excellent ballet schools in the area."

"I'm sorry and apologize for not having someone brief you earlier. My daughter is off-the-charts smart; we can't even test for her IQ. She's also on the spectrum. She can't go to a normal school as she has outbursts and is prone to anger. We've tried a few times to get her into a more social environment with no luck. The only thing that she likes is dance. However, none of the teachers we've tried have worked."

"Why not?"

"Not a good fit." Spencer didn't elaborate further.

"What do you want me to do?"

"I watched you teach yesterday, and I've seen some of your more recent performances. You have a strength about you that most dancers lack. However, I first need you to connect with her."

David stared at Spencer then at Leia. The whole thing seemed like a waking dream. He'd agreed to install covert surveillance equipment for the US government and return to Toronto. Now he's being asked to teach a billionaire's daughter. Leia was the student they wanted him to teach. "I can't promise anything."

"I've read your resume, and I'm confident you can." Spencer walked over to the door of the studio. "When she's not moving like this, she watches ballet on YouTube. Before we begin, I need your word that there will be *no* impropriety between you and my daughter."

"No. Of course not."

"And there will be no outside contact, email, or texting outside of the time dancing. All the training will happen here. Agreed?"

"So, I take it you are offering me the job?"

Spencer laughed. "To teach dance to the employees? Yes. As for teaching my daughter, I'd like to see if you can connect with her enough for her to follow your instruction. Let's go in. As you will discover, she's not overly communicative."

He pulled the heavy wood and glass doors forward and walked inside. David followed.

The room was long and wide, about forty by fifty feet by his estimate, meaning about two thousand square feet. The floor was covered with thick Marley vinyl. The tall windows looked out onto Lake Washington.

"We can see out, and no one can see in. Too many paparazzi are trying to take pictures from boats on the lake."

Leia stood under a halogen spotlight that highlighted her silhouette. Her legs were like little twigs in black leggings, and her arms followed suit.

David noticed a bandage wrapped around her forearm.

"We have a problem with self-harm. I'm told she does it to feel something," Spencer said.

He motioned David to stay at the door. "Leia? There's someone here who would like to meet you." She continued to swing back and forth in time with invisible music and didn't stop or look at her father. Her hair, in contrast to her father's, was jet black.

"Her mother was Japanese, so luckily she didn't get my looks." Leia still didn't acknowledge or notice that her father and David were in the room.

"This is the tricky part—to get her attention without setting her off."

"What kind of ballet did you say she watches?"

"Anything really. Anything with music and movement. Most nights, I shut her access to the internet off so she can get some sleep."

"Do you know if she has any favorites?"

"She likes classical ballet. Pointe shoes and full tutus."

David pulled out his smartphone. "Do you have a way to play my phone through the room?"

"Yes. There." He pointed to a tiny shelf with a cable and a few buttons. David connected his smartphone to the system and started a song. Immediately, a soft strum of trumpets filled the room.

"What's this?" Spencer asked.

"Bolero."

David walked into the middle of the studio, ignoring Leia, and moved into first position. He raised his hands and moved his body. Step, step, step, leap. Pirouette and again step, step, step, pirouette. He moved through an entire routine he'd choreographed a few years ago for the fun of it. A man dancing differs from a woman. Shorter, more decisive moves. More definite and angular. Women sometimes have more precise and gentler moves. Not so for men.

He never looked at Leia and instead kept his attention on the piece. The trumpets of Bolero rose, and he moved with them. Leia stopped moving, and out of the corner of his eye, he saw her paying attention. Finally, after a few minutes, the piece ended, and he recovered his smartphone. He realized he had a surveillance bead to insert. Though inside Spencer's house would be good, he didn't want to press his luck.

Leia ran over to her father and whispered in his ear before running out of the room.

Spencer looked shocked, as if this was the first time she'd ever done that. Perhaps it was.

"What did she say?" David asked.

"She said she liked you. The job is yours if you want it."

Chapter Ten

Westin Hotel, Seattle

"You took the job?" Fitz asked. He looked like David's father did when he told him he wanted to be a ballet dancer.

"I did."

"Teaching Spencer's daughter ballet?"

"Afternoons. In the morning, I teach two classes for employees."

"And he's flying you to his house every day via helicopter?"

"Much less traffic to deal with." He smiled at the thought of his newfound station in life. Fitz hobbled around the hotel room, stabbing his cane into the carpet. David worried the news might either cause a stroke or have Fitz spontaneously combust. Maybe both at the same time.

Westlake sat back in the wide chair and smiled. "This may be a good thing."

"What do you mean, a good thing? This was a quick in-and-out. No muss, no fuss, no guns. He's planted all the bugs, and now you want him to go back for a god-damned job?" Fitz said.

Fitz's voracity surprised him. The old Brit rarely cussed and was the poster boy for upper-crust civility.

"No, Asher. I didn't say that. David working on the inside might help uncover the truth."

"What exactly has this company done again?" David asked.

Westlake turned and said. "It's not what they've done. I'm more concerned with what they might plan to do."

"You mean like selling arms to Iran and using the money to fund South American wars?"

Westlake glared with his good eye and finally broke out into as much of a smile as David had ever seen.

"Before my time, I'm afraid. My higher-ups worried that Spencer's company is doing one thing to get to another outcome, like how a magician misdirects the audience."

"And you have no idea what it is," David said.

Westlake shook his head. "Call it a hunch."

Fitz piped up. "What's your famous CIA hunch telling you?"

"That something is going on that we won't like when we find out. And we might be too late to do anything when we find the truth."

"What category are we talking about? Animal, mineral, or vegetable?" Fitz asked.

"Medical, we think."

"Bio-warfare?" Fitz asked.

"Not sure. Not yet. Selling security secrets is too much on the nose for a software company. However, we are getting a whiff of biotech in some intelligence, but nothing conclusive. One red flag is that Spencer has no history. He first appeared twelve years ago after creating some revolutionary software and started a company that took on and beat a large group of security software vendors."

"What do you mean, no history?" David asked.

Westlake pulled out his phone and squinted with one eye. "In situations like this, we run background checks on the principals. We found some history, and it's a bit thin."

"How thin?" Fitz asked. He hadn't planned to tell Westlake what he'd learned from the Hardy Boys.

"The intel says he was an only child, and his parents died when he was young. No information on relatives or adopted parents. We have records of schools he attended, along with his report cards and grades.

Nothing out of the ordinary other than the parent information is missing. No US-issued driver's license. He pays his taxes and votes by mail. Our biggest issue is we can't positively confirm the man in the big house on Lake Washington is, indeed, Nolan Spencer. He gives no interviews, and no one but his staff has been close to him. Except for you, it seems." He glanced at David.

Fitz turned to David and said, "What's your assessment of him?"

David shrugged. "He's a doting father, calm, considerate, and thoughtful. I didn't detect any weirdness if that's what you're thinking. . You said biotech before. What do you mean?"

"Rumors mostly. We had intelligence that when he lived in Japan, he worked for a biotech firm, except we couldn't confirm it either way. SCS has nothing to do with biology—just security and analytics. We found his software protects eighty percent of personal health data worldwide and a large share of banks and governments. There are many ways that security or broken security might tip the scale in a conflict or even a country's economy. Hacking into a government computer and holding it for cyber ransom might trigger several outcomes. We just want to make sure he's not rigging the deck for profit."

"...not unlike the way the US Government usually does," David said.

Westlake glared at him but didn't disagree. "Yes. If anyone is going to rig the deck, we want to be the one dealing the cards."

Fitz hobbled over to a small chair, sat down, and poured himself a cup of tea from an insulated container. As Fitz sipped the hot liquid, David could see his body visibly relax.

"How much did they offer you?"

"One hundred and seventy-five thousand dollars plus benefits." David almost couldn't contain his smile.

Fitz raised his eyebrows. "If I'm correct, you'd be one of the highest-paid dance teachers in the country."

"Probably in the world."

"Now that you've been in the literal belly of the beast, is any of the old spy's intuition coming through?" Westlake asked.

He glared at the government agent and shook his head. "The memories are gone. I told you that before." David poured himself some tea from Fitz's container and sat down. "I hate to say it, but there was something odd about the entire process, from the interviews to the job offer. There's no way they should pay that much for a dance teacher. They'd have a line a block long waiting to interview. And I'm not a teacher. I'm a dancer that can teach a class."

"Then why you?" Fitz said. "Any ideas?"

David shook his head. "None."

Fitz stared out the window of his room in The Seattle Westin. The hotel was a great place for a tourist visiting the city. He wanted a line of sight to the SCS building, and this room worked fine.

The window overlooked downtown and Puget Sound. To the left sat the cruise ship terminal and to the right was the Seattle Aquarium. Maybe someday, he'd visit as a tourist and relax instead of experiencing the usual anxiety that came with running an intelligence operation. "Anything?"

Westlake glanced towards him and shook his head. He peered over the shoulder of his tech as information scrolled up on a laptop screen.

"I woke one sensor up and kept it quiet. We expect a large broadcast from a hidden device might set off some alarms in the building," said the tech.

"What kind of signal do you use?" asked Fitz.

"A modified wireless telephone frequency. As it's not receiving, only sending, the range is good. We can pick up audio, or if the bug is close enough, we can grab some of the wireless network traffic. If the device detects anything, it opens a channel to us."

"What do you hope to get?" Fitz said.

Westlake turned to Fitz and said, "Anything is better than nothing. A Japanese-born computer science grad agreed to help us about six months ago. After his first interview, he boarded a plane to Japan the next day, and we've heard nothing from him since."

"Is he still in Japan?"

"We don't know. Our intel from Japan is even weaker than what we have here. He was spooked or bought off. In most companies, people aren't hired that fast unless there's something illegal going on."

"Why was he helping you to begin with?"

"His father was in prison; we offered to help reduce his sentence."

"Is his father still there?"

"No. That's the kicker. Another law firm re-opened his father's case, and he was released a couple of months ago. Fresh DNA evidence was presented."

"Convenient, don't you think?" Fitz said.

Westlake raised his hand towards Fitz. "We are picking up email traffic. At least the bugs are working as advertised."

The tech typed on the keyboard, and blocks of text appeared on the screen.

"We are converting it to English."

"Anything important?"

Westlake looked down at the text and his eyebrows rose.

"Perhaps."

Chapter Eleven

ON HIS FIRST DAY, David spent the morning in a company orientation for new employees. After signing a multiple-page employee contract he didn't read, he was given a thin SCS employee ID card with his picture on it and a thicker plastic encased the access card that would get him into the building and elevators. He slipped the employee card in his wallet and took a seat in a large training room filled with Japanese men and women in business attire.

He wore jeans and a black t-shirt.

During the morning, well-manicured executives spoke about the company vision, culture, and products. One executive spoke about Spencer with near-religious fervour. However, the executives glossed over the history of the company; anything they would say seemed thin.

He found out that SCS had their headquarters in Seattle and ran large data centres in Virginia, Germany, and Tokyo to serve customers around the world. Most of the time, the execs talked about the need for security—both for the products and the company. Although most of the technical detail sailed above his head, one module caught his attention. Social engineering, the executive said, was a top security issue that no amount of software could fix. He gave an example of how a fast-talking salesperson could get past the guard and into the elevator to sell floor by floor.

Precisely at noon, a lunch lady wheeled around a cart of bento boxes and delivered one with precision to each new employee. Marisa met him after his mind-numbing orientation. She was still his handler.

"As you aren't from Seattle, we have provided accommodation for you within walking distance of the office."

"Really?" He hadn't given much thought to his accommodation as he'd only planned to be in Seattle for a couple of days and after yesterday's fear of being tossed from the helicopter, he wondered if he'd make it past the end of the week.

She smiled. "It's furnished, and as you will be busy, our service can stock your refrigerator with fresh food or supply a chef to cook your dinners. You also have a daily food allowance if you prefer to eat outside the apartment." She handed him an envelope with a key and an address. "Let me show you to your office."

"Office?" He followed her into the elevator that delivered them to the same floor as the rehearsal studio. In a corner office sat a custom desk, a high-end chair, and an open laptop.

"This is yours," she said and didn't give him any clue what they expected him to do with the computer. Email perhaps? Since the accident last year, his surfing habits had changed. No longer was he interested in posting about his life to strangers on the internet. His brain now cautioned him that broadcasting his life was an excellent way to get killed. Instead, he became consumed with world political events, who was in power and who was not.

Yet as he sat down in the custom chair and desk, he noticed the smile on his face hadn't disappeared since Marisa had handed him the key to the apartment.

What rabbit hole had he fallen into?

He realized he was the only employee stationed here. SCS had outfitted the entire floor as an exercise and wellness area with Japanese-style locker rooms complete with hot and cold pools, and separate washing stations with wooden stools. At lunch, he found a few of the male employees soaking in the hot pools with small towels perched on their heads. He wasn't planning to check the woman's side.

There was nothing else for him to do. As the classes and his first day with Leia started tomorrow, he left early to check out his new apartment.

After following the address with his smartphone, he ended up north of Pike Place Market in an area known as Belltown. In Canada, a dancer's salary usually afforded a basement suite in an older building filled with unpleasant smells. As he stood in front of the building that matched the address, he realized his apartment wouldn't be like that.

There must be a mistake. Brick, steel, and glass with a freshly restored vibe. However, after holding the key fob to the access panel, the door clicked open. "2205," the note said. A few minutes later, after a silent elevator ride, he stood in the front hallway of his apartment.

Gorgeous vistas of Puget Sound opened up from the living room. A five-foot TV screen hung above a gas fireplace, and there were granite counters and stainless-steel appliances. Inside the refrigerator were fresh vegetables, meat, eggs, and cheese. Six bottles of beer on the bottom shelf. A note was attached to a small bottle of milk in the door. "Enjoy with your coffee — Marisa."

As he opened a beer and walked out to the terrace overlooking the water, he wondered if he had signed away his soul with his employment contract. He decided he didn't care.

Later, he walked into the warm Seattle evening following a zigzag security protocol route until he slipped into The Westin's parking lot and met Fitz in his hotel room. As he walked him through the day's events, Fitz couldn't believe the company supplied an apartment.

"By all means, enjoy your place. As the suite might be bugged, don't break protocol. No contact from within the walls."

David nodded. Too much of a good thing usually spells trouble. However, he liked the prestige so far. He kept the meeting short, took the back stairs to the parking garage, and slipped back into the Seattle evening.

David's first classes began at 10:00 a.m. and noon the next day. Both were small, with women ranging barely out of their teens to a couple under forty.

His ten o'clock class started uneventfully as they filed in, bowed, and smiled. Six women in pink tights, ballet shoes, and black hair in neat buns. Marisa followed with another woman behind her in a long dress and heels. The woman bowed and smiled.

"Sensei, this is Sakura, and she will play for your classes."

"Does your name mean Cherry Blossom?" David asked.

Sakura covered her mouth and giggled.

Marisa smiled and said, "Have you been studying Japanese?"

"No. I must have read that somewhere." He wondered why some words seemed familiar. Had Jonathan ever traveled to Japan? He'd ask Fitz later. He didn't want any more surprises or to find out that the spy had been a secret Teppanyaki chef.

Sakura took her place at the piano in the corner. The dancers stood at the barre against the mirror, facing the water.

"A 3/4, please," he said to Sakura. He grabbed the barre and demonstrated the warm-up as she played a slow melody that mirrored every dance class he'd ever taken. His goal was to get to know the dancers and give the appearance that he knew how to teach.

During the exercises, he increased the complexity and noticed the dancers followed without difficulty; Marisa had told him the truth.

However, the class appeared more stoic than he expected, and he wasn't sure if they had volunteered or were told to attend his class. However, his next one was different. Six women arrived, again dressed in tights with their hair tightly wrapped in buns on the top of their heads. Unlike the morning class, the women all smiled, bowed, and giggled as they walked into the studio. Without direction, they took their positions at the barre and waited. He moved up to the front of the room and again started the warm-up. From his viewpoint in the mirror, he noticed smiles on all his students.

For the first thirty minutes, the dancers followed his progressively harder exercises. He brought them into the center for the second half of the class, and they performed several small pieces he'd put together.

Just like every class he'd taken since the age of eight.

At the end, he bowed, and each woman bowed and said their name. The last dancer looked so excited he expected her to levitate off the floor. "Sensei, my name is Amai." She giggled, and her hand covered her mouth.

Being called sensei or teacher felt strange. Instead of letting it go, he said, "Call me David."

That elicited giggles from the rest of the dancers. She bowed and said, "Ok, David-san!"

He wasn't sure if he'd ever adjust to being called David-san.

At 2:00 p.m. precisely, he followed Yoshi into the helipad elevator and onto the waiting helicopter. It was a ten-minute flight to Lake Washington, same for the walk from the helicopter to the house. Spencer met them at the door, brought David to the dance studio, and then disappeared. Leia stood where he'd first met her, swaying to the music and looking out to the water.

"Good afternoon, Leia." He took a position at the barre along the wall. Once he started the music, he began a slow warm-up.

He held onto the barre facing the water and worked his feet and legs to an easy pattern to the front, side, and back. He extended his left arm to the side, bent forward at the waist, and recovered to a straight position. He repeated the side bend, recovery, and back bend, always in time with the music. At the end, he rose into fifth position and balanced with his arms to the side.

He caught Leia staring at him. He ignored her and kept going.

She moved to the ballet barre, and he could tell she had taken hold of the polished maple.

"Your turn," he said without looking at her.

She followed his movements as he repeated from the beginning and he narrated as he moved. "Stretch to the front and flex and point, close to fifth. Out and close. Out and close."

She moved. Her movements were not as refined as he had expected. However, there was a lightness in her step and an urgency about her.

She followed his directions as any good student would. After a few minutes, he realized she had the potential to be a beautiful dancer. "Now turn to the other side, and let's repeat the exercise with the other leg."

As he waited for her to turn, she stopped and shook. Her hands dropped from the barre, and she raced out of the studio.

Was she coming back? He wondered if he did something that upset her but couldn't think of what it was. As he unplugged his phone, Spencer appeared with an enormous smile. "Well done. She has never gotten that far before."

"We weren't finished."

"I'm delighted with how far she went. She might have gotten overwhelmed by the music, the movement, or you."

"Me?"

"She watches ballet incessantly on YouTube and pours through her collection of ballet DVDs after I turn off her internet access. Her doctor and I will review the video of your interaction with her today to see if he has any suggestions."

"Video? You never told me you were taking video."

Spencer's face grew tight. "I'm sorry. That's my prerogative. This is therapy, not just a dance class. She seems to like you, and I'm hoping we can make a breakthrough."

David said nothing. He wasn't sure how he felt about being recorded without his knowledge. From her father's point of view, he understood, yet something wasn't quite right.

As a father, Spencer wanted the best for his daughter, including flying a ballet dancer to teach her every day. The story sounded plausible. His daughter did have challenges; one to one dance training might be the way in. However, her father didn't seem like a whiter version of an Italian mob boss. Just a smart guy that struck a vein of software gold the world needed. Maybe Westlake and the US government were all wrong. Except, for an operation like this to be authorized, they would have needed more than a hunch.

"Yoshi will escort you back to the city. I expect you tomorrow at the same time," Spencer said and walked out of the room. The parent-teacher meeting was over.

Two minutes later, a smiling Yoshi came to the studio and ushered him out to the waiting helicopter. He noticed Spencer standing at a window, watching them leave. He wondered what else he did during the day besides watching over his daughter. SCS was a big operation. If Spencer was here, who was running his company? Nick Moore, the man afraid of homeless people?

Chapter Twelve

Nick Moore looked out of the penthouse window of The Four Seasons hotel with a glass of Glenmorangie single malt in his hand. He loved the place and its discretion. He'd discovered through a former assistant that all employees signed non-disclosure agreements about guests and their habits. They guaranteed his anonymity as long as he wasn't doing anything illegal.

He ignored the view of Puget Sound and sipped the scotch. Everything pissed him off today, especially being forced to live in tourist-heavy Seattle instead of the all-business Manhattan.

However, what upset him the most was Spencer.

"Who is this asshole again?" Moore asked. His private investigator had laid out a series of photographs on the mahogany table near the window. The top picture showed an old white man in a tailored suit inside a cafe. A smartphone was in his hand.

"As you know, we track the new employees you've identified for the first few weeks to protect SCS from any social engineering attacks, rogue programmers looking to steal company secrets—that sort of thing."

"I remember. I set it up."

"Yes, sir. Naturally, we do this as a matter of security. Ninety-nine out of a hundred times, we find nothing. This case is unique, and because of our findings, we needed to notify you directly."

Moore looked over at him and said. "A geezer drinking coffee? He doesn't look like he'd get through the applicant tracking system."

"Correct. You didn't hire him." He pulled out the next picture. "Your company hired this man." The photo showed a younger, blonde, and buff man sitting directly beside the older man at another table. "His name is David Knight."

Moore frowned and set his scotch on the mahogany table. "Doesn't seem likely for either guy. We only employ Japanese landed immigrants. Are you sure?"

"Mr. Spencer hired him to teach dance to the employees."

"When?" Moore said.

"Last week."

"Dance?"

"Ballet. Unusual, I know. Many Silicon Valley companies retain yoga teachers to help reduce stress, so dance isn't much different. However, the old man beside him got our attention, and it took us a bit to find his identity. His photograph didn't connect us to any social media service. We couldn't find a LinkedIn profile or even a Facebook page."

Moore picked up the picture and stared at it. "Maybe because he's a grandpa."

"He's past retirement age, yes. However, it's unusual to have no online presence at all. Even though he's using a high-end smartphone, he's a ghost in the electronic world. An internet search of someone's face usually brings results. Not this time."

"Did you find him?"

"Mr. Moore, our firm is good at what we do. If I can get a picture of someone, they exist. We just had to figure out where to look."

"And?"

"Funny enough, in the covert community."

Moore sipped more of the scotch and resisted the urge to gulp it down. "You mean like the Russians or Germans?"

"Not exactly. Intelligence for hire. Governments or companies that need off-the-books information." He set the picture back down on the stack and said. "His era was when spies rode dinosaurs. Microfilm and dead drops behind the Iron Curtain. He peaked about ten years before the wall came down. The old man's name is Asher Fitzsimmons."

"Wall?"

"Berlin Wall."

Moore nodded. He remembered watching it come down in high school. The whole situation irritated him, and he wanted this guy out of the room as soon as possible.

"You presented me with a picture of a retired geezer spy drinking coffee beside a new employee. Congratulations."

The man said, "Correct."

Moore swore to himself and wanted to light up a cigarette in the worst way. He took a breath to calm his nerves.

"We watched for several minutes. From what we can tell, they talked. Possibly just a couple of guys striking up a conversation over coffee. However, we think there's more to it. I found news about Knight being caught up in something a year ago. Fitzsimmons appeared to sustain an injury around that time as well." He pointed to the cane beside the chair. "Our intel concluded he never used a cane before. This leads us to believe he'd been in an accident."

Moore stared at the photograph, trying hard to come up with a plausible explanation other than the US or some other government was poking around in his business. A business that he'd carefully organized to prevent things like this from happening.

"We did a background check on Knight. Ballet dancer from Toronto. Canadian. No military record or anything else. No family. We don't think he'd ever been out of Canada until last year."

"Where did he go?"

"He performed in Europe and then went missing. Local authorities accused him of drug offenses and homicide. They dropped the charges."

"Why?"

"We can't tell. Unfortunately, there are limits to our intelligence gathering, especially when it ventures into the hidden side."

"But you connected our newest employee with an old spy specializing in information gathering."

"Correct."

"And Spencer hired him."

"Yes. From what we've gathered after reviewing your HR department's notes on the hiring process, Spencer gave the green light himself."

Moore drained the glass. "Thanks for your help. I will arrange payment the usual way." He extended his hand towards the door. The man took the hint and left the suite after first leaving the photographs and a folder behind.

Moore gathered the photographs together and pushed everything into the room's safe. He had a few hours of relaxation planned, and today he needed it. Spencer was trying to screw things up again, and Moore tried hard to overlook it. But this time, Spencer crossed the line and could bring the entire house of cards down on them. Moore sent a text and placed his phone and tablet into the safe as well and locked it with a four-digit code.

The other window peeked towards Lake Washington. Almost a direct diagonal from this building to Spencer's fortress. He wished he could order a cruise missile from room service like he did the scotch. It would circumvent a lot of problems, however, he needed to unplug for a while.

He heard a soft knock at the door. Right on time. He let the girl into the suite, she fit his profile perfectly: tall, curvy, and luscious.

The room service in this hotel was the best.

Chapter Thirteen

Dogenzaka, Shibuya, Tokyo

THE LOVE HOTEL Yumi chose the night before was short on love and short on windows. An elaborate, almost pornographic painting against one wall inside the room could slide out to reveal a tiny fire escape into the back alley.

In the morning, she craved a cup of Jasmine tea, but there was nothing in the room. The lobby only contained a set of loveless vending machines that supplied only warm tea, packaged food, carbonated alcohol drinks, or sex toys to fit most Japanese fetishes.

She'd dozed with one eye open in a bed that probably never saw a full night's sleep. She fantasized about boarding a plane, leaving Japan, and feeling safe enough to lean back and nod off. Maybe she'd sleep the entire flight.

After showering and dressing in different clothes, she left the hotel at 8:00 a.m., grabbing a taxi instead of the subway. She didn't feel like fighting the morning rush and didn't need to. She didn't want to take the chance of any spotters at the stations noticing her and broadcasting her location.

A white-haired taxi driver smiled at her as she climbed into the backseat of the older Toyota and said, "Shinjuku Station, please." She decided to only speak English from now to practice living somewhere else.

Her only goal was to empty her safe deposit box. Any bank could supply American dollars, but a couple of years ago, she'd chosen to store her valuables securely with a private company. All the benefits of a bank but without all the excessive regulation and control. Fully automated, the Tokyo Personal Deposit was always available. A key card and fingerprint gave her access to the facility any time of the day or night, and a robot retrieved her box. An admirer from a few years ago set her up with a ten-year rental for the occasional trade of her time and services.

The taxi dropped her at the subway station and the Tokyo summer heat had already come on strong. She had decided to wait until morning to ensure she could disappear into the rush hour crowd if she needed to. She walked several blocks through the humidity and the employees heading to their white-collar jobs. At one time, she'd considered becoming a salary worker and shivered at the life most of them lived. Eat, work, sleep, and repeat. She wanted something more—she just wasn't sure how to get it.

However, this morning, she chose an office worker outfit, ditching her white ball cap and party girl clothes for neutral coloured skirt and jacket. She'd fit in at any Tokyo office and challenge her pursuers to find her in a sea of similarly dressed employees.

The facility was a plain building three blocks south of Shinjuku Station, far away from the neon depravity of Kabukicho. Each floor housed some kind of business: lawyers, importers, finance, or mortgage brokers. Her destination was the basement.

She entered the building and waited as a few men and women filed into an open elevator. Once the lobby cleared, she pulled on the door to the basement and stopped. The stink of cigarette smoke wafted up from below. She stuck her head inside and peeked down the stairs. Two men in suits leaned up against the wall. Half-smoked cigarettes hung out of their mouths.

The stairs only led to Tokyo Personal Deposit. Nothing else. Men hanging around and smoking meant either they were waiting for someone that was already inside or they waited for someone else to appear.

Based on the night before, they were waiting for her.

She closed the door quietly, slipped out of the lobby, and back into the throngs of people heading to work. Life presented an ongoing series of obstacles, and she already had her fair share. Not getting access to the facility changed things. She'd kept an alternative passport and a set of credit cards in the box. She worried her real ID might raise a security flag, and she'd never make it to the airplane. Another identity would speed her escape and on to her new life.

She had no other choice. She needed another passport, or the vampire would get his teeth in her once again.

Fake identification was easy to obtain in Japan. They just couldn't be Japanese. She knew of a few backroom operations that could supply the right documents. However, she had limited time and little trust. There was only one place that would be acceptable. After disappearing back into the subway station and grabbing some food, she took a cab to Akihabara that dropped her in front of the tall Sega sign. She walked with purpose through vast groups of tourists looking perpetually lost as they wandered around the morning streets of Electric Town.

Block-long electronics stores pumped driving music with every outside wall covered in advertising for food, movies, video games, and anime girls in knee-high stockings. Between the stores were BBQ, sushi, or ramen shops, all getting ready to feed lunch to the throngs of tourists and residents. This level of commerce seemed commonplace in Japan. She wondered how she'd react to a country that wasn't trying to sell something 24 hours a day.

She threaded through a narrow alley and up an even narrower staircase until she buzzed a button beside a red metal door at the end. As she got close, she noticed several round dents on the surface, as if a customer had head-butted the door. Knowing who she was visiting, someone might have rammed the door with the customer's head.

The door opened, and a large man looked down at her and smiled.

He asked no questions before waving her in. "I have an appointment this time," she said in English. She needed all the practice she could get.

Boxes and shelves covered both sides of the hallway as she made her way to an inner office. She found the little gnome of a man sitting in his chair, peering through a magnifying glass, painting a small robot with a brush. A tray of colors sat on his desk. His English name was "Mr. Continental." She thought he had picked it because he always liked the old American luxury cars, but she couldn't be sure.

He looked up at her and frowned. She tried her best smile. "I need another passport. Plus, credit cards."

"No, good morning. No, how are you?" He kept painting and switched colors a few times while she waited for him to finish. A large comic book sat open on the other side of his desk. She noticed the pages contained detailed pictures of robot and tentacle pornography.

"Good morning. How are you?" she smiled again. Her cheeks were hurting.

"What happened to the passport I made for you three months ago?"

She smiled again. "I'm adding to my collection. I need one in Spanish and maybe Portuguese."

Mr. Continental snorted. "You don't look Portuguese."

"Swiss then. I speak some German," she said.

"Give me a second." He opened a large drawer beside his desk and rifled through a large stack. "I have one from the UK. The woman has black hair and is your height. Okay?"

She shrugged and said yes. A UK passport would allow her just to use English if stopped and let her leave the country without being detected.

"300,000 yen," he said with a straight face. Close to $2000 US dollars. She wasn't in a haggling mood, and he was the only vendor. He would have paid the pickpocket that stole it from an unsuspecting tourist around $50 American dollars. Nice profit margin.

"Three months ago, I gave you 150,000 yen."

"Inflation. Prices rise. Police cracking down on my suppliers."

His pickpockets, she thought. She opened a thin wallet and counted out the exact amount. She'd expected the increase and used three cards she'd grabbed from Leather Pants the night before at three banks for the cash. If she had just gotten to her safe deposit box, she wouldn't have needed this.

"When do you need this?"

"I'll wait here while you do it."

He looked over his glasses. "Why the hurry? Tokyo is nice with this heat." He chuckled at his own joke. A modern air conditioner on the wall delivered cool air into his little place—a far cry from the sweltering heat outside.

"There is no one else here."

"You are in luck. My morning is free." He laughed again and stood up. "Follow me," he said.

The narrow hallway where she met him blocked a larger, hidden work area. Clean and organized, with wire shelves stacked with neat and well-labeled boxes. Very different from the entrance.

"What is stopping the police from coming to see you and asking questions about all this?"

He grabbed a camera and motioned for Yumi to sit on a stool with a plain white background behind her. "Look into the lens. Don't smile." He snapped some pictures, connected the device to a laptop, and fiddled with the image. "I provide many services for lots of people. Many police and politicians. Everyone is in the boxes." He nodded to the shelves. "Police don't want to look because they won't like what they find."

A small printer in a corner whirred.

She watched as he pulled on magnifying glasses and expertly cut and pasted her likeness over the original photo. He slipped the page into another machine several times and pressed a button. To Yumi, he was aging the paper slightly to erase evidence of his work.

"Good passport. Japanese woman. We could have kept her picture, but you didn't look much alike. Better to have your picture." He flapped the passport in the air before handing it to her. "Now tell me why you need it so fast?"

She just smiled and took the document. She leaned in and kissed his forehead. "Thanks, Grandfather."

"Wait. One moment." He left the room for a minute before returning with another document. "Another Japanese woman. Very fresh. Can you use it?" he handed her a deep blue Japan passport.

She looked at the picture and smiled. "Thanks. This will work fine."

The old man handed her the wad of cash she'd given him. "I think you need this more than me, Granddaughter. Stay out of trouble."

"That's what the passport is for."

The old man wasn't her real grandfather, but he was the only one she had. She'd met him when she needed it the most. She was pregnant and on the run from the white vampire and he helped her. He asked nothing about her situation or even who the father was. He just helped find the woman that took her baby. Maybe she reminded him of a relative or his own daughter.

He helped again. She hoped this would be the last time.

A taxi took her from Akihabara to Tokyo Station and then to the Narita Express. She'd booked a trip online during the hour-long train ride and boarded the first United Airlines flight to Hawaii two hours later. The trip was uneventful. Just a bored rich girl from the UK looking for excitement in the westernmost state in the US.

She eased her way through immigration out of Japan and through customs at the Honolulu International Airport. One of her patrons had given her a hotel gift card that covered an entire week of sun and palm trees. She'd booked herself into a Waikiki resort at the far end of the beach and spent the first few days lying by the pool and walking barefoot in the sand.

She reviewed her cash and gift cards that she'd purchased using Leather Pants' credit card until it maxed out back in Tokyo. The money might last her a month even after she'd paid for her next flight somewhere. She needed to find a base of operations in order to start her new life outside of Japan.

She had a few friends working in clubs in Honolulu and Waikiki and picked up a few nights as a hostess under a different name. She hadn't planned to return to the role except for Japanese tourists who still wanted the Japanese experience along with palm trees. The tips were better, and two men made offers to take her with them. She considered a few of them until she'd found a suitable destination.

Lisbon, Portugal.

The man was older and shorter; she towered over him in her heels. Polite and educated, he appeared to be like many of her other patrons; smart and lonely. He didn't push for any physical interaction; he just wanted her company. That arrangement suited her fine.

The plan was to leave Honolulu, fly to Vancouver, hop to Montreal, and then take a direct flight to Lisbon. A long series of flights, but he only traveled in business class, which meant sleep and good meals.

She could do it. She could do anything if she got a fresh start.

The man's name was Tetsu Fujita. She checked and double-checked his credentials secretly. Widower and no children. He'd built a business and sold out to a larger competitor, allowing him to travel the world but, without a partner, it wasn't as fun.

And she didn't care if he dumped her once they got to Portugal or if she dumped him instead. She just needed to start over. However, indentured servitude isn't a bad way to go, especially if he gave her a credit card of her own.

Chapter Fourteen

Daniel K. Inouye International Airport, Honolulu

AN OLDER JAPANESE gentleman walked into the Honolulu airport from his business-class seat on ANA Airlines. His grey suit complemented his hair. If he'd been born in this century, he would have carried the label of having obsessive-compulsive disorder. However, what society calls an affliction, he credited it as the very thing that made his success. Well-laid plans needed backup and contingencies. His projects always did, thanks to his OCD. He called it being pragmatic. Operations went off the rails almost all of the time. Why not just fold that error rate into the calculation?

A commercial flight from Narita to Honolulu worked fine; he didn't need the convenience of a private jet. Travel was part of his job and his life. The longer flights were a little tedious, but the destinations and the completed operations usually made up for it. He's prearranged his return with the Gulfstream waiting in a hangar for a special passenger to arrive before flying back to Tokyo.

His associates arranged a car to pick him up from the airport. He'd used the same service before and liked their discretion. On his way to the hotel, he reviewed the meticulously tracked logs of successes and failures until their success in finding the girl.

As he read through the documents, he developed an admiration for her. She was smart, fast, and improvised well. Using a subway bystander as an unwitting shield was brilliant. If the situation were different, he would have recruited her into his organization. Talent like that was hard to find in this era of always-on internet and 24-hour surveillance culture.

But the gentleman had to admit that technology just made things easier, plus data science, and a little intuition rolled turned out to be the winning combination.

The team started with extensive electronic legwork. They hacked the stolen passport reports from the Tokyo police databases and cross-referenced U.S. entry via an immigration portal. They also checked other countries, but he had a hunch about the U.S. Once they found one used to enter the U.S. in Hawaii, all they had to do was search every hotel on the Hawaiian Islands. Hotel policy recorded foreign guests by passport numbers. When that turned up initially negative, the team repeated the initial search, and checked other stolen passports against hotel records in Hawaii.

Yet when they finally got a hit, the team had to hustle. The hotel reported she'd only booked the room until tomorrow. She might be moving hotels or leaving the country using another set of identification. Once they narrowed their search, they put the plan into operation.

Japanese staff are common in Honolulu. They noticed she'd ordered a single margarita at the hotel bar every night and charged it to her account. They called her and offered to deliver a pre-dinner drink and appetizer to her room so she could watch the sunset and experience Hawaii from the comfort of her spacious balcony. She gladly accepted, and a team member, disguised as a room service attendant, delivered a tray with a handwritten thank you note. All they had to do was wait.

The undetectable camera they'd placed in her suite the day before showed her sipping the drink and swaying to the live music rising from the bar below. She sipped again and sat down on the immaculate couch near the window. They watched as her head slumped to the side as the sedative took effect.

A team of three came into the room and quickly packed her belongings into her suitcases. It had to appear as though she checked out early. A guest disappearing but leaving all their belongings would trigger alarms from the hotel and the local police. No, just a guest checking out a day early to continue their trip. They wheeled a large trunk marked "Audio/Visual" into her room and placed her gently inside. They could move the case through most parts of the complex without causing trouble.

They wheeled the case into a white panel van parked in the delivery area. "Honolulu Sound Design" was stencilled on the side. There was no such company other than a website and email address to confuse any potential witnesses.

The older gentleman didn't have to wait long in his car, now parked in the private hangar. From inside, he watched while they eased their special guest from the AV trunk into a thin gurney that two of his staff carried into the Gulfstream, complete with a nurse to monitor her vital signs on the trip back to Tokyo. Once the team had completed their task, he boarded and checked on her well-being himself. He wanted nothing to happen to the girl; they'd been looking for her for a long time.

Chapter Fifteen

Renton, Washington State

THE PROJECT MANAGER waited at the warehouse with a tablet in hand. The constant stream of jets overhead, landing or taking off, didn't bother him. He liked the proximity to SeaTac; it was more straightforward to get in and get out, and less chance of traffic jams at critical moments. He watched for confirmations of the team's arrivals; date, time, airline, and terminal. Everything a team leader needed.

The client had arrived unannounced a few weeks before. An older Japanese gentleman that spoke English like a scholar. His two bodyguards looked like they'd stepped out of a bad yakuza movie: black suits, white shirts, and dark sunglasses. The client wore a grey suit that complemented his grey hair. He also smiled when he talked, which struck the PM as odd. Was this person the client or a decoy? He'd mentioned he'd just landed and would stay close to give the green light and not leave until the operation was completed. "I won't be interfering," he said. "This is your operation, and you are being well paid for success." He asked if there were any questions.

The PM pushed the questions out of his mind and said, "No, sir." He didn't need to clog his thinking or upset his thin moral veneer with the why. He kept a focus on the who and how. The client smiled and clapped him on the back. The PM suddenly felt that failure meant the client would smile as he slipped a long knife between the PM's ribs. Maybe it was nerves, but he spent the next several hours rechecking the plan to ensure he covered all possibilities.

The base of operations had been an old aircraft parts manufacturing plant at the bottom of a dead-end street. The company moved to Mexico or maybe Ohio. It didn't matter. The only thing the project manager needed was power, water, sanitation, and anonymity. He'd wheeled in a food truck and two industrial refrigerators. No cooks. He kept the food stocked, and each team member would prepare their own breakfast and lunch and clean up after.

The client finally gave the green light with the date and time forthcoming. The project manager had started the clock, and within a couple of days, all the vetted contractors began arriving. A massive operation for a city this size. Usually, the team had more flexibility with the timing and the planning, but in this case, double the money meant a shortened ramp time. Fast, cheap, or good. The project manager could only pick two. Fast and good meant it wasn't cheap.

None of the men were local. Local meant loose lips. A buyer's market in this economy and the project manager chose from a group connected with private military; all had been soldiers. Different armies and different countries; A few from the Middle East, three from Central America, and one flew from the Romania via Heathrow.

Once the team had arrived, they started their training with cash-based motivation. Better money meant stronger engagement. No fucking around. The men knew the stakes and would stand to make their usual month's pay in a week or two, with a success bonus paid after.

The project manager gave the team leaders a rough outline and schedule, but he kept the timelines loose until the client provided the last details. He knew the big picture and kept it to himself.

He divided the team leaders into offense, defense, blocking, and tackling. The teams were cross trained to pick up the ball in case of a problem. He'd select the starting team on the day, yet he needed all the teams to be equally sharp.

The quote 'No plan survives first contact with the enemy' rang in his head. He added the next part: 'then everything goes to shit'. He planned for the inevitable shit storm and managed the risk as best as possible.

He'd mapped logistics with multiple scenarios to manage risk vectors. Simulations with maps provided a variety of computer-generated scenarios. Different dates and times meant traffic patterns needed to be factored into entry and exit alternatives. The event at noon required a lighter touch than at 5:00 p.m. He simulated and tested various options. He liked the exercise, like playing a chess game ten moves ahead.

The men slept in trailers parked at one end of the cavernous warehouse. Besides the food truck, he ordered daily gourmet dinners and rotated drivers for retrieval in a freshly washed white panel van. The catering company got high marks for the food choices. They thought they were feeding a top-secret film project crew.

After a week of training, the men got antsy. "On each other's nerves," one of them said. He allowed the men out at night two at a time, with strict limits to the activities and behaviors outside the warehouse. Any infractions meant ejection from the operation and being blackballed in the industry. And that would be the least of their problems.

A smaller building connected to the main building housed the vehicles. If the catering van drove past, they would see a production company ready to shoot a movie, especially with the number of cars they'd ordered. He even had all the correct permits. With his budget, the car suppliers were happy to procure and deliver to his specifications.

Finally, the green light came. The client had called him personally and said everything was now a go and the blockers to operation had all been cleared. Dates, times, and sequences were checked and rechecked. All the equipment was tested, cleaned, and oiled. They could shoot a film for real—the amount of action and mayhem about to be delivered to the city should qualify for at least an Oscar, if not a Golden Globe.

Chapter Sixteen

Downtown Seattle

NICK MOORE SIPPED his after-dinner espresso in his private dining room and pushed his chair back from the table. The remains of a flank steak and some bites of local organic vegetables were all that was left of his meal. He re-read the hand-written note. Moore didn't trust emails for these kinds of things. Too discoverable.

The note detailed the dancer's movements after work. Same thing every day. Arrives back from Spencer's via helicopter, walks to his Belltown apartment, eats out for dinner, alone, spends the evening walking around downtown Seattle, and frequents Starbucks and other cafes, then shops for clothes. Surveillance loses him for thirty to sixty minutes, then he re-appears. Moore couldn't determine if the dancer did this on purpose or if the team was incompetent.

He flipped through a stack of pictures. No more meetings with grandpa spy. Moore shook his head; something seemed off. The dancer was young and good looking and didn't go out. He didn't meet any women or men.

Every night, he disappeared for an hour.

What the hell was he doing? Was he a robot in disguise?

Moore left the dining room for his office and grabbed his tablet from his locked desk drawer. He brought up the application he'd instituted to track the movement of all SCS employees via RFID chips embedded in their access cards and a network of sensors embedded in the walls. He hadn't told Spencer about the sensors when the building was constructed; he just had it done under enhanced security. Spencer didn't need to know.

In Moore's mind, proper security meant preventing nasty things from happening, plus ensuring every asset provided the most value. The most important assets were his people. Going all Big Brother on his employees was a legal grey area. However, Moore didn't care. The great unwashed gave away their privacy when the first iPhone came to market. GPS tracking found lost phones, lost spouses, and if employees weren't where they should be. His solution was a private version of a new product SCS planned to release later that year. In his experience, Japanese employees didn't worry about tracking. Their work ethic leaped and bounded over their USA counterparts.

A year ago, Moore added video.

He'd set the dancer up as a trackable asset. The system acquired him at the entrance and fast-forwarded him through the day. A building map beside the video tracked his location.

Moore set it for 5X speed and fast-forwarded the teacher taking the elevator, teaching dance, taking a crap, teaching more dance, exercising, eating a free lunch, and then flying off in Spencer's fucking helicopter.

No clandestine meetings with other employees or trying locked doors that he didn't have access to.

Moore frowned and reviewed some of the other days. Same time. Arrive, teach, eat, crap, and travel like a Rockefeller in the helicopter. In his head, Moore started to calculate the cost of each trip and then stopped. The real number would just piss him off.

He knew something was up with the dancer. Growing up in Boston and his time in the army gave him a good bullshit detector. From what he could tell, the dancer was full of it.

Moore jumped ahead a few days and slowed things down. The dancer ate lunch in the cafeteria by himself. Later in his first week, his students started joining him with smiles and laughter as they ate together, covering their mouths when they wanted to talk, like all good Japanese girls.

After a week of video, something still bothered him. The dancer would eat lunch every day and the women would join him. The smiles grew into business hugs. They wanted physical contact. He knew about that need and noticed it in their eyes. Smiling. Affection. Probably lust. The dancer would business-hug back. Nothing improper. He imagined the women's attraction to their new teacher. They spent an hour a day with a buff gaijin. What's not to like? Moore thought maybe he was jealous for a fleeting moment before remembering his bank balance. Good looks came and went. Money was hard to get and even harder to keep. He'd done both well.

He set the tablet down on the desk and examined the facts. Spencer hired this random guy to teach dance to employees and his daughter. He even spent a fortune adding a dance studio on one of the top floors.

Why?

He knew Spencer supported a few charities, but Spencer never struck him as overly generous. Wealthy people mostly gave to the needy for the PR. Spencer didn't want the exposure. Spencer had founded a dance scholarship, and Moore didn't know why. Any donations to the arts were tax-deductible. However, the more he thought about it, he figured Spencer had a hidden agenda. He just didn't know what it was.

He opened his laptop to review the plans. Years ago, when he struggled with his anger, a therapist had told him to journal to organize his thoughts. He had and decided to keep the content locked up and double encrypted with a couple of unbreakable keys.

He had continued to journal and poured his heart and soul onto the secure electronic pages. Most of his thoughts weren't safe for other eyes. However, over the last two years, his entries had turned into a plan that took logical shape. Once the first draft was complete, he reviewed it and realized his ideas made sense.

The plan. Started ten years ago as the company's prospects rose straight up, and Spencer's irrationality began. Small eccentricities by Spencer—like no milk in the building—seemed off but harmless. However, as the behaviors became more extreme, Moore knew he needed to act. Except Spencer's "Howard Hughes" gene kicked in, and he disappeared for days at a time at his Lake Washington fortress. Out of sight meant Spencer didn't cause trouble. At least none that Moore knew about.

Moore reviewed the plan and the status of each phase. Every part, task, resource, contract, and payment seemed on schedule. However, the presence of this dance teacher complicated the scenarios. And the meeting with the old spy could mean trouble. Too much coincidence to believe a new unconventional and un-vetted employee had coffee with an old geezer spy. Moore didn't trust in chance.

And he took none without adequate review of the odds.

He added another entry to the plan and a corresponding entry in his journal. Steps needed to be taken and taken quickly.

Chapter Seventeen

Belltown, Seattle

DAVID LOVED the apartment and waking up in the Pacific Northwest. His local espresso shop made a great morning latte for his walk to work. If he meandered, he could finish in case the company's lactose intolerance sensor prevented him from entering. Visiting Spencer's house every day gave him a new appreciation for the finer things in life. Spencer's success was because of software, just like his neighbour Bill Gates. Was it too late to give up the arts and move into programming?

He also realized last year's stress had evaporated, helped by his newfound income, glitzy apartment, and daily commute by helicopter.

He'd take it as long as it lasted.

At Fitz's request, he installed more bugs inside the company walls, even though Westlake said they had found nothing actionable. Old wonky eye said they'd captured an incriminating conversation on the first day. Except instead of a smoking gun, they uncovered an employee's email to a sibling in Japan heading to jail because of some low-level drug trafficking. Nothing that implicated SCS in anything.

Westlake wasn't happy with the lack of progress. David wondered if he was only pleasant when he stole a kid's lunch money.

The lack of evidence didn't bother David. Fitz negotiated a contract extension, depositing more cash into an offshore bank account. No need for the IRS or the Canada Revenue Agency to get involved.

Every evening, he met with Fitz to report anything out of the ordinary. Usually, the ex-pat Brit asked for any observations and David usually said nothing. Any workers he saw appeared healthy and adhered to the Japanese ethic of hard work. They spoke English during business hours with the occasional lunch conversation in Japanese. Nothing suspicious. The employees looked so happy and productive that he wondered if Moore had implanted them with a microchip to control their emotions.

The only thing unusual was the nightly surveillance. Three teams of two. They acquired him when he left his apartment for dinner and followed throughout the evening. David loved disappearing for his thirty-minute Fitz meeting to confound his shadows, only to reappear in places they didn't expect. He didn't detect any danger, just surveillance.

"Someone doesn't trust you," Fitz said.

David shrugged. "I got hired for too much money and have daily access to the founder. Maybe it's the SCS security team ensuring I'm not a threat."

"I thought your double-wide Japanese friend was their corporate security."

"Yoshi? He's Spencer's personal security, as far as I can tell. And he doesn't talk much during our daily commutes."

Over the first few weeks, his morning routine stayed the same. Dance class at 10:00 a.m., followed by a thirty-minute break before his second one at noon. He considered what would happen when his contract ended. Should he audition at other dance companies? After a brief discussion with Fitz, he decided he wanted the time off. Six months at a minimum. He'd go back to the National Ballet, meet with Jo, and convince her he'd conquered his demons and was ready to work.

On the Friday of his third week, his noon class was short by one dancer. Amai was missing; the cute and excited dancer who bounded into every class. Today had no bounding and no Amai.

"Where is Amai-san this morning?" David asked.

The other dancers looked at each other. One said, "She wasn't allowed to come this morning."

"Wasn't allowed?" David said.

The girl's face blushed red. "No, sorry. I meant she couldn't come. She had a sore stomach."

David nodded. "Let's continue without her."

The music, the movement, and the views were held together and produced a great class. The dancers worked extra hard maybe to make up for Amai. He realized that even though it had only been a couple of weeks, he missed her energy. Kind of like missing a little sister. He didn't want her to push her to attend if she wasn't feeling well, so he decided to find her desk and check to see if she was okay.

His company laptop said she worked on the 60th floor in a department called 'Information Management.' He had no real idea what that meant.

He assumed the 60th floor would be like other floors. Rows of cubicles with lots of space, a kitchen/tea area in the middle, with washrooms near the elevator. Except once on the floor, he wondered if he was still in the same company. Smaller cubicles crammed tightly together. Lines of men and women wearing wired headsets talking simultaneously. Did he stumble into the SCS call centre? The collection of voices was so loud he thought he heard yelling. He also caught the stink of stress-generated body odour.

He guessed she sat on the west side, near the window. Since he was in unfamiliar territory, he took the long way around to see if he noticed anything Fitz or Westlake might deem important. The CIA wonk remained convinced they'd find dirt. However, David saw nothing except a strong work ethic and Japanese stoicism.

Yet as he continued his tour of the 60th floor, he detected something else. Not just body odour.

Fear.

A holdover from the reptilian brain. Predators sense prey through fight-or-flight pheromones. The air stank like they had pumped it into the air conditioning system.

Most of the employees were women. A higher percentage than he'd seen in the cafeteria or as he randomly counted entering the building in the morning. Maybe as high as ninety percent, which seemed outside the norm. Each woman typed furiously away on a laptop while talking to someone on headphones. All of them. Little automatons. And an absence of happiness. A few men in white shirts and black ties walked around like floor bosses, scanning the women's work as a teacher would during an exam. The whole thing felt odd.

He found Amai's empty desk near the corner separate from the rest of the female crew. She had two large monitors side by side and a stack of books on her counter that had titles like "Corporate Governance" and "Securing Confidential Information." His student was a security geek apparently. Her yellow backpack sat by her desk. He looked around and saw her sitting in a small office near the centre of the floor. Her body language had shrunk, and she looked scared.

What could scare her in the analytics department? Math behaving badly?

Then he saw it. A muscular guy with spiked hair and bad skin stood in front of her, yelling and jamming his finger into her face.

He'd found the source of the yelling.

As he got closer, he saw big tears running down her face. David didn't know what was happening, yet the sentiment was clear. He opened the room's door, and the guy stopped.

He turned to David with a snarl. "It's forbidden for you to be here!" Muscles strained against the guy's white shirt. He was a few inches shorter than David but carried ten or twenty pounds more muscle.

David forced a smile and noticed a dense band of tattoos peeking out from the strained cuffs of the guy's shirt. He had seen no one else in the company inked like that. "I have an important message for Miss Amai. It's confidential, and I have to give it to her."

He glared at him like he didn't understand. David held his hand out to Amai and said, "I have to talk to you about something. I'm sure you can spare some time to hear it."

Confusion crossed her face for a second before wiping her tears and standing up. The guy yelled at her, spit coming out of his mouth. Even though the Japanese came fast, some words seemed familiar, like listening to a cell phone with poor reception. The guy said, *"Fushidarana on'na!"*

The man had just called her a slut.

A pinprick of pain hit David and without thinking, he pushed up to the guy's nose causing him to step back with a look of surprise as if no one had ever done that before.

"If you *ever* talk to her again, I will have you fired!" David took Amai's hand, helped her up, and walked out of the room. He didn't look behind him.

He handed her yellow bag to her and walked her to the elevator. She was shaking and crying as they descended to the lobby. "I am going to HR. He can't bully you and get away with it."

She grabbed his hand. *"No!* Please don't tell anyone what happened. No one can know." She continued to beg with big tears running down her face. He wanted to be the white knight and save this woman, except he couldn't. She wouldn't let him. Instead, she bowed and thanked him before leaving the building. He watched her walking towards the mall, her yellow backpack on her shoulder.

He just hoped he hadn't made things worse.

After lunch, the helicopter ferried him to Spencer's house, and he taught a distracted class to a distracted Leia. She grasped the structure of the exercises and goofed off between each one. After an hour, he announced the class was over. She curtsied and disappeared into the depths of the house. Spencer was missing from the end of class, and Yoshi escorted him back to the helicopter and into the office.

"I saw a manager yell at a student of mine before lunch, and I intervened."

Yoshi sat stone-faced and didn't look at him. "You must not get involved in company business, David-san."

He was about to argue but had a better idea. "I wouldn't normally. I don't even know what she does. Perhaps she stole something or made too many copies on the printer."

"She couldn't have stolen anything. That's not possible."

"He yelled at her enough to make her cry."

Yoshi nodded like that was a regular occurrence. "You shouldn't have gotten involved."

"I think of her as a younger sister. What would you have done if a man called your sister a '*Fushidarana on'na?*'" He repeated the Japanese word to make sure he had the pronunciation correct.

That got his attention. He turned, his eyebrows raised, and said, "I would probably kill him." And then turned away.

Good thing David had only threatened to go to HR.

Chapter Eighteen

"Did Brooks ever travel to Japan?" David said.

He'd met Fitz the last couple of nights in Fitz's hotel after giving surveillance teams the slip. He wondered how he could do so easily.

Fitz frowned and said, "Why would you ask me that?"

"Just a feeling. I'm understanding a few Japanese words." He didn't elaborate about the bully.

"Watching too many anime cartoons as a child, perhaps?"

"No. I read books."

Fritz sipped his tea and sat the cup back down. "Are you experiencing any new memories?"

"No. I told you in Toronto, nothing is showing up and your boy hasn't stepped in and taken over, if that's what you are asking. However, some skills have hung around. Like losing the surveillance teams trying to track me. "

Fitz looked out the window of his hotel room. "Jonathan visited Japan, but I know little more than that."

"How long was he there?"

"I don't know. Maybe six months."

David looked Fitz in the eyes and said, "That is unlike you. You seem to have a supernatural view of where people are and what they are doing. How could that information escape you?"

"Jonathan and I had a falling out, and he broke off contact. I worked to reestablish our relationship and when I did, whatever happened in Japan was long over. I suspect he probably picked up a few words here and there. Perhaps, that's what you are experiencing."

"Perhaps," David said.

"Anything else?"

It was David's turn to look out the window before saying to Fitz, "I encountered an employee that might be a Japanese gangster."

"Yakuza?"

"That's what I'm trying to figure out," David said.

"Encountered, as in, bumped into him in an elevator or something else?"

"Something else." He waited a beat and said, "He's a manager and screamed at one of my students today. Intricate designs covered his forearms. I'd only seen that in movies where the yakuza are the bad guys."

"Tattoos on millennials don't seem that unusual."

"I agree, but as this man is Japanese, the tattoos looked more cultural versus a regrettable fashion statement."

"Based on your descriptions of the workings of the company, it seems unlikely an active member of the yakuza would be in their employ. However, I will pass it along to Westlake. The lack of actual evidence is upsetting him and maybe looking for a Japanese organized crime connection might be the distraction he needs."

Chapter Nineteen

Pike Place Market, Seattle

AFTER TWO WEEKS as a corporate lackey, he needed a Friday night distraction. As the weatherman predicted a chance of summer rain, he grabbed a small SCS-supplied umbrella as he left his apartment.

He indulged in a great close-by sushi restaurant and texted Fitz he had no updates and needed a night off.

South of his place was the area for music. As he didn't need to trade his body for money anymore, maybe he could find someone willing to do an exchange for free.

As he walked by the giant red letters of Pike Place Market, something caused the hair on his neck to rise. He stopped and turned around. He'd expected to notice the tail he had for the last two weeks, but he felt as if a different person was tracking him—he was sure of it. Maybe the feeling was a holdover from the caveman gene. Spotting a bear before they spot you is an excellent trait to pass on to your children. David suspected the echo of the memory implant might play a role; double the caveman, double the fun.

As he tried to see who was following him, his heart raced like before a performance; excitement mixed with fear. The only problem was the tail was invisible, and he just felt the butterflies.

Before Amsterdam, he'd always avoid rough areas. Any block that looked sketchy, he'd bypass if he could.

Things were different now. The implant, the situations, and the intense pain following the memories had changed something inside him. He now liked the dance between prey and predator.

He craved danger.

Odds were on Mr. Spiky-hair as his new stalker. He'd pissed the guy off for yelling at Amai. No other person came to mind, as he hadn't been here long enough to get on anyone else's bad side. After the incident, David wondered how the guy got hired. The HR department would have checked his references before the first interview.

His original plan was to find a club, grab a place at the bar, and listen to some music. Nothing too crazy, and as he'd discovered an alcohol allergy as a teenager, drinking wouldn't kill him but would sure make him extra uncomfortable. For him, a night out meant tonic and lime mixed with ice in a tall glass. However, the implanted memories left behind an intense taste for scotch. He'd satisfy his craving and order a single malt to sniff between sips of his soda.

His plans had changed. He ducked into Post Alley, fighting the fear of being prey against his desire to fight. As he moved deeper into the tourist area, the sense of being followed hadn't gone away. He heard his heart pounding in his ears as he threaded his way through a nearby walkway. However, after several minutes of walking and switching back, no one that would fit the description appeared. Maybe the implant gave him a false positive.

Dusk had given into the night, and the city had come alive with people roaming the streets looking for love or a good time. He ventured south towards Pioneer Square and snaked down another alley after seeing neon and hearing booming music at the far end. As he neared the middle of the narrow passage, he heard leather scraping against brick and stopped short as a fist came out of the dark and grazed his shoulder.

David stepped back as Mr. Spiky-hair exploded at him with a series of wild punches. He blocked the first couple until the bully landed a hard one and rocked him back. The guy's muscles weren't just for show. On the next swing, David ducked and jabbed left and right into the guy's face causing him to step back, dazed from the hit to the head.

Behind David, a larger and wider version of the bully appeared with his arms crossed, blocking David's exit. Both the bully and his friend wore identical T-shirts straining over steroid muscles.

"Are you sure you want to do this?" David asked.

"You should not have interfered today," the bully said. He had his fists up and kept looking at the larger version behind David.

"You shouldn't be picking on women," David said. "It's bad for your health."

The guy stared with as much hate as he'd ever seen before. In hindsight, walking down a narrow alley with someone stalking him probably wasn't his best decision. He didn't have superhuman strength, nor could he leap a tall building. All of his fighting experience belonged to someone else. Yet, even with the immediate threat, the old spy's presence didn't appear like a year ago. Same as in front of the Toronto strip club. Maybe Jonathan's memories had left forever. David saw no flashes of other places. No visions and no pain.

The spy who left me.

However, he felt no fear. As he faced the two men, he just felt anticipation.

The guy launched forward, weaving like a boxer, and yelling fast Japanese. His friend laughed, and David ignored him. He kept focused on the guys' eyes. They never lied.

All at once, the guy shifted his stance and lashed out with a front kick. David expected the move and pivoted before grabbing the guy's outstretched leg and pulling him off balance. He followed with a left hook into the guy's nose and heard a satisfying crunch. He swept his other leg, and he crashed face-first into the asphalt.

"I told you," David said, "bad for your health." He kept the friend in view and the friend shook his head before crossing his arms and leaning against the wall. The friend wasn't a player. Not yet anyway. Perhaps a mugging was a rite of passage for the guy to join their beat-up-a-dancer club.

The bully grunted before pushing himself up from the ground and wiping his forearm across his bloody nose. As expected, the guy could take a punch and didn't like it very much.

"If you just walk away," David said, "I won't even tell HR that a ballet dancer beat your ass." Something inside him wanted the fight to continue. Just a little. And he didn't know why. He looked up and down the narrow alley. He hoped someone might call the police, but the passage stayed empty.

The bully smiled, pulled a six-inch blade, and moved into a crouch, scything the edge back and forth. Blood poured out of his nose onto his shirt. The knife looked like something a local Walmart would sell.

This changed things. A knife meant business. Outside of a kitchen, a knife was used to stop a person from doing whatever they were doing. Often forever.

This wasn't just an unfriendly visit to debate office politics.

Shit. Why did he walk down this alley? If he lived through this, he had to have a serious conversation with his brain. He pulled out the umbrella from his back pocket and held it up in front. Not the most effective weapon, but better than air. The friend stayed still and kept quiet. He looked like he was there for adult supervision.

Knife fights weren't the same as in the movies. Hard to block a blade with just your hands. A knife in a fight increases the chances of someone getting hurt or worse. He couldn't let the fight continue any longer than he had to.

The bully had a crazy look and kept spitting Japanese words fast at him as he swung the knife back and forth, forcing David to step back.

"Look," David raised his hands. "I want no more trouble."

The bully yelled in English, "I'm going to kill you, gaijin!" and swung the blade close.

David slammed the umbrella into the knife and leaped back. The guy grunted and stabbed the blade forward towards David's stomach. But David blocked with the umbrella and pushed it to the side, locking the guy's wrist in an arm bar. Without hesitating, he twisted further and snapped the guy's wrist with a crack, and the blade dropped to the ground. David pivoted and dislocated the bully's elbow like snapping a chicken bone. The bully screamed and clawed at him with his free hand.

David followed up with a right cross to the jaw, dropping him to the ground.

A look of surprise crossed his friend's face. He didn't take off or move forward; he just waited. The unconscious, broken, and recently disjointed bully had fallen between David and the friend and stopped the bigger guy from coming closer.

"Take him and leave. I've got no problem with you or him anymore."

The friend said nothing as he reached down, grabbed the bully's working arm, and struggled to stand him up before disappearing back down the passageway. Both men wore similar tattoos on their forearms. An intricate fanged snake, dense with multiple colors and fine details on the scales.

David rubbed his hand and checked his arms and hands for any cuts. In the heat of a fight, sometimes you didn't know you got hurt till after. The only issue was the jab in the bully's face broke some skin on his knuckles. He leaned back against the wall and felt the drip of adrenaline slow. Why was he attacked in the first place? Because he stood up for one of his students? The response seemed exaggerated. He could see the guy wanting to settle a disagreement outside the office, except he came armed with a knife with no problem using it, and he looked like he had some skill.

The bigger question was how David survived. Last year, the memories turned him into a marionette and saved his life from people trying to kill him. He winced at the memory of himself killing his attackers more than once in the heat of battle.

This fight was different. He didn't fear his opponents. He moved with the confidence of a dancer on center stage in a well-rehearsed pattern. Yet, he also improvised—something that doesn't occur in classical ballet. His body reacted, and he was firmly in control—no one else was pulling his strings.

He waited a few more minutes and calmed his heart rate before picking up the fallen umbrella that had saved his life. A club a block away still boomed out music, oblivious to the near-death experience only a few feet away. He entered and found a seat at the end of the bar. He desperately wanted a real drink as a reward but ordered a tonic and lime with a side shot of single malt. After the bartender set the tall glass in front of him, he relaxed and downed half the drink in one gulp.

The cover band started with a song he didn't recognize. Minutes later, he knew David Bowie sang the lyrics. Another memory was just out of his grasp. A memory of a memory. He didn't want to know the science, even if the occasional déjà vu drove him nuts. Tonic and lime would not kill the offending brain cells, regardless of how much he drank.

The tattoos puzzled him. Japanese culture frowned on body ink and wouldn't allow tatted men in public bathhouses or pools. Both long revered and now demonized, a tattoo like that said he belonged to an organization that wasn't the Rotary Club.

This organization dealt with drugs, extortion, and prostitution.

Yakuza.

Why would SCS have a yakuza member in a management position?

Chapter Twenty

Monday afternoon, Amai arrived at the studio quiet and somber. As the class progressed, her mood lightened to the point of smiling. At the end and after the other women had left, she came toward him and said, "Thank you for your help Friday, David-san," and bowed.

"I'm sorry I interfered. It wasn't my place."

Amai bowed again. "I'm glad you did."

"Did anyone say anything about what happened?"

"No."

"Was the manager in the office today?"

"No."

"Do you know when he will return?"

"No. He has gone."

"Gone?"

"Yes. I was told he went back to Japan." She didn't say or want to say anything more. She just smiled and bowed again before leaving.

David ran into no more problems as the week continued. Other than the Friday night fight with sharp objects, life was pretty good. He loved his apartment, job, and students, and Leia was growing on him. During the evening meeting with Fitz, he shared details about Friday's rumble in the alley and said the guy was a school bully who finally lost the playground fight. David held back the part about a large knife waving around; he didn't think Fitz needed to know. The memories hadn't returned, but apparently, the skills never left. Fitz asked a few more questions and casually said Westlake was still upset they could uncover no evidence of illegal activities.

Tuesday morning, he surprised Amai with flowers, and her face lit up. While there, he walked around her floor and noticed a lack of fear and general lightness. Maybe the bully was an anomaly; someone's cousin, or the guy just lied on his resume.

As he led the class through the first exercise on Wednesday, he realized he enjoyed teaching more than expected. His students worked hard and smiled throughout. Yet, with each class, he was left with the feeling something was missing. Like an amputee still sensing a phantom limb. Did he miss the grind of his daily class and rehearsals or the intrigue of a spy's life?

He wasn't sure.

In the evening, David detected no surveillance; the teams shadowing him were gone. Either they'd given up, or he'd gotten soft. For fun, he continued his random routes to dinner out of habit. While waiting for an Uber, Fitz called him.

"I'm leaving Sunday," Fitz said and didn't elaborate. "Westlake doesn't need my help, and you seem to be thriving in your newly minted career, other than pissing off the occasional manager."

"What did Westlake say?"

"He's not happy I'm leaving."

"Is Westlake ever happy?"

Fitz said nothing for a few seconds. "Not in my time with him. He's convinced that SCS is hiding something and wants to catch them in the act. He also wants you to resign from your teaching position."

"You can't always get what you want," David said.

Fitz laughed out loud—probably one of the first times ever. The old Brit said, "I know this is the end of our contract, and it's been lucrative for both of us, but don't let your guard down. I don't hold the same level of paranoia as our one-eyed friend. However, I suspect your employer is not entirely clean."

David thought for a second. "I understand. This job feels like a fresh start, and I'm happy for the first time in over a year. I'm not sure how long it will last, but I'm thankful you pulled me out of my slump and self-pity party."

As he ended the call, he had the strangest sense of never seeing the old man again.

———

The next day, he ate his sushi lunch alone in the cafeteria, the usual group of his students was nowhere to be seen. He realized no other SCS employees interacted with him. No hello, smile, or even the occasional nod. Was it because he was the lone dance teacher in a sea of programmers or that he was on a first-name basis with the CEO?

The only exception was Nick Moore. One morning, he entered the building at about the same time as the COO. When Moore saw him, his face twisted up in a half snarl. He wondered if Moore's parents kept him in a cardboard box until age ten.

After finishing his bento box, he smiled at every employee he encountered to test his hypothesis. They met his smiles with ambivalence. He didn't know why.

SCS employees spoke English while inside the building, with some lapsing into Japanese during the day. He noticed if he overheard those conversations, he'd recognize one or two of the words, leaving him with tiny pinpricks of pain.

When this operation started, Fitz and Westlake asked if he had any residual memories. He hadn't lied; he only experienced flashes of fragments but didn't tell the boys that. As for the Japanese, he only picked up the occasional word; complete sentences remained unavailable. Maybe Brooks took a few Rosetta Stone lessons on a flight once.

During his evenings, he'd researched Leia's condition. Spencer said she was "on the spectrum." Most had an incredible focus on things that caught their interest. Some had trouble with eye contact. A few had social interaction issues. Most were super bright.

Leia fit the description with a side of OCD. Spencer said that after obsessively organizing her room in the morning, she'd choose black clothes and black eye makeup for her daily tutor session. He never elaborated on why she didn't attend private classes; he could afford the whole damn school if he wanted. However, every afternoon, she transformed into a dancer. Hair in a bun. Leotard, tights, and dance shoes with the Hello Kitty backpack on her shoulder as she entered the studio.

He thought Spencer had lied about the morning goth look until he saw a picture of her and a teacher in a small frame in the corner of the studio. She must have smuggled it inside her backpack. The picture showed Leia standing beside a teacher four feet away without a smile and her arms crossed. Some kids on the spectrum had similar troubles with social contact.

Yoshi opened the door, and David expected to see Spencer at the top of the stairs for a daily pre-brief.

No Spencer.

"Where's Nolan?"

"Spencer-san is on business trip," Yoshi said.

"Where did he go?" David asked. Yoshi just smiled and directed him upstairs. The studio was dark. No lights. No music. No Leia.

Where was she?

"I find her. Wait," Yoshi disappeared down a hallway. The upper floor of the house was octagon-shaped, with heavy timber posts connected to wide wooden beams joining up to the ceiling.

The studio sat on the far left of the building, facing Lake Washington. A large living area to the center and a series of smaller rooms to the right side. He'd never walked through this much of the house before.

Spencer either had good taste or hired people that did. Several grand works of art hung strategically on the walls, and each piece bore the same bar code sticker near the bottom of the frame.

"Teacher will bring her up," said Yoshi, who materialized behind him.

"Any chance of getting a tour of the house? I've only seen the dance studio."

"No." His usual smile faded. "Go to studio. Daughter will be there soon."

He shrugged and wondered if he could get building plans for the house and understand the layout. Something in the back of his head tingled like a spider sense. He wondered what secrets Spencer kept away from prying eyes. Should he ask Fitz and restart the paranoia? Fitz said he was leaving, and Westlake had found exactly nothing.

An older woman, impeccably dressed, appeared with Leia in tow. Spencer's daughter wore full goth makeup and had a large bandage around her right forearm. She stared at David with a look of fear in her eyes, but he realized she feared the woman. Not him.

Leia backed away and tried to pull the bandage off her arm. The teacher turned her around and pulled her back towards the studio and away from David. He heard Leia half-complaining/half-yelling but gradually she calmed down.

"There was an incident last night," Yoshi said.

"What happened?" David asked.

"She found a razor."

David knew a girl from his ballet school a few years ago who landed in the ER for cutting herself. He didn't understand why kids cut, but it had become a "thing" with some teenagers. Depression, anxiety, problems at home, or all three.

"Time for lesson," Yoshi said. David followed Leia and the teacher to the studio's entrance.

David asked, "Is she okay to dance?"

"Yes. The wound will heal," the teacher said.

"Was her father here when it happened?"

The teacher looked at Yoshi and back to David. "No. Mr. Spencer had left."

Where had Spencer gone, and why so secret? Spencer had always been in the house during dance lessons. His daughter seemed his to be his chief focus, much more so than the company he founded and built up to a billion-dollar business.

He'd text Fitz later to help feed Westlake's conspiracy theories. A billionaire that leaves his house occasionally; break out the tinfoil hats.

A business trip seemed likely, but the silence pointed to something more salacious. A secret affair with a mysterious woman, perhaps?

Spencer didn't seem like the type, but with his wealth, he probably kept his movements as quiet as possible.

Leia and the teacher left for a couple of minutes and then reappeared. Tights and a leotard replaced the goth look. Leia looked towards Yoshi and handed David a piece of paper.

"I want to go," she said and walked back into the studio as she twisted her hair into a bun.

She'd handed him a laser-printed announcement for the premiere of a ballet tomorrow night in downtown Seattle.

Leia stuck her head out the door and said, "I got tickets."

The teacher said, "You did what?"

"We have box seats for him and me. You can't come," she said. She pointed at Yoshi. "You can come but can't sit with us."

"That's just not possible. Mr. Spencer isn't here, and I'm under strict orders..." the teacher said.

David turned to her. "How did she get tickets?"

"Mr. Spencer is a patron of the ballet and owns a box, but he would never allow his daughter to attend," the teacher said.

"What is he worried about?"

"Mr. Spencer worries about his daughter's mental health. The ballet is crowded and noisy, and there's a security concern," the teacher said.

"There are many people but it's not like an English football match. Ballet goers are usually quite calm. As for her safety, I will be there. Yoshi will be there, and I'm sure we can find some other security staff to help, don't you think?" David said.

The teacher shook her head. "I can't allow it, and Mr. Spencer certainly won't allow it."

Yoshi said nothing, but two seconds later, his cell phone rang. "Sir? Yes. Yes. I understand. I understand."

He slipped the phone back into his pocket. "Mr. Spencer is traveling but has the box seats reserved. He thinks a night out would be fine with the usual safeguards."

David kept stone-faced but glanced around for any cameras, even though he'd never spotted them. Big brother never slept if he had any doubt before. He checked the time. Right now, he had a lesson to teach.

The afternoon lesson was all over the map. Leia couldn't focus, and she broke into an uncontrollable giggle during every exercise.

"Excited about tomorrow?" David asked.

The face she usually wore during class burst into a huge smile. "Yes!" She almost levitated during some jumps he had her do.

David stopped the music. "That's all for today. I will see you tomorrow."

She turned and ran out of the room, saying nothing more. Her teacher didn't reappear either and the helicopter flew him back downtown without Yoshi. When he landed, he realized he wanted to text Fitz but held off. He'd been asked to escort his student to a ballet. Security would tag along. It was as if he was teaching the president's daughter. Nothing nefarious or out of the ordinary. He was a well-paid babysitter to a little girl he enjoyed instructing.

Should he text Fitz and tell him that Spencer was on a business trip? A billionaire traveling by plane. Alert the FBI. Perhaps he visited a mistress, an unmarried man with a lot of money, meeting a woman for sex and companionship. Someone call the Pope.

He shook off the feeling, put his phone away, and walked to his apartment. He gulped down a bottle of water from the refrigerator and realized he needed to release some stress.

The place came with a membership to a local gym. He looked up a class schedule, grabbed some exercise gear, and took part in a group boxing workout thirty minutes later. The class comprised of a small collection of people doing cardio, jabs, lefts, hooks, and uppercuts; first into the air and then into heavy bags. A row of ten men and women all beating the hell out of leather bags and working up a sweat with a couple of trainers helping with corrections on angles, making sure there were straight wrists and full turns with jabs.

After the class, at the front desk, he booked a private session with a cute trainer named Verena, lied about his training goals, and instead ducked, weaved, and hit her boxing mitts as she called out combinations for the next thirty minutes.

"One, two, three, four." Right jab, left jab, right hook, left hook. He danced in, jabbed twice, right hook, left hook. She called out other combinations and circled him like in a boxing match. The more sequences she called out, the more he did with ease. He hadn't boxed before in this lifetime, but the movements and the timings came naturally to him. He found he loved the sweat, the timing, and the hitting, especially the hitting. After they finished, he realized he felt a familiar glow of a tough dance rehearsal.

"Have you ever boxed professionally?" Verena asked with a big smile. Her short black pixie haircut dripped with sweat from the workout.

"No. Just for fun."

She half frowned and smiled at him at the same time. "Next time you want another workout, I'm up for it."

He showered and changed, and as he was about to leave, she walked up and handed him a card. "Here's my number if you'd like to work out again." He slipped the card into his pocket and thanked her. He might call later.

After dinner at another sushi restaurant, he thought about giving the trainer a call and decided to wait a couple of days. The urge to contact Fitz remained, even after the workout. He looked at his phone and saw a text from the old man.

"Westlake might have found something. I might delay my exit."

Yeah, right, David thought. He wrote a quick reply. "Spencer is traveling. Going to the ballet tomorrow night." He pressed SEND and didn't want to engage anymore. He'd done his job and installed a bunch of bugs. It would be up to the government to hunt out any witches; that wasn't part of his contract.

Fitz didn't reply. He pulled out the boxing coach's card and stared at it. *Verena — Personal Coach. Boxing and Yoga.* A telephone number along the bottom. No email. He texted her to see if she wanted to get together for a drink, even though he'd keep with tonic and lime. A few minutes later, she responded. "Love to. Your place or mine?"

"Mine." And he sent the address. If he were still under surveillance, he'd give them something good to watch.

Chapter Twenty-One

Seattle Center, Seattle

THE NEXT DAY, after David taught his classes, Yoshi texted him to take the afternoon off and return to the office at 5:00 p.m. At the prescribed time, he met Yoshi, and they took the elevator to the waiting helicopter. Yoshi said they would drive with Leia to the ballet; David didn't know what that would entail.

Fifteen minutes later, as they walked toward the house, three black Cadillac Escalades sat in the wide, paved driveway. Leia sat in the back of the middle one with the door open, wearing a beautiful dress and her hair done up. Her Hello Kitty backpack sat beside her. As he climbed into Leia's truck, a guy in the back vehicle stared at him, causing his body to go on high alert.

He didn't know why.

As he buckled himself beside his student, he saw a thin bandage covering her arm where she'd cut the night before and a smaller bandage on her other arm that looked like it covered the site of an IV or blood donation. He hadn't seen that before. Was she diabetic? Spencer had said nothing about it before, and neither had anyone else.

"Have you ever attended a ballet before?"

She shook her head as she kept her gaze out the window. Yoshi sat beside an unfamiliar white driver. The Cadillac in front carried four men, including the driver. He assumed the rear car would be the same to balance the security.

The configuration looked logical. A presidential-level security detail. He glanced at the car behind. He was right; four people. Three Japanese and a white driver. The security team mirrored Yoshi's stature. The driver appeared shorter than Yoshi, but equally imposing.

The trip led them to 84th Ave NE and the 520 westbound. As they weaved their way from the house to the road, David saw a series of cameras installed high in the trees. Razor wire sat on top of the tall iron fence encircling the property. He'd only ever seen Yoshi for security. Either the other guys kept hidden during his lessons with Leia, or someone had ordered 'rent-a-muscle' for the evening out.

A guard at the gate let them through to the road. The estate contained tighter security than he'd realized. Something about this situation picked at him, just out of his reach.

Leia looked oblivious to any danger he imagined. Her smile stayed on the entire ride as the big SUV weaved through traffic across the 520 bridge over Lake Washington.

As they hit the I90 south, the Seattle skyline came into view. The Space Needle rose to the north of downtown, and the massive skyscrapers tried to overshadow the magnificence of the Pacific Northwest. The entourage exited the highway and traversed the city streets west. As they got closer to the theater, David noticed several white trucks parked along the road. Heavy cables converged into an older building, with bright lights on cranes. It must be a motion picture crew or a big-budget TV show.

A few minutes later, the drivers took a left to Seattle Center and pulled into the main entrance.

Yoshi exited and opened the door to allow a high-heeled Leia outside. She wore a knee-length pink dress with her hair tied at the top and her backpack hanging from one shoulder. David had chosen a suit jacket, a white shirt, and no tie. The day after he started, he bought a good-looking pair of Christian Louboutin sneakers. Yoshi looked the same as always in his black suit, tie, and white shirt.

However, as he walked beside Leia, David's vigilance was on high. Everything stood out. The woman by the fountain reading a book. The homeless guy on the sidewalk pushing a shopping cart. The tall black man in jeans wearing a hoodie leaning against a wall talking on a cell phone. David's brain kept doing automatic threat assessments that he couldn't turn off.

"This way," Yoshi said, directing him and Leia into a side entrance. No one scanned any tickets. David's mouth went dry as they entered the lavish floor-to-ceiling glass lobby of the McCaw Hall; a fading sun streamed into the building from the west. Yet, the fear they were walking into a trap wouldn't back down. He wondered if Yoshi perceived the same thing.

Two years ago, a dancer had told him her brother had a sixth sense for trouble; he was a bouncer at a Toronto nightclub and could tell before a fight was about to break out, or worse.

David's own alarm kept going off. The voice hadn't returned since Silicon Valley, yet whatever remained inside him was spooked by something out of his perception. Something dangerous.

He couldn't see what it was, but he knew it was there.

The three of them took the elevator from the lobby to the first level. Best seats, best sound, and best privacy. The guards from the other Escalades had disappeared. He assumed they'd spread out inside and outside the theatre. Yoshi pointed down a narrow hallway to the box closest to the main stage. A red EXIT sign glared at the end of the hallway.

Yoshi took the rear guard and checked behind him. *He must feel it too*, David thought. Like when birds sensed an earthquake before it happened. If it were up to him, he'd grab Leia and carry her kicking and screaming to somewhere far away.

He shook off the sense of doom. The implant was just messing with him. She had a more extensive security detail than the president. They were in a public place. He was in front, and Yoshi was behind. Zero chance of anything happening other than his charge overdosing on sugar during the intermission. He'd taken a job teaching dance in a software company and giving private lessons to the CEO's daughter. It paid well and he traveled by helicopter like the King of Spain.

So, why did he want to throw up?

A man that could be Yoshi's thinner brother waved the three of them into the last door at the end of the hallway. David hadn't seen him before. Maybe Spencer owned the theater instead of just renting the box. However, he knew the billionaire rarely went out in public even though he had money to buy anything he wanted.

Back in Toronto, David would have enough cash left over for a large latte after paying rent. Some months he'd add a muffin to the order. He'd never had the resources to purchase a regular seat at a show like this. Box clientèle breathed different air.

The Japanese guard bowed slightly as they entered. Leia found a seat in front and pointed beside her. "You sit here," she said to David. Yoshi stood near the back as they waited for the show to start.

Opening night for any ballet was special. Civic dignitaries, critics, celebrities, and the rich walked on the red carpet. The local news and social media might talk about them if they were lucky. The more famous the ballet company, the more famous the people.

He looked down into the theater. The crowd had dressed up; women displayed elaborate dresses, and men wore smart suits. A premier usually included a gala after-party that gave wealthy patrons a chance to rub shoulders with the talent. A few wanted more than rubbing. He had heard rumors of dancers boosting their bank accounts with little extra effort. David remembered the girl that had stuffed money into his wallet in Toronto. Was there much difference?

Leia grabbed his arm and snapped him back to reality. She vibrated and squirmed as the orchestra warmed up.

The show was about to start.

Apparently satisfied that the theater was secure, Yoshi sat in the back. David took an aisle seat with Leia beside him. She seemed oblivious to any actual or imagined danger. She stared with a mile-wide grin lodged on her face.

He gripped the armrests as the house lights dimmed, and a deep feeling of dread engulfed him. The curtains parted, and the dark stage appeared. The violins rose in pitch, and movement began. Men and women appeared in wild costumes and elaborate face paint, danced across the stage. He saw the audience laughing and heard nothing as if he had become instantly deaf. He turned to Leia. Instead, he stared at someone else.

Elizabeth. Jonathan's wife. Utterly stunning. Brunette. Soft makeup. Luscious and red lips. Plunging neckline. She laughed at whatever performance they watched together. David was there instead of Jonathan. Elizabeth was his and his only. His heart wanted to burst as every memory of her flooded his psyche. He squeezed his eyes shut and pushed back against the feelings that weren't his.

Then different music started. A warmer sound. Slower and coming from a string instrument. He knew immediately the music was from a Japanese Koto. A younger woman had replaced the image of Elizabeth. Petite. Soft makeup and ruby lips. Black hair. Japanese.

Yumi.

She turned to him and smiled, big brown eyes looking into his.

The memory evaporated as David tried to speak. He was back in his seat with Leia beside him, watching the stage with an intense gaze as the ballet dancers appeared and took their place. As the music began, she grabbed his hand and held it tight, leaning forward as if she wanted to fly down and join them.

The image of Yumi didn't fade in his mind, but he couldn't recreate her presence. The memories would only play once. He was in Seattle at a ballet premiere and not with a woman he didn't know but felt Jonathan deeply loved.

He shook off the images of both women. Jonathan's visions had returned. He'd been lying to himself that the memories were gone. He had ignored the night sweats and the feelings of dread. Jonathan hadn't left; he'd just dived deeper, hiding his psyche away from the world.

Happy recollections were free. Anything to do with tradecraft cost him in a currency of pain; both physical and emotional.

He shook his head and focused on the stage. The first performance was classical ballet. Women wearing tutus and pointe shoes, their hair pulled into tight buns. Stage makeup sharpened their features. Tall men with ripped muscles and transparent leggings, lifting their partners over their heads like they were made of paper.

The movement transfixed Leia. Her teacher worried about the noise and people would overwhelm her. Tonight, was different; Leia wanted to be at the ballet and wanted to experience everything. The lights, the music, and the movement. Once the show started, she became focused and intent.

"He will lift her and spin twice," she whispered. He'd seen variations of this choreography but hadn't performed it. Yet Leia knew it, as a dancer might. Almost on cue, the male soloist lifted his female partner effortlessly in the air and spun her twice before setting her back down like a fine piece of crystal.

"How did you know that?"

She shushed him. "YouTube."

He smiled. Spencer had said she only viewed ballet videos and must have learned this performance step by step.

The premier proceeded with a mixture of classical and modern pieces performed by a talented company to exacting standards. He pressed his lips together as the show continued, filled with conflict. All he had ever wanted was to perform. He should be on stage instead of watching as a highly paid babysitter. Yet, the longer he observed Leia's expressions, the more he recognized he was giving her something that her father or other teachers couldn't: a direct connection to the dance world.

The last piece ended, and the curtain came down as the house lights rose. Intermission. Fifteen minutes. The audience would get up, stretch, go to the washroom, and maybe grab a drink or snack. A few would venture outside for a quick smoke.

Yet even with the movement and music stopped, dread welled up inside him and he found it hard to breathe. Leia didn't notice his distress. She jumped up and twirled on the carpet behind the seats. He knew trying to stop her would be a mistake, and instead, he faked a smile as she moved like the dancers below. Yoshi stood near her, blocking any view of her body from the other boxes or below. After a minute, she sat down and leaned over the balcony, watching the audience milling around.

David needed a few minutes. He told Yoshi he'd be right back, but he wanted to escape the building as fast as possible. Instead, he'd settle for the bathroom.

The security guard outside the door let him pass. A thin cord ran from the guard's ear to a hidden radio, all secret-service-like. As the box sat dark during performances, the bright light from the corridor shocked his eyes.

His awareness felt sharp and turned up to eleven. He noticed everything. The lemon smell from the freshly cleaned carpets and the slight tang of the Seattle air mixed with air conditioning.

Unnatural fear coursed through him. It didn't make any sense. They had brought a security detail that rivalled most heads of state and he didn't want to check if they were stationed in strategic positions or not. Instead, he wanted to throw water on his face and regain some control.

A sign pointed to the washroom on the opposite side of the building, and the familiar murmur of the intermission crowd one floor down calmed him. He could do this. Take some breaths, wash his hands, and return to the box. Easy.

The hallway mainly sat empty as the patrons on this level probably sipped champagne in the privacy of their spaces. He told himself he shouldn't expect any funny business. Almost inconceivable in such a public place.

He slipped into the ornate men's room and the hair stood up on his neck again. He heard hard footsteps and a man's voice saying, "Be quick." In the mirror, he saw two white men in dark suits moving fast. As he turned, the first man launched toward him like a linebacker.

Without thinking, he grabbed the man's arm and pivoted right, swinging him forward and smashing his face into the mirror. The other guy jabbed a black baton at him, sparks flying from the metal end. Instead, David blocked the stick, stepped in close and grabbed the baton, pulling the guy off balance. He directed the stun rod into the other guy, raking his body with high voltage. He elbowed his attacker's throat, jammed the stun rod into the guy's neck, and then more into the first one for good measure.

Leia. They were after Leia.

He sprinted down the hall, the private boxes still quiet as the inter-mission continued. At their box, the large security guard lay uncon-scious on the ground; the earpiece pulled from his ear. Inside, Leia and Yoshi were gone.

Where are they? He looked over the balcony and saw people milling back from the break. No screaming or chaos. Three bells chimed as the intermission was ending.

He raced out of the box and through the EXIT door to the lobby. Their abductors would time their escape for the performance to restart; carrying a screaming girl with hundreds of patrons finishing a last drink might be challenging. Grabbing Yoshi seemed an impossible task, yet he saw no blood or any trace of struggle. Was the big man part of this? He pushed past slightly tipsy people sipping wine and swiveled his head, looking for any sign of Yoshi and Leia. He still didn't see the other guards they'd brought from Spencer's estate.

Where the hell were they?

Shit. His sixth sense had been right. The lights dimmed twice, signaling the show was about to start, and his cell phone vibrated. "Ballet shop. Basement. Come find us." The text from Yoshi.

He pushed his way down another flight of stairs past the crowds of people into a large store selling posters, books, jewelry, and photographs of the dancers. As he entered, Leia waved to him with a big smile and a bag of something she'd purchased. Yoshi stood behind her, looking nervous.

At the back of the shop, an EXIT sign hung over a door marked "Employees Only". He had to get them out of the theater. Once they'd cleared the building, he'd figure out the next step.

Yoshi looked troubled. Troubled the guys in the washroom hadn't grabbed him? The shop had thinned out and left only a couple of grandmother types poking around the jewelry counter.

"We have to go!" he yelled at Yoshi, running towards them. He heard two pops, and Yoshi fell back to the floor, a red bloom just below his collarbone and one in his arm. His security escort had stopped moving. A man appeared under the back exit, grabbed Leia, and dragged her back through the door.

A thick arm reached around David's neck and squeezed, cutting off his breath. His attacker stood six inches taller and probably fifty pounds heavier. "Don't struggle. We don't want to hurt you."

David pulled on the man's forearm, sidestepped to the left, and hammered his fist into his attacker's groin. The guy crumpled to the ground. He must have been Yoshi's assassin. He followed Leia and her abductor through the exit and saw Leia sink her teeth into her abductor's arm. Her Hello Kitty backpack still hung around her neck. The guy ignored the bite and dragged her through a door marked "Receiving".

Multiple attackers. Coordinated event. Why wasn't he dead? They shot Yoshi without warning. One death was already murder. A second body wouldn't matter.

David whipped into the storage room and through the open exit door, caught sight of the man pushing Leia into the rear of an SUV as she screamed and kicked her legs. A second man pulled her into the back before the truck squealed out towards the street.

As he burst out into the receiving area, a guy in tactical gear stepped in front and blocked his path. David leaped and kicked him in the chest, dropping him to the ground. But from either side, two guys grabbed his arms, and one punched him in the head. He managed a sharp kick to one man's kneecap as another punch glanced off his shoulder.

The guy on the ground pulled out a Taser, and yelled, "Hold him!" David wrenched one of his attackers off balance as sharp hooks shot from the gun and buried into the man's face. Electricity blasted through the wires and the guy jitterbugged before falling to the ground.

David twisted, punched his other attacker in the throat, and then unleashed a kick to the Taser man's balls.

A second SUV sat running with the doors open. He jumped into the truck and stamped on the gas. As the SUV with Leia turned right on to the street, he matched the movements and chased after it.

Chapter Twenty-Two

FITZSIMMONS SNIFFED the air and scowled. This regurgitated Holiday-Inn used a pine-scented cleaner, he assumed, to remind customers of the trees of the Pacific Northwest. Or the cleaner was cheap and the housemaids had lost their sense of smell because of using this horrible chemical for years. Regardless, he wrinkled his nose, opened the meager windows, and engaged the fan in the bathroom. He'd planned to be here only a few more days until his trip home.

He'd removed his suit jacket, pulled off his tie, and unbuttoned the top two buttons on his shirt. He had booked the hotel online as his security protocol dictated. The reviews mentioned the establishment had been a Holiday Inn in its former life. Now refurbished, the place re-opened as The Hotel White. If he'd known his stay in Seattle would be this long with such little danger, he might have arranged an Airbnb or even rented a short-term apartment.

The clock on his phone said David would soon be entering the theatre with his charge in tow. Westlake would also be back shortly with fresh intel the old spook was securing from an insider. He still hadn't gotten used to the gold bracelet on his other wrist. Maybe he didn't like the weight or that it looked too ostentatious for a man who made it a point not to stand out.

Over the years, he had rarely had an insider like David during an operation. And none that commuted daily by helicopter to the belly of the beast. From what Westlake said, the James Bond tech David installed had provided nothing of interest other than evidence of a suffocating corporate bureaucracy. Were all Japanese companies this way?

Fitz had changed hotels three times since he'd first arrived in Seattle. Longer-term residents brought questions, and an older man staying longer than a few days meant someone could bribe the bellhops for his room number.

He'd moved from the Westin to the old Palace Hotel, within spitting distance from the palatial Grand Hyatt. Older hotels suited him better than the newer ones and felt better to Fitz's older bones. Except for this one. The Hotel White had all the ambiance of a 1980 Toyota Corolla. The bed had the same number of miles.

Even though he hoped the room service would be passable, he steeled himself for disappointment. He'd ordered a poached chicken breast, asparagus, and a small house salad. Protein and some vegetables. A dinner roll provided carbohydrates. Smaller meals agreed with his constitution.

Someone knocked on the door. He peered through the door's viewer and saw a man in a white coat holding a tray. As he withdrew the chain and twisted the handle open, the wood slammed into his chest and sent him sprawling back over a chair and off-balance.

He clawed for his pistol on the coffee table, but three men dressed in serving jackets jumped on him and held him to the ground.

A needle pinched him in the neck, and his eyes fell dark.

Westlake waited for fifteen minutes on a bench south of Pike Place Market. Public, well-traveled, and tourist heavy. He preferred an urban space for a first meeting; the next one could be less popular if the contact established some level of trust. Light rain in the morning gave way to afternoon sun and a stunning evening, making Seattle sparkle like a diamond.

Earlier in the day, he watched the crowds of visitors sipping their coffees, watching burly white men toss fish from buckets to ice-filled display cases. He marvelled at the men's accuracy in tossing and catching the slippery things.

He sipped an espresso and hot water from a local vendor he had discovered on his last trip. Mario's Coffee, a one-man shop. An older, balding Italian proprietor stood behind a geriatric espresso machine lodged into an alcove the size of a closet and made the best coffee outside Italy. This late in the day, he chose decaf.

The brew was hot and intense. Westlake added a full teaspoon of sugar because he liked it that way. No chemical sweeteners for him. Mario supplied cane sugar, which seemed a rarity, plus a dollop of cream.

As he continued to wait, his patience waned. Usually, whistle-blowers looked the part, nervous and constantly checking their shoulders as they circled like hawks around the prescribed meeting place. Westlake saw none of that. Just tourists gawking at the Seattle sights scrunched in with city residents moving into their evening.

He wiped a tear dripping from his blind eye. Doctors kept telling him he needed to replace it with a prosthetic one. However, unless his condition put him in danger, he'd continue to swallow their pills to keep the pressure down. Nothing more. He secretly hoped to live long enough to get a robotic eye but doubted he would.

The man he waited for was 'a friend of a friend of a friend.' He said that he had damaging information about SCS and more on Spencer. The only outstanding question was how much money it would cost the government to get it.

Westlake's management called for discretion. Bad news about a large US cyber security firm that the state relied on to keep the criminals out wouldn't turn out well for anyone. His boys had delivered a deep analysis of SCS's customer base and discovered many branches of the US government and almost all the states had licensed it. Even if the US wanted to replace all their security software, the project would take months or years, depending on the system. They didn't want to put the entire US at risk. Westlake was the first to suggest prudence when deciding a course of action. However, they needed verifiable data. A decision shouldn't be made on gossip or rumors.

So, he waited.

He marveled at how well-placed the dancer was in the company. Hard to believe it was a coincidence that his covert agent would be offered a role in teaching the CEO's daughter. Too much of a stretch, even for Westlake. However, he saw no downside.

During the operation, he hoped the old spy's memories would appear again, yet the dancer swore the implanted skills had evaporated, making plans for further testing not viable. The science boys still wanted to know why he was the only one who survived the implant. Blood type? Family of origin? Maybe because he was Canadian. Regardless, creating a spy-on-demand was an attractive idea to an old dog like himself. Yet some things might resist modernization forever and always require traditional training methods. Westlake had been on too many similar flights of fancy in his career. And he was about to chalk this meeting up as another one.

Then he felt it. Someone brushed him from behind. He didn't even see who it was. A nudge and a squeeze. Like someone bumping into you accidentally. He turned his head to find out who had touched him. However, there were too many tourists around him. He rubbed the back of his neck and looked at the drop of blood on his fingers. He'd been stuck with something.

A wave of panic set in. What was he injected with? Poison? Paralytic? Whatever it was, he wouldn't have much time to get to an ER. He pulled his phone out of his pocket and tried to dial, but his hand shook, and he couldn't even unlock the screen. He tried to voice dial, but nothing came out, like he was underwater. He gasped and dropped his coffee cup to the ground.

The tourists initially gave no notice of his discomfort. He clawed at his throat as it closed, and he collapsed onto the sidewalk.

Chapter Twenty-Three

MOORE SHOULD BE SHARING a great dinner with a beautiful woman. Steak perhaps. Rare. Plus a red Merlot from Argentina, light salad, and a guaranteed desert. Instead, he sat in his office, with an earbud wired into his cell phone. Bluetooth was too easy to crack, his assistant told him. So, he suffered with a wire from his cellphone to his ear. He ran his company old-school, rule from the top and with strict management. However, as he listened to the report, his careful plans turned into amateur hour.

Fuck.

He usually farmed out this kind of work. Better for everyone all around. At least two degrees of separation. Work paid from bank accounts in the Caymans. His orders had been specific; he'd planned out the operation himself. Yet they had fucked it up. Whatever losers and lowlifes his contractor had used had made a big mess.

"Stop," he said, and the voice on the phone went silent. He gulped from a bottle of extra fancy ionized water that wasn't helping. His mouth and throat were bone dry.

The report spiked his heart rate and, more worrisome, his blood pressure. He kept pausing the guy every couple of seconds to try calming himself, to stop him from stroking out.

"One right colossal fuck-up," Moore said. The voice agreed and assured him the operation could not be traced back. He ended the call without thanking him. The man hadn't caused the problem; he was just the compartmentalized messenger.

During the call, the guy had provided detailed colour commentary as to the events, but more detail didn't help. Prior to the call, Moore had received a pre-arranged text with a code word for the operation's success or failure. The first message must have been a mistake. He had requested confirmation.

He didn't like the answer.

Fuck.

He should have led the operation himself. The army taught him how, and he knew he could have done a better job. He'd aged and put on a few pounds, yet he knew in his bones if he'd ran the damn thing, he might have prevented the screw-up.

Who could have predicted the outcome? And that it would have gone this sour. The fucker had been prepared. So prepared that several of the crew lay dead. Dead leaves a mark that's hard to cover up. Moore took extraordinary precautions to prevent any blowback from a screw-up, but his guts still churned. He was more worried about the company being dragged into it. SCS hadn't gone public. However, customers didn't like bad news and the uncertainty that came with it.

And everything was uncertain.

He watched the video feed twice from his cell phone. Shit. He'd underestimated that fucker. Never again.

The other crew came away with a partial win. No resistance and no trail. Partial was better than nothing. Like a good sales rep, he liked winning and wouldn't take no for an answer.

He gulped some more of the fancy water and hoped the ionized oxygen molecules were roaming his body, gulping the free radicals in his cells like candy.

The whole situation forced him along a path and course of action he didn't want. He hung up and made another call, this time with another phone.

Chapter Twenty-Four

South Lake Union, Seattle

THE SUV SCREAMED out of the delivery ramp, and David made a hard right turn onto the road. A blue Volvo swerved and honked, and he ignored it. He turned on Mercer Street and punched the gas. The black SUV with Leia inside barrelled ahead about a quarter of a mile.

He white-knuckled the steering wheel, his heart pounding as he threaded in and out of traffic, his hands and feet moving on automatic as though he was the passenger instead of the driver. After a few seconds of Fast and Furious driving, he reminded himself he didn't even have a driver's license. He never needed one in Toronto, yet he drove as if he'd taken lessons on a Formula One track.

The old spy's skills had continued to surface and without the pain of before. Happy to take one and not the other. For the last year, the skills must have been on vacation somewhere. Maybe in Ibiza or Nice. He wished he were there right now.

He yanked his focus back. Someone had grabbed Leia with an over-the-top abduction. Grabbing a girl with a thousand cameras and police nearby meant the probability of a screw-up and failure was triple-extra high.

The crew didn't seem to care. They had pulled out all the stops to nab her.

Law enforcement would respond fast to shots fired. Two minutes at most for the closest cop.

Just then, lights blaring from two Seattle police cars passed him going in the other direction, oblivious to his own journey. With an active shooter in the theatre, the SWAT team would be close behind. With all the chaos, the cops wouldn't realize for several minutes what had really happened.

The SUV ahead took a sharp right. He punched the gas and skirted through a yellow light to catch up. He didn't see the other car until it smacked into his back bumper and jarred him. His SUV swerved and spun in the intersection. An older American model had hit him. He got a glimpse of the driver pulling out a gun and aiming at his truck.

Shit.

David stamped on the gas and heard bullets strike the side of the SUV. None fired at the driver. The shooter could have killed him and didn't. Instead, it looked like he had tried to shoot the tires and missed.

Why not take out the driver chasing after the billionaire's daughter?

David spun the SUV around and smashed the back of the truck into the attacker's driver's side door , and then took off.

Eight men so far. Four at the ballet. Three in the truck in front and now this guy. Eight of them so far. Large crew just to grab a little girl and hold her for ransom. With all the DNA, fingerprints, and video evidence, how could they expect to get far? David figured the best abductions were silent; a quick in and out, with no traces left behind, and a minimum of killing with a money transfer at the end. All business.

Leia's abduction was different, and he couldn't figure out what it was. Maybe his newfound driving skills would morph into something more useful.

He caught up to the black SUV as it took a corner. He sped up and drifted around the corner after it. He was about to overtake it, too, until another truck pulled out and smashed head-on into his SUV. The airbag deployed and smacked him in the face, dazing him for a few seconds. He shook his head and two men in tactical gear jumped from the truck and came toward him. Both men carried the same black batons as the man in the men's room. 20 million volts on a stick.

Ten men now, but still with no guns. They want to stop him, not kill him?

He had no weapons other than his hands and feet. He glanced around the cab and found a Glock in a holster stuck in the crack of the passenger seat.

As the first man jabbed the baton through the driver's side window, he grabbed the Glock and twisted it towards his attacker. Electricity jolted David's left arm as he pulled the trigger and caught the guy in the throat. The guy dropped to the ground, blood spurting out onto the asphalt.

The gunshot deafened him, and his left arm wasn't moving. As the other guy pulled the door open and jammed a second baton at him, David grabbed the baton with his right hand as sparks came close to his face. He pulled and brought his attacker close enough to drive his elbow into the man's throat. He twisted the baton and jammed the sparking metal into the man's face. The guy shook as every nerve and muscle in his body short-circuited until he dropped to the ground.

David's left arm regained some feeling as he unhooked the seat belt and got out of the truck. The second assailant lay dazed on the ground. He jammed the baton into his chest and pulled the trigger, and watched the man shake like he had palsy. That should keep him quiet for a minute. The first guy was probably already dead.

A cop car pulled up with lights blazing. He dropped the baton and raised his hands. A lone cop jumped out of the car and pulled a stainless-steel Colt pistol out of his holster. "Keep your hands up!"

"A girl was just abducted from the theater. I was chasing them when these guys smashed into the car," David said.

"Turn around, hands behind your back."

"They are getting away!"

The guy didn't blink at the men lying on the ground in tactical gear. At the very least, the cop should call for reinforcements.

"What station do you work for?" David said. He knew nothing about the Seattle police.

"Turn around. Hands behind your back," the cop said.

David didn't move. The cop fussed, trying to get shiny handcuffs out of a new belt.

"You aren't really a cop, are you?"

The cop raised his gun at David's head. "Hands behind your back!"

The Colt's safety was on. David jammed his hand forward and up, pushing the gun away from his head, and twisted it out of the cop's hand. The cop swung a haymaker, but David blocked and hit him with a left jab and a right cross, dropping him to the ground.

Moving down to the second and third stringers, he thought. From the ground, the man grabbed his leg. He shook off the man's grip, grabbed the baton from the ground, and jammed it into the guy's neck before jumping into the running cop car and taking off.

The cop car wasn't a cop car. No laptop in the center console or other weapons. No radio either. Just a late model Crown Victoria with no extra features. Someone had done a quick paint job and jury-rigged some lights for the top back window. A guy in uniform would complete the picture.

He remembered the movie trucks he'd seen as they drove in from the highway. The crew must have used the movie shoot as the alibi for the snatch and chase. A few of the trucks were still sitting on the street. The police wouldn't know if it was real or scripted.

A lot of effort to snatch a twelve-year-old.

He didn't have a uniform and didn't look like a cop. It wouldn't be too long before someone caught on to a fake cop car and called 911. The last thing he needed was the real police with loaded guns chasing after him.

He was all out of options.

The looming Space Needle stood on his right as he headed south on Broad Street. He drove a couple more blocks until he found what he was looking for. The police would be at the theater, trying to make sense of the chaos and dead bodies. They wouldn't be looking for a fake cop car that wouldn't stand even to a cursory inspection.

He pulled into the underground parking lot of one of the cheaper chain hotels. No ticket attendant or anything. Just drive right in. There might be a camera, but he didn't care. The police weren't looking for him. Not yet anyway.

Dim lights punctured the gloom of a crappy parking garage. He drove down to the lowest level and parked in the corner.

The men had Leia. There was nothing he could do about that now. He didn't think they would hurt her; it didn't look like that kind of abduction. Instead, they were a group of men with a well-executed plan. He had chased after the SUV and Leia, but he failed. Too many other things conspired against him.

He still didn't know why he wasn't dead.

They had opened fire on Yoshi without compunction. Why not go for a doubleheader? He wore no Kevlar, and any of the three that tried to grab him in the back of the theater could have done it.

He had jeopardized the capture of Leia. They should have killed him in the bathroom, not used a Taser or a fake cop as a backup plan.

What the hell was going on? He couldn't come up with anything that made sense.

He searched the car for anything useful. A first aid kit sat unopened in the trunk, and there was nothing so much as a cell phone inside the Crown Victoria.

He wiped his fingerprints from any surface he touched, walked up the stairs to an empty lobby, and slipped into the men's room. As he washed the blood from his face and hands, he realized he had no plan. He took a breath, calmed his monkey mind, and willed the voice to reappear. He stood quietly for almost thirty seconds until he opened his eyes.

Nothing.

No secret voices in his head or automatic writing on the mirror using a bar of soap. Just as quickly as the skills appeared and saved his life, they evaporated like water on a hot pan.

Shit. He was all alone. Again.

Surveillance cameras at the theater would show a tall blond man kicking the crap out of three attackers in the delivery area. Similar surveillance might have caught him doing the same in the men's room on the second floor. The police wouldn't know from the video who he was. He'd be mistaken as part of Leia's security detail.

The police would find the damaged SUV and check for fingerprints. The US government had all his details and SCS or Spencer would confirm he worked there. It was just a matter of time before the authorities knew who he was.

He looked in the mirror. His new suit jacket was in tatters and dirty from various altercations, with a few streaks of blood, none of it was his.

He still had his cell phone. He tried Fitz first. After several rings, his call went to voicemail. Weird. Fitz always picked up. He looked at his contact list. His phone had only one more number on speed dial.

No way around it. He dialed Westlake's number and after five rings, a female voice answered. "Hello?"

"I think I've got the wrong number," David said, but frowned. This was Westlake's number. He'd used it before.

"Who are you trying to reach?"

"Arthur Westlake," David said.

"There's been an accident. Mr. Westlake was injured. I'm a nurse at the Harbor View Medical Center. We need to contact his next of kin. Are you a relative?"

"No."

"Can you tell me about his employer at least? All we have is a driver's license and a couple of credit cards he had with him."

"What happened?"

"He arrived at the ER unconscious. When the EMT found him on the street, he wasn't breathing. He's in the ICU. If you can provide any..."

David clicked END. This situation kept getting worse. Leia's abduction now looked like something larger. Much larger. Westlake was in intensive care. Fitz wasn't answering his phone. He dialed again with the same number of rings before going to voice mail.

Even though he was on a first-name basis with the billionaire, he didn't have Spencer's number. Yoshi was his only way to contact him.

He had three options: try to contact Spencer through SCS, go to the police and tell them what happened, or try to find Leia himself.

Fitz's voice replayed in his head. Operations frequently went sour. Fitz drilled it into him during his first two days in Seattle in the hotel room. A memory from deep down replayed the same set of instructions from Fitz.

Stick to the plan.

His apartment was out of bounds. If someone had hurt Westlake and Fitz, they might be waiting for him.

The image of the old Brit went through his head. Where was he? Was he in the same shape as Westlake, or worse?

He slipped out of the hotel and discovered a thrift shop still open on the next block. No one batted an eye as he walked in. Most of the other patrons looked in worse shape than he did. After rummaging around for a few minutes, he found a passable pair of jeans, sneakers, a T-shirt, and a hoody that didn't smell. After paying, he changed clothes in a back alley, stuffed his old stuff in a plastic bag, and left it in a dumpster.

A few days of work, Fitz said. No guns, he said. Easy money. Suddenly, easy money came at a higher cost than he wanted to pay.

Chapter Twenty-Five

Boeing Field, Seattle

THE TWO MEN held the target from either side as she kicked and bit and screamed. The third drove and considered himself the lucky one. They had to get her quiet and fast. The man on the right encircled her little body in a hug while the second pushed a gag in her mouth and tied her hands. They were under strict rules to not hurt, hit, or injure her, which turned out to be more challenging than expected. Once they finished, the man on the right pulled out a small canister and said, "Ready?"

The men all held their breath as he sprayed an aerosol into her nose. One spray in each nostril.

The screaming stopped, the straining against the straps ceased as her body relaxed. The driver unrolled the windows for several seconds before raising them. One guy checked her pulse. Strong and regular. "She's down for the count," he said.

"Clear."

The driver touched his earpiece. "The other target escaped in the second SUV and was pursuing us. However, he was interrupted by the third team." He didn't know what happened to the 2nd team and didn't hear an overall outcome.

The project manager would handle it from here. Every crew member knew about the contingency plans, and this was one of them. The three men kept focused on the endgame. They might worry if cops gave chase, or the other target got close. So far, they were on track.

The truck took a steep right turn onto another side road. The instructions were not to speed, and the vehicle's tinted windows and plain wheels looked like government issue. Better to take it slower and zigzag out of downtown. The girl wasn't a problem anymore, either.

The driver took the I-5 South ramp. No one followed. No police, FBI, or vigilante hot heads that got it in their mind to take a run at the Dirty Harry trophy.

He adhered to the pre-arranged route to the Boeing airfield. Five miles south of Seattle, the airport housed cargo and private jets. After he exited the highway, a quarter mile later, he pulled the SUV into an open hanger and stopped in front of an unmarked Gulfstream jet.

They exited the SUV, unhooked the girl, and cut the tie around her hands. A woman in a uniform came out from the plane and put two fingers on the girl's neck.

"Bring her in and lay her on the gurney," she said.

The first man entered and checked out the interior. It still had the new jet smell. The second man carried the girl inside and laid her down gently.

The woman said, "You are bleeding in my airplane." She pointed to the wound on his arm.

"A wild animal bit me."

"You should get it looked at. It might have been rabid."

He glanced down at their target. "Quite possibly."

The last man held up a tiny, brightly colored bag with a cartoon cat printed on it. "What about this?"

"Give it to me. It might help when she wakes up."

"I wouldn't count on it."

The woman glared back but said nothing. She waved them out of the jet.

They climbed into the SUV without a thank you or good luck from the woman and didn't expect one. As they drove away, the woman closed the door and the engine spooled up. One speculated she was a nurse for hire. The other thought she was just a flight attendant for this kind of work. Both decided they didn't care. Their destination was Spokane, far east of Seattle. They stopped only long enough to get bandages, gauze, and antiseptic liquid to handle the bite. Once in Spokane, they would dump the truck and grab flights to different destinations. They'd probably never see each other again, which was a benefit of their profession.

Human bites were usually more poisonous than many wild animals. The men agreed on the story if they got stopped and asked why one had been bitten. A large dog bit him, not a pre-teen girl with a Hello Kitty backpack.

Chapter Twenty-Six

DAVID PULLED the hoodie up and shuffled downtown. His jaw hurt from some hit he took, and he shook from the massive amount of adrenaline his body had pumped into his bloodstream. He stumbled and half-staggered along the sidewalk until he collapsed on a street bench, dropping his head low and slowing his breathing. Adrenaline was a killer post-conflict. Not like in the movies. James Bond couldn't fight four men and then calmly have tea with the Queen. It didn't happen that way.

He'd read something about it once. Or maybe the other guy did. Adrenal glands ramp up at the first sign of danger and dump a heroin-like substance into your blood. The chemical turbocharges your brain synapses, muscle fibres, and lungs to boost your strength and acuity for a limited time. Once you escaped the lion trying to eat you, the chemicals hung around like teenagers at an overnight party. Hard to get rid of and it causes lots of problems.

Nausea, for instance. He leaned over to keep blood in his head instead of rushing to his limbs that no longer needed to flee from the tiger.

The series of events replayed in his mind. A highly trained team grabbed Leia from public space with lots of noise and some casualties.

Likely, every movement the abductors made was captured by internet-accessible cameras everywhere. The police would review all the streams and find out what had happened.

Yoshi, his security escort, was dead or injured badly. David had disabled several of the attackers. However, he didn't know how many had escaped in the chaos.

The memories confirmed one thing: the operation had deep pockets and hired professionals. All but the fake cop had done this before. Amateurs would have failed immediately.

The question was why?

"Are you okay, sir?"

He looked up and into the face of a female police officer. She wasn't smiling but wasn't going for her gun. David dropped his head again. "Yes. I'm ok."

"Are you using?" Her tone wasn't judgmental, more like, "Did you get up this morning?"

"No, Ma'am. I lost a friend today."

She knelt down and put her hand on his back. "I'm sorry. I don't want you to follow the same road as he did." She made an assumption based on his clothes and appearance. She wasn't wrong, however.

"I won't," he said, and he meant it. These bastards had grabbed Leia and likely killed Yoshi, and he wasn't going to let it go.

"I haven't seen you downtown before. New in town?"

"Yes. Just a couple of weeks ago." He wasn't lying.

"There's a shelter on 4th if you need a hot meal and a place to sleep."

"Thank you."

David watched her leave. A city beat cop, no cop car, on foot only. She would have gotten the call about the theatre, however, she looked more like a social worker than an officer of the law.

The nausea finally lifted, and he stood up to get his bearings. The first order of business was to find Fitz.

Chapter Twenty-Seven

Industrial District, Seattle

FITZSIMMONS REMEMBERED nothing for the first few minutes. His thoughts felt messy and out of alignment. The stink of industrial fluid filled his nose. Gasoline or oil, maybe. Then, like focusing a camera lens, everything came into view. At least some of it. He'd been at a hotel and ordered room service, and then his memory stopped. A server brought his food. No, they forced the door open and stuck him with something. Three men. Three men to overpower a geriatric spy with a limp? His hand-to-hand combat days had left his calendar years ago. *Poor form,* he thought, although he'd probably make the same decision.

Abduction never went out of style in the covert world. A black bag covered his head. He sat in a hard chair with his hands zip-tied behind him. Police used plastic ties for single use and for protesters. He didn't think he was protesting anything.

His abductors weren't law enforcement, and he worked at arm's length for the CIA. Was there a hostile takeover in Westlake's department he wasn't aware of? Seemed unlikely, as they had found nothing incriminating at SCS.

What about David? The dancer-turned-spy was chaperoning

Spencer's daughter at the ballet. Did they grab him, too? He suddenly felt a pang of regret convincing him to travel across the country for a simple job. If they hurt David, Fitz would never forgive himself.

Or them.

He wondered briefly about Westlake and dismissed any concern. If the old spy got hurt, it was his fault.

His wrists and hands had lost all feeling, and his shoulders ached from being pulled back. He heard footsteps and someone removed the bag. Gently, not the yank seen in most spy movies.

"Fitzsimmons, isn't it?"

A man he didn't recognize stared at him, large and imposing with a three o'clock shadow and long sleeve tactical shirt, and one percent body fat. Even in his glory years as a field operative, he had never had the self-discipline to get that lean. He focused on his other talents. He shook his head, "No, I'm not, and whoever you are, I'm not who you want."

Fitz tried to appear scared, but he was never much of an actor and was too old to start now.

"What's your name?" the man said.

Fitz stared at his captor and deadpanned, "Why am I not enjoying dessert in my hotel?"

He watched him frown as if he had just received an order to climb to the top of the building and jump off.

"You are Asher Fitzsimmons. That's clear."

How did they know his name? He'd hidden his ID as per his usual travel protocol and checked in under an alias. He glanced around the facility. They had brought him to some kind of dilapidated warehouse. Large pieces of steel bars sat piled up in one corner. Metal walls. Some enormous machine on the opposite side. That explained the bouquet of engine oil and disrepair he woke to.

Cue torture music.

He tried moving his fingers and rolling his shoulders; the movement caused him more pain. He hated his age with a red-hot denial. He was getting older. He should be the lord of a manor in the country with a Welsh Corgi at his feet and a beautiful maiden looking after his needs.

He was far away from that fantasy. An industrial area meant an excellent setting for interrogation; cleanup was a snap, and no noisy neighbors. Probably south of the city center a few miles if he was still in Seattle.

As he moved his fingers and hands more, he noticed his gold bracelet was missing. Someone from the rent-a-thug group had grabbed it.

"You can't trust everything you find on the internet," Fitz said.

"This is going nowhere. Let me soften him up a bit," the man said, but not to Fitz. Either he was crazy, or he was talking to another person remotely. As the fellow turned, Fitz noticed an earpiece. Remote control interrogation.

"You *are* Asher Fitzsimmons. What is your relationship with David Knight?"

"I don't know who you are talking about," Fitz said.

"The dancer we have seen you with. And..." the guy was silent for a couple of seconds, "the police are looking for him."

Fitz kept his cool. Interrogation meant bluffing with information you didn't have, yet his curiosity got the better of him. What did they want?

"Why would I care about the police searching for a man I don't know?"

"He's a suspect in the abduction of Nolan Spencer's daughter."

"Who's that?" Fitz said. He wanted to shrug his shoulders and couldn't.

The hulk scoffed before staring up to the right, nodding his head. Fitz guessed more invisible instructions were being relayed via the earpiece.

"Why doesn't your puppet master show himself instead of employing an overstuffed Pinocchio to repeat his words?" Fitz said.

The big guy sneered, and he looked like he might wind up for a smack when a door opened, and another man walked in, shorter and in a suit, with a bald spot, in his mid-forties.

"Asher Fitzsimmons. Former British Intelligence. Implicated and never charged in several high-profile covert break-ins and a few equally significant assassinations. Military adviser to one side in Vietnam and the white South African government before Mandela took over. You've had quite the career. It would be a shame to go out in flames."

He looked closer at the man, manicured nails, expensive tailored suit, pricey shoes, herringbone white shirt, no tie.

He smelled like money and was the same man David saw yelling at a homeless couple on the day of his first interview.

"You are Nicholas Moore," Fitz said.

Moore's eyebrows lifted and nodded. "Very astute. I'm Nick to my friends."

"I suspect I'm not in that category."

He waved his comment off. "Of course, you are." He gestured to the other man. "Please release him. I'm sorry we had to do this. I didn't think you would have come if we just asked."

His muscle-bound captor pulled out a knife and cut the tie holding Fitz's hands. The relief was almost agony as blood flowed into his arms and shoulders. The Chief Operating Officer of the company the US Government paid him to spy on stood before him with the appearance of legitimate operational information.

"I'm here to tell you that your boy, David, is in grave danger."

Fitz kept working his arms around with the faint hope he could fight his way out of the room if he had to. Thirty years ago, he might have tried. He looked back at Moore. He'd played this 'I'm here to help you' game many times before the man had even been born. Chances are whatever he'd disclose would be a falsehood clothed with a smell of truth.

"David Knight? He's hardly my boy."

"How do you know him?"

"We met in Europe last year, and I've taken a liking to him. I try to help him out now and then," Fitz said.

"Well, he needs help now. He's in deep trouble."

"He's a ballet dancer and a teacher. I can't think of a less dangerous career."

Moore shook his head. "Doesn't matter. The police are looking for him, and it won't end well if he's on the run."

"Does that mean you tried to overpower him like you did me and were unsuccessful?"

Moore snorted but didn't smile. "No."

Fitz rubbed his wrists back and forth. "I'm a little out of the loop since your boys pulled their rendition on me. What happened?"

"While your boy escorted Spencer's daughter to the ballet, a team of heavily armed men stormed the theater, shot several people, and abducted the girl."

Fitz raised an eyebrow. "Who are they?" He didn't need to ask why they grabbed a rich man's offspring. Even his larger captor would understand.

"I have my suspicions. It appears they wanted David along with the girl. That's the only reason I think he wasn't killed during the abduction. However, we don't know if he's still alive."

Another pang hit Fitz's gut. He pushed away the feelings. Emotional manipulation was on page three of the interrogation playbook. "What do you mean?"

"Public places are flooded with surveillance and record everything. The police have a video that shows the attackers trying to capture David and being unsuccessful."

"How can you tell they tried?"

"Because he wasn't killed immediately. The attackers shot several of the security guards, a few fatally. They had the opportunity to take him out and didn't. Instead, they tried capturing him and failed. Logic suggests they wanted him for something."

Fitz said, "I don't believe you."

Moore pulled a tablet out of a small bag and touched the screen. "Have a look."

Fitz watched a video of David entering the men's washroom and two men in suits following him inside. Stun rods were visible in their hands. A few seconds later, David ran out of the room. The men didn't.

He was both surprised and unfazed but didn't reveal his feeling to his face. Contrary to David's assertion, Jonathan's memories might not be lost.

Moore touched the screen again. The view changed to an outside camera of a delivery area. David burst out of the building a few minutes later and took out three additional men with fists and feet. Another camera caught Spencer's daughter kicking and biting while being pulled into a black SUV. After the truck took off, David jumped into a second SUV and pursued the vehicle out onto the street.

There was no doubt in Fitz's mind that the memories were back. Perhaps David had lied to him all this time.

"That's the only video showing the girl. However, he failed to catch the SUV, and another team stopped him several blocks away. They tried to capture him again and failed." Moore squinted and said, "I want to know how a dancer with no military training takes down two men inside and three armed men outside?"

Fitz looked up at him and smiled. "Training for a ballet can be quite grueling."

Moore snorted. "No way."

"Then I suspect he got lucky. Adrenaline is a wonderful drug. When they kidnapped his student, any fear would be replaced with anger. He's in shape as well," Fitz said. He needed to sow doubt in Moore's mind about David's perhaps reborn abilities in case there was an ulterior motive.

Moore turned his head and looked at the pile of metal stacked up in the corner. "I'm showing you all this because I need your help."

"You have a funny way of asking."

"I have to protect myself and SCS."

Fitz raised an eyebrow and rolled his shoulders again while waiting for Moore to continue.

"Why is the US government investigating my company?" Moore said.

The question of the day. Moore probably knew everything, however, that didn't mean Fitz should show his full hand.

"For potential wrongdoing which seems more likely than a day ago. But it's not 'your' company really. Spencer is still the majority share-holder if I'm not mistaken," Fitz said.

A pained expression crossed Moore's face. "Things can change. Quicker than you'd expect."

In any negotiation, there was always a give and take. Fitz looked him in the eye and said, "Why should I tell you anything?"

Moore smiled again and said, "Because if you don't, David may die a horrible death."

Fitz tried to maintain his composure. The wealthy man who abducted him by force now wanted to save David's life if he was still alive to be rescued.

"You said that you had suspicions of who is behind the abduction."

"I do."

"Care to enlighten me?" Fitz asked.

"Spencer."

"Spencer what."

"Spencer engineered the whole thing and kidnapped his own daughter in a very public and expensive operation."

Fitz frowned. The image of David being at risk because of a billionaire weighing less than one hundred and forty pounds seemed crazy.

"That makes no sense at all."

Moore raised his eyebrows. "I know, right? I couldn't believe it as well, but my team has found an electronic trail that confirmed Spencer is behind the whole thing."

"That's the craziest thing I've ever heard. How do I know this isn't some kind of elaborate con you are trying to pull?"

"You can't. All I can say is that over the last few years, Spencer has become more agitated and Howard Hughes-like in his approach. He's rejected every new business strategy and keeps himself locked up in his lake fortress with no visitors. David is the first in a long time. My team built a psyche profile and based on his break with reality, we think he's behind this whole thing and grabbed his own daughter to create a specific outcome."

"Which is?"

"Destroy the company and me at the same time."

Fitz took a breath and waited for a few seconds to process what Moore had just said. "That does sound crazy. But even if he did engineer the operation, why would he want to kill David?"

"As leverage to force the sale of the company and assets to pay an enormous ransom to himself. Tax free, I might add. We suspect if David had been captured at the theater, he'd murder David in some public way to gain support of the public. Once he'd received the ransom, the now grieving billionaire would pin the abduction and your boy's murder on me."

"Where is Spencer now?"

"We don't know."

"What about David?"

"We don't know, and the police don't either."

"He will surface," Fitz said.

"That's not my worry. I'm more concerned about who he will contact."

"He will try to contact me."

Moore held a phone out to Fitzsimmons. "I tried calling his number, and it went to voice mail. Do you have another way to contact him?"

"No."

"How do you two communicate?"

"He calls me at the hotel. Since this isn't the hotel, he probably doesn't have this number."

"Where's your cell phone?"

"At the hotel."

"We checked. My guys couldn't find it."

"Pity, you hired the budget mercenaries. I would have upgraded."

The big guy beside Moore chuckled and stopped. He must have figured out Fitz's insult faster than expected.

"David is at risk. Unless we can find him, Spencer will, and then his life will be in danger."

Fitz heard a text on Moore's phone. The COO pulled the device from his pocket, read the screen, and swore to himself. After typing furiously for a minute, he made a call to someone. "Yes. I got the same text. Looks like we are going for a ride."

"What happened?" Fitz asked.

"I have a few people on retainer for various activities around the city. I was just informed that an unconscious pre-teen girl was seen being placed on a gurney and carried aboard a private jet at Boeing Field. The plane took off about thirty minutes ago. I have people looking for the flight plan. If the girl is Spencer's daughter, David can't be far behind."

"How do you know it was Leia?"

"The source reported that the girl looked like she was wearing some kind of formal dress and had a Hello Kitty backpack with her. Sound like anyone you know?"

Chapter Twenty-Eight

Pike Pine Area, Seattle

TWO MINUTES after his nausea lifted, the sky opened, and rain poured onto the Seattle streets. David's hoodie kept his head dry, although, after a few blocks, he looked like a wet dog.

Fitz had moved to The Hotel White on 6th and Pine a few days ago. Usually, an older inn meant only harsh-smelling soap and squeaky beds. Fitz told him he discovered the place had been a mid-tier Holiday Inn that had been sold to a new management company. Yet, the hotel provided anonymity and ease of access, both attributes Fitz liked.

David leaned against a wall under a concrete overhang across from the building and watched. His thrift-store wardrobe rendered him invisible. With a skateboard and facial tattoos, he'd be up for homeless guy of the week.

He shivered from the dampness and checked his phone again. No calls and no texts. Fitz and Westlake were the only ones who had his email, and his inbox was empty. He'd only given his cell to Yoshi, but he didn't need it anymore. How in the hell had he gone from flying daily to a billionaire's estate by private helicopter to resembling a drug addict in the space of an hour?

His only consolation of the attack was watching Leia sink her teeth into the arm of one of her abductors, like a Hello Kitty pit bull.

Part of him wanted to run. Escape to Canada and hide out in a cabin near Whistler. Or maybe find someone in Vancouver to stay with. He knew enough dancers in the city that would shelter him for a few days. However, that was a no-win scenario.

After watching the hotel and the surrounding streets for several more minutes, he detected no overt surveillance. His eyes darted back and forth, looking, evaluating, and dismissing anyone walking nearby. He didn't have to think of the attack vectors or possible exits, he just knew. The autopilot-driven memories and skills were back, but without the pain.

Why not?

He didn't miss the ice pick jammed into his brain after a memory activated to save his life or kill an attacker. Yet a year later, the memories seemed under his control; knowledge and directions appeared when needed. A ready-to-go spy-on-demand.

As he waited, he couldn't stop thinking about his failure to protect Leia from her abductors. He went over it again in his head. If he'd carried a weapon, he might have stopped them. However, the only real way he could have saved her was not to have taken her to the ballet to begin with.

He glanced across the road and fingered a plastic hotel key in his pocket. He wanted inside Fitz's room; their protocol dictated this would be the first option if he was ever compromised.

This was one of those times.

A bored bellman stood at the front door, watching cars and people. If David timed it right, he could make it to the lobby. However, based on his current thrift store fashion choices, he might get challenged by an employee and prevent him from getting further without a ruckus. This time, he needed to be invisible.

A thin alley ran to the left of the building. As the rain slowed to a drizzle, he angled across the road away from the building. He caught the bellman's stink eye he undoubtedly gave to other street people. Probably a required skill for the job.

David ducked down the passage and into the garage marked "Hotel

Parking Only". He pulled off his hoodie and stuffed the soaking mess into the waste bin by the door inside. He slicked his hair back and pressed the plastic key to an access panel for entry into the building. He rode the elevator to the 6th floor without incident. Fitz's room was on the 7th.

The hallway was empty. Protocol directed a suite as far to the end as possible. He dialed Fitz's cell phone and again it went to a nameless voice mail. Powering off the device was a deviation from his operating procedure. Fitz said his strict adherence to procedures had saved his life several times over.

He slipped to the end of the passage and gently opened the stairwell door. He heard voices one floor up and the squelch of a radio bounced on the concrete walls.

Shit.

David knew the hotel wouldn't attract anyone with a security detail, and he saw no police cars. That meant they were something else and not the good guys.

He'd planned to check the room first, but he didn't want to brave a security gauntlet to knock on the door.

Time for Plan B. When Fitz walked him through the spy-in-a-day handbook, David had mentally rolled his eyes at all the cloak and dagger the old man wanted him to learn.

Today, he appreciated the benefit of hard-won experience.

He tapped his other pocket for the other key. Room 514. The opposite side of the hotel and two floors below Fitz. A backup room.

The elevator took him to 5th and twenty seconds later, he slid the plastic card into the door at the other side of the hotel. The Do-Not-Disturb sign hung on the handle. Booked separately, David had checked in about an hour after Fitz had, two days ago. Standard operating procedure. Backup plans to backup plans.

One room. No hidden guests.

He'd messed up the bed when he first entered and hung a wet towel over the shower bar. A closed suitcase full of his clothes sat on a luggage stand. A shaver and toothbrush in the bathroom. He'd left the place dirty as a window dressing, preferring to sleep in his new apartment. A room booked and not touched would stand out in a chambermaid's mind. A dirty one would be cleaned and forgotten as the housemaids moved on to the next one.

Another bag rested in the closet full of items David had pilfered from this hotel and others. They'd probably come in handy. He just didn't know when.

A second cell phone hooked up to a charging cable laid on the side table. Standard operating procedure.

He twisted the deadbolt shut and jammed a rubber wedge into the bottom of the door. Attackers would have a hell of a time breaking through.

Stripping off his wet clothes, he showered. After, in the mirror, he surveyed the damage. Twin welts rose from his arm courtesy of an attacker's stun rod. A red strip ran across his chin where another man smacked him. He tested the rest of his joints and limbs. Other than his hearing on one side that hadn't returned, everything worked.

Why didn't they kill him? They killed Yoshi without hesitation. *Why was he alive?*

After dressing in his backup clothes, he downed a cold cola from the mini-bar and sat in an armchair, staring at the door. He noticed Jonathan's autopilot creep away, the twinges of awareness waning. He laid his head back against the back of the chair and fell asleep.

A knock at the door woke him up. Someone jiggled the handle and knocked again.

"Housekeeping," a female's voice spoke from the other side of the door.

"Thank you, we are fine," David said.

"Hola. Thank you."

He heard the chambermaid knock and yell her greeting at the next room until he heard her enter a room across from his. Her standard operating procedure had made his heart skip a beat.

He'd forgotten something. Something to check. Something Fitz had told him about.

He unlocked the safe and pulled out one custom tablet supplied by

Fitz, that ran a modified version of Android, with extra encryption and a few other special features. After typing in a password, he wirelessly connected to a tiny camera Fitz had stuck to the top of a painting in his suite two floors up.

A similar layout to his own room appeared, empty and messy. The contents of Fitz's expensive luggage were strewn on the floor. The mattress had been tipped up to the window during a frantic search of the room. Like the U2 song, they hadn't found what they were looking for.

He dragged his finger on the screen to backtrack the video. Surveillance technology has reached the app generation. He backed up the timeline to roughly when he and Leia entered the ballet. Fitz sat in a chair reading a newspaper. He rose and walked to the door as it burst open and smacked him back into the couch. The old guy reached for a pistol on the table before two men strong-armed him to the floor and jabbed him with a needle. Five seconds later, Fitz's body relaxed, and the guys grabbed the gun.

David swore to himself as he watched and felt a burning behind his eyes, the same kind he felt when they had dragged a screaming Leia into a truck. Rage from bullies that wielded power over people that shouldn't need to worry about such things. He watched the team search the room, turning his suitcase out and looking under the mattress and getting progressively agitated at their lack of progress.

They found nothing. No computer and not even a cell phone. The largest brute fireman-carried the old guy over his shoulder and five minutes after they had arrived, they closed the door with an unconscious Fitz in their possession.

He re-watched the show twice. Something was bothering him, and he didn't know what.

David opened Fitz's shiny leather briefcase and withdrew the laptop. The operational procedure was to store everything somewhere else. Extra protection—like wearing two condoms.

As Fitz didn't steal the Maltese Falcon, they probably wanted his computer to search emails, documents, sound files, contacts, and any other messages. He understood why, but the big question was who.

SCS was the common element. Leia was Spencer's daughter, and

Fitz led a covert operation to find dirt on the company. The evidence pointed to someone from SCS being behind Fitz's abduction. The timing between Leia's and Fitz's abduction would infer they were connected. But why would they grab Leia?

Nothing made sense.

David reached into the safe and extracted a few passports, credit cards, and driver's licenses, some fake fingerprints for fooling fingerprint scanners at the airport, and cash: US, Canadian, and Euros. Ten thousand dollars worth. With it, he could rent cars, arrange flights, and book hotels. He stuffed everything into a small shoulder bag he pulled out of his suitcase. He added a black baseball cap at the last minute.

He checked one last time. No gun. "Not that kind of operation," Fitz had said when he'd first arrived. He couldn't have been more wrong.

David rubbed his eyes and jabbed his fingers into his temples. His head ached, and not from the use of another man's memory. Just a normal result of an adrenaline spike coupled with low blood sugar. As he ran through the sequence of events, his gut told him they'd been played from the beginning. They abducted Leia in a highly orchestrated operation that would have required planning, the right crew, a staging area, and lots of money. Timed with Westlake's injury and Fitz's abduction. Someone had played them. Someone with incredible resources, yet the reason remained elusive.

Westlake hired Fitz and David to look for a smoking gun at SCS however, he found nothing, other than a strong and driven workforce and a capable company culture. Other than the mistake of letting a yakuza member slip into a single management position, he found it kind of a boring organization. The only thing he discovered was that Spencer preferred Japanese workers. If the company was as dirty as Westlake surmised, no employee knew anything about it.

Westlake had told Fitz about a meeting today with a whistle-blower. Was he hurt during the encounter or did his heart give out? Still too much of a coincidence for the three of them to be out of commission at the same time.

However, the yakuza connection troubled him. Fitz suspected a rotten apple slipping through the hiring gauntlet, and his student returned to her bright and cheery self. No repercussions.

It didn't matter. An armed team took Leia. Someone grabbed Fitz and hurt Westlake. Three, two, or just one player. David couldn't tell at this point.

He watched the video until he realized what he'd missed. The gold bracelet was still on the old guy's wrist. He zoomed in and saw the glint of the fashion statement part tradecraft.

"It's multipurpose and not so pedestrian as the big tech companies want you to wear." Fitz showed it off when they'd met at his hotel room. "Some communications and standard things like heart rate, O2 level, and a tracking GPS. Everything an aging spy needs."

David opened the 'Find me' app on the tablet and after a few seconds, located the location of the bracelet over the last sixty minutes. 6:55 p.m. hotel. 7:10 p.m. a few blocks south. 7:20 p.m. south along the I-5. At 7:30 p.m. 7:40 p.m. and 7:50 p.m.—the bracelet hadn't moved from what appeared to be in an industrial area south of the stadium.

Interrogation time.

He had to get Fitz out of whatever shit he'd been dragged into. He felt like a grandson to the old Brit. When he first met him in Amsterdam, he wanted to kill him. Now he looked up to him and echoes of the spy's memories told him Jonathan had also liked him.

David had limited options. The police would need more than an anonymous tip that a pensioner was being held hostage. The cops would want to know who he was, and questions would slow things down. He needed to help Fitz and needed to help him now.

He just had to get out of the building alive.

David filled one of the small rolling bags with some items he thought he'd need, slicked his hair back with some gel, and pulled on a hotel jacket he snatched the day before during one of his nightly meetings. After filling a tray with a couple of bottles of water, he left the room for good.

So far, so good. It was a Saturday night, and the hallway was empty. Most of the guests were out for dinner or exploring Seattle. He walked to the elevator and pressed the down button.

The display climbed from 2nd to 3rd and finally the 4th.

At the end of the hallway, the stairway door opened and a large man with a thick beard and hair walked toward him. He had on a dark suit, no tie, and was wide and stocky, he looked like someone on the second tier wrestling circuit. 'The Alaskan' maybe, or 'Mountain Man Mike.'

He walked towards David, his arms swinging back and forth. David turned and smiled. The man stood behind him as the elevator chimed and the door slid open.

"After you, sir," David said.

He nodded and took the offer after looking David up and down.

"How long have you worked here, son?" The man had a faint British accent.

"Going on two years, sir." The hotel jacket he'd stolen made him look like the perfect valet or bellman. Except for the jeans and his prized sneakers, he'd worn to the ballet. They'd come through the attacks and chases relatively unscathed. He pressed P for parking.

"Are those shoes regulation?" the man asked. As the door shut, the man reached out to grab him, but David wasn't there. He pivoted, swung his leg behind the man's knee, and pulled, taking him off balance. As the man lost his footing, David whacked the tray hard into his skull and he dropped to the floor.

A minute later, the door opened into the parking garage and David left the body on the elevator floor. He slipped off the bellman's coat and pulled on a leather jacket from the rolling suitcase. Minutes later, he drove Fitz's shiny rented Toyota out of the hotel parking garage south through downtown. He planned to get close to where Fitz's signal gave up its location. He hoped the owner was still there.

As he kept driving, Leia was on his mind. She'd be safe while the abductors executed their plan. Money or leverage drove abductions. These days, ransom could be paid in cryptocurrency or electronic transfers of real money. Except the kidnapping didn't feel like a cash abduction. Too public. What would they force Spencer to do? Providing software to a rogue country or something more mundane, like interfering in an acquisition of competitor? Westlake worried SCS was selling encryption codes on the black market. Russians? North Korea? David wasn't sure if any of the abductors were European or not. He mostly got an American vibe from them. The guy in the elevator sounded like he was from the UK. Same crew? He couldn't tell. Not yet.

What would the abductors do? Hold her ransom until they received a text message with encryption codes?

He shook his head. He was clearly out of his league as to their motivations. But one thing was clear, he didn't know where to look for Leia. He'd lost the scent an hour ago.

Fitz. He needed to find his old and new friend.

As fast as he could.

Fitz's last ping originated from south of downtown. David kept the tablet open and drove through a part of Seattle that was undergoing a renaissance of sorts. The software boom brought more people to the area, and more companies arrived to take advantage of a more affluent consumer. The city-built stadiums replaced warehouses, and what was left was converted into tech-hubs with exposed wood and high-tech glass.

However, not all areas made the cut, and some waited like dogs in an adoption shelter. The map took him to a seedier area, and he drove by the address of Fitz's last known location. Similar to other unkept structures nearby, a stiff wind would cause problems.

He parked a block away and pulled out his tablet again. He reviewed the video from the hotel room and checked the time the three stooges grabbed Fitz. Close to the time when he and Leia had arrived at the ballet. Made sense. Snatch the old guy first, quick, easy, and quiet, then go for the prize in the middle of a crowded theater. They must have counted on the chaos the people would cause for the police and how they would the chase. When he chased after Leia, the police headed towards the chaos and not after him.

The public snatch still made little sense. A carefully choreographed abduction would have worked better at Spencer's estate, costing less and with a higher probability of success.

He double-checked the location. Down the road a block with an empty lot beside it. It had one level with a metal roof, making the building look like something out of a dystopian video game. Corrugated steel walls, intact windows, hunks of metal in rough piles dotted the outside. Weeds grew through cracks in the concrete and a chain-link fence encircled the place. Most of the surrounding neighborhood appeared abandoned except for the odd auto-wrecker and towing company.

Let's see if anyone is home.

No signs of movement. No lights, no cars, no nothing.

He had to work smarter. Maybe he could threaten to go to HR again. That worked so well the last time.

The silence made him uncomfortable—butterflies in the stomach uncomfortable. No lights meant no people. No cars meant no people. No activity meant it was either empty, or a large, corrugated mousetrap.

Were they the same guys that took Leia? They must be linked, yet he couldn't see how.

He plugged an earbud into the tablet and connected it to the bracelet's electronics. At the hotel, he could only get a GPS signal. Now, up close, more options were available. The device's tiny microphone picked up no sound and the embedded camera showed only a black screen. Yet, everything appeared to be working. However, as seagulls screamed at the ocean, a muted version of the bird's cry came through from the tracker.

Let's ramp it up a bit, he thought.

He pressed a button and forced the bracelet to ring. He listened for talking or swearing and heard nothing. Still no sign of any activity. Making a noise like that should bring a henchman or two to the window, at least. Even for a quick glance.

He let it ring for ten minutes and then stopped. No one home.

Maybe they went out for burgers and fries.

After finding a suitable window to break and enter, David stood inside the warehouse full of piles of steel beams and racks of rusty rebar. The place didn't look like it had been used in years.

A metal chair sat in the middle of the room. They had tied Fitz to it. Broken zip ties on the concrete. At some point, his abductors cut his bonds.

Why?

No blood or body parts anywhere. No snot, spit, or any other fluids. A couple of empty water bottles sat on the floor. All they needed was a blanket and sandwiches, and they could have a picnic.

He poked around more and found nothing else. Three men grabbed him, stuck a needle in his neck, carried him outside to a waiting car, drove him to an industrial park, cut his bonds, and shook hands?

Something smelled rank.

He didn't see the bracelet until he rang it again. Over in the far corner, tossed under a broken pile of wood pallets, he found it. The scratched and bent surface implied they had discovered it and tried to break it and couldn't. Fitz said the manufacturer advertised it would work even under extreme stress. A jingle showed up in his head. *Takes a licking and keeps on ticking.* He didn't know what that meant.

He tilted the bracelet towards the sun, peering through the windows near the top of the roof. No blood on the metal. In fact, David found no liquid or body fluids anywhere. What kind of interrogation served milk and cookies?

He brightened up at the thought Fitz might still be alive, yet he wasn't closer to finding Leia.

David slipped out of the building with the bracelet in his pocket and made his way to his car. He swivelled his head to check for surveillance and detected none.

He found a coffee shop with Wi-Fi about a mile away. He needed to make a call.

Chapter Twenty-Nine

DAVID PULLED into the parking garage beside the coffee shop and parked against the adjoining wall. He wanted to keep invisible if any cops needed a stimulant refill.

He connected his tablet to the place's free Wi-Fi and linked it to an anonymous internet telephone service to make the call. He didn't need police swarming his location because he used his cell phone.

He didn't have Spencer's cell phone number. Any contact outside his daily trips to the billionaire's house was through Yoshi.

Fitz had walked him through various ways to find information on people but kept coming back to a shadowy service called the Hardy Boys. David visualized a group of pimple-faced teenagers drinking Mountain Dew by the gallon and hacking banks and governments between studying for their chemistry exams. He turned on his cell to check for messages. As he was about to connect to their site, his phone rang.

He looked at the number. It was from an area and country code he didn't recognize. Probably a robo-spam-caller telling him his Windows PC had a virus and only they could help.

He pressed 'end' on his phone.

Five seconds later, another call from another area code and number. He frowned and ended the call again.

Three seconds later, a third call came in. This time, he answered.

"David, this is Nolan."

A chill went up David's back. He said nothing.

"David. It is important we meet."

The call caught him off guard. He swallowed and said, "I tried to stop the men from taking your daughter."

"You weren't successful." Spencer sighed into the phone. No emotion. No rage. No anger. Just the truth.

"Did they contact you yet?" David asked.

"Who?"

"The people that took your daughter?"

"I have bigger problems."

David said, "What the hell are you talking about? Someone grabbed your daughter."

"They won't hurt Leia, but they want me dead."

David grimaced. "Who does?"

"Who doesn't is a better question. Few have the balls or resources to pull it off. This one has both."

Spencer sighed through the phone. This time tinged with sadness and a touch of desperation. "My entire operation is compromised, and I don't know who to trust. My security team is gone. Yoshi is in surgery, and I'm exposed."

Yoshi in surgery? That meant the semi-happy sumo security guy might still make it. He felt a tiny spark of hope. "Mr. Spencer, I think I can—"

"And you, Mr. Knight, ballet dancer and teacher. How did you get out of there alive?"

David stopped for a beat and said, "Luck. And adrenaline. I chased after Leia after they shot Yoshi, but I couldn't stop them." David heard Fitz's voice in his head say, *reveal nothing unless it's absolutely necessary.*

"They could have killed you."

"And they didn't," David said. He didn't know why he was still alive, either.

"Are you injured? I've been monitoring the police channels and watching for anything suspicious at the hospitals. Since you hadn't surfaced, I thought you might be dead."

"Did you tell the police I escorted your daughter to the ballet?"

"I haven't talked to the police."

"Why not?"

"I'd be signing my death warrant."

"Why?"

"I told you. I don't know who to trust, and I don't trust the police."

"Don't you think the best..."

"No! Not going to happen. Look, I need your help. My chief of security is out of the picture, and I don't have anyone else to turn to."

"Mr. Spencer, I'm a dance teacher. And how do you even know to trust me?"

"I don't. But we need to meet anyway."

He checked the address Spencer gave him. Not the SCS office, his estate, or even the helicopter. No gauntlet of security to pass through. Just a street name and number. Drive north on the I-5, take the exit from Northgate to Lake City Way. An internet map showed a nearby pawnshop, a cannabis store, and a strip club. Not Spencer's usual hangout.

What the hell was he doing there?

A full moon punctuated the summer night sky. He drove the speed limit on the fast-moving highway heading north, slowing near the University of Washington exit and on to Northgate. He kept a baseball cap and clear horn-rim frames on the entire trip.

A large Nordstrom marked the exit, and after a few minutes, he took a left down to Lake City Way and arrived on a street that time had forgotten. All the restaurants, car dealerships, strip joints, and pawn shops looked like they'd been frozen in the 70s and had just thawed out.

A mile down the street, he passed the address Spencer gave him. A red neon *Lake City Motel* sign hung on the building, a single level, with a wood frame, and early crystal meth decor. Best location in the area to stage a drug deal. Not Spencer's usual haunt. Not by a long shot.

David searched for any surveillance and detected nothing. No police or mercs-for-hire waiting for him to appear. Didn't mean there wasn't any; he just couldn't spot them.

He parked facing the main road and circled the building, checking all exits. He didn't even think about doing it, he just did. A convenience store and a thrift shop sat on either side. A medical marijuana store stared at the motel from across the block. On Yelp, they would vote the place "Most likely to be stabbed in."

A lone beater sat nose in. No quick getaway was planned unless the Mesolithic Taurus had a jet engine makeover. No rust. It looked like a police ghost car from the 90s.

Room six, Spencer had said. End of the line. The Taurus faced the door. Not the most secret of hideouts.

He looked back and forth and knocked. After a couple of seconds, an eye peered through the blinds, and the deadbolt slid open. Not much security if SWAT came calling. A nosy chambermaid could force her way in.

Nolan Spencer looked through the crack in the door and said, "Come inside."

David entered, and Spencer slammed the door, locked it, and wedged a chair under the handle. The usually quiet and well-dressed billionaire looked like a hundred miles of bad road.

A laptop and a small leather courier bag with a broad strap, sat on the bed. The local news played on a tiny flat-screen TV with no sound. A grainy picture of Leia taken from a security camera at the theater was displayed on a bottom banner.

"The police are looking for you and want to talk to me," Spencer said.

David said nothing. He checked the bathroom and glanced around the room. Just the two of them and only one way in.

"I'm alone if that's what you were checking."

He was about to say something and didn't. He needed to hear Spencer's story.

"Thank you for trying to save my daughter. The TV is showing a video of the attackers. I'm surprised you weren't hurt."

Either no surveillance cameras recorded his heroics, or Spencer hadn't seen them yet. Either way, he wasn't offering any information. "Who took her?" David asked.

"Nick Moore."

"The head of your company? Why would he do that? Don't you pay him enough?"

"He has delusions of grandeur. Always had. I boosted his equity and raised his bonuses, and it still wasn't enough. He wants to take the company in a different direction. A much different direction."

"How do you know it was him?" David asked.

"He's the only one that knows Leia is worth billions, or even trillions. I've only started doing the calculations."

David frowned. "What the hell are you talking about?"

"Her blood contains the secret to curing a host of cancers. I'm estimating the potential is five hundred billion to start. That's why Moore grabbed her."

He stared at Spencer and tried to process the information, but it didn't make sense. At least not to him. "I don't believe you."

"I understand how that sounds. Complete science fiction but it's true. She carries an extremely rare combination of antibodies and some special proteins that are like anti-virus software for cancer. Hunts and destroys. I've seen the data myself."

"Moore abducted her for a pint of her blood?"

"No. It's more complicated than that. He wants to harvest her blood and use it as a treatment and make it only available to individuals with money. He doesn't want to cure cancer for the world, just for people that can afford to pay."

David suddenly wondered if Westlake had any inkling of this. Old wonky eye thought the company was selling encryption codes. Selling a cancer cure wasn't breaking the law. Kidnapping and murder was.

"He wants to start at ten million dollars a treatment. Far out of reach for normal people, and insurance companies would just laugh at the cost. However, if he's got the only source, it's supply and demand. And the demand will be high."

David looked around the room for a non-existent chair and kept standing. "Why wouldn't you both work together to bring this out?"

"I considered it initially, but I won't submit Leia to the testing. It's too invasive and she's fragile enough. He grabbed her to force me out of the company because he's a raving psychopath. I've feared for my life and Leia's. And everything I've dreaded has come true."

"Why am I meeting you in this drug dealer motel and not your estate?"

"After you and Leia left for the ballet, Moore's goons stormed my house."

"Yoshi said you were on a business trip."

"I came back. There was no need to let anyone know I was there."

David wondered how Spencer could have returned with no one knowing. He didn't play the invisible man very well. "What did they want?"

"They wanted me dead. That's the reason I can't trust anybody." He pointed to David. "Other than you."

"You know nothing about me."

Spencer shook his head. "Correct. I don't know how a ballet dancer survived an attack by a gauntlet of armed men while trying to save my daughter. Or why you disappear every night after dinner. None of that matters right now. I need your help to find Leia and put Moore in jail."

The billionaire opened a tiny refrigerator, pulled out a white bottle, and swallowed. David saw Spencer's face relax as whatever was in the bottle took effect.

Affecting what, David didn't know.

"And you asked before, why didn't I go to the police?" Spencer said.

"Yes. Why not?"

"It's complicated."

"Try me," David said.

"I met Leia's mother when I worked in Japan. She was young and beautiful, and I fell deeply in love with her. We dated for a while, and when she found out she was pregnant, she stopped all contact. I tried to locate her and couldn't. Later, I discovered she gave birth to Leia and found a woman that would locate a family that would take her baby. But it took some time."

Why?

"Mixed-race children don't adopt well in Japan. Couples don't want to raise children that aren't theirs. Half white and half Japanese have a stigma attached. They move from foster parents to foster parents. Some end up in institutions."

"What did you do?"

Spencer looked down at his shoes. "I stole her."

"You did what?"

"Not me directly. I hired someone to grab Leia from her crib while the adopted mother was out for a few minutes."

David imagined a new mother leaving an apartment for ten minutes to get some diapers and discovering her baby was taken. He couldn't believe Spencer was so callous.

"Did she not think it was you? You shouldn't have been hard to find."

"I had a different name then."

"A different name? Like a different identity?"

"Yes."

This keeps getting better and better, David thought.

"Why?"

Spencer looked sheepish, like he was caught with his hand in the cookie jar. "I was a smart kid and started programming when I was ten. At university, I breezed through the courses. While there, for fun, I wrote an application for some bad guys to help them steal from banks. They paid me a lot of money and I also got caught. I ratted them out to the police to save myself from going to jail. The crime boss threatened to kill me, but with the money I'd made, I moved far away and changed my name so they couldn't find me. When I discovered the crime boss had died in prison, I returned to the US.

"And the mother never found you after?"

"No. But I'm always afraid she will. That's why I don't do any interviews or have any pictures of me on the internet."

"Did you discover the truth about her blood before or after you stole Leia from her mother?"

"After. A fluke, really. Look, I know how this looks. A white guy knocks up a Japanese girl, takes the baby, and abandons the mother. But that wasn't my intention. She was the love of my life, and I love my daughter. I knew I could show her a better life and her mother wouldn't let me. I made my decision."

"How did you find her blood cured cancer?"

"When I got to Japan, I wrote software for a biotech company to search for specific proteins in sequenced DNA. We were paying random Japanese citizens to test their blood. That's how I met her mother. After I returned to the US with Leia, I updated the application and found her mother's blood contained part of the protein that had been predicted, and after I tested Leia's blood, more of the proteins were there. Her blood was a better choice to create a serum."

David followed most of what Spencer said and focused on his student's blood containing a key to killing cancer.

"Why do you need me?"

"I don't have anyone else. I'm telling you all this because I believe I can trust you. My daughter likes you, and you tried to stop her abduction. I'm also a good judge of character. If I had the choice, I'd rather have Yoshi, but he's recovering. You also work for me. That's why I need you with me."

"And go where?"

"I discovered Moore planned to take her out of the country. She's probably already in the air."

David heard a car drive by. He peeked out of the blinds and watched an old pickup belch smoke as it passed.

"Tell me about what happened at your place after we left for the ballet."

Spencer stood up, washed his hands in the tiny bathroom sink, and dried them on a threadbare towel.

"I told Yoshi to proceed as if I was still away. I stayed in a different part of the house. Yoshi arranged for a replacement security team to arrive after the three of you left. Ten minutes later, a team of Moore's men took over the house and killed the cell service and Wi-Fi. They must have had a jammer."

"How did you get out? Your place doesn't exactly have exits on every floor."

"I own a security company, don't I? I write security software and security scenarios. I'm prepared for this kind of situation."

"That your security would be compromised, and you'd have to escape?"

"More or less. I left through a hidden exit and grabbed my getaway car."

"A Taurus."

"Yes. Blends in and always starts. I had it ready to go in case I ever ran into a situation like this."

David rubbed his chin and stared back at Spencer. He looked as though he was made of paper that could crumple at any time. He maintained that he had fled from men who had tried to abduct him or worse. It didn't seem possible.

"Do you think they would have taken you hostage, too?"

"No. They were there to kill me."

"How do you know?"

"I just knew."

Spencer said nothing more, and David didn't press him. He wondered if Spencer's mental health was moving into Henry the Eighth territory. His profile fit; rich and isolated by choice, perhaps delusional. Yet, there was no way he'd be able to kill an armed group of men before they killed him.

"How did you get away again?"

Spencer closed his laptop and started stuffing some things into the gym bag on the bed. "A more accurate statement would be did the men that tried to kill me get away?"

"You killed them?"

Spencer laughed. "No. I'm not a murderer. I hid in my safe room, and once all the team was inside, I released fast-acting knockout gas that covered the whole house. They all went to sleep. I escaped via a secret passage to a hidden garage."

"Your Batcave had a Taurus in it?"

"Something like that."

David looked at Leia's father and frowned. He could visualize the guy hiding under his desk, but that was it. *Never judge a book by its cover,* he thought, *especially a billionaire one.*

"Moore's grabbed more than just your daughter."

Spencer frowned. "Like the old spy you've met with?"

David shook his head. He should have put an announcement on Craigslist. "Yes."

"The one that had you install surveillance tech inside my company?"

"That's the one."

"The tech is impressive. I'm curious who developed it—it's much too clever for the US government to create. I still don't know why they made you install it."

David had to admit the old guy had him cold. He could lie or tell the truth.

"Your Chief Operating Officer appears to be a psychopath and wants you dead. Wasn't that enough?"

"What reasons did the government give you?"

"They wanted evidence of illegal business practices. I never knew the full story. However, it appears they weren't far off the mark."

Spencer looked up at the ceiling. "Interesting. Well, it makes sense. Moore always just skirted the edge of the law. It is about time he was discovered."

"It's you that has the most to lose."

"You and I both have something to lose," said Spencer.

"Then Moore grabbed Fitz and Leia," said David.

"Yes."

"Who attacked Westlake?"

"Who?"

"Arthur Westlake. The guy paying the bills. Tall with a crazy eye."

Spencer frowned like the name meant nothing to him. "I don't know an Arthur Westlake." He stuffed a few more pieces of clothing into the bag.

"He's in intensive care. He was injured about the same time Moore grabbed Fitz."

"Then Moore may be getting rid of anyone that can derail his plans."

"If he has Fitz and Leia, I'm going wherever they are," David said.

Spencer's phone beeped, and he looked down. "I just got confirmation. I know where Moore's taking Leia."

"Where?"

"Japan." He looked at the phone again. "Tokyo, to be specific." Spencer's shoulders slumped as if another weight had dropped on him.

A ripple of fear ran through David when he heard Japan, and a bigger one when he heard Tokyo. Why? Japan wasn't Iraq or Pakistan. Everyone raved about the place, the people, the culture, and the food. He couldn't think of a safer destination.

Except the thought of going made him nauseous.

"I can't go to Japan," David said.

Spencer looked at him like a man caught in the jaws of defeat. "I can't do this alone."

Nausea hit him again. "You need to go to the police and come clean about Leia."

"I can't. Look, I'm paying your salary and I can give you a bonus when we find Leia if you are worried about that."

"It's not the money, I just..." Bile came up in his throat and he wanted to lock himself in the bathroom.

Spencer looked like a man that had just been shot. "I don't have anyone else. If we don't find her, Moore will lock her away and drain her of as much blood as they can get away with. She's not like other kids. She's fragile. She might not even survive the first test. I can't let him go through with it."

David took a deep breath and remembered how excited Leia was at the ballet. The size of the smile on her face and her passion for dance. *On the spectrum* meant she experienced 150 percent more than anyone else. He thought about her kicking and screaming as the thugs dragged her into the SUV and his anger burned away any trace of his nausea. The same anger that had helped him take out the three men waiting for him by the delivery entrance.

He replayed the incident and connected it to Moore. How the man that had everything still wanted more. How the man would sacrifice an innocent child to build his fortune.

Fuck it, David thought. He didn't trust Spencer or Moore, but it didn't matter. Leia's life was at risk, that was clear. He'd go to Japan and handle anything thrown at him.

"What do you need me to do?" David asked.

Chapter Thirty

Seattle-Tacoma International Airport, Seattle

SPENCER DROVE the geriatric Ford to SeaTac as David followed and dumped the rental car. Once they met at the ticket desk, Spencer handed him a boarding pass and passport.

"We are on the next flight to Tokyo, leaving in an hour," Spencer said.

David looked at both documents. "David Weller?"

The US passport with the same name had his picture that was used for his SCS ID badge.

"When did you create this for me?"

"I run a company specializing in security. I plan for scenarios like this," Spencer said.

David just looked at him. The billionaire appeared more capable at the covert side of the business than he gave him credit for.

They breezed through the gate into international departures, with the TSA agent giving only cursory looks at their fake documents. They boarded an older airplane jammed with a large tour group returning home. The last-minute ticket squeezed him between two Japanese sisters that wouldn't trade their existing seats for two beside each other.

Spencer sat a couple of rows ahead and looked uncomfortable being this close to other people.

As the flight reached cruising altitude, the sisters talked non-stop as if David wasn't there. Drops of sweat trickled from his forehead, and a migraine gripped his temples. A kind flight attendant supplied him with a pain reliever that lessened his suffering. As the sisters continued their conversation, each word drove a spike into his head. After wedging a couple of earplugs into his ears, the pain stopped long enough for him to fall asleep.

He woke after the attendant dropped a Japanese meal of rice, chicken, and vegetables on his seat tray. He'd been dreaming again of another man's life, but the dreams felt more real than before. More of Jonathan's memories. Buying a pint of whiskey at a drugstore and picking up an order of Chinese food. The old spy's time at university. Some big US school. Texas seemed likely. Other visions surfaced as well. Kissing a drunk nursing student in a dorm room. Standing at the grave site of a mother he didn't know. Random and disconnected images climbing their way from somewhere deep in his psyche.

He blinked the sleep from his eyes and tore the aluminum foil off the chicken and rice dish and ate it with the supplied chopsticks, drank hot green tea, and enjoyed a tiny mango cream desert as the sisters on either side of him both snored. Their batteries had finally run out. He felt better. The migraine had disappeared, and the meal helped. He realized he hadn't eaten for a while.

He dozed for a few more hours, getting up twice to stretch. The pilot announced in English and Japanese that they were preparing to land. As the plane descended, his stomach did barrel rolls, and it wasn't from the food. A few rows up, Spencer didn't look much better. He squirmed at every cough and movement. Poor guy. His billionaire life had been ripped away from him and thrown into a cesspool.

David could almost relate.

Almost.

Chapter Thirty-One

A SHORT TIME after he'd agreed to help, Fitz faced backward in an SUV, alone with his initial brutish interrogator and shiny chrome handcuffs. Moore said David was in terrible danger and needed Fitz to help stop the worst-case scenario. Moore said Spencer was behind the whole abduction. Fitz wasn't so sure.

He had agreed to help to keep him in whatever game was being played. As in most games, the balance of power could shift fast.

Moore declined to tell him their ultimate destination. They pulled into a secluded hangar beside a private jet, and he struggled to walk to the jet's stairway. He wished they'd abducted his cane as well as him from the hotel. Once he made it up the stairs and into the posh interior, he noticed Moore was missing.

"Are handcuffs necessary? I'm an old man."

His nursemaid didn't respond. Fitz tried another tactic. "What's the movie on the flight?" and smiled his best British upper-crust smile. He didn't ask about the destination. Not yet anyway.

The guy had the personality of a porcupine and ignored him. He led Fitz to the back of the plane and handcuffed him to a leather seat that faced backward.

"We can do this easy way or the hard way. The easiest thing for me is to stick another needle in your neck, and you go out for the duration. Long enough for me to get some shuteye and not have to listen to your jabbering. Or you stay quiet."

Fitz considered the offer and said, "I will keep silent, my good man," before leaning his head back and closing his eyes. He still didn't know if Moore had made it onto the plane.

The window shades were down, preventing him from watching the takeoff. A private jet would dictate Boeing airfield. SeaTac would be too busy, and ground staff would notice a man starting a trip in handcuffs.

As the plane took off, he willed himself to relax. He heard a curtain closing, separating him from the rest of the passengers. He assumed Moore had arrived and merely neglected to say hello.

Even though they had chained his wrists to the seat, he tilted it back. He'd learned the old army lesson many years ago: eat, sleep, and pee when you can. You might not get another chance. True to form, his breathing slowed once he closed his eyes and fell asleep in under five minutes. He'd had a busy day so far.

Bumpy air woke Fitzsimmons with a start. He needed a shower, a change of clothes, and a covert strike team to be available when he landed. He rubbed his eyes with his free hand. His jailers had given him enough chain to allow him to eat and drink. Just then, a flight attendant came in with a paper cup.

"Coffee or tea?"

"Tea, please."

She handed him the cup, and the lovely smell of Earl Grey filled his nostrils. "I'm forever in your debt, Mademoiselle."

She smiled and ignored his restraints. Blonde, beautiful, and freshly scrubbed, she looked about thirty. "Once I complete all my business, can I repay the favour with dinner?" He smiled his best old man smile. Viagra provided remarkable augmentation as long as the body was willing. His was, especially for this lovely lass. Yet, the question was more to gauge her reaction than a May-and-very-late-in-December date.

Her face changed to neutral, then a frown. "No, sir. I don't think that will be possible." She turned and left the tiny back cabin to the front where the rich and infamous traveled.

He hadn't expected a positive reply. However, her reaction and demeanour told him a lot. This was a corporate jet with a trained flight crew, not a couple of pilots plus Moore's underlings. They would be on retainer to fly when needed and provide in-flight services. She didn't react to the chains, which meant this wasn't the first time she'd served a passenger in handcuffs. Her response to his dinner invitation might indicate previous guests never made the return trip, or at least others in the same circumstances never did. His hypothesis didn't change the game he'd played many times before. As he sipped his tea, his mind returned to the main question: where was David?

Fitz continued to doze and estimated they'd been flying for the better part of the night, at least nine hours or more. An hour later, the plane banked and started a slow descent. With the window shades down, he couldn't determine what city, country, or hemisphere they were in. The flight time guaranteed they weren't in the US. Based on the company's hiring policy, he expected they'd land in Japan if he had to guess. Tokyo, probably but Osaka might be a consideration. As they flew in a private jet, any airfield would accommodate them. Spencer's business seemed centred on Japanese culture; Fitz could see no other destination.

The cute flight attendant pulled the curtain between the cabins and opened the window shades. She looked in his direction without an expression. Landing meant she was on the job, ensuring passengers were belted, calm, and safe. Safe in the air, at least. Once he left the airplane, he wasn't as sure.

They needed him for something. His death would be far easier if completed in Seattle, no expensive flight to somewhere, therefore, his presence was useful. He'd try to be useful for as long as possible.

He caught sight of buildings and water through the open window shades. They were landing in a port city. Singapore, perhaps. If they landed in Japan, then Haneda Airport would fit the bill. Narita

International Airport was two hours from Tokyo and fifteen miles from the ocean.

The jet's wheels screeched at touchdown as the pilot applied the engine brakes, moving him forward in his seat. A few minutes later, the plane taxied into an enormous hangar that looked like a twin of the one in Seattle, private and secure. Fitz didn't expect any customs officer to review his passport, which he neglected to obtain when he was snatched from the hotel room.

His nursemaid unlocked his wrists. "No funny business or you will wish you were somewhere else."

"I already have that wish," Fitz said. His jailer ignored the quip.

Three black Mercedes SUVs greeted the jet. He wondered if criminals ever considered another color palette. At least, they could have arranged Japanese versions to blend in.

His nursemaid directed him to the middle one. He limped towards the truck and watched Moore and two others enter the first truck. Moore must have felt too important to talk to the hired help during the flight, which told Fitz a lot about his character. The crew would undoubtedly take the last SUV to a hotel somewhere on standby if Moore and his cronies needed to leave Japan in a hurry.

Pity. He fantasized about dinner with the flight attendant here or somewhere else. There was always the possibility of a ride home. Fitz had made a habit of spoiling other people's plans for him.

Chapter Thirty-Two

Narita International Airport, Japan

DAVID AND SPENCER breezed through customs with their false passports. The billionaire grimaced as he walked but didn't complain. They exited into the Narita arrivals hall and the main building. No bags to wait for. David's only luggage was the small bag that carried his tablet, a cell phone, and Fitz's emergency cash and credit cards he stowed in a hidden compartment. Spencer had a computer bag and wore the courier pack over one shoulder.

Jammed into a middle seat for the last twelve hours had taken a toll on David's tall frame and he felt like death warmed up in a microwave. However, his migraines had subsided. His companion swallowed a large pill with the help of a water fountain. Spencer drinking from a public spigot seemed unheard of. He was the poster child for germ avoidance. Had a life model decoy replaced him?

He picked up a couple of DoCoMo SIM cards from an airport kiosk. He'd need internet access before too long. As they exited customs, a pale man in a suit held a sign with the SCS logo. No English or kanji characters. Spencer nodded and the guy led them outside to a waiting car.

David wiped the perspiration from his forehead and looked up at the sky. It was grey and dreary with lots of humidity, like Toronto in the thick of summer. The combination of the heat, sweat, and jet lag wasn't a great start to their search. A few minutes later, they pulled up to a four-seat helicopter sitting on a helipad near a set of buildings at the far end of one of Narita's many runways.

"At this time of the day, Tokyo is a ninety-minute trip by car," Spencer didn't elaborate on their destination, and David's unease started rising.

The pilot bowed and took his position at the controls. They sat behind him, each pulling on headphones.

As Spencer spoke to the pilot in Japanese, sharp needles dug into David's temples. What the hell was going on? He hadn't suffered pain like that for over a year, and that was only after he'd killed someone. If the torture lasted much longer, he might do it again. Spencer continued in fast Japanese until David tore the headphones off and stared out the window. The loud droning from the engine and blade calmed his torment.

Fifteen minutes later, the farmland between the international airport and the city gave way to tiny, single-family houses, apartment buildings, and busy streets. He watched a never-ending stream of cars on the highways injecting themselves into the street arteries that made up Tokyo proper.

The helicopter descended into an empty parking lot of a low-slung industrial area with only an SUV and some people waiting to greet them. He realized they must be in Kawasaki prefecture. He swore to himself. How long had Jonathan lived in Japan? The memories were like drunk texts from an ex-girlfriend; you never knew when they would appear.

To the south sat Tokyo Bay, with planes dotting the air at the nearby Haneda Airport. The memories had been here before. Nothing else surfaced.

Once the chopper landed, he got a better look at the welcome committee. Twin beefy Japanese men dressed in suits, white shirts, and no ties stood beside a black Lexus SUV. A third, skinnier man with slicked hair and sunglasses exited the truck and threw a half-smoked cigarette to the asphalt. He'd call the guy Slick.

I'm trapped in a Japanese gangster movie, David thought. These guys didn't look like they were the kind to provide help. As he squinted at the reception committee, he shivered. Slick rang a distant memory bell, except with no information on when, where, or why. Had Jonathan gotten mixed up with the yakuza?

The muscle looked fresh out of Japan Central Casting. Probably not hired because of their SAT scores. As looks could deceive, he decided the first studied history, and the second liked science. Both were struggling students, glowering and beating up people to pay for school.

As they exited the helicopter, David said, "Who are these guys?"

"Former business associates."

"If they are escorting us to the bad guy convention, I forgot to bring my sunglasses."

"They've offered to help find Moore and Leia."

David wasn't convinced.

As they walked towards the SUV, the helicopter's engine wound up, and the pilot lifted off like he had a train to catch, leaving only the acrid smell of jet exhaust and the stabbings-r-us welcome committee. Spencer moved toward Slick, and their body language showed neither man liked the other. For a friendly business meeting, you didn't bring bodyguards.

Spencer stood in front while David assumed the role of hired help. History and Science each stepped forward, positioning themselves on each side about ten feet from him. A tall chain-link fence surrounded the parking lot with an open gate at one end as the single way in and out. If the conversation slid south, they had little choice for an escape plan.

David's breath caught in his throat, and he rubbed his fingers against his sweaty palms. He pulled off his backpack and sat it on the ground. He realized he wasn't afraid. He felt the same emotion as he did before he walked on stage—anticipation.

Spencer directed rapid-fire Japanese at Slick. David expected the pain to ramp; instead, the words sounded more familiar, although he didn't get their meaning. The guy stood, relaxed, his arms crossed and rubbing a nicotine-stained thumb and forefinger together like he wanted another cigarette. He noticed part of one finger was missing, and there were several half-smoked cigarettes on the ground. They'd been waiting for a while.

More angry Japanese between Spencer and Slick, but with aggressive, confrontational tones, or so David thought. Each word and response became more familiar, like tuning into a frequency on the radio. Finally, as Slick jabbed a finger at him and Spencer spoke, he understood the conversation. Spencer said in Japanese, "My employee doesn't speak the language," nodding his head towards David.

"Supenser-kun, yakusoku o yabutta na!" Slick said.

David heard, "You have broken your promise!"

In a flash, he understood. Jonathan must have lived here and learned enough of the language to get by. The pain and the words surfacing made sense.

As Slick and Spencer ramped up their rhetoric, the two thugs shifted closer to him. Crap. He looked for a way out of this mess. He didn't want whatever this was. Or did he?

Science turned to History with his hands out and said in quiet Japanese, "Two fucking gaijins to deal with. Your turn or mine?"

"Mine," History said.

"How?" Science said.

"Sleep, I think. Blondie is too pretty to hit. He might cry." He chuckled and flexed his biceps through his suit.

A larger guy usually has the advantage in a fight. Strength plus weight easily overpowers a smaller opponent. If the planned outcome is final, a larger guy can grab the opposition with one hand and plunge a knife into his ribs with the other. If History wanted to use a sleeper hold, he wanted to capture, not kill, for interrogation with a side of pain. Good plan overall. Subdue the blonde gaijin, and the thinner Spencer would fold like yesterday's newspaper.

David breathed in and relaxed as History lunged towards him. The big guy would expect David to run, and Science would stop him. With no place to go, History would have the advantage. He probably would use a sleeper hold. If not, a right hook would suffice.

As History reached out, David's body exploded forward, closing the gap, and smashing his head into his attacker's nose with a satisfying crunch. The guy reeled back as David swept his leg at the knee, pushing him off balance. Science reacted, running towards his falling friend, realizing too late that he had underestimated the gaijin. He grabbed at David and found his wrist twisting back as he threw Science over History like a top-heavy bowling pin. He followed with a blow to History's temple and a kick to Science's face.

Slick yelled and pulled out a revolver from his jacket. A gun, really? Firearms were rarely used in Japan. Gun law violations delivered extreme sentences. The gangster didn't seem to care. David leaped forward and smashed his elbow into Slick's head as the gun fired.

The revolver dropped and Spencer staggered, falling back. David stopped his fall and pulled him towards the SUV, a red bloom spilling out from behind Spencer's hand. He lifted and shoved him into the back of the bad guy's SUV. As the three bloodied men on the ground stirred, he threw the bags they'd brought from Seattle into the truck and took off. In the rear-view mirror, he saw Science raise his head as blood poured down his face.

Spencer groaned. "Why did you do that? He was going to give me Leia's location."

"The big guys planned to knock me out and grab you."

"How could you know that?" he grunted in pain.

"They were talking about it," David said.

Spencer looked distressed like he'd just swallowed a bug. "You don't speak Japanese."

"I've got to get you to a hospital."

"No!" Spencer said. "No hospitals." He held his hand to his side. "We won't find Leia if we do. They will find me." Spencer lurched over to the side of the window and groaned.

"Who will find you?" He looked back. Spencer's eyes were closed as it appeared he had slipped into unconsciousness. What was he going to do? He had to take Spencer somewhere.

He tried to orient himself in the Tokyo traffic. His memories surfaced like a map torn into little pieces, only some areas in focus. A hospital popped up in his mind, close to their location. He could drive up to Emergency and drop his passenger off, hoping the doctors would save his life and not put him in jail when they discovered who he was.

The police would match his fingerprints and ask why a US billionaire that had just entered Japan under a false passport was shot within an hour of landing.

Another image appeared in David's mind. He stepped on the gas, racing along the side road until he merged onto the highway towards Shinjuku.

"Where are we going?" Spencer had regained consciousness—at least for a while.

"I know a place," he lied. He didn't know a place. Jonathan did. The red stain on Spencer's shirt was growing. He hoped the bullet had missed any major arteries or organs and guessed he had a few minutes of grace before his passenger died.

David grimaced as another nail jabbed into his temple, except he wasn't losing control like last time; the memories seemed to guide him more than anything.

The image of a place reappeared in his memory. As he pulled into traffic, he drove with a vague sense of the right direction. The mammoth city's organization returned in staccato fragments. Other than he'd never been there before, he wasn't doing half bad.

He threaded the Lexus SUV towards the centre of Tokyo when the name of the neighbourhood popped into his head like a long-forgotten friend.

A groan came from the back seat. "Where are you taking me?"

Chapter Thirty-Three

THANKFULLY, someone, Fitz's nursemaid or Moore, didn't think it was necessary to blindfold him or keep his hands locked. Maybe Moore realized an old man that needed a cane to walk wasn't a flight risk.

Once they started driving, he understood why. He'd only visited Tokyo a few times before, and neither had a mental map of the city nor knew what direction the convoy traveled. Not expecting a free trip to Japan, he'd forgotten his tourist map. He felt more like carry-on luggage than a hostage.

During the flight, he had considered that Moore was telling the truth. Except he didn't believe him for a second. Too many times in his life did another person try to convince him of an alternative fact. Most of the time, the motivation was greed or manipulation. Moore would score high on both counts.

He rubbed where his handcuffs had squeezed his wrists for the flight over. He briefly fantasized about reciprocity to Moore and the nurse-maid but decided to wait. Opportunities were always available. Most took patience. What Fitz didn't have in youthful vigour, he made up for with the unemotional endurance of a Russian.

He stared out the window, watching the unfamiliar streets, signs, and people. Their driver kept his eyes on the road and said nothing. His original big and brutish interrogator, devoid of any personality, sat in the front. He preferred the seating arrangement as he wasn't in the mood for any witty banter. A hot shower and a bed to fall into was his only wish. A visit from the flight attendant would cap off a perfect evening. He wagered none of his wishes would come true.

He knew they'd landed at the Haneda Airport, which gave close access to Tokyo proper. With almost fourteen million people and eight hundred and fifty square miles, David could be anywhere in the city or Japan if Moore's information was trustworthy.

Fitz had shied away from work in Asian countries. He'd visited Vietnam and Cambodia during the 60s and 70s. Once he left his government employers, he limited his activities to Europe and North America. Besides the King's English, he spoke French, German, and some Spanish. In his business, communication meant everything. If he didn't speak the language, he'd falter, and people could die.

Jonathan, however, was a polyglot since birth and picked up any Roman-based language effortlessly and Japanese after spending only a little time here.

Yet, his former partner held the title of leading conflict magnet. He never looked for trouble—trouble found him. He spent six months in Japan before returning to the US. Fitz had told David the truth. Jonathan had never revealed what happened over here.

Something always happened with Jonathan around. Fitz imagined his old friend saw himself as a knight-errant. Solving problems that met his own "code."

He missed the son-of-a-bitch and, weirdly, felt a similar affection for David. More like a parent instead of a co-worker. He kept imagining bits of Jonathan's personality leaking out of David here and there but didn't know if David was a bit of an asshole before the implant or not.

And with his dying breath, he would save David from anything unsavory. He'd let Jonathan die with that old German on the Amsterdam bridge without support. He'd be damned if he was going to let David suffer the same fate.

His nursemaid turned, looked at Fitz, and said, "We're almost there. I want no funny business, or your next trip will be in the trunk."

Fitz ignored him and peered out the window. The man waited for some kind of response that he wouldn't give.

The brute grunted and faced forward. *Just as well,* he thought. *If he stared at me any longer, I'd consider jamming my thumbs into his eyes.* He'd get at least one; both if he was lucky. That would serve him right for underestimating someone who survived the Cold War, regardless of how old he was.

The buildings thinned out to larger and wider structures. More highways this time and back to an industrial area. Why couldn't clandestine operations run out of a Hyatt or a Four Seasons? Much better room service.

He laid his head back and closed his eyes, the hum of the ride putting him to sleep. He wished he'd been more prepared and thirty years younger. However, he'd work with what he had.

The car slowed and pulled into a large garage. The other cars emptied first. He glimpsed Moore disappearing through a doorway. Finally, his nursemaid opened the door and offered no help getting him out.

"Hurry up, old man. We have a sighting."

"A sighting for what?"

"The dance teacher and Spencer. Moore needs you to get them."

Fitz dusted himself off and looked into the goon's eyes. "And exactly how am I going to do that?"

The driver of his car and another man took Fitz's arms and directed him through the door. "Don't worry. Moore will give you a few tools to find them, plus some extra motivation."

Fitz scowled. He was still a prisoner, and having these young chaps push him around didn't bode well for his future role in Moore's operation, or if they'd planned for him to return to the US in anything other than a box.

Chapter Thirty-Four

Nishihara, Shibuya, Tokyo

"Konnichiwa. I need your services," David said, switching to English. He had tried speaking Japanese and found it distant and unreachable. Jonathan's memory worked, and then it didn't.

The memories had driven him to Shibuya. He'd snaked through a rabbit warren of tiny streets and tinier houses until he pulled into the back of a small building needing repair. Upkeep takes money, he thought, and the owners looked like they were a little short. He'd hoped the memory guiding him was accurate.

He pulled Spencer out of the car, half carrying him up the stairs, and knocked on a scratched and pockmarked door, crying for paint. A crack appeared, and a short, balding man frowned at them. Very few Caucasian men ever came to his door, and even fewer probably had bullet wounds. The man looked older than David expected. A familiar smell wafted through the open door, but he didn't know what it was.

"My friend is bleeding," David said, hoping the man understood.

He squinted at Spencer and the bloom of red covered by Spencer's hand. "Hospital two miles that way." He pointed behind David and said nothing more.

"We can't go to the hospital," David said. The man kept his right hand hidden. He probably held a baseball bat.

"No help, sorry." David wedged his foot in the crack as he pushed the door closed.

"We have money."

The man hesitated and still shook his head. "No. We don't do that anymore. Too many problems."

David took a deep breath and said, "Jonathan Brooks told me you owed him a favor." He'd grabbed a wad of yen from Spencer's wallet and thrust it into the man's face. "Please. We have nowhere else to go."

The man frowned as if he'd just eaten a bug. "Brooks-san? He's not here. You aren't him."

"He's my uncle. He told me you owed him a big favor."

The old man squinted at David and said, "Why do we owe Brooks-san a favor?"

"He helped your son."

The man dropped his head and grimaced before nodding and waving them inside. Spencer's legs gave out, and David carried him through the door. *Weird*, David thought. He was light as a feather. Too light for a full-grown billionaire.

An older, stout Japanese woman stood grim-faced, first looking at David and then at Spencer before shaking her head. David felt the heat radiating in his chest as if his mother had walked through the door. He had to look away as tears welled up inside him. What the hell was going on?

She spoke to her husband in Japanese, too fast for David to translate. He guessed she shared her husband's unhappiness.

"In there." She pointed to a room on the right that looked vaguely medical. Vinyl covered the floor, and hard white tiles rose against the walls. Cardboard boxes littered the exam table. The woman spoke to the older man, and he cleared the table and disappeared with the cartons.

David laid Spencer on the table, and she washed her hands before pulling on latex gloves. She checked his pupils and listened to his heart. The older man plugged in a fluorescent light with a reflector and moved it close. He remembered the house's distinct smell, a combination of hair spray and jasmine.

"He should be in hospital," the woman said in accented English.

"That's not possible." He fought an urge to hug her.

She sighed and pulled out a plastic box, extracting a pair of scissors to cut open his shirt and expose the bullet wound.

As he tried to watch, she shooed him away. "Wait in the kitchen. This takes a while."

He found the room and sat at a low table and chairs. The older man poured him a cup of tea before disappearing again. He noticed the little white flowers on a jasmine plant overflowing on the window ledge, looking into the alley. The source of the aroma and the memory.

They were back and showed up at random times. Maybe he hadn't paid for the upgrade for full memory access. His Japanese comprehension appeared only occasionally. Sometimes he could speak like a native. All the other times, he was a dumb tourist. No rhyme or reason.

Why would he expect anything different?

Last year, his rage was a mix of Jonathan's and his own. Anger at being violated by another man's memories and fighting for his life throughout Europe and Silicon Valley.

Then the craziness ended, and he returned to Toronto, ready to slip back into his old life. Yet, the anger simmered below the surface and was ready to blow. Now he knew the memories stoked his rage, remorse, and sadness all hidden by a thin layer of smoldering embers that might catch fire.

He pulled out his tablet and phone, switched to the Japanese SIM cards from the airport, and got back online. The screen displayed US news sites covering the attack and the abduction at the Seattle Center. Nothing about Spencer, Leia, or anything else. He found a grainy picture of him fighting the men at the back of the theater. He was described as a "person of interest," and the police asked anyone who saw this man to call the non-emergency number.

That's great, he thought. *I'm wanted by law enforcement again. How in the hell did this happen?*

Lucky. A thought appeared like a tweet from his subconscious.

"Go fuck yourself," he said out loud.

The older man brought him a bag of rice crackers, then disappeared into the back of the house.

A gunman shot Spencer, mercenaries grabbed Leia and Fitz, and someone hurt Westlake, with all roads leading to Moore. He'd first seen him when he threw a fit at a couple of panhandlers. David didn't like him from that single interaction.

Spencer said Moore was pulling the strings for Leia's abduction, which led to the death of several people. Moore was an asshole, but why the public and costly operation? Spencer said Moore was the bad guy. He was sure Moore would say the same thing about Spencer. He felt jerked around as a rage built up inside him. He swallowed some tea and ate a handful of the spicy rice crackers.

And he was on the run in a foreign country with a billionaire that spun an unbelievable tale of curing cancer. A billionaire that couldn't reveal himself. A billionaire that couldn't use his money. A billionaire with secrets. David watched from the kitchen as the woman used more gauze and bandages to clean Spencer's wound.

A billionaire that bled like the rest of us.

In Japan, a gaijin didn't blend in. In Amsterdam, David looked Dutch and could pass as French in Paris. A tall blond Caucasian stood out in Tokyo, towering over most Japanese. In the sea of bodies at a subway station, all the police would have to do is look and say, "There he is."

With this forced detour, he wasn't anywhere closer to finding Leia. And Spencer, who had promised magical help, was out of commission.

David looked through Spencer's things that he'd brought from Seattle. The computer bag had a laptop and a power supply. He powered on the laptop and was met with a Linux login screen with an SCS logo. The courier pack wasn't any more interesting. He found a powered-off cell phone and a wallet stuffed with yen. Lastly, he found a small white envelope with a single photo of Leia staring off through one of the large windows onto Lake Washington.

He wished he was at the estate, about to start another lesson. He slipped the picture into his coat. The older man kept things clean in the makeshift operating room while the old woman sewed stitches professionally into an unconscious Spencer. His breathing looked slow and steady.

"I gave him something to sleep. He lost blood." She'd hung a saline bag from a hook in the ceiling. A thin tube snaked into his arm. "But not too much. Fluids will help," she said.

He watched her finish the stitches and bandage the wound. "Change the dressing every six hours. He can stay the night. Tomorrow you both leave." She pulled off the blue latex gloves and dropped them into a garbage bin. David followed her and the husband into the tiny kitchen. "How come you say you are Brooks' nephew? Brooks said he's an only child. I heard he was killed." The words stung him, like calling his mother fat, and he didn't know why. "Are you sure you aren't his son? You look old enough to be."

"No. Not his son."

Internal debate time. He felt Jonathan trusted this couple. Could he trust them too? They had helped him with only a little prodding, and he couldn't move Spencer for a few hours. He didn't see any harm in telling them about what had happened. Whether they believed him was up to them. Spencer was still unconscious, and David didn't want him to know any more than he did.

He breathed and closed his eyes for a second before bringing up a memory "2003. Brooks had been wounded. And was bleeding to death." He made a cutting motion across his stomach. "You fixed him up, and in return, he helped your son escape the yakuza clan he was a member of."

The old woman's eyes opened wide. "He promised he'd tell no one."

"He didn't. I just know."

"How is this possible? He must have told you."

He needed their help for a few days and decided to trust her. "About a year ago, Brooks was killed, and I was implanted with his memories." He tapped on his temple. "Against my will."

The woman frowned and waved off his description. "That is bull dung. Not possible."

David closed his eyes again and said, "Jonathan stayed here for three weeks. You brought him ramen and eggs. He paid you in cash every day for each bowl. He extracted your son from the yakuza clan and resettled him in the US. Changed his name. Had the tattoos removed. Gave him fifty thousand dollars to get him started. All because of the kindness you showed a gaijin who would have died."

The woman's face turned white.

"How would I know this? How would I know to come to you?" David said.

"You carry his memories?"

"Yes, except they show up when they want to. They cause me problems and protect me at the same time."

She frowned at him and said, "Good story. It might be true, even. Brooks wouldn't have told you this story if you weren't important to him."

She left the kitchen and went back into the living room where Spencer lay. He followed. "We can take care of your friend for a few days. Not too long. We are old and not fast."

"Understood. I have to leave for a few hours if you don't mind."

She nodded, and he stood for a second before hugging her. She looked surprised but didn't return the hug.

"Thank you. Brooks-san appreciated your help, and so do I." He grabbed his bag and slipped out the door. A memory was driving him somewhere, and he wasn't sure where. He'd know when he got there.

David navigated in the stolen SUV through the late afternoon Tokyo streets. The image of the building and the road appeared in his mind, yet he didn't have the exact directions.

Before his trip, he unlocked his phone and reviewed the measure to prevent eavesdroppers from listening in or determining his location. He checked messages and sent the code word to Fitz they'd agreed on in case the old guy was still alive.

Nothing from anyone.

A year ago, he never worried about security. His friends knew where he was, and his girlfriends did too, which caused him problems a few times. He'd never cared.

When another billionaire dropped his life into a blender, everything changed. He went all Fox Mulder on his data. And as bad luck followed him, another billionaire was trying to fuck up his life again.

Returning to Toronto, he overhauled his information with a

vengeance. He stored his data in private locations, double encrypted to ensure the big software companies couldn't track him. Extra security protocols took time, and he knew someone trying to crack his identity would find it more of a challenge than they expected.

He pulled onto a side street and killed the engine. He searched the SUV and found two thick wallets stuffed with yen and three cell phones. Following his yakuza theory, maybe the goon's day job was collecting protection money from local businesses. Regardless of the source, he figured he had an equivalent of five thousand American dollars.

He'd parked a quarter mile from the destination his memories led him to. A group of teenagers stood on a street corner, talking, laughing, and smoking. One kid had a long piece of hair gelled and lacquered into a curved mohawk and wore a black leather jacket with chromed chain.

In English, he said, "Konbanwa. Could you watch my car for a few hours? I can't find parking."

Mohawk frowned at him and said in halting English, "Is this joke? I don't want car from no gaijin!"

David used his best smile. "I will ask that group up there if they are interested." He pointed further up and pressed the button on the key. All the lights on the ride lit up.

Mohawk tilted his head and smiled. "No. No. We take it. When coming back?"

"Two hours." He held up two fingers.

He dropped the keys into the kid's hands along with two thousand yen and walked away. He'd hoped they would steal or take it on a joy ride. If the vehicle had a GPS tracker, they could take the yakuza on a wild goose chase, at least for a while.

Akihabara, Tokyo

Akihabara, or as the locals knew it, Electric Town, started in post-World War II Japan as a black market for electronics, radios, and other household goods. More recently, and anchored by the train/subway station, the area had morphed into all things computers, anime, and manga.

For David, the place seemed both foreign and familiar. Like déjà vu on Red Bull. He'd felt the same way in Amsterdam and Paris. Familiar and uncomfortable, like a pebble in his shoe.

The same pebble had come back, and it was in both shoes and under both eyelids.

Ahead of him loomed Akihabara Station, where you could take a train or subway anywhere. He tried pulling up the memory fragment again and only saw a couple of images and a red door. Great. No address or even a business name. He re-framed the visions like a treasure hunt, where the prize was a little girl's life.

Nothing appeared. He walked around to see if anything tweaked his cognition.

After a block, he stood in front of an enormous neon sign that lit up the sidewalk. Across the road, similar LED and bright tubes outlined almost the entire area.

The place made his head swim. All the spoken Japanese drove his senses crazy, and the wall of bright signs coupled with the crowds of people was too much. He walked towards the subway, zigzagging around tourists and shoppers. Sweat trickled down his back as the day's heat escaped from the sidewalks into the humid air.

Nothing came as he crisscrossed the roads and alleys, looking for a hit. Most of the smaller shops sat across the street from the Akihabara station. He walked through a passage to an older building that didn't look like it had changed in twenty years and felt his eye twitch.

Jonathan had been here before.

He climbed the stairs to the second floor, into a narrow hallway to another staircase leading to the third level. At the top, he faced a closed metal door painted red. Was he in the right place? He was flying blind, without a paddle or a net, just a wobbly memory from a dead man to guide him this far.

Chapter Thirty-Five

He stood in front of the door and pushed the small button on the right side. A camera bubble stared down from the ceiling. The hallway walls cried for a coat of paint or a flamethrower.

David held the button and looked up.

"*Hai,*" came through a hidden speaker.

"I'm here to see Mr. Continental," David said.

In halting English, a voice said. "Go away. No Mr. Continental here."

"I'm a friend of Jonathan Brooks."

Silence for twenty seconds. He counted, to be sure. The man behind the door might need to call someone to verify or wake the old guy up to check. Whatever happened, it took about twenty seconds.

"Raise your hands and turn around."

David complied.

"No tricks, gaijin." The door buzzed, and a wide man opened the door and gestured David's arms up to frisk him before letting him squeeze into the narrow hallway. He reminded David of a large guy in Toronto named Bob that sold ramen noodles from a tiny shop near the ballet school. He'd call this guy Sumo Bob, except not to his face.

He walked past a floor-to-ceiling set of shelves jammed full of electronics, cell phones, printers, computer parts, and DVDs. Some looked new and were still in the box, while others seemed destined for the scrap heap. Prints of sexy girls with kitten ears fighting horrible demons with tentacles, covered the hallway's walls.

The end of the narrow hallway opened into a darkened office with a small gnome-like Japanese man sitting at a desk and a burning cigarette hanging from his mouth. He looked through a magnifying glass as he painted a figurine with a tiny brush.

"Brooks-san owes me five thousand dollars! Did you bring it?" He stabbed the smoke in a small ashtray as he looked through the magnifier.

"No."

"Who the hell are you? His son, or maybe his grandson." He chuckled at his joke.

"No. Not his son. A friend. He told me you can help fix things."

"He told you that? That's generous. He still owes me five grand." He flipped his fingers towards the door. "Get out."

Sumo Bob smiled and gestured towards the door. He expected to get about seven seconds of grace before he was assisted.

"Jonathan says he's sorry that he hadn't paid you. There were circumstances beyond his control."

"I don't care."

"Being dead was beyond his control."

The man looked up at him with surprise on his face. "Dead? Like for real?"

"Yes."

"Who the fuck are you, and why are you bothering me?"

"I need help. Jonathan told me you can find things."

"Like what?"

"A girl."

"Plenty girls here; look around. You can find them yourself. No charge."

"No, this is a special girl. Half white, half Japanese."

"Half breed." The man snarled.

"She was brought to Japan against her will."

"Most foreign women are. They don't know it at the time. That's what causes divorce. Girls wake up."

"She's only twelve," David said.

"It happens," he said. "Bad but big business."

David shook his head, "No. Not like that."

"Who then?"

"A rich American."

"Name?"

"Nick Moore."

"How did she get here?"

"Private jet. Today or late yesterday." David said.

"There will be a record. Impossible to be invisible now. One time, yes. Many cameras now. Too many."

"How much to find her?" David said.

The man looked up at the ceiling and smiled at Sumo Bob. "Five thousand dollars."

How convenient. The same amount Jonathan owed him. Curious why he owed him that much. He'd save that conversation for later. He pulled out the wad of yen from the stolen SUV and placed it in Sumo Bob's catcher's mitt of a hand. He figured it should be closed. "Cash, okay?"

The old man laughed. "We sure as fuck don't take Apple Pay." He nodded to his oversized helper to count it.

"Hai," Sumo Bob said. Twenty seconds later, he gave five thousand yen back. "Too much," he said. Nice to see someone was honest.

"Need picture," the old man said.

He pulled out the picture from Spencer's bag and handed it to him. "She was on a private jet. It probably landed in Haneda with lots of gaijin with her from Seattle. Can't be too many of those lately."

He looked up at David over his tiny glasses and nodded. "You're probably right."

Chapter Thirty-Six

As he left the tiny office and descended to the street, more fragments surfaced. He wasn't sure if the image was from Jonathan or some bad gangster movie he'd watched growing up.

Mr. Continental was a Japanese version of Switzerland, neutral overall and providing services for the right price.

Capitalism for the digital age.

What day was it again? Saturday or Sunday? The jet lag had messed with his head. He rubbed his eyes as exhaustion swallowed him up.

He needed to find a place to rest or he wouldn't be any good to anyone.

The stairway emptied onto a tiny lane packed with a rush hour crowd. Girls dressed as anime characters were selling guided tours for the area. Although he didn't detect any overt threats, his paranoia hit a new high, as he figured out quickly, he was lost.

He'd discovered the Red Door by feel, and now, standing in the middle of a busy street, his heart pounded. Instead of signs pointing to the subway station, he was engulfed in a multitude of people walking, shopping, and smoking among shops selling all kinds of electronic components.

Across the street, girls in bright-coloured anime costumes handed out brochures to cafes where your favourite character would serve you coffee and pastries. He desperately wanted to be a tourist and have one of them take him to a theme cafe. Instead, he backed into a tiny corner hidden from the crowd and tried to contain his overwhelm by slowing his breathing. Even after a few minutes, he barely prevented himself from running away screaming.

He had to pull it together. He brought up an image of teaching Leia in his mind and watched her anxiety calm as he slowed the music and took her through deliberate and thoughtful movements. She'd come into the class hyper and leave gentle and graceful.

He needed to recreate her relaxed state, or he'd never find her. Gradually, his heart rate dropped, and his vision sharpened. He wanted to maintain this level of calm as long as possible.

Mr. Continental had promised to text him with any leads on Leia. And even with a nagging feeling that he couldn't trust the guy, he had no other choice. As he slipped back into the stream of people and turned the next corner, he saw the signs for the subway. Two blocks east of him.

Easy.

The smell of grilled meat and fish hit him as he walked by a couple of hole-in-the-wall restaurants. Food sounded like a good idea. Five minutes later, a tiny ramen shop provided a bowl of hot noodles and pork, and he enjoyed the salty goodness.

From his window view, he noticed a group of teenagers up ahead. One of them was the guy with the mohawk. The same leather jacket with chrome chains. They kept searching back and forth on the street like they'd lost something.

Shit. More than likely, they were looking for a tall, blond, white boy. He wasn't exactly hard to find in Tokyo.

He swallowed the last of the noodles and slipped out the door, away from the group and towards Akihabara Station. If he got into the subway, he'd disappear in a minute.

The crowd grew as he neared the station. His paranoia rose as he felt others staring at him. A white man wasn't unheard of in Tokyo. However, there wasn't a surplus either. Then he heard it. Someone was yelling behind him. "Gaijin! Gaijin!" He turned and caught

Mohawk pointing at him and screaming like his pants had caught fire.

He figured the guy wasn't trying to return the SUV. Instead, gangsters probably found their vehicle and forced the kids to search for him. If he sprinted towards the subway through the crowd, he might make it unless the dark suits waited for him at the entrance.

His plan of blending in wasn't working too well.

Maybe there was a third option.

He'd read that Akihabara was the center of *otaku* in Japan. *Otaku* was the term for people with obsessions with things like anime, manga, weird robots, and demons. David understood obsessions. He had one with dance.

Today, *otaku* might be useful.

He veered away from the subway and down a narrow alley filled with stores selling books, figurines, and shiny comics in clear plastic bags. He vaulted up a stairway beside a shop onto an entire floor of what looked like a horror museum married to a robot factory. It was full of incredible spaceman costumes and weird rubber suits with tentacles for arms. Japanese *otaku* culture at its finest. He dug through the aisles until he found what he was looking for. After paying for the costume and some other bits and pieces with a clerk that didn't look up from his computer, David slipped into a changing room and pulled on a red samurai robe and a matching rubber demon mask, complete with a samurai top knot stuck to the top of it. He wanted to fit into the *otaku* crowd and escape by hiding in plain sight.

He emerged from the dressing room and saw no exit save the stairs he entered from. One way up and only one down.

Security screens transmitted the street activity on the wall behind the clerk. Mohawk pointed up the stairs to men in black suits who were either well-dressed criminals or funeral directors. He decided he didn't care to meet either vocation.

A set of wooden weapons rested against the counter. *Bokken* flashed in his mind. Training swords were made of bamboo. They wouldn't stop a bullet, but guns were rare here. He remembered being surprised when Slick pulled a revolver at the heliport. Maybe the bad guys saved them for VIPs.

As he grabbed the sword, his hands automatically reversed his grip before he swung up and around. He'd never touched one, yet the sword felt comfortable. He grabbed a second one and slipped it into his belt.

Did he wait for the men to come up the stairs to fight, or did he rush them with the high ground advantage? Any store commotion would bring the police—something he wanted to prevent.

The clerk looked at him over his glasses as words appeared in his brain. He said, "*Hijouguchi ga arimasu ka?*"—*is there an emergency exit?*"

The man stared at David and glanced at the security feed. His eyes widened.

"Hai!" he pointed to a corner of the store. Slutty cats and femme fatale costumes hung on large racks. David rushed past silk jackets and female wigs into a hidden exit behind a drape. He slipped the second sword through the handle to jam it closed and ran down the darkened stairs leading to the ground level. He adjusted his mask and pushed the bamboo blade into his belt as he made it to the street.

He fit into the rest of the cosplay kids just fine.

Once he arrived at a busy road, he waved for a taxi. After a few minutes of halting Japanese, the cab driver said, "Hai," and drove him out of Electric Town.

Chapter Thirty-Seven

Sitting in a Tokyo cab wearing a samurai costume and a barely breathable mask wasn't as fun as it sounds. He provided the address to the driver. Even with the shot of adrenaline, his energy reserves were dropping. A memory surfaced that his destination should give him some options to rest yet still be close enough to Spencer.

He kept his eyes forward and caught the driver looking in the back mirror. David nodded, and the guy ended up smiling with a little laugh.

Probably not the weirdest fare he'd picked up in Akihabara.

Finally, he pulled off the mask and slipped on a pair of Clark Kent glasses and a hat he'd grabbed at the *Otaku* shop. He turned the red samurai robe around and wrapped the all-black cloak over his shoulders. Nice. Almost a complete Goth-like appearance. All he needed was to spike his hair with gel, and the disguise in plain sight would be done.

The driver glanced into the rearview mirror and looked surprised as if David had just teleported in from New York City.

"Konnichiwa!" the guy said and laughed. He took the next left and, after twenty minutes, let him out once he produced enough yen.

Ikebukuro.

One of Tokyo's many shopping and entertainment districts, Ikebukuro sits on the northwest corner of the Yamanote train line.

Around the area where the cab dropped him, he saw restaurants, bars, and small Japanese 'love hotels' rented by the hour or the evening, usually with little sleep. However, they offered what he wanted: discretion and privacy.

He adjusted his glasses and hat and slumped his shoulders, trying to shorten his six-foot frame a few inches. He added a limp and held an arm crooked like he'd had a stroke.

As un-dancer as possible, he found an older hotel near the subway station. A matronly woman at the desk smiled and narrowed her eyes when she saw he was alone.

"Girl? Get for you?" she said.

He didn't try his Japanese this time. "No, thank you. I need a few hours of sleep."

She shrugged her shoulders and took his cash before handing him a large metal key connected to a hard-to-lose thick plastic disk. He followed her, limping down the hallway to a medium-sized room with a mirror on the wall and the ceiling.

"No girl?"

"No," he said.

"Man?" She looked hopeful that she might help arrange a guest for a few hours and take a small commission for the service. He smiled and closed his eyes, faking sleep. She chuckled at the white foreigner that came to a love hotel not looking for any. She nodded and shut the door.

He took off the samurai coat, cap, and glasses and lay on the futon. The thick cotton bed could have been made of concrete and it wouldn't have mattered; he was asleep in under a minute.

Strange dreams plagued him. Yumi again, the woman from his vision during the ballet with Leia. Japanese, petite, straight bangs, pretty, demure. He walked with her in the rain, her fingers interlocking with his and her touch electric. He saw red lipstick marks on an empty wine glass. In the next dream, she wasn't there. He ran down a tiny street at night lit with neon, searching doorways for her as water poured down. And then nothing.

He realized why he hadn't wanted to return to Tokyo. Jonathan had lost Yumi here and couldn't find her. That explained a lot of what he'd been going through.

The room's telephone woke him, and he checked his phone. 9:00 p.m. He'd slept for two hours. After calling the front desk and asking for another half hour, he jumped in the shower and let the near-scalding spray boil his body. After ten minutes, he cut the hot water and let ice-cold needles knock out any remaining cobwebs. The dream felt real, as did the deep anguish from losing a woman he'd never met. Something seemed familiar about her, and he couldn't tell what.

He left his room and walked outside The area around the hotel had come alive in the evening with people, restaurants, and bars all hustling with activity. After a quick meal of pork and rice from a street food vendor, he hailed a cab and headed back to Spencer. He'd hoped the billionaire hadn't expired while he was gone.

The taxi dropped David in front of a rabbit warren of residential streets and walkways that looked impeccably clean. No litter or other garbage, freshly washed sidewalks, no leaves, grass, or anything out of place. Residents parked their tiny cars in equally small spaces. He noticed a couple of unlocked bikes behind buildings. Unheard of in any other city.

He checked his phone. Nothing from Mr. Continental. After all that had happened, he needed Spencer awake enough to come clean about why the welcome committee at the heliport wanted to snatch them.

And Leia. He didn't want to imagine her terror. Instead, he tried his rage at being unable to stop them and not finding her yet. He wasn't sure she was even in Japan. However, if Spencer was taking him on some elaborate treasure hunt, he didn't understand why.

The sleep from the no-love hotel helped his mood, and the food boosted his energy. He walked a few more blocks and stopped. In the distance, police lights flashed, and a group of people clustered near the end of the street near where he'd taken Spencer.

That wasn't good.

Twin ambulances roared down the road and turned into the tiny alley past the police cars. David stood in the shadows and waited. Minutes later, the gurneys reappeared, carrying the old couple gesturing in the air. The man had a bandage across his temple, and the woman looked pissed off.

Shit.

This was his fault. He brought harm to people that wanted a peaceful retirement. He'd try to make amends if he got Leia out of the country alive.

Someone had forced their way in and attacked them. Did the helipad welcome committee track Spencer somehow?

He waited for the police to pull another body from the house. After twenty minutes, he breathed a tiny sigh of relief. No third gurney in or out. Spencer wasn't there. He might not be dead. At least, not yet.

Could the billionaire have escaped on his own? The gunshot wound left him weak and unable to hurt them, even if he wanted to. They must have tracked the SUV to the location or tagged him at the airport. Did someone bump into him at the airport and plant a tracker? Maybe Spencer already carried it.

Spencer had held on to his bag and refused to let it go, even when he was almost unconscious. Maybe he led the attackers right to him.

Another cop car drove by and slowed down. Maybe the noisy neighbours spotted a gaijin sneaking around and called it in. He didn't want to explain anything to the Tokyo police department. He turned into a tight alley and took off at a run.

At the next garbage can, he ditched the glasses and hat and sprinted until he reached a major intersection and found a Starbucks. He figured that he might stand a chance of blending in.

The cafe sat half full. Two fresh-faced female baristas bowed as he entered, giving him big smiles. He ordered a large cappuccino in passable Japanese with an extra shot. He took a seat in the rear with his back to the wall. The only exit was back through the front door. After pulling out his tablet, he checked his phone. No messages.

He sipped his drink and watched for the police or anything else out of the ordinary. The memories of another man were like a bad dream.

He wished he'd never left Toronto. He could have found another job, and Fitz would be safe.

Maybe.

Fitz was the wild card. He'd been so caught up in finding Leia that he wasn't sure if the old guy was alive or dead. Yet, a memory told him Fitz had more lives than five cats.

As he took stock of his situation, he faced reality; he was mixed up with dangerous people and alone in a strange city. Again. He wondered who he'd pissed off in a past life to elicit such a karmic payback.

Yet, the image of Leia with her Hello Kitty backpack burned into his mind, and he knew that getting her to safety was his only goal. The late-night caffeine and an overabundance of stomach acid fuelled his anger. However, he resisted the urge to find someone to punch. Highly inappropriate in the Japanese version of America's coffee shop. As he walked through the events, he realized his irritation stemmed from the nagging feeling that he'd been played.

But by who? Spencer? He didn't see how or even why. A well-financed team had grabbed Spencer's daughter, and he had asked for help. Now in Tokyo, David was ten thousand miles away and alone.

An idea appeared, and a bad idea for sure. He shook his head. No, he shouldn't. Except he found the number on his tablet. A local call, even. He ordered a refill as he hoped more caffeine might help him decide.

Back at his table, he dialled the number. After several rings, he hung up without leaving a message.

He'd try again. Or not.

He walked through again what Spencer claimed: Leia's blood cured cancer and Moore snatched her because her blood was worth billions. The billionaire offered no proof of either.

Spencer said he got a woman pregnant while working in Japan, and the mother had planned to give the baby to an adoption agency, but mixed-race children didn't adopt well. Too much racism and xenophobia. David verified it with a Google search. Childless Japanese couples wanted offspring that looked like them. Instead of letting her abandon the child, he stole Leia from the mother and brought her with him to America with no thought for the mother's well-being.

Too many loose ends. His bullshit detector had rung back at the motel. Now in Tokyo, the bell kept ringing and didn't stop. Had Leia's mother planned to use an agency, or was Spencer lying?

He connected to the cafe's Wi-Fi, and he did some research. Techno-geeks around the world liked the minutia stuff about their heroes. Like what their Silicon Valley idols did before they discovered software gold. Some wannabes wanted to walk in their favorite nerd-Jesus footsteps, mirroring their education and first jobs in the hope they too could be anointed with the oil-of-silicon.

Bill Gates' Wikipedia entry contained everything from parents, to schooling, and early Microsoft—an open book. Amazonian Jeff Bezos had the same level of detail with school, career, and family. All information, all the time.

Not Spencer. He was limited to a Wikipedia page with no history, no career info, and only a few links to a few conspiracy rumors, limited data on SCS with no social media presence. Until about thirteen years ago, Spencer and SCS didn't exist. At least not on the internet.

He couldn't confirm or deny what Spencer told him at the motel in Seattle. Spencer said he changed his name to escape some mafia boss but didn't provide any details. Everything Leia's father was saying could be the truth or a lie. David didn't know and frankly, didn't care. His focus was on Leia: where to find her and how to get her away from whoever had grabbed her.

Nicholas Moore, however, had an internet history. Boston born and raised, his father, a cop, he joined the Army in the Signal Corps to get a university education, worked in the Army Cyber Command before becoming a civilian and joining Spencer to form SCS. There was little information about his tour of duty, but anytime over the last fifteen years meant Iraq or Afghanistan.

David remembered Moore yelling at panhandlers outside the head-quarters. Not the salt of the Boston Irish. More like an arrogant son-of-a-bitch that enjoyed the fruits of someone else's work.

He checked his personal email that kept him in contact with the rest of the world to see if anyone was trying to contact him about the abduction. As he scrolled through ads for low-cost Russian girlfriends, one appeared with the subject: "Tokyo. Critical." In clipped sentences, the email said his life was in danger and he should find Kando Nakamura if he was in Tokyo.

That was it. He checked the email header. An anonymous email service.

He replied, "In Tokyo. Need help. Will look for Nakamura." At the end, he typed, "Who are you?"

No way to identify the original sender. He agreed with the invisible person's assessment that he was in danger. An internet search of the name displayed several pages of results. Some musicians, two actors, and additional terms of Tokyo and software produced nothing different. When he added cancer, an article appeared about an oncology research scientist in Tokyo that had disappeared. He clicked for more news and translated it. "Scientist missing after break-in at the lab."

Cancer. Oncology. Break-in. Leia's abduction. If Spencer was telling the truth, there was much more at stake than control of a security company. Moore could be involved.

How were security software and cancer research connected? Seemed like one thing was not like the other.

He only had an internet view of the human genome and cancer. When they diagnosed his father, he felt powerless to do anything more than watching him waste away.

Cancer cells invade the body and trick others into becoming cancerous. Converting the cells like the Mormons at your door tried to do. As he kept reading, he discovered tech companies like Microsoft and IBM applied technology to find fresh ways to detect the source and presence of cancer, treating them like modern computer viruses.

Spencer said Leia's blood was like an anti-virus for the disease. Research, detection, and treatment collectively cost more than the GDPs of some smaller countries. Lost productivity attributed to cancer patients wasn't counted. A company that cured cancer with lower cost, more accessible treatment, and wide distribution, would be worth a lot. Billions or trillions, Spencer said.

Moore wanted to provide treatment only to the wealthy. The neighbor's child with leukemia couldn't afford it, but the Wall Street stock trader could.

The rich get richer and live longer lives.

David dug into the biotech name from his internet search. They had a good track record of discoveries and an impressive employee pedigree. Then ten years ago, the company's stock and valuation dived and never recovered.

At about the same time, Spencer first appeared in the US, and SCS became an unknown software startup.

Interesting. He couldn't ask Spencer about any of this. He knew everyone had an angle. What was Spencer's? He was already one of the wealthiest men in the US that no one knew. He didn't need more money. For a guy that commutes in a helicopter, more money wouldn't buy him anything more than he already had.

He also didn't seem to be the money type. Just a brilliant, doting father to a special-needs child. Nothing more. Other than a few billion dollars, of course.

And that billion-dollar man might be dead or worse.

David was leaning to the worse side of things as two Tokyo police officers entered the cafe.

The cops came in the front door. The place had gotten crowded. Mostly Japanese with a sprinkling of Indian and Filipino. He put everything into the backpack and drank from his empty cup. He was pretending to be back in Seattle, drinking coffee, staring at his phone, and not looking guilty of anything.

Leaving wouldn't be wise, especially if the cops wanted to find a blond gaijin as a person of interest.

The police showed no trace of happiness. They were all business. One stood near the door and gave the place a once over, while the other ordered two coffees. The barista bowed slightly, took the order, and moved the cups up front, jumping the queue. David glanced at them as he sipped from his empty cup. The second cop might have checked him out. He couldn't be sure. It didn't matter either way. If they wanted to see his ID, he'd be happy to show it. If they wanted him to go outside with them, he'd need to choose his course of action.

Two women had sat at the table near him, with tall cups of something with a dollop of whipped cream on each. Both giggled as they sipped their drinks. The one facing him continued to steal glances at him and smile, and the other turned a few times. They repeated for a few minutes before getting serious. One produced a set of cards and showed the other one by one. Finally, he realized one girl was drilling the other in English words.

David picked up his cup and his bag, squatted down by the women's table, and gave them his best smile. "Konnichi wa. I see you are learning English." Both girls nodded and put their hands over their mouths and giggled. He pegged them to be eighteen or nineteen.

"My friend has test tomorrow. I try to help her," the woman said in passable English.

"Would you like some help? I'm an English teacher." David didn't lie. He was a teacher and spoke the language.

She smiled and translated to her friend in rapid-fire Japanese. David understood 'cute man' and 'teacher.' The second woman nodded and invited him to sit down. Out of the corner of his eye, the one officer scowled and grabbed his two queue-jumping coffees.

He spent the next twenty minutes helping with pronunciation. The police loitered outside with their drinks until finally leaving, perhaps deciding a white English teacher in Starbucks didn't fit the description of who they were looking for.

At the twenty-five-minute mark, David stood and bowed. "Thank you for the opportunity. I must go to my next appointment."

The girls bowed, and he left. More police had congregated down the block. With no plan in his head, he walked toward the subway.

As he reached the stairs, dozens of people were coming up. He'd just hit the late rush hour.

He heard yelling and turned. The police from Starbucks were a hundred yards away from him. His teacher impersonation either didn't work, or they had a better description. He saw more cops on the run from across the road, rushing towards the entrance.

He vaulted down the steps and over the turnstiles as a train pulled in on opposite sides. Crouching over, he zig zagged between the passengers until he jumped into the end car as the police arrived at the platform. He squeezed against the wall of the car and kept out of sight.

As the train pulled out of the station, he watched constables scanning for him. If they considered him a threat, he had little time and couldn't take a room at the Tokyo Hyatt.

Get control surfaced in his consciousness. His words or someone else. It didn't matter. No question. He needed control and had a good idea of where to start.

He looked at the train map. The longer he remained on, the more time the police would have to station constables. It was not a straightforward thing on a Friday night in rush hour to mobilize a police force to find a person of interest.

Shinjuku was the next stop. The largest subway and train station. A million people walked through it every day. Hard to locate one person. But a tall blond Caucasian was an easier target in Japan than in Toronto or New York.

He hustled off the train at Shinjuku, fished out a wool watch cap he'd grabbed from his bag, and tucked his blond hair underneath as best as possible.

His instinct took him out of the terminal and to an area filled with smaller retail stores, sushi restaurants, and higher-end retail shops. After another block, he found the place he needed and hoped it was still open.

A middle-aged man in a white coat frowned as David entered the barbershop. The guy must think he was an alien, which he was. He took off his baseball cap, rubbed his long hair, and said, "Shave?"

The man shook his head and shrugged his shoulders.

David frowned, looking out the window and back at the man. Words appeared. "Atama o sotte kudasai" and rubbed his head. *Can you please shave my head?* he thought to himself.

The barber smiled. "Hai!" and waved him to a middle chair. Once he'd placed a white sheet over David's body, he pulled out an electric razor and got to work.

He watched in the mirror as the guy went full Vin Diesel on him, cutting off his blond hair in long strips before covering his head with a thin layer of shave cream and using a straight razor to complete the look.

Cut, shaved, and polished. The barber finished with a moisturizer with a slight color added to keep him looking like a corporate hockey enforcer.

Beside the barber, an optometrist was about to close when David entered and quickly purchased a pair of black horn rims with clear lenses. On his last stop, he found a men's wear store and bought a business suit with a generous fitting jacket and pants. He wanted to appear like an American salaryman and distance himself from the frat brother, jeans, and T-shirt set. Serious and businesslike to confuse his pursuers and to give him an edge. He used the Fitz-supplied credit card. No need to make it easy for people to find him.

At another cafe, he ordered a fruit juice. He needed to do a few things, and he didn't want to be out wandering the streets any longer than necessary.

First was information. He only had one source and didn't know where the Hardy Boys were located or if they were men, women, or precocious children. Fitz had said to count on them for any information or requests. The more you provide, the better their results.

David worried about full disclosure, but he had no choice. He had to trust someone, even if it was an invisible group hiding on the internet.

With his tablet, he connected to The Hardy Boys website. He needed in-depth intelligence on Spencer, Moore, and SCS. Everything that Google couldn't find. Even gossip, rumours, or whispers. He needed everything.

Bitcoin from Fitz's account provided payment, and he hoped for a quick response. Now all he needed was a place for the evening. He considered the Love Hotel again. However, Shinjuku had hundreds of hotels within about a mile radius. He'd blend in better, especially in a suit.

After the shave and glasses, he figured he could pass for Dutch. From the secret compartment in his bag, he withdrew a credit card in the name of *Jens Jamison* and booked an upscale hotel close to Shinjuku Station. He never wanted to walk into a hotel and take a room at the rack rate; a memory told him that situation would be too easy to spot. However, a clerk wouldn't look too closely if the room was booked online. A confirmation came back for a suite with two queen beds.

Jens' MasterCard bought a small rolling suitcase, a few more clothes, some boots, and a few extras he might need later. He also stocked up on some electronics and a burner smartphone. He'd give Spencer the bill if he were still alive. If not, he'd have Westlake pay for it. It was his fault he was here.

After forty minutes, David wheeled his new bag into the lobby of the Hotel Century—walking distance from the Shinjuku Station. The elevator opened at the 23rd-floor entrance, covered in granite and tile. Other businesspeople filled the lobby, an even split between white and Japanese. Some had glasses in their hands. Perhaps an international sales meeting with drinks after. The more mixed men and women in the area, the better. He'd blend in for the first time in the city.

The clerk gave him his passkey. A few minutes later, he entered the room, slid the drapes closed, and sat on the bed.

The room looked clean and contained a light fragrance he couldn't identify. He pulled one drape open and stared at the top of the massive Shinjuku Station. At this time of the night, all the street and office lights stayed on; building-sized signs flashed and promoted Japanese products. Too bad he wasn't a tourist.

He wondered if he was dreaming and almost pinched himself to wake up. Why in the hell was this happening? Dance teacher yesterday, international spy today. Both different and the same as last time. A year ago, he was running for his life. Today, he was trying to save a little girl.

In Amsterdam and Paris, Jonathan's memories had pushed and pulled his body like he was a marionette. Now, the memories seemed more integrated and part of him, although sometimes he didn't know if the memory was real or implanted. Anything outside of Canada was easy—he had traveled little as a kid. No money for big vacations meant driving to Niagara Falls. Motels instead of hotels. Fast food instead of restaurants.

He remembered once when all the cheap motels were full, forcing his dad to upgrade the family stay to a real hotel. The place came with a free breakfast of sliced fruit, tiny cinnamon buns, and a waffle machine producing dinner plate-sized waffles in three minutes. Heaven for a ten-year-old and a far cry from his helicopter commute to a billionaire's house.

He thought about his father and felt an ache for his mother. She'd died when he was a toddler. His only parent had worked in construction and hadn't taken too kindly to his son wanting to dance.

The memory came and went. An internal clock kept ticking. He had little time to find Leia. After connecting to the Wi-Fi, he reviewed The Hardy Boys' response to his questions.

"Specifics about Spencer and Moore challenging. More time is needed. Excellent information on Nakamura. He's connected to SCS. Lots of people are interested. Good and bad. Be careful."

As David read the information, a memory flashed to microfilm and telephone books with paper so thin you could wipe your nose with it. He shook the images away. They weren't even his.

The memory was so old, he figured spies probably rode dinosaurs to work, yet the cause of the problems of prejudice and entitlement hadn't changed: power, control, greed, hate, and of course, money.

The service attached a group of documents from various sources. Mostly Japanese translated text, which sometimes made for strangely worded sentences. Nakamura had received a Ph.D. in Genomics from MIT. However, something had happened, and the university rescinded it before the US deported him back to Japan. No reasons were given. All published papers were deleted.

Not a good start for your resume.

David scrolled through a recovered listing of Nakamura's papers. All dealt with things like blood proteins, enzymes, and human leukocyte antigens. One caught his eye. "Searching for unique blood proteins in monolithic DNA database repositories."

In his paper, Nakamura advocated mining DNA databases for specific genetic combinations and harvesting the owner's cells for immune drug creation. Besides breaking all kinds of laws for access without consent, Nakamura proposed a scenario to find people with suitable DNA and use their blood or other body parts to create drugs to fight disease such as liver, gall balder, pancreas, and bone marrow. Sort of like a reverse Doctor Frankenstein. He understood why MIT had gotten upset. Nakamura promoted the farming and vivisection of lower-class humans to prolong the life of more "worthy" people. Worthy meaning "rich."

During his father's battle with cancer, David stumbled across the story of Henrietta Lacks and the HELA cell line. Some of her tumor cells biopsied before her death in the 1950s lived on without her. They generated millions of dollars in revenue for the companies that used the cells for research, yet nothing flowed to Henrietta's estate.

Nakamura also suggested limiting drug therapy to the individuals contributing to society, which David took as either racist or limited to the one-percenters. One paper went on a rant about the overhead consumers place on critical people. More racism, prejudice, and power imbalance. Nice. Harvest bodies for their organs and blood and sell the parts to the highest bidder. Extreme capitalism. He noticed the scientist skirted over the issues of who exactly would do the work if a large percentage of the population was only suitable for keeping the others alive.

Nakamura must be working with Moore if what Spencer told him was true.

Nick Moore, one of the wealthiest men in the US, used his money to fund a cancer cure only for the right people. The people that could pay. And he had to abduct a twelve-year-old girl to do it. And from what Spencer had said and Nakamura's writing confirmed, blood wasn't the only thing they wanted.

What a piece of work.

The last information said Nakamura owned an apartment in Shin-juku under a different name, and they'd obtained the code to enter the building and his suite.

Chapter Thirty-Eight

Shinjuku City, Tokyo

NAKAMURA'S CONDO sat six blocks from his hotel in an expensive area of Shinjuku.

A quick real estate search showed condos in the area cost from $800,000 to $1.2 million US dollars. The address for the building showed suites closer to the $1.5 million level.

Nakamura couldn't afford that on a researcher's salary. No inheritance either. His disgrace in America would impact his finding work when he returned to Japan. His dead mother's name was on the title. Where did he get the money from?

The building's security had been recently updated with the best and most up-to-date technology. Everything was electronic.

The Hardy Boys provided an app. His hotel and the condo used RFID cards for entry. He uploaded their app to his phone, along with the security codes for his hotel. After he touched his cellphone to his closed door, the lock sprung open.

He loved technology.

After pulling on his suit jacket and threading a tie around his neck before exiting the hotel, he crossed several blocks of roads until he stood in front of the Shinjuku Park condo complex. English and Japanese signs dotted the exterior. Rental apartments for ex-pats looked like the target market. Quick access to the Shinjuku subway, a gateway to everything in Tokyo.

He held his phone to the building access panel and touched the screen. After five seconds, the lock clicked open, and he entered through a heavy glass door. Inside the sizeable and empty lobby, a stream of water ran through a thin dip of rocks surrounding the outside glass. A desk for a concierge that hadn't looked used in years sat empty.

The elevator required the same key access. He pressed his smartphone against the panel and touched the screen. A minute later, the doors opened to the 22nd floor. Nakamura's floor. Expensive carpet and narrow grain, solid wood doors marked the suites. At the end of the hall, he used his phone again, and Nakamura's entrance popped open.

He didn't enter at first. Instead, he stilled his breath and listened, hearing nothing except for the low hum of air being conditioned, cleaned, and circulated. He entered and locked the door behind him.

The apartment was massive by Japanese standards. Three large bedrooms. Two enormous bathrooms. Four families could live here comfortably. Yet everything looked staged and sized for westerners. Showroom-grade furniture in the living area, Martha Stewart style kitchen, granite-like counters, a full clothes closet, hotel room level of organization. He looked out the window to a similar view of Tokyo from his hotel room and the city lights that went on forever.

People didn't live like this. Even the most anal person left some trace of their life.

He checked all the bedrooms. The last one was dead bolted and had a reinforced door. He couldn't open it up without some specialized tools, and he didn't want to come back.

Nakamura would have a key and, based on the information supplied, he would have hedged his bets. He probably kept an extra one in the apartment.

He searched through the drawers and cupboards and found everything was too tidy. Nothing in any of the bathrooms. As time passed, he started feeling anxious that he had already overstayed his welcome.

In the refrigerator, he found sealed bottles of juice and green tea. No food. He checked in the freezer. Frozen meals. A bag of gyoza dumplings, a ten-pack of grilled rice balls, a bag of fried rice, and a frozen container of thick ramen noodles. Microwave and serve. From underneath everything, he pulled out a white envelope secured inside a freezer bag. Inside was a key. There must be something worthwhile in the room if he went to this much trouble to hide it.

The frozen key unlocked the door. Inside, a large workstation with twin screens stared back at him. A Herman Miller office chair and a large garbage can full of crumbled paper were also inside. The room stunk of stale human sweat. Several cans of a Japanese energy drink sat on a shelf. Weird.

He touched the keyboard, and the computer came to life. No password, which seemed strange considering all the other security.

Windows in English. Every file and folder had an English name. Probably for Moore's benefit. The web browser automatically connected to Japan Genomics—the company Nakamura had worked for. David logged in with a saved username and password. Time saver and security breaker. However, he wasn't about to chastise an invisible man on his password practices.

The page opened into a detailed data explorer, with graphs, reams of data, and current simulation loads. Impossible to download from the web page. Instead, he inserted a USB key he'd purchased when he became Jens in Shinjuku and copied all the folders and documents from the desktop.

Each folder was named after a Greek myth: Odysseus, Theseus, Prometheus, Perseus, and Andromeda. Five in total.

He didn't know what they referred to without deeper reading. The USB key dropped into his pocket. As he was shutting everything down, the door to the outside hallway jiggled, and then someone knocked before more rustling of the door handle.

He closed the computer room quietly and pocketed the key. Someone wanted into Nakamura's suite, and unless it was an unnecessary house cleaner, the person rattling the door might have valuable information. In for a penny, in for a pound. He adjusted his jacket and tie and opened the door to three Japanese men in dark suits.

An older, shorter man with gray hair stood in front, and two taller men in the back. One of the taller guys looked middle-aged and wore a blue tie. The last guy looked the same age as David and wore a red tie. All three wore sunglasses inside the hallway of a building, at night.

Was this a kinder, gentler version of the helipad welcoming committee? He looked at the three of them without a trace of recognition. Jonathan hadn't met them before.

"Good evening. Can I help you?" David said with a big smile.

The older man looked startled, and the two others stepped back a couple of inches like they weren't sure what to do.

The older man removed his glasses and said, "We are looking for man." His thick grey eyebrows looked like caterpillars.

"You don't look like my type," David said and smiled again. The best defence was an offence. The older man's expression didn't change. David thought he didn't appreciate Canadian comedy. "I just moved in."

The older man frowned, like David's statement made little sense. "I'm looking for Nakamura-san. He..."

"Nope. Not here. Look, guys, I'm meeting a friend if you will excuse me."

Everything David had found sat on the USB key in his pocket. He pulled the door shut, and it locked automatically. "Hope you find whoever you are looking for." He gave a little wave and walked towards the elevator.

The older man yelled something in Japanese, but David didn't understand. The two men looked like smaller versions of the guys from the helipad. Were they also yakuza? He jabbed the elevator button, and the door slid open. The men followed behind him.

Crap, David thought. *This would not end well.*

The two men provided no greeting or acknowledgment; both just smiled and held the door as the older guy walked to the elevator. Three against one. As the door closed, the two guys grabbed David's arms and held tight. David didn't struggle; the Shinjuku Welcome Wagon might have something valuable.

"What do you want? I don't have any money," David said, feigning fear.

"We want Nakamura-san," the youngest guy said. The older one gave him a dirty look.

"What were you doing in Nakamura's apartment?" the old man said.

"Don't know him—"

Blue tie punched David in the stomach, doubling him over. He expected the strongarm treatment and had been ready, but the punch still knocked his breath out. Yakuza membership seemed like a straight-line career path for most Japanese schoolyard bullies. Blue tie had given him a good hit. He might not expect a victim to hit back.

He planned to test that out.

"Guys, please. I don't know any Nakamura. I just rented the place."

This time, red tie wound up and punched David in the stomach. He needed to do something soon.

"He has something of ours," the older man said.

The elevator started moving. They could only hold it for a couple of minutes before the automatics kicked in. As Red tie turned and jammed some buttons, David acted.

Fighting in an elevator was a challenge. Nowhere to run. Hard to get momentum for a hit or a kick. Close quarters grappling, with lots of angles—like sizing up a shot in a game of pool. Three against one. Two of them outweighed him. The third guy wouldn't count.

No contest.

He didn't feel fear. Instead, he had to solve a physics problem. He guessed the modern yakuza rarely had to fight. Their reputation and size scared most people into paying or giving up what they wanted.

He wasn't one of those guys. He stamped on Blue tie's foot to get his attention before swinging his right arm up, breaking the man's grip before head smashing Red tie in the face and pushing him off balance into the old man. David turned and hit Blue tie with a left hook and right uppercut and pulled him off balance before smashing his elbow into the Red tie's chin. Both men collapsed to the floor.

The older man in front of him shrunk back into the corner.

"You and I are going for a walk," David said. As the doors slid open, he grabbed the older man's elbow and walked him out the door, leaving his dumb-shits-for-hire unconscious in the elevator. He felt fire across his stomach where the men had connected. He almost wanted to go back and kick them both in the head, but the disgrace of having a can of whoop-ass opened on them by a gaijin would have to make do.

The nice thing about a highly secure building was the money was spent on technology and not personnel. Chances were the elevator had cameras, so a security team or the police should be on their way. Five minutes would be the maximum the residents would allow. David figured he had four to hustle the older man out.

A black Toyota had parked in the half-moon driveway, and the old guy glanced towards it. The driver sat, eyes forward. His eyes widened when David pulled the older man to the car.

"Get in," David said and pushed the man into the back before sliding in after. He felt his Japanese returning. "Harajuku, onegaishima-su," he said to the driver.

The driver looked back, and the older man nodded. The driver pulled into the street and turned right at the first corner.

"What does Nakamura have that you want?" David asked.

"You know him. You said you didn't."

"I lied. What do you want with him?"

"He promised something. He has not delivered."

"What?"

The man scoffed and stared forward. David considered opening the door and pushing him out into traffic. However, he thought he'd try another tactic. "What would you trade if I found him?"

The man pulled a card from his jacket and gave it to David. "Call me. We work something out. Money, girls, drugs. Whatever you want."

David looked at the card. Japanese characters. David focused on the card for a second and saw instead *Takeuchi* and a telephone number. Nothing else. "I'm looking for a little girl brought to Japan by force. Leia Spencer. Daughter of Nolan Spencer. Half Japanese. Half white. Nakamura is involved," David said.

The old man scoffed. "Never heard of her. Nakamura is bad. No honor. Puppet of rich US man. If he's involved, she might be already dead."

Anger flared in David's eyes. He didn't want to consider that scenario. *Fucking Moore,* David thought. He'd kill that son of a bitch.

"What does he owe you?"

"Information." the old man said nothing more. The car kept moving like nothing interesting was happening.

David asked more questions, but the man wouldn't respond. As the driver continued, the hair stood on the back of David's neck. "Stop the car." The man kept going. David pulled his tie off and looped it over the driver's neck, pulling it tight.

"Pull over now."

The car slid over to the sidewalk. David opened the door with one hand, and the other held the tie tight around the driver's neck. "Find the girl, and I will find Nakamura," he said before jumping out and watching the car speed off. He didn't know where the driver had initially intended to take him, but he knew they weren't on the way to Harajuku. He suspected the destination was to meet a group more capable than the two losers in the elevator.

Two blocks away, he hailed a cab to take him back to Shinjuku Station. He walked the last couple of blocks to his hotel.

Once inside, he slipped a chair under the doorknob. He didn't think they had followed him, but he might have missed a tail.

He sent a text to the old man from the taxi. "Find Leia Spencer for me, and I will find Nakamura."

He checked his email. Nothing from Spencer, Fitz, Mr. Continental, or even the Hardy Boys.

Seattle news said more attackers were in custody, and there was additional speculation about the abduction. The police wanted any information on Spencer.

The most interesting thing was the lack of anything. Other than a grainy picture of him fighting the team outside the delivery area, David hadn't been identified by name. Not in Canada, Seattle, or Japan. Good news, or at least he thought it was good news.

No one was looking for him except for the Tokyo police, and they were searching for a blond dancer, not a bald businessman. He fantasized briefly about grabbing a train to Narita and taking the first flight home. Air Canada to Vancouver, then to Toronto. He'd couch surf for a couple of days and then get a job at Starbucks like half of the millennials out there. Take daily ballet classes and see the therapist again. The money from Fitz and a few weeks' salary from SCS would buffer him for a few months.

Easy peasy.

A memory of the terror on Leia's face as the men pulled her into the car surfaced. He snapped out of his dream and realized he was tapped out as he lay on the bed. He had no more ideas. His Japanese had deteriorated. He felt like a tourist and would have problems navigating around the city outside the major areas.

Leia's face appeared in his mind again. He had to help her.

After staring at the number he'd called earlier, he dialled and waited. After several rings, a sleepy voice answered in English. "Hello? Moshi moshi?"

"Razor, it's David."

David heard nothing on the phone except for some laboured breathing. He pictured his friend, Frederic Razour, lying in a bed with the phone to his ear.

No one ever called him Frederic.

"Razor? It's me. I'm in Tokyo."

"I can tell from the number," Razor said.

David's spider-sense told him Razor wasn't overjoyed to hear his voice. A deaf and blind monkey would come to the same conclusion.

"What do you want?"

"I need help," David said.

More silence, and then a heavy sigh.

"Not more James Bond crap, I hope. I can't deal with that shit again. Please tell me you are here dancing, on vacation, or chasing a girl, and you've lost your passport or something."

"I'm chasing a girl, but not how you think."

"Tokyo is a long way to come for that."

"I taught a girl in Seattle. Someone abducted her and brought her to Japan."

"This doesn't sound like the type of girl you normally need help with."

"I need someone to help me find her."

"Find her? What do I look like, Lost and Found?"

"I need someone who knows Tokyo to help me find her."

"David, this is not a good time. "

"I can pay you." More silence on the phone.

"I don't care."

"Razor, I wouldn't have called if I didn't need the help."

"The last time you asked for help was in Amsterdam. Remember?" Razor said.

David winced at the memory. He'd called Razor to get him his passport. Instead, his friend had been injured and started him on his downhill trajectory.

"That didn't go so well, did it?" Razor said.

"No."

"I've had time to reflect on that phone call. If I hadn't answered, I'd still be performing. Maybe even be a soloist by now."

"And I might be dead," David said instantly regretting what came out of his mouth. "I'm sorry. You have a right to be angry."

"It was my fault. I was always happy to help and was the one that paid the price."

"Razor, I know you are angry, and I wouldn't call if I—"

"Don't call again. Enjoy Tokyo."

Razor hung up.

David stared at the phone. He'd talked to his long-lost friend for precisely two minutes, thirteen seconds. The longest discussion he'd had with him since Amsterdam.

Razor didn't hide his anger. He had every right to be upset with him. Amsterdam had screwed up David's life and Razor's even worse. Razor had become collateral damage to David's memory implant escapades. His friend's injuries received by thugs-for-hire had fucked up his personality, balance, and life.

But David still needed help. Leia needed help. He needed to try one more time.

The following day, at David's request, the Hardy Boys dug out Razor's last address in Tokyo from a combination of cell phone billing and bank records. David didn't want to know how in the hell the group had access to any of that information and didn't want to ask.

Razor lived in a teacher's apartment complex near the old Tsukiji fish market, where tons of frozen tuna had been auctioned off to the highest bidder every morning since 1935. However, the buildings were aging, and the government was worried about sanitation and earthquake resistance. The primary market moved, yet the area still drew tourists year around.

After his conversation, David could tell Razor was different. His friend had a constant edge in his voice. When they attended the National Ballet School in Toronto, Razor held the title of class clown. He made the other boys laugh, the girls giggle, and elicited stern looks from the teachers.

Razor wasn't that guy anymore.

As David left the Tsukiji subway station, he threaded through streets jammed with tiny grocery and food stores and an abundance of sushi restaurants. Per the Hardy Boys' directions, he walked past the outside market, turned at the first left, and walked another four blocks.

As he was getting his bearings, his smartphone beeped. "Kabukicho tonight. I have information on the girl." The text was from the old man from the condo. He needed help now more than ever.

He stood outside an Indian tandoori restaurant with a sign written in English. Razor had loved Indian food while in ballet school. David wondered if he had rented above an Indian restaurant by accident or on purpose.

Was he doing the right thing? Razor had been through enough. He should just head back to the hotel and call the police instead.

"You can't leave well enough alone, can you?" Razor called at him from a second-floor window. "How in the hell did you find me?"

"Let me in, and I'll tell you."

Razor pointed to a small set of stairs at the side of the building. At the top, his friend stood in a miniscule kitchen, pouring boiling water over green leaves jammed into a tea strainer over an open teapot. He wore a thin blue silk robe tied at the front.

"Take off your shoes," Razor said.

David felt a blush of sadness. His last good memory was in Amsterdam when Razor had filled himself with recreational drugs before exploring the infamous red-light district.

That didn't turn out so well. Thugs attacked him, and David and Razor were injured again trying to help David to escape back to Canada, and he never bounced back. A head injury was tricky to diagnose and harder to heal. Plus, he knew Razor experienced some lingering PTSD from the attacks. Worse, the trauma screwed with Razor's balance and timing. The National Ballet of Canada couldn't use an injured dancer. They had moved him into an administrative position until he had just quit.

David hadn't seen him since.

Unshaven and heavier than he'd ever been, Razor looked like he outweighed David by twenty pounds or more. Before, David had always outweighed him.

"You look like shit." Razor handed him a cup of tea.

"I've had better days."

"What's with the serial killer's look?"

David ran his hand over his polished head and chuckled. "I needed a change."

Razor razed his eyebrows and smirked. "What are you here for? You said someone grabbed a girl?"

"A student of mine."

"You lost her?"

"Did you see the news about a girl abducted in Seattle?"

"The one with the rich daddy?"

"She was my student. I taught her dance every day."

"Taught? In Seattle? What happened to Toronto?"

"The National Ballet laid me off, and I took a job teaching dance." He left out the part about commuting to a billionaire's house in a helicopter and installing surveillance equipment for the US government.

"Someone abducted your student?"

"Yes. And I couldn't save her."

"I'm sure you tried."

"I did."

"And she magically appeared in Tokyo."

"That's what her father believes."

"He's all over the news. The FBI is looking for him. I just read they are looking for some guy that escorted her into the theater and fought the abductors...oh." He sipped more tea. "You're the guy."

"I'm the guy."

Razor sat on one of two chairs in his meager apartment and peeked out the window.

"Jesus Christ. How do you get into these situations? Why can't you just be a dancer?"

"I tried. It's not working out. Look, I need your help. I have no one else to turn to."

"Did you go to the police?"

"No."

"Why not? You aren't James Bond, swooping in to save the damsel. Get with the program and stop being a dickhead."

This conversation wasn't going anywhere. He wasn't sure what he expected, except it wasn't this. "I'm meeting with a guy tonight in Kabu-kicho who knows where she is."

"A guy. I thought you didn't know anyone here."

"I don't. I bumped into him in an elevator." Which was technically accurate. He didn't want to elaborate.

Razor poured more tea and looked at him crosswise.

"Who is this elevator guy?"

David thought for a minute, and while he didn't want to lie to Razor, telling him the whole thing would dig him in deeper than David wanted.

"I think he's a gangster."

"You mean yakuza? For fuck's sake, David, what in the hell are you doing? Those guys are dangerous. Even if they don't beat your ass, they can screw up all kinds of things for people like me living here. Like a job or work visa, for example."

"Razor, I'm in a tight spot, and this little girl's life is on the line. If I don't save her, they might kill her."

"Who will kill her?"

"The guys that grabbed her."

"And why did they grab her? To get rich daddy to pay?"

"No. Look, it's a long story. I need someone to watch my back."

Razor set his tea down and looked at him. "You won't learn, will you? For some reason that escapes me, you didn't die a year ago. You must think you are invulnerable, and you aren't. If you mess with these guys, you will get hurt. Go to the police. They can help. I can't. I've got too much to lose."

David stared at his friend for a long second, then stood up, pulled his shoes on, and said, "Thanks for the tea."

He returned to his hotel in under an hour and sent a series of requests to the Hardy Boys.

First, he needed to find out as much as possible about the old man. The cell phone number and the name on the card both went to the shadowy service. Maybe they could point him in the right direction.

Second, he needed something on Nakamura he could trade with. He inserted the USB key he'd used to steal data from Nakamura's condo into his tablet. The info wasn't doing him any good just sitting on the key. After considering his options, he uploaded all the information to his virtual helpers with a request to review.

David also needed a best-case and worst-case plan if he was meeting the old man tonight in a busy part of Tokyo. He spent some time war gaming potential scenarios and then did an internet search on the kinds of extra electronics he'd need, just in case.

Later in the afternoon, he made another quick trip to Akihabara dressed as a bald and white office worker instead of a blonde dance teacher. The business suit rendered him as invisible to the shoppers as the samurai cloak from a couple of days ago.

He hadn't heard anything from Mr. Continental either and couldn't be sure if he was the one that alerted his pursuers of his location. He texted the little gnome of an information broker just to be sure.

"Any update on finding information on Leia?"

He waited for a couple of minutes to see if he'd get a reply, otherwise, he'd try again later.

Chapter Thirty-Nine

Kabukicho, Shinjuku City

DAVID ARRIVED in Kabukicho about an hour before the meeting. He would have preferred two hours; one would have to do. The Hardy Boys could only provide sketchy information on the old man and the name on the card. The phone number only had a few calls to and from, and they couldn't determine cell number ownership. They also said Takeuchi could refer to a yakuza clan or a business that buys and sells data. Some may be tied to intellectual property.

Everyone was buying and selling something.

Lovely. Capitalism at its finest.

David was surprised the old man had dug up info on Leia in less than eight hours, considering he professed he knew nothing about Spencer and his daughter. Something didn't quite jibe. However, this was the only lead he had.

Kabukicho, early evening, nice and public, crowded with tourists and salarymen looking for food, drink, and companionship. He climbed subway stairs and faced a neon wave of noise and people.

The area held the title of Tokyo's red-light district, yet the brothels moved out years ago, replaced by dimly lit bars supplied with Chinese girls eager to work off their visa and transportation costs. The places sold overpriced booze and used Nigerian hawkers to encourage visitors inside without delay. Black men selling a good time in downtown Tokyo seemed an odd choice, but there were quite a few.

David received a text with the location. The tiny street would be busy this hour of the evening. He saw police roaming the area to ensure drunks caused no problems and that the yakuza stayed in their own lane. The cops and the Japanese mafia kept an uneasy truce. If their business interests didn't interfere with the general population or visitors, the police left them alone unless they broke any of the recent laws the government had created to curb the yakuza's influence and actions.

As he walked around, the smell of sizzling meat, fish, and vegetables from the many restaurants permeated the area. Coupled with the humidity, he almost felt he was on an exotic vacation.

Except he wasn't. Leia's life was on the line.

Before leaving the hotel, he replaced the horn rims that Jens Jamison wore with a similar pair he'd picked up in Akihabara. The frame contained tiny LEDs that emitted invisible infrared light to foil facial recognition systems. He didn't need a Tokyo computer system squealing on him. After wandering around and getting a feel for entrances and exits, he reached the location. No cars. Walking only. The old guy stood on the opposite corner with men different from the ones he had brought to Nakamura's apartment. The wider and thicker men wore black suits and dark sunglasses.

Nice and easy, David thought. A new goon squad to watch his back. That's all. Just a trade of information.

Two other guys dressed the same came up from the other direction and stopped. Four goons in total plus the old guy.

Shit.

The old guy walked into the middle of the street and stopped.

"The auditions for the Matrix are one block over," David called out. They ignored him and stood stone-faced. Maybe he should have worn sunglasses instead. "You said you had information on Leia," David said.

"Yes. And you have information on Nakamura."

"Where is she?" David said.

"What do you have on Nakamura?"

The Hardy Boys had delivered on his request. "He used a credit card in Osaka yesterday. At a hotel."

"That's all?"

"There's more. What do you know about Leia?"

The old guy waved one of his goons to come near and whispered something to him before saying, "Girl arrived at the airport two days ago and brought to a clinic in Ginza. Wheeled on a gurney into the building."

"What did she look like?"

"Young. Twelve or thirteen. Short hair. Long dress. Fancy dress. Hello Kitty backpack."

David said, "I need an actual address."

A Cheshire cat smile broke out on the old guy's face. "What's the name of the hotel?"

All negotiations were give and take. Give a little and get a little back. "Hotel Nikko. What's the clinic's address?"

The four goons fanned out to either side. David yelled, "Don't come any closer."

The men stopped and yelled back at him. He just heard gibberish. His memory-implant-auto-translation had quit for the evening. *This will end badly.* Except he didn't know for whom. Two other men in suits came up from behind him.

He'd miscalculated and now was the star of a bad Japanese movie, about to be attacked by the sales team of Men's Warehouse. He'd figured the guys he'd smacked in the elevator might be there, and he'd have to deal with them. Instead, he'd made a mistake and hadn't expected this level of response to trade information. The old guy wanted something more.

What? Was he pissed he had smacked his guys around?

The man spoke rapid-fire Japanese to his goons, but no one moved. They remained stoic with their hands at their side. The man didn't move and kept silent.

He was boxed in. He had no weapons other than his body, and the Men's Warehouse team looked like they were waiting for something.

Then he heard it. Scraping sounds coming from behind and in front. Two skateboarders with bright t-shirts, hats backward, and wide pants skated along the narrow passageway towards David. He thought he might knock one of them over, grab the skateboard, and use it as a weapon to escape.

But he still needed Leia's location.

"Give me an address, and I will give you the room number." He lied; he had nothing but wanted to keep negotiating to stall for time. No police in the area either. Where were they when you needed them?

The old guy smiled and stared. David turned his head, and the front skateboarder slalomed close. As he shifted to hockey check the kid and grab the board, the kid feinted and barreled towards him.

Almost too late, he saw a syringe in the kid's hand. He pivoted, grabbed the kid's wrist, and twisted the needle away. He didn't see the other skateboarder jam a needle into his thigh, but he felt it. His leg instantly went numb.

The four goons surrounded him and the skateboarders and blocked the view of any passersby. He grabbed the fallen board and swung it back and forth while the second skateboarder tried to jab the needle in again. David smacked him, pivoted left, and almost lost his balance. Depending on the chemical, if they got another syringe into him, he'd probably collapse within seconds.

The front goons fell to the ground. Razor stood behind them, his fists balled up. He'd shaved and wore a tight T-shirt. What David thought was fat turned out to be muscle.

One of the other goons ran towards his friend, but Razor shot a vicious kick to the man's gut and followed up with a blow to the head. He followed up with a roundhouse kick to the skater boy's face. The fourth man jumped close to Razor, except David smacked the skateboard into the man's gut. Razor leaped close with a sidekick into his head, dropping him to the ground.

The pedestrians had scattered, and the old guy backed away as his guards were down. Razor grabbed David's arm over his shoulder and half carried him to Yasukuni-Dori avenue separating Kabukicho and Shinjuku and a line of green and black taxis lined up for late-night travelers. His friend pulled open the door of the first cab and helped David inside.

No one followed.

As the cab pulled into traffic, David rubbed his frozen leg where the skater had jabbed him. Razor gave the driver the destination in Japanese. David understood this time. Everything.

Nice timing, Mr. Implanted Memory.

"What the hell happened?" Razor said.

"What the hell happened to you? Where did you learn to do that?"

His friend leaned back into the seat, breathing fast and sweat dripping off his temples. "When I moved here. I was determined not to let what took place in Amsterdam happen again."

"That was only a year ago."

"I'm in the dojo all my free time."

"It shows."

"I followed you here. I wasn't planning on doing anything. Everything came flooding back when I saw those guys ready to gang up on you. I just reacted."

"They could have hurt or killed you!"

"I'm hurting now." Razor leaned forward, his head in his hands. "Because of my concussion, I'm in pain after an exertion like that with no warm-up." He swallowed a couple of pills with help from a bottle of water he'd pulled out from his backpack. "I will be okay once the drugs kick in. A head injury takes a long time to get over." He leaned back into the seat. "What did those assholes want, anyway? Why were they trying to grab you?" Razor asked.

"I don't know. Mercenaries tried to grab me in Seattle when they abducted Leia, and I don't know why. When I landed here with Spencer, a group tried the same thing. I thought it might be for leverage or a bargaining chip. I'm not so sure now."

"Is there something in the memories they want like last time?"

"No, at least I don't think so."

David looked out the window of the cab. A light rain had started, and umbrellas were popping up like flowers. Someone tried to grab him again and he couldn't figure out why.

"I got confirmation of one thing."

"What?"

"Leia is here in Japan, and if the guy wasn't lying to me, I at least have a place to start looking."

Chapter Forty

THE CAB DROPPED them a couple of blocks from the hotel, and they walked the rest. David didn't want any direct connection to where he was staying. He used an app on his smartphone to mark a route back to bypass any surveillance cameras and kept his head on a swivel to ensure they weren't followed. He needed to get them both to safety and help. His leg still felt all pins and needles. Whatever they injected him with wasn't yet out of his system.

Razor's lips were pulled tight, and his face was drawn like a prisoner of war. He'd knocked down some attackers, and the effort had taken a toll. His friend squeezed his eyes shut as they waited for the elevator.

"Can you make it to the room?"

"Not much farther than that."

The main elevator took them to the lobby, and a large crowd of guests milled around with drinks in their hands. They ignored them both as they snaked their way to the next elevator.

They were a fine pair; he dragged one leg, and Razor looked like he was auditioning for a zombie movie. When they reached the room, he touched his key to the door and entered. Inside, he heard, "Hello, David."

A somber and tired-looking Asher Fitzsimmons forced a smile from the chair near the window. His face seemed drawn and sunken. Dark rings hung under his eyes. His ordinarily sharp white shirt looked dirty, and his trousers needed serious attention from a dry cleaner. A scratched and beat-up cane leaned up beside him.

David should have been surprised but wasn't. Relieved was the closer emotion. He wanted to hug the old man and decided against it. There would be time later.

"You appear to be one step away from being tossed out of here as a vagrant," David said.

"Nice to see you too, but you boys also have seen better days." Fritz managed a frown. "And you've changed your hairdresser."

He chuckled and ran his hand where his hair used to be. He'd almost forgotten about his newly shaven head. Razor looked at Fitz out of one eye and grunted before collapsing on the bed. "If you are going to kill me, can you at least wait until I get some sleep first?"

Fitz didn't respond, and after thirty seconds, Razor started snoring. He wasn't that worried. David limped to another chair and sat down before draining a bottle of the hotel water from the table.

"Do you mind bringing me up to date?"

Fitz nodded. "Your arrival at the ballet in Seattle coincided with three thugs bursting into my suite and jabbing me with a knockout drug."

"I saw the video."

"You followed our protocol?"

"I made it into the hotel and into the second room. Your abductors left some backup thugs, presumably for me. And I agree, the video showed those men weren't that welcoming to a man with your"—he smiled—"maturity level. I almost didn't make it down to the elevator. I had to improvise." David frowned. "Did Moore grab you?"

"Indeed. He started with a full interrogation setup and wondered how a dancer made it out alive through an armed gauntlet of mercenaries. I suggested your ballet training and adrenaline contributed to your survival and stayed silent for other reasons."

He frowned. "Were you on the same plane as Leia?"

"No."

"Where's Leia now?"

Fitz lifted his eyebrows. "I don't know. Moore is looking for her, too."

"What do you mean? He's the one that orchestrated the operation and grabbed her at the ballet."

"No. That's incorrect. He does not have young Miss Leia."

"He does! Why do you think I came to Tokyo with Spencer?"

Fitz narrowed his eyes. "Spencer brought you here?"

David nodded.

"I'm old enough not to believe anything without proof. What did he tell you?"

"That Moore tried to have him killed and was behind Leia's abduction."

"If Moore wants Spencer dead, why does he need the daughter?" Fitz said.

David shrugged and said, "Spencer told me a story about Leia's blood containing a rare protein that can reverse cancer and claimed Moore plans to use her blood and organs to extract the protein and sell it to wealthy patients as a cure. He brought her to Tokyo because he's got a scientist named Nakamura who can do the work and has no problems using people as spare parts for the rich."

Fitz shook his head. "Sounds a little fanciful to me. Like a bad Bruce Willis movie."

"I had the same thought. Except I received an anonymous email telling me to find Nakamura. I broke into his apartment close to here and found evidence that backs up the curing cancer story."

Fitz leaned back in the chair in obvious discomfort. "Moore told me a different story. He said when Spencer couldn't force him out of SCS, he created an elaborate ruse to kidnap his daughter and pin it on him. He wanted to grab you and Leia at the ballet and use you to squeeze SCS for an enormous sum in exchange for Leia. He'd planned to kill you for negotiation theatrics. Moore needs to find Spencer and clear his name."

"Kill him, I think he means."

"Yes. I suspect that's a likely outcome of Moore finding Spencer."

David shook his head. "But there's no news about either one around Leia's abduction. The police have no leads, and only a few thugs are in custody. This is crazy. Spencer told me Moore took her, and now you tell me that Moore told you Spencer took her."

Fitz squinted at him. "One or both of these men is playing a shell game, and we are being conned." Fitz glanced out the window. "Or maybe they are working together."

David's head spun with this possibility. He'd never considered it. "Why would they be?"

"No idea, but I've seen similar confidence scams during the cold war," Fitz said.

David noticed something blinking on Fitz's ankle. "Looks like you've picked up some high-tech jewelry."

"Yes, lucky me. A gift from Moore. An incentive, he called it. Any attempts to remove it will trigger an immediate detonation. I don't plan to abandon my current vocation to become a pirate either. Our best-friends-forever relationship didn't last very long, yet he's giving me some freedom to bring you in."

"Can't he tell where you are?"

"Maybe. I overheard the tech telling him he couldn't get the hardware working with the DoCoMo phone network. That also may be a ruse. However, I need to return within a time frame to prevent my foot from leaving my leg. And you have to be with me."

"What does he want?"

"He thinks you are in league with Spencer and can provide his location. I told him I could find you. That's why he let me go; this grenade on my leg is insurance that I return."

"After I failed to stop Leia's abduction, I went looking for you. Your expensive bracelet led me to your last location." David reached into his bag and handed Fitz the once shiny GPS device he had found in the abandoned warehouse. "Try not to lose it next time," he said with a smirk. "When I couldn't find you, Spencer contacted me. We met at a fleabag motel in North Seattle. He said Moore engineered Leia's abduction and that he barely escaped his estate with his life. He said Leia's blood is worth trillions as a cancer treatment, and Moore grabbed her to experiment on her and perfect the cure."

"Where's Spencer now?"

"I don't know. He's AWOL." He didn't want to explain any further.

Fitz pointed to Razor. "I see you have reconnected with an old friend."

"I had no other option. He helped me out tonight in Kabukicho. More than I expected," David said.

"He's been studying martial arts since he arrived. He's got a natural gift. Once I discovered you were here, I thought you might find him," Fitz said.

"Why didn't you mention to me you knew how he was doing?"

Fitz frowned as if an eye had just opened in the middle of David's forehead. "Do you wish me to tell you everything that goes on? Even when it doesn't concern you? I took an interest in your friend after last year's incident and realized he could use a little help. For instance, I arranged a teaching position over here for him."

David shook his head; he didn't want to argue. He had other things to be upset with. Like that, his leg wasn't back to normal. He rubbed and massaged it as best as he could.

Fitz watched for a few seconds. "What happened?"

"I was jabbed with a needle that paralyzed my leg."

"I'd change dentists if I were you," Fitz said.

David said nothing as he thought about the cluster fuck Fitz had unwittingly dragged him into. He took off his shirt and looked at his bruises. His forearm had gone purple, and bruises covered his knuckles. He'd come out okay, other than the bum leg.

David turned to Fitz. "We've been played. Both of us. Or all three, if you count Westlake. And I don't care who's behind it. I need to rescue Leia from whoever has her and let Spencer and Moore fight it out. I've had enough of rich assholes doing whatever they want."

Fitz grimaced in pain as he grabbed his cane to help him up. "Let's look at this objectively. We have two dueling billionaires fighting over a cancer cure and both trying to implicate each other in the abduction of one's daughter."

"Yes, that about sums it up."

"And the one billionaire is missing."

"If he already had Spencer, he wouldn't need to lie, would he?"

"I can't see a reason. He's told me a lot of things and I'm hard pressed to parse what's true and false."

"And if I don't come with you, he will blow your leg off."

"Yes."

"He's bluffing."

"He might be. However, they showed the device working on a now one-legged mannequin where they held me. And he strapped its twin on my leg," Fitz said.

"Do you believe he'd do that?"

"He's got some Army in him, so he might."

"If he blows your leg off, you will die and won't be any good to him."

"Yes, I'm sure he'd get all emotional about me being dead."

"See, you have nothing to worry about," David said.

"I'd still like to not take that chance."

"How much time do you have left?"

"Ninety minutes," Fitz said.

"Do you have a plan?" David asked.

"You should know me better than that. I always have a plan."

Chapter Forty-One

David ordered rush room service and noticed his leg was almost back to normal.

"We are sorely lacking intel on the situation." Fitz bit into a bacon, lettuce, and tomato sandwich. He looked at his phone and sent a text to Moore.

"What did you say?"

"That I've made contact and waiting to meet you at a train station."

Fitz's phone beeped seconds later, and he read out the message. "Chop chop. I need you back in an hour. Or not, if you don't mind limping."

"I've been engaging with your shadowy detective twins. Your bitcoin bill might be high," David said.

"The sky's the limit with that group," Fitz said.

David wasn't sure what that exactly meant. His initial inquiry cost ten thousand real dollars in cryptocurrency. He wasn't sure what they'd ask for the second pass.

He fired up his tablet and wrote a terse message to The Hardy Boys for more information. It was a broad request for anything more they could find on Moore and Spencer, plus any businesses they may be connected to. A typical search firm would take hours or days to research;

however, the internet bloodhounds didn't work that way. Either they had a wizard on staff or remote-viewing Russian telepaths. He didn't want to know.

Fitz's cell phone chirped again. "David, I hate to be a bother, but if we don't meet Moore soon, I will be auditioning for the next production of the Pirates of Penzance."

Koto City, Tokyo

David left Razor a note and a Do-Not-Disturb sign on the door. He helped Fitz walk to the front of the Shinjuku Station and hailed a cab. Fitz texted Moore that they were en route.

Moore responded, "Better hurry."

Traffic in Tokyo mirrored every other major city in the world. At least the drivers were polite.

"Sounds like Moore considers himself the white knight in this situation," David said.

Fitz shook his head. "I'm sure he's just brimming with the milk of human kindness. I'm still trying to understand who's the mastermind in all this. SCS's success seems to be tied to Spencer's programming genius. However, Moore appears as more of a blunt object in a suit. Neither Moore's nor Spencer's story sounds the least bit plausible."

"Spencer told me he wants to take back control of the company and send Moore to jail."

"Moore's story matches that narrative." Fitz raised his leg on the seat and grimaced in pain. "Is this entire operation just an elaborate plot to entrap Moore?"

"Did he say anything about hurting Westlake?" David said.

Fitz raised his eyebrows. "What do you mean?"

"He's in the hospital in Seattle. I called his cell, and a nurse answered. She wouldn't tell me anything other than that he was in the ICU. Near as I can tell, someone injured Westlake about the same time they grabbed you," David said.

"That points to the same team in a coordinated event," Fitz said.

"Or a big coincidence."

"It could happen. If Spencer engineered and paid for Leia's abduction, he might have dealt with Westlake to cut you off from any support," Fitz said.

"If you were running a covert operation that included kidnapping a principal and pinning it on someone else, what would you do?" David said.

"The same. Loose ends will kill you. Perhaps Moore beat Spencer to it. He said they tried to grab Spencer to force him to sign over the company and weren't successful."

"Spencer said Moore's goons attacked him at his house when we left."

"How did he escape?"

"Good question," David said. "He claimed he flooded the mansion with knockout gas while he hid in an airtight safe room." Out the cab window, the light rain filtered through the ever-present neon lights and looked a bit like Christmas in the summer. "Where are we going?"

"To an industrial park devoid of any Japanese charm."

"I'm sure it's voted best place for an ambush on the yakuza-r-us website," David said. Fitz sighed and kept silent.

The taxi took twenty minutes and stopped at a large white building. No windows. A lone light above a single reinforced door. A camera stared at the entrance, and a single intercom hung off the side of the door. Not even an overhang to keep the rain off them.

David said to the driver, "*Nijuppun o matte kudasai*" and handed him ten thousand yen.

"Hai!" the driver said.

"What did you say?" Fitz asked. "How can you speak Japanese and then can't?"

"It comes and goes. I don't know why. I told him to wait here for twenty minutes. I'm hoping we won't need that much time."

"I just want this bloody grenade off my ankle."

As they approached, the metal door swung open, and a disembodied voice in English said, "Inside."

David fought against an inner memory, trying to stop him from entering. Images of similar entries into buildings flashed in his head.

Some large, some small. Most memories recalled a door going in. He didn't remember any exits. The voice guiding them sounded like it came from everywhere.

Fitz waved him close and put his arm around David's shoulder. He had his cheap cane in the other hand. "I can't walk any farther with this damn thing on my leg." He pulled up his pants, and his ankle had swollen red. David helped him through the door.

Once inside, the voice ushered them down a hallway filled with a low-level electric hum. He guessed they were in a data center, probably owned by SCS. Thousands of the customers' confidential information sat protected in this bunker. Tight and secure and away from the prying eyes of bad actors and teenage hackers.

He had learned a few things as he sat through a mandatory employee orientation on his first day at SCS. Few people worked in their facilities. Instead, robot maintenance crews kept the electronics running, which meant a machine disconnected and pulled the misbehaving computer server and replaced it with a new one.

A door opened at the end of the hallway, and a large white guy waved them inside. His T-shirt stretched around his thick chest and arms. David saw no holster or other weapons. The guy probably thought the muscles would be enough. Or he didn't expect any funny business from a dancer.

"Raise your arms." He ran rough hands over David's body. The man grunted when he did the same to Fitz before pushing them inside.

A thin Japanese man with a toolbox stood nearby. A buff Japanese man stood at the other side of the room wearing a better-quality shirt with no tie, and no weapons that he could see on either of them. Fitz told him the guy was Moore's assistant, Jacob.

"Sit down," the thin guy said.

David helped Fitz to the chair and stayed behind him. Another door opened, and Nick Moore walked in with a big smile.

"Mr. Knight, so glad you could come," Moore said.

"I'm here. Get this thing off his leg."

Moore nodded to the thin man. After a few minutes, he unlocked the anklet, and Fitz groaned while rubbing his calf furiously. The man carefully split open the device and removed a small block that looked like white clay. He packed the block into another box before packing up everything and leaving the room. The white stuff looked similar to a C4 explosive. Moore hadn't been bluffing.

"So, you are the famous dancer I've heard so much about," Moore said

"What do you want? I'm pissed that you planned to blow Fitz's foot off if we were late in traffic."

"The world revolves around incentives, Mr. Knight. I needed you here. Your partner needed an incentive to ensure you would come with him." Moore pulled out his phone and typed something on the screen. "Why do you think you are here?"

An annoyance grew inside him. "I haven't got time for a thousand questions. A girl's life is at stake."

"Ah, yes. The young Leia Spencer."

"Where is she?"

Moore's demeanor changed. "I don't give a shit about the daughter. Where is Spencer?"

David frowned. "I just want Leia, and then we can all go our separate ways."

"I don't have her, idiot. Spencer does."

"You grabbed her in Seattle and killed people. Is she in this building?" An instinct kept forcing him to push Moore as hard as he could.

"I grabbed her? Is that what that old fuck told you? You are stupider than I thought."

Fitz hobbled over, his leg still dragging to one side. "As you requested, I've brought David here to help you, but you need to tell us what's going on, or we are both walking."

"You guys are incredible. Do you think you can waltz in and out of here?" He nodded to the two other men. The big white guy moved behind David while the assistant went behind Fitz.

He'd been watching them both. The big guy moved well, even though he was muscle-bound. Moore's assistant had a boxer's body, yet looked relaxed, like he didn't consider either visitor a threat. He stood behind David and kept him from going anywhere.

Fitz said Moore couldn't believe a dance teacher evaded the mercenaries at the ballet. Moore's brutes had no weapons. Just their size, strength, and overconfidence.

In any other situation, the muscle would win. They'd never expected their prey to fight back. Especially someone half their weight.

As the big guy grabbed for him, David pivoted to the right, grabbed his wrist, and twisted hard away from the thumb, driving the guy down. David smashed his knee into the guy's jaw and the man collapsed to the concrete floor.

The assistant looked surprised, like he couldn't believe what he saw. He shot toward David, except Fitz stuck out his good foot and tripped him. David lashed out with a front kick into the assistant's head, dropping him alongside his unconscious colleague.

"We are getting out of here," David said. Moore ran towards him at full speed, snarling, and launched a barrage of punches. He had some skill. David ducked and weaved close into Moore's circle and head-butted him, knocking him back on his heels. He wanted to savor hitting this asshole again, so he waited for his rich opponent to shake off the hit and come at him again.

Moore opened with a left jab. David ducked, spun backward, and smacked his elbow into Moore's jaw. The executive stumbled as David followed up with two left jabs, a right hook, and an uppercut, dropping him to the floor.

He yanked an ID card off Moore's neck and wallet from his pocket. As he used the ID card to open the door, Moore grunted from the floor, "You are fucking dead. You are fucking dead!"

"You are the one on your ass," David said. As an afterthought, he grabbed a handful of zip ties he noticed sticking out of the big guy's pocket and bound each man's hands behind their backs.

He took more time with Moore and drove his knee into his neck as he yanked the little man's arms back and zip-tied his hands together before walking out with Fitz and away from the screaming executive.

Chapter Forty-Two

David's smartphone beeped. Mr. Continental had finally responded.

"Security video showed a girl with a backpack landed two days ago. She was asleep. Men carried her to a van and drove to a clinic in Koto."

"Address?" he wrote back.

"None so far. I will let you know. Might need more money."

Nothing about who grabbed her. David thought he should have been more specific about what he wanted before handing over the cash.

But he said she was taken to Koto City and not Ginza. The old guy in Kabukicho lied. This meant Moore didn't have her, but David searched the other offices in the data centre anyway while Fitz waited. After a few minutes, he found nothing. Maybe the old gnome from Akihabara was telling the truth.

Moore said Spencer engineered the entire thing, except David couldn't believe one of the wealthiest men in the US would want to hurt his daughter and go to the trouble of such an enormous ruse.

The cab took them to Shinjuku Station. The hotel was a ten-minute walk. David didn't want anyone tracking them.

Razor was asleep. David sat down and realized after hitting the guards and smacking Moore he hadn't felt the surge of adrenaline usually generated from a fight-or-flight situation. Almost like he was getting used to kicking ass without the physical and mental toll.

Fitz said nothing. He took off his shoes, lay on the second bed, and fell asleep in a minute.

David worried about Leia. He wasn't any closer to finding her or even uncovering the truth. Was she even in Japan? He needed more help. After logging into his tablet, he received a request from the Hardy Boys: they wanted to chat online in real-time. They attached several documents to the message. The first one detailed all GPS-capable devices tied to Spencer used for tracking.

David typed, "I'm looking for specifics on the devices."

"Good morning! We hope things are well." The pleased-as-punch customer service seemed out of place from a company hidden on the dark web. After a few seconds, the chat continued. *"The data you uploaded helped us to prioritize our searching. However, to answer your first question, SCS owns several shell companies that use the devices. We successfully hacked their system."*

"What did you find?"

"Most are US based and centered in Seattle. To be clear, they are for tracking assets; cars, machinery, and people."

"Does SCS manufacture them?"

"No. Another company does. The technology is so advanced the military doesn't even have it. We estimate each would cost several thousand dollars to produce. When we hacked into one, we discovered they report their location to a central system."

"The ultimate stalker device."

"Yes. A key piece of tech is the battery."

"Why?"

"Large batteries can be detected. Small electronics with no perceivable battery are harder to find. Several are currently active in Seattle and a few in Japan. They are small enough to hide in plain sight or inserted into a passport or even sewn into fabric."

"Show me the ones in Seattle." A map appeared. He zoomed into a cluster in Belltown. His apartment. Fitz was right to have him keep to the protocol. No talking or texting inside his place. Several lit up in what looked like his bedroom. Did someone sew it into his clothes?

"Show me Tokyo." Two locations: Shinjuku and Asakusa. His heart pounded. Could Leia be this close to him? He zoomed in and stopped when he reached his hotel.

"Crap." He dug through his small backpack and stripped.

"What's this? A Chippendale audition?" Fitz said. He must have only slept for a little while.

"I'm being tracked." He checked everything. His clothes and shoes were all new. Finally, a memory surfaced. His wallet. He'd carried it with him the entire time. He'd swapped out his credit cards, but he found a thin SCS employee ID card with his picture on it. There was nothing else it could be. He held the card up to Fitz. "Son of a bitch. You hired me to install tracking devices in this company, and they've been tracking me all along."

Fitz looked stone-faced. "We don't know who initiated it. Spencer, possibly as the profile Westlake created, said his paranoia was turned up to eleven. As you were his daughter's teacher, adding surveillance that you would carry wouldn't be unexpected, yet this may not be the smoking gun. Moore knew much about you as well. You were being tailed every night. That might have been Moore's doing."

David looked back at the tablet. "What about the other one?"

The Hardy Boys typed, *"Asakusa. The last ping was about a day ago. The tracker is in a shielded building or has been found and destroyed. We took the liberty of reviewing the device's movement. Started at a location on Lake Washington until a few days ago when it traveled to the Seattle Center and then to Boeing Field. The device left Haneda Airport in Tokyo and hasn't moved for a few days."*

Leia. She had a tracker on her.

"Do any of these locations look familiar to you?"

"Yes. Both."

"If it was Spencer, then he had Leia's location as soon as we landed," David said. "But our pit stop at the heliport screwed things up."

"And if it was Moore, he didn't care where Leia was. He wanted Spencer," Fitz said. "I think it's prudent to play along and keep the card with you for the time being. Whoever is tracking you, we don't want to alert them until we have some leverage."

David slipped it into his bag. "I've got a better idea." He went back to the online chat with the Hardy Boys. "Have you found answers to my other questions?"

"Yes. Curing cancer. That and erectile dysfunction are top searches on Google. Current research shows the disease is both genetic and random. One vector is looking for a key to immunize against it."

"Why is Moore so interested?"

"We can't tell if Moore or Spencer is the one interested. Your data wasn't specific about who is funding the research. We know that SCS produces sophisticated security software that finds and patches system vulnerabilities. We've found fingerprints of their programs searching DNA databases for certain patterns. Breast cancer, for example, has been tied to a specific gene expression. There's a belief that a particular combination of DNA can give rise to distinct cancers through the interaction between the various genes."

He didn't tell the Hardy Boys about Leia's blood. Fitz told him he could trust this disembodied group of people across the wire, but he held back. "Is the person examining the data looking for a cancer cure?"

The screen sat silently for almost thirty seconds until the agent typed again. *"Perhaps. We've discovered a series of companies SCS has discreetly acquired. We have concluded SCS is betting on a line of research from a discredited Japanese scientist named Kando Nakamura."*

"I told you about him," David said. "I broke into his apartment, and I stole this." He showed Fitz the USB key. "I uploaded all the data to your boys."

"Nakamura has a severe right-wing ideology bordering on xenoracism. Early in his career, he researched genetic advantages in certain races with a lens on racial purity. Publicly available analysis does show minor genetic differences between races; however, real advantages are random. A heavy smoker in the US doesn't get cancer, but his neighbour does. The accidental mutation prevents the first man's cancer. Nakamura's investigation showed cancers could be prevented or even removed by fortifying the body's protection. Like strong anti-virus software," the agent typed.

"And Spencer's company knows how to do that."

"They do. With some help."

"What?"

"Your data points to precise enzymes and gene combinations that can interact to build this cancer shield and hammer. We have evidence of searching multiple DNA databases for exact combinations."

Fitz said, "Ask him if they are random or inherited?" David keyed in the query.

"Could be a combination. Some gene expressions like eye colour are inherited, and some are random."

"Are they looking for people with these combinations?"

"Yes. If our research is correct, the searcher believes they found three people with the right mix of enzymes."

"Only three?"

"Only three people in all the databases they searched."

Fitz said, "Ask them what sources?"

David typed in the question.

"Based on the data you provided, they've combed through every available DNA database maintained by government security, police, hospitals, etc., and all the for-profit DNA tracking companies that find long-lost cousins or discover your father isn't your father."

"How in the hell were they able to do that?" David typed.

"All those organizations around the world use SCS software to safeguard their data. There must be a back door for secret access by people with the key."

"Even private companies that track your ancestry via DNA?"

"Yes. Those companies also utilize the SCS software to protect their customers' privacy."

"Isn't that breaking the law?"

"Yes. Accessing this kind of information without permission is breaking every privacy law in the books. Like what we do here!"

David nodded and kept typing. "Who are the people?"

"A woman in Japan—whereabouts unknown. She's off the grid. We think her birth name is Yumi Hattori."

Yumi, David thought. "Jonathan knew her." He turned and looked at Fitz.

"How do you know that?"

"I saw her in a dream," David said.

"The second is another female. Mixed race. Japanese and Caucasian. Whereabouts unknown."

David typed. "Any relationship between the first woman and the second?"

"The first woman is the mother of the second."

"And who else?"

"Unknown. We believe they have identified the person. Caucasian. However, we haven't found a name."

"Does each person's blood contain the cure?"

"Only a portion."

"What happens when these people get together? Do they need blood samples or something?"

"We don't know. The blood alone won't be enough. Leukemia, for example, needs a bone marrow transplant from a donor to the patient."

"So, they will need their bone marrow?"

"Yes, and maybe parts of their livers, pancreases, and gallbladders. Full removal, of course, would lead to death."

David rocked back in his chair and looked at Fitz. "What in the hell did you get me involved in?"

The conversation from the Hardy Boys continued. *"We discovered some deleted emails outlining the planned procedure. Patients will gain access to the treatment at a high cost. Until they can clone all the organs of the three subjects to make them self-sufficient, blood from the three together is the cure."*

Fitz had David type, "Why would this company do this? Even if they charged several million dollars a patient, SCS still makes significantly more money from software."

"Yes."

"What then?"

"Spencer has an untreatable and rare form of cancer himself. We are guessing he will be the first patient."

Fitz transferred enough bitcoin to settle up with the Hardy Boys with some extra in case they needed more information. David downloaded all the relevant material.

As he read the material, a lump formed in his throat. He, Westlake, and Fitz had been played like a chess game, a hundred moves ahead. And Spencer was the grandmaster.

"There's one thing that's been bugging me. Why am I here?"

Fitz shook his head. "What do you mean?"

"Don't you think it's convenient that Westlake wanted to investigate a company needing a ballet teacher? And that I was available?"

"I agree. The situation bothered me. The spook wasn't concerned. He saw you as a way in."

"Why didn't he use one of his agents to lie on the application and obtain an interview?

Fitz looked at David as if he was going to say something and stopped. "I've seen that look before. Out with it."

"I'm such a fool," Fitz said.

"What do you mean?"

"Westlake had an agent apply with a padded backstory and never got an email response. His guy even had some dance training. Westlake engaged the services of an HR recruiter and couldn't get through the door. That's when he turned to me, and I turned to you."

"Doesn't that strike you as fishy?"

"In the context of our present situation, yes. Westlake was overjoyed when you took the role; I was upset. However, you settled into the job, and I hoped you'd found a real calling. But now..."

"They set us up. They wanted me to interview, and I don't understand why. When they grabbed Leia, they tried to grab me, too, and failed. Earlier tonight, mobsters tried to abduct me as well. They could have just killed me if I had been in the way. Doesn't that strike you as odd?"

"Yes, no one tried to kill you." The old Brit forced a smile.

"Why would Spencer do this?"

"Westlake wanted to discover why you didn't die from the implanted memories. Would Spencer be interested in that research?" Fitz asked.

David hadn't considered that. However, it seemed out of the range of what SCS and Spencer cared about. He'd believed the reason he didn't die from the implanted memories was a fluke. "I almost died. Several times." David's head was swimming. "If Spencer wanted me, why go to all this effort in bringing me to Seattle? Why wouldn't he have some guys grab me in Toronto?"

"Too much risk. He ran the risk of you going on the run, or injury or any number of things. No, he wanted you to come to him. Perhaps he enjoyed putting a plan like that together and seeing it executed."

"He didn't expect I'd put up a fight at the theater."

"And drop three of his goons," Fitz said. "Did you mention anything about your European adventure last year?"

"No. I told him I took karate as a kid. He might wonder how I understood Japanese or took him to a back-alley clinic in a city I'd never visited. He was out of it and might not remember how he got there."

"Did he tell you his plan once you landed?" Fitz said.

"No. I felt like a mushroom. We flew in a helicopter into Tokyo and met up with a yakuza a cappella group that seemed pissed with Spencer for something. Two thugs tried grabbing us. I declined their offer.

"Did they know about your skills?"

"No. The goons weren't prepared." David rubbed his eyes. "Even with all this, I still can't understand how Spencer could turn his daughter into a cancer medicine factory," David said.

"I suspect we will find out soon enough."

Razor stirred in the bed, moved his feet to the ground. "What did I miss?"

Chapter Forty-Three

Hilton Hotel, Shinjuku, Tokyo

THE FOLLOWING DAY, as per Fitz's advice, David booked a new hotel for him and Fitz and ensured there was an extra bed if Razor stayed. He'd saved David from the thugs and simultaneously delivered a can of whoop ass. He'd be handy to have around.

This time, David picked a big American chain with many white men and women coming and going. This made it easier to blend in. The place stood about a quarter mile from the old location. Easy to walk to and not out of the action area. After the revelations from the Hardy Boys about Spencer, he decided on a different option for the tracking card. As they checked out of the room, he stuffed it into the bottom of a housekeeping cart in the hallway under a stack of towels. Fitz watched and shrugged. He'd appear to be still in the same location, but that was all.

They talked about the next phase. Blending in was paramount. They purchased new clothes and shoes, leaving their old stuff in the department store changing rooms.

David continued as Jens and kept the suitcase. They entered an expansive lobby, checked in, and dropped their bags. They needed food to boost their energy. Nearby, they discovered a long and narrow passage lined with tiny restaurants, most with a few empty seats. They spotted a place that would work. He ordered sushi, Razor chose a bowl of ramen, and Fitz settled on chicken barbecued on bamboo skewers.

The aromas triggered a happy memory, like waking up on Christmas morning and holding hands with the petite and beautiful Japanese girl again. The vision overtook him, and he shivered from the touch of her hand on his, giving him butterflies in his gut as she kissed him lightly. A peck at first, then full lips that tasted tart cherries.

He shook the image away to get back to reality. The spy bouncing around in his head had been more active than David suspected. James Bond-level action, except this woman seemed more than a dalliance.

He knew Jonathan had searched for love, craved it even, during a career that would have challenged any man. As the image of his wife, Elizabeth, flashed past, he pushed that down. He didn't want to revisit the pain like he was forced to a year ago. Yet, the heartache was apparent. The ache of wanting to bask in another person loving him. He almost couldn't determine whose memory it was. His or Jonathan's.

He ate his sushi from a platter on a chest-level counter; the wood scarred from the thousands of plates over the years, with Razor nearby. Fitz settled into a lone seat in the back. The place only had eight seats in total.

The alley sloped to the exit. With chopsticks, he grabbed a piece of sashimi, dabbed it with wasabi and soy sauce, and popped it in his mouth. As he savored the salty and spicy fish for a second, he almost forgot why he was here. His eyes tracked people walking past the shop, and he couldn't turn it off. Like a new car's collision avoidance system, even if the tuna and salmon he ate were the best he'd ever eaten, he'd still be on high alert.

As he finished, he swiveled his head. Razor seemed better, and David appreciated his help.

Some guys had gathered outside. All were tall with gelled hair sticking straight up. They stood in clumps of two or three. Only one man wasn't sucking on a cigarette. Maybe he'd quit that day. Everyone was on a cell phone.

They were waiting for something or someone. The group looked like they'd popped out of a yakuza dispenser. He watched them, trying not to look at him at all. A trio of white males in Tokyo would garner at least a peek. They got instead an intentional ignore.

Which team were these guys on? Red or blue? Shirts or skins? *Which group of assholes did they belong to?* He waved Fitz over, and after the old man hobbled to the counter, he looked out. "What do you think? I left the tracking card at the other place."

"Maybe it's not needed. They probably used low-level spotters. Three white men that matched our descriptions might be easy to find."

"What is your assessment?"

"My bet would be on a standard follow and take down. No one has tried to kill us yet, but the night is young. Perhaps they believe we hold information."

Razor stopped slurping his ramen. "What are you talking about?"

"We may need to leave." He put down about seven thousand yen on the counter. The front of the alley took them to the hotel through sidewalks and side streets. The back of the alley faced a busy street.

"I'm wondering who they work for." His stomach was in knots, and he fought against Jonathan's instincts to kick ass now and ask questions later. He felt like he did in Amsterdam; a passenger in a car driven by a maniac and trying to grab the wheel every chance he had.

"Moore brought a small team with him. A local squad would be hard to mobilize that fast."

"What about Spencer?"

He shrugged. "He might be dead."

"The guys are yakuza gang members. Look at their tats." Razor nodded his head in the direction of the men.

David squinted, and as one of them raised a cigarette to his mouth, a dark snake tattoo was wrapped around his wrist.

"They are gangsters or wannabes," Razor said. David pushed back from the counter. Razor grabbed his arm. "What are you going to do?"

"You are a bit outnumbered, old boy." Fitz said.

"I'm just saying hello, but you should pay for your meal." He borrowed a pen from the cook and wrote something down on a restaurant receipt.

This time, he consciously willed Jonathan's presence into his body.

Seconds later, he felt like a large dog had jumped onto his lap, followed by a burst of so much confidence he could hardly breathe. His heart pounded, and his breathing elevated to the point he had to do something, or he'd explode.

"Get ready to move," he said. He slipped off his stool and walked twenty feet to the largest thugs. The other men turned to watch the proceedings. Their purpose might be more crowd control.

The two guys in front of him looked like enforcers.

"*Konichiwa*. Are you looking for me?" He moved in close to the first man, as an aunt would that didn't understand personal space.

A look of surprise turned to a scowl. "Get lost, gaijin."

The second guy stepped behind David, reaching around with a chokehold. David caught the guy's wrist, twisted down, and spun his elbow into the guy's head, knocking him into a line of stools.

"Now that's over. What do you want?" The front man threw a haymaker, but David throat-punched him first and followed with a headbutt into the guy's nose. The guy dropped to the ground in a bloody mess.

"I'd like to meet your boss. Have him text me." He jammed the piece of paper from the restaurant into the guy's jacket.

He said to Fitz and Razor, "Let's go," and the three of them disappeared out the end of the alley. The crowd control guys just stepped aside and let them pass.

Chapter Forty-Four

Although the Hilton was clean and modern, the lobby stunk of sweat, fatigue, and anger as a tour group of Americans poured into the hotel from a large bus.

They entered with Fitz limping with the help of a new cane he'd found when they purchased new clothes. He detected no surveillance and expected staff wouldn't notice three more men out of a group of North American tourists.

Hide in plain sight, Fitz always told Jonathan. As they entered the room, David still couldn't grab hold of the situation.

"Why is the yakuza involved in this thing at all?" Razor said. "I thought a couple of rich guys were after you?"

David said nothing at first. He was trying to pull the pieces together.

Fitz sat in a chair while Razor and David peered at the tablet.

"Spencer said Leia's blood can cure cancer and Moore had grabbed her for it. Moore said Spencer abducted his daughter so he could extract money from SCS tax-free and send Moore to jail.

"Yes, the billionaire's version of he said, he said," Fitz said.

"But they want you too, don't they?" Razor said.

David nodded. "I don't know why. If what Spencer said is true, Moore abducted Leia for her blood. Any other abduction would include ransom demands. Maybe Spencer is telling the truth if there is no ransom note."

"Except if Spencer is as rich as reported, why make Leia's abduction so public and brutal?"

"You told me she was a shut-in at his mansion. If he wanted to bring her to Japan, he could have just booked a private jet, and no one would have known," Razor said.

A text message chirped on David's cell phone. He'd given the number to one of the bleeding yakuza.

"*Good afternoon, David-san. We have something in common,*" the message said.

The person has my name, David thought. Moore and Spencer wouldn't be that formal. He typed a response. "Do we?"

"*A girl. About twelve.*"

"Okay." David held back from saying anything other than simple answers.

"*She's fine and sedated.*"

"That's probably a good idea."

"*We are interested in a trade.*"

"For what?"

"*We want to trade the girl for you.*"

David showed the text to Razor and Fitz. They said nothing for a couple of seconds.

"Why do they want you?" Razor said. "Is there more information in your head bouncing around like last time?"

"No," David said.

"Biotech doesn't seem to be a logical vocation for Japanese mobsters to pursue," Fitz said.

"Their business has always been protection, girls, and drugs," Razor said.

David noticed Fitz had aged considerably since this operation started in Seattle only a few weeks ago. However, as Fitz spoke, his voice became clear and engaged. "Let's look at the abduction. Seems way out of bounds for a group that prides itself on staying under the radar. Were there any Japanese as part of the crew?"

"No. Mostly white. A couple of African Americans and some Latinos. Maybe a few from the Middle East or Central Europe," David said.

"America is a melting pot. However, someone that is trying to fake being an American might slip up in the heat of an operation. I still don't see the value in grabbing Leia. From what I've seen and what you've told me, a crew that size would be pricey and a huge logistical challenge." Fitz looked at him and sipped tea he'd made from the kettle in the room. "How many men?"

"At least ten, if not fifteen."

"That's at a million or two, plus travel and incidentals. Most high-stakes abductions are a simple cost-benefit analysis. The target's worth versus the amount the other person will pay for their return. A large upfront cost means a substantial return, especially with the risk of something going wrong."

Razor said, "I watched some videos online from the road cameras. I thought they were filming a movie."

The fights and the chase flashed back in David's mind, and he felt the burn of shame as he remembered watching Leia carried off by her attackers and he couldn't stop them. He wanted to remain dispassionate and think logically, but his anger rose again the more he remembered the events.

"Big upfront and big risk point to a big payday."

"Yes."

"I'm not seeing any ransom note, real or virtual."

Fitz checked the Seattle news on David's tablet. "Still nothing on Spencer or Leia or, thankfully, you. Other than they are searching for persons of interest."

"The simplest explanation is they want Spencer to pay up. A billion dollars or more. That kind of cash can't be withdrawn from an ATM and dropped off somewhere."

"And Spencer isn't anywhere to be found."

"They said they'd trade me for the girl. What do they want with me?"

"Retribution for beating up their guy in Seattle? Maybe he was the son or grandson of someone important," Fitz said.

"The return on their investment isn't there. I'm not worth anything," David said.

"How much exactly is Spencer worth?" Razor said.

"Good question. From the size of the estate and helicopter daily flights, I'm assuming Bill Gates and Warren Buffett's level of wealth," Fitz said.

Razor pulled his phone out and stabbed around on the tiny screen. "I'm reading an article from a financial website saying that SCS's valuation is a house of cards. Revenue and expenses can't be what's been leaked."

"Could this entire thing be a shell game to keep SCS going?" David said.

Fitz glanced at Razor's phone and sped-read the article. "Revenues are estimated to be up, and so are costs. It says because it's a private company, information is hard to find. However, debt can kill a company as quickly as a bad product.

"Then why grab Leia if they are so willing to trade her for me without a fight?"

"We need proof of life before we go farther," Fitz said.

David swallowed and didn't want to consider the possibility Leia was already dead. "Why would they kill her if the operation cost so much to obtain her?"

"They wouldn't. Not intentionally. An overdose on the knockout drug, for instance. The dosages need to be correct, and if someone without training filled the syringe, anything is possible," Fitz said.

David hammered out a text, "Proof of life required," and pressed send.

A few minutes later, a video arrived. An awake and pissed-off Leia screaming at the camera to fuck off and get me out of here. David figured the abductors would have their hands full.

"This is not a normal abduction. She's upset and screaming at her captors. That kind of behavior is usually not tolerated."

"What the hell is going on?" David said.

"I think we need to set up a meet," Fitz said.

David received a text plus a map on his phone. "Meet in three hours. Tokyo Train Station."

"There will be lots of people around," David said.

"Chaos at rush hour," Razor said.

"Public places are good for us. It makes it harder for them to do a smash and grab if there are a hundred thousand citizens nearby."

"True. I expect to receive new coordinates once we are there."

He needed a few things, and Razor suggested a couple of shops close by. Fitz wanted time to rest. He said an old man wasn't cut out for the same activity level as the other two.

He looked at his watch. "We need to be back in an hour."

Sixty minutes later, David and Razor stepped into the room with some large bags in hand. Fitz wasn't there.

David checked his phone. No text or message. Fitz's clothes sat folded on top of a cabinet.

As the boys started to consider other possibilities, the door opened, and an English voice said, "Good afternoon." Fitz walked in wearing a long white bathrobe. "I just popped down for a bit of a sauna. Heat does wonders for the blood and constitution." He finally looked and sounded like the man David knew.

"We don't have much time," David said.

"Give me five minutes."

David turned to Razor and said, "You don't need to come. You've helped enough. I can't ask you to do anymore."

Razor looked at him for a long minute and said, "As it appears you might get your ass kicked if I'm not around, consider me a good luck charm."

He smiled. "Let's get to work."

Tokyo Station, Tokyo

The Tokyo Station handled over four thousand trains per day along with the high-speed Shinkansen bullet trains that carried residents at up to 200 miles per hour in comfort.

The guy who messaged David had set the meeting for rush hour, which in Tokyo was almost any time of the day. At the station, thousands of men and women in suits walked to catch a train or subway to get home, meet a friend, rendezvous with a lover, or just shop.

They entered the station from the south end, made their way to the Yaesu Central Entrance, and waited. Hundreds of people passed by them as if they were invisible. And they were. Three white men in a sea of black hair. Noticeable but ignored.

David's cell phone buzzed. "Lobby. Tokyo Station Hotel. Ten minutes." A vague memory invaded his brain. Razor called up a map on his phone, and the group kept to the right side of the walkway to reach the hotel.

The Tokyo Station Hotel was one of the oldest hotels in Tokyo, with work completed at the same time the station opened in 1915. The iconic structure had been designated a historic site and sat a couple of steps above the usual chains.

As they entered the lobby, two bellmen bowed. An old man with grey hair, wearing a dark suit, sat in an overstuffed chair. As David approached, the man smiled and waved him over.

"Mr. Knight, please, you and your friends, sit down."

David glanced around and didn't detect any overt threats. The bowing bellman seemed too skinny for any violence, and behind the main desk, two women in impeccable suits stood waiting for the next customer.

"Hello, Asher," the man said.

Fitz bowed. "I run into you in the strangest places. Vienna, I think was last time?"

"Berlin. Friedrichstraße."

Fitz nodded and didn't elaborate on what had happened in Germany. Jonathan hadn't been there.

"I'm here. And you are?" David said.

"Masamoto or Mass for short." His English was impeccable and with only a hint of an accent. "David-san, your new hairstyle looks good."

David ignored the comment. Mass must have seen pictures of him before. "Where's Leia?"

"You should travel more, David-san." Mass laughed. "When I was younger, I left my native Japan and traveled to Germany, France, the UK, Canada, and the US. I miss my home when I'm gone. Even though Vancouver has sushi that rivals here." He narrowed his gaze. "You didn't come here to talk about cold fish."

David said, "I'm not here for travel tips either. Where the hell is Leia?"

Fitz stood close and said nothing.

"She is fine," Mass said.

"That's not what I asked you. Where is she?"

"You don't think it would be that easy, do you?"

A memory hit David in the temple like a stone shot out of a gun. A younger Mass. Masamoto-san. Grey hair made him look older. A don't-trust-him feeling washed over him. Not dangerous. Not yet. *Same business as Fitz, with a stake in the yakuza business.*

Percentages, the memory said. He thought that Mass was a medium risk. A memory said Mass was trustworthy if it was to his advantage. *If this geriatric Japanese spymaster is here, there's something in it for him.* All the memories of Mass were here in Japan.

Mass leaned over and talked in a lower voice. "What's it like?"

"What do you mean?" David said.

"Having Jonathan's memories bumping around in there." He tapped his head.

David said nothing. He didn't want to provide any more information than necessary.

"I'd learned about Jonathan's exploits many years ago. After a Paris operation, this man"—he nodded to Fitz—"wouldn't allow me to meet him, so I made arrangements and invited him to come to Japan." He looked back at David. "Come now. You're an urban legend. A young man gains skills from an old spy. Few know the complete story. I do." He smiled again.

David sighed. "It's a colossal pain in the ass. Like a pebble in my shoe that I can't remove. Uncomfortable and unwanted."

"Most of the time," Mass said.

David raised his voice. "All the time. If it weren't for these memories, I'd be performing in Toronto and not dealing with any of this shit."

The old spymaster laughed and said, "Look at all the fun you'd be missing."

David looked at him and agreed. Life before was boring. Staid. With the occasional affair with a female dancer from the company or elsewhere, his life was only that of a performer. Music, ballet class, endless rehearsals, and sleep. Rinse and repeat.

Two years ago, he would have never imagined this. Now, the brain cells of another man bounce around in his head like balls in a pinball game. As they were in Japan, maybe Pachinko would be a better description.

"What do you want?" David asked.

"What does anyone want? Love, happiness, long life. Today, you are on the menu."

"Why? What do I have?"

"Many things. However, my goal is to show the dead Jonathan Brooks that I will never forget what he did."

Another memory smacked him in the head. Jonathan was part of an operation in Tokyo at Mass' request. He'd been asked to save one guy and kill a few others. However, one of the team was injured, and Jonathan couldn't prevent it. He watched as the kid bled, and the light went out from his eyes. The kid was Mass' son. His only son.

"Mass, I'm sorry."

The old man's smile faded, and his face was contorted by rage. "You remember, don't you? When you caused the death of my son. When I found out, you were long gone. Like all the others, you became a ghost. And I think I'm talking to his ghost now, aren't I?"

David nodded his head, and another man's tears ran down his face. Overwhelmed, he let Jonathan take over. His voice changed in timbre, and his consciousness moved to the back seat. In a different voice, he said, "Mass. I'm sorry about your son. He was covering the escape. He wanted to show you he could handle it. I tried to prevent his death and couldn't."

A flood of regret and sadness washed over him. Jonathan's memory and presence slipped out of David, but the feeling and shame of another man stayed with him. He wiped his eyes and pushed away the sense that he was responsible.

He wasn't.

Jonathan's guilt wasn't his. He didn't have to take on the burden of someone else.

He had to find Leia.

"I'm sorry about your son. I truly am. But I'm here to get Leia back," David said.

"You will see her, but not how you expect." Mass nodded, and all the people in the lobby, from the doorman to the two women behind the desk, pulled out Tasers and pointed them at the group.

"You are all coming with us for a ride. We'll see how this plays out."

Chapter Forty-Five

There was no use. No use at all. Although guns were rare in Tokyo, the gangs used other incentives to force people to comply. Tasers wouldn't kill you; however, they'd make your day unpleasant. David considered his options. He might have dodged the twin fishhooks on high-voltage wires and gotten close enough to fight the two doormen or maybe the women behind the front desk. If he was by himself, he might have tried.

Razor could have followed his lead. He'd proved his ability in Kabukicho. Fitz was the issue. He didn't want to jeopardize either by trying a take down or an escape. He owed both of them too much even to consider it.

And he still needed to find Leia.

Against his better judgment, he raised his hands. His companions followed.

Three separate cars appeared at the hotel entrance as men in police uniforms held traffic at bay. They directed Fitz to the first car, David into the second, and Razor won third place.

He looked at Razor and shook his head. How could he be so stupid to let him join their spy boy band? Yet, all wasn't lost. However, his plan to save Leia could be going better.

The cars drove away in a perfect line like a presidential detail. They traveled south towards the water for twenty minutes and then pulled into a large warehouse with a gate and rotund guard waving the cars inside. He wore no gun. Only police and government security could legally carry handguns.

Their captors had them exit the rides in a prescribed fashion. Each man had Tasers pointed at them. Fitz and Razor had two. David warranted top billing and had four escorts. All Japanese. All in suits. One was the guy that had bullied his student and tried to knife him in a Seattle alley. A bandage covered his nose. David smiled and touched his nose with his finger.

No memories surfaced about this place, yet some men appeared familiar. David knew an older one with a flattop haircut and horn-rim glasses. Or Jonathan knew him a dozen years ago.

The building looked ready for manufacturing something. Polished concrete floors, shiny walls and gleaming equipment. Not precisely a manufacturing line; more like a high-tech prison. David couldn't tell what they manufactured.

None of the handlers spoke as the three were led through computer-controlled doors with reinforced glass and heavy locks. This was no ordinary office complex.

Still no Moore, Spencer, or Leia.

"Where's Leia?" he asked out loud. He wasn't sure if he was going to get an answer.

Mass' men took the three of them through a heavier set of doors, and once they closed, the outside hum of the building stopped. No more sound. Although he was chosen for this drama, they still brought the old spymaster and an English teacher. Maybe for leverage later.

The room looked and stunk like a hospital as the pine scent of floor cleaner assaulted his nostrils. The last time he entered a clinic against his will, a billionaire injected him with the memories of a dead man. He still didn't know why Mass brought them here. If he had aimed to kill them, he could have saved time by just killing them all in the hotel lobby by the train station.

A short, middle-aged man in a white coat appeared from another door. He kept his gray hair close-cropped and wore a jet-black goatee low on his chin. Small square glasses sitting on his nose completed his look. He bowed towards Mass. "Are these the right gaijins this time?"

Mass nodded slightly and smiled. "Hai."

The man didn't meet David's gaze. Instead, he examined Razor first and then David like he was looking at a zoo animal.

"Which is the dancer?"

"We both are," they said in unison.

The man's eyes went wide and fired off a string of fast Japanese swear words that he couldn't quite follow, but he got the context.

Mass pointed to David. "He's the one."

The man's demeanor changed. He smiled before bowing to Mass again. "Thank you, Masamoto-san."

"And who the fuck are you?" David demanded. His anger rose and wanted to start smacking people. This asshole would be the first in line.

The man sneered. "I am Kando Nakamura. You should be honored to be chosen for such an important opportunity."

David had broken into the guy's condo and stole all his files, and a yakuza gang was looking for him. He might save that nugget for later. "For what?"

Nakamura pointed towards the door. "All of you out and take these other two gaijins with you. I don't need them."

"We will wait here," Mass said and bowed with a smile.

"No!" Nakamura said. "Not possible. We can't begin until everyone is out."

"Then don't begin," Mass said. "I don't care either way." He stood like an immovable object.

"Begin what?" David said. "I showed up to trade myself for Leia. I don't see her here. Therefore, you guys are full of shit."

Nakamura sneered at his response and looked him in the eye. "She's here, gaijin." He pulled open a sizeable gray curtain that hid four beds. An unconscious Leia lay strapped into the first bed, breathing slowly. Several small bandages were across one side of her stomach. A woman lay on the second bed with a similar dressing on her stomach. Nakamura's assistant blocked David's view of her face. Some kind of metal headband ran across Leia's forehead. Nolan Spencer lay in the third bed. His skin looked gray and clammy like death warmed over. Worse than when David left him at the back-alley surgery.

The fourth bed sat empty.

"Is Nolan a prisoner or a patient?"

"Patient, thanks to you," Nakamura said. "You screwed up the pickup at the airport and got Spencer-san shot. You should be happy he's still alive, or you wouldn't be."

Why is the world full of people who can't do more than threaten? David thought. "Unlock me, and we can work out this threat of yours."

Nakamura laughed. "There's no need for anger. That will come later. Spencer woke up in a back-alley butcher shop and contacted us to come and get him. You are lucky the old woman didn't kill him from infection."

David remembered seeing the old couple taken out on stretchers, still lively. He'd need to make it up to them if he made it out alive.

"Why does Leia have a bandage on her stomach?" David said.

"Her cells are important," Nakamura said. David figured it must have been a biopsy if the Hardy Boys were right about cloning.

"What's that device on her head?" Fitz asked.

Nakamura turned to Fitz and smiled. "You are all full of questions. It's electronic sleep. My invention. No chemicals. Better for everyone." He turned to Mass. "Spencer-san is worse than we expected. We wanted more time for testing; instead, we are going ahead."

"Go ahead with what? I missed the last episode of Evil Genius High School."

Mass said, "Spencer-san has a rare form of cancer. He discovered it several years ago when he worked in Japan together with Nakamura-san."

This confirmed what the Hardy Boys had found and fit the narrative of Spencer's intense germaphobia, including no handshakes and loss of weight.

Nakamura spoke this time to the room like he was holding court. "When Spencer-san found out about his cancer, he talked to me. I'm the leading researcher in genetic engineering, and we wrote an artificial intelligence program to analyze his disease and simulate every viable treatment. Our AI proposed we search for specific antibodies in blood that could cure his cancer. That bitch lying there was the first one we found that had them." He pointed to the woman lying beside Leia.

"The first one you lost, you mean," Mass said, "Twelve years to find her after your stupidity. She gave your team the slip every time." Mass didn't seem to care if he antagonized the scientist. However, he spoke like he admired the woman.

"I let the man responsible for her escape go," Nakamura said. David suspected he had let the man go from the top of a building. "When we couldn't find the woman, Spencer found her baby she'd put up for adoption and brought her to America. The baby kept Spencer alive."

The woman in the second bed moved, and David looked at her better. Another memory kicked in. Sharp like an arrow through his head.

Yumi.

A flood of emotion engulfed him, and his knees weakened as images, sounds, and smells buffeted his brain. Yumi Hattori. The mysterious woman he remembered during the ballet performance in Seattle and the only other woman Jonathan loved. He met her long after his wife, Elizabeth, was murdered. He'd moved to Japan to get as far away from Europe as possible and met her by accident. He thought she was a soft Japanese girl but instead discovered her to be strong and self-reliant. He dated and wooed her and bought her gifts. He thought she must be a witch to take him over like that. He had no resistance. Everything about her was wonderful and different from other relationships.

Here he was, a middle-aged man who found love again in a career that shunned connections. He didn't care. He longed for her touch and her light kisses.

Then everything stopped. She didn't return his phone calls. She moved from her apartment. Her email address was deleted. He checked every legal and illegal source of information he had access to. She disappeared like a ghost.

The memories faded, and David snapped back to the room that stunk of pine-scented cleaner.

"Why did Spencer want the baby?" David said.

"Daughter has the similar antibody type as the mother." Nakamura pointed to Leia. "Spencer-san had to use girl's blood to slow cancer, but it wasn't a cure. He needed time to find the mother and the last piece of the puzzle."

David screwed his face up in disgust. "Spencer bled his daughter like a vampire?"

Nakamura laughed. "Not his daughter, stupid gaijin! Other gaijin sired the girl."

David looked over at the unconscious Leia. All the time he'd known her, he'd noticed a strange connection to her. Wanting her to do well and wanting to protect her from any or all threats. He hadn't understood why he'd felt that way. He'd guessed that she reminded him of all the other young dancers that showed up at the National Ballet school to be trained every day and cloistered away from the world and their friends and parents.

She was the on-the-spectrum daughter of a billionaire. As he stared at this half Japanese, half Caucasian girl lying in a hospital bed beside her birth mother, he remembered her eyes tracking him when he demonstrated in the dance studio. She had the same eyes as Yumi. Spencer had lied the whole time. However, he didn't know the truth. No one knew the truth except for David. She had disappeared when she found out she was pregnant.

Leia was Jonathan's daughter.

"I came to trade myself for Leia. I'm here now. Let her go with Fitz and Razor," David said.

Nakamura laughed like David had told a joke. "She can't go, and neither can you."

Fitz said. "I understand why you want the women. Why have you gone to such great lengths to obtain Mr. Knight?"

Nakamura smiled. "He's the last piece of the puzzle."

"What the hell are you talking about? How am I part of your little Halloween experiment?" David said.

Spencer turned his head from the last bed and said, "I told you I needed your help."

"What help?"

"Found your...DNA." Spencer's voice drifted off again.

"Found my DNA? What in the hell does that mean?"

"You were a needle in the haystacks, gaijin. Spencer-san found you,"

Nakamura continued. "Your blood contains the third enzyme his software predicted. Impossible to find. Like a unicorn. Spencer found one match in the US Government database, but the subject had died. After another search, your DNA appeared on a hospital database in Amsterdam."

As it sank in that Leia was Jonathan's daughter, David pushed down the urge to break free, find a large knife, and gut the bunch of these sons of bitches for all the pain and suffering they'd caused Leia and Yumi.

Nakamura grabbed David by his arm, turned it over, and looked at the veins. "The blood test results were uploaded to their computer protected by Spencer's software. You carry the missing protein to cure Spencer's cancer. We confirmed when your blood was tested again during your interview at Spencer-san's company."

David remembered the HR woman requiring him to submit to a blood test. He couldn't have installed Westlake's surveillance devices if he hadn't. He should have declined, left the interview, and flown back to Canada. However, even without him, Leia might have still been brought to Tokyo against her will.

"I remember when Spencer found you. He almost lost hope when he found out the other subject was dead. You appeared out of nowhere."

David glanced at Fitz. The old Brit raised an eyebrow; Fitz had figured it out, too. David survived the implantation of a dead man's memories a year ago. The other two test subjects didn't. Silicon Valley mad scientists extracted Jonathan's brain tissues, mixed them with a radioactive secret sauce, and injected the goop into him against his will.

He figured the back-alley memory procedure must have passed to him whatever unique enzyme Jonathan's blood contained. After he'd collapsed in Amsterdam and was brought to an ER in the old city, the doctors would have tested his blood for illegal drugs. Spencer's software picked up the test and identified the enzyme coursing through David's blood stream.

But there was a problem. Even though they had a recent test and the enzyme appeared to be in his blood, it might be like a radar ghost; showing something was there but really wasn't. Spencer was betting his life that David was the real deal and carried the enzyme in his body since birth. Instead, it was jammed into his system a year ago. There were risks and their precious curing-cancer-for-money plan might not work quite how they expected.

But he wasn't going to tell them that.

"Spencer-san planned to bring you to Seattle. Even planted clues with the government to get them interested," Nakamura said. "I told him to send a team to Toronto, and he said no. His way was the best. And here you are."

David shook his head and looked at Fitz. "We got played, old man."

"Evidently."

Nakamura said, "This treatment was going to take place in Seattle until she was grabbed and brought here." He nodded to Mass. "We were lucky that Masamoto-san snatched her from Moore and brought her here."

"Happy to help Spencer deliver on his promise," A smile crossed Mass' lips.

Moore didn't mastermind the abduction. Mass must have. But David still didn't know why.

Nakamura frowned and snarled at David. "Because of you, Spencer-san almost died."

He wondered what Spencer had promised the mobsters from the heliport. "You've gone to all this trouble for my blood?"

"Your blood is the first step. We need much more from all of you. We've taken the initial cells from both women," Nakamura said.

"And what if I don't agree?"

"We take what we need and keep you all asleep with the headband. Everyone stays alive and makes it easier."

"On you or us?"

Nakamura ignored him. David said, "Why didn't Spencer just ask me? I would have done what I could to save his life."

Mass said nothing. Nakamura said, "Fucking gaijins, always not getting it. It's not just your blood we want."

David didn't feel it coming. The unconscious impulse to escape, fight back, and hurt anyone in the way. Without warning even to him, he exploded and spun backward, driving his elbow into the jaw of the closest man who'd kept a Taser pointed at him. The man dropped and the high voltage gun rattled to the ground.

David held on as Jonathan's memories and skills raged like a ball of lightning. He twisted out of the way as another Taser shot forward, and just as he stepped to land a front kick at Nakamura's chest, twin fish-hooks bit into his back, firing fifty thousand volts through his body. He collapsed to the floor, shaking, and twitching as every nerve short-circuited.

The last thing he heard was, "Get a band on his head. I don't want problems with the procedure."

<hr>

Fitz was surprised at the speed of David's attack and his ferocity, no warning and almost zero chance of success, there were too many guards and no way to escape. He expected Jonathan's memories had calculated the odds of their overall survival and took a last stand, regardless of how futile the effort was.

One of Nakamura's assistants pushed a metal headband on David's head and pressed a button on a small device. His body stopped shaking and his eyes closed.

He was out.

Nakamura had created an interesting device. With a timer, the device could usher in a revolution for insomniacs. His assistant pulled the electric fishhooks out of David's skin as Nakamura barked out orders in Japanese. The little man had taken a good kick in his chest from David, and he struggled to get up from the floor. Two larger guards lifted David's unconscious body and placed it on the empty bed between Leia's mother and Spencer.

The Hardy boys had said other parts of the body would be involved. Spencer told David that the plan was to clone the key organs and turn them into anticancer factories. However, the scene looked more like a makeshift blood donor clinic than Dr. Frankenstein's laboratory.

Fitz found it odd having so many people watching a medical procedure like they'd watch a sumo match. The doctor inserted IV needles into both arms of each subject. Thin tubes were next, running from each arm into a central machine. Once everything was tested and checked, Nakamura nodded, and his assistant flipped a switch. Blood first flowed from one arm of each patient into the machine, and then the blood was pumped back into the other arm of each patient.

Fitz said, "What exactly is going on?" He kept his anger in check and made sure he didn't act out the same way David did. He preferred other ways to seek retribution if he made it out alive.

"The three of them have the same blood type. Their white and red cells are being mixed and exchanged between the four of them. Spencer is undergoing a complete transfusion with the help of the other three."

"How will you know if the procedure is successful?"

"If they all survive."

Chapter Forty-Six

DAVID REMEMBERED the anger just before everything went black. Angry enough to find a flamethrower and fry all the bastards. But awareness slipped away, and he dove down into the blackness. He woke briefly with fever and chills, then sank back into the depths.

Finally, bright lights pierced his consciousness. He tried to cover his eyes but couldn't; they chained his hands to the bed. He decided never to step into another hospital or clinic ever again.

As he grew accustomed to the light, he fought against a raging headache and an incredible bout of nausea. He wanted to either throw up or die and wasn't fussy about the choice. After taking some deep breaths to fight the sickness, he realized he was alone.

No nurse. No doctor. No Leia, Yumi, or Spencer. No Fitz or even Razor.

Where was he?

He could be dead, and heaven appeared as a vaguely medical-looking room with brighter-than-average lights. Or he might be in hell. No way to tell until he tasted the food. He struggled to move, and he felt a sharp pain. A couple of bandages covered part of his right side, just like Leia and Yumi.

His eyes closed and everything went dark. Again.

He woke up sitting in a moving wheelchair. They had dressed him in a hospital robe. He couldn't see who was pushing him. He wondered how they had gotten him into the chair.

He and his faceless escort arrived back at the room where they had started. Nolan Spencer rested in a chair and studied a clipboard. He wore a bathrobe and real pajamas, whereas David had a dollar store version. Spencer must have pre-ordered the business class option. Leia and her mother weren't around. Mass and the team that had grabbed them at the train station remained at one end of the room like they were waiting for something.

"How are you feeling?" Spencer sounded surprised he was moving at all.

"I'm alive."

"I almost didn't recognize you with your new hairstyle. However, I wasn't at my best. And to preempt your question, we mixed my blood with the mother and daughter before filtering it through your body and back to me. If you aren't feeling a hundred percent, there's a reason."

That would explain why he felt like an elephant had trampled over him. "Do I now have your cancer?"

"No. That's the beauty of it. The blood cocktail fought my cancer easily. You are the only three people I could have used to make this work."

"I'm trying to contain my excitement." A wave of nausea hit him again and disappeared. "Why are my friends and I not all heading back to North America in first class?"

"We aren't yet sure how to deal with your compatriots."

Spencer flamed a spark of anger in David; he could see how this conversation was going and it might get worse. More nausea hit him. He'd hoped if he vomited, he might at least hit Spencer.

"I just saved your life. You owe me."

"I'm grateful and will be sure to fund a scholarship in your name." He stood up and walked around the room. David could tell Spencer wanted to jump up and down by his body language. "I want to know how the procedure affected your mental capacity. I don't want my prized assets to go all psycho on me; it might impact the outcome. And Nakamura-san here,"—he nodded to the man beside him—"expected the process to have an adverse effect on the subjects. That's why we took some biopsied key organs as part of the plan."

David remembered the sharp pain and the bandages on his side. "I can't wait to have an adverse effect on all of you."

Spencer laughed. "I see it hasn't taken the fight out of you. That's good. What's my daughter's name?"

"Are you serious?"

"Just checking your cognitive abilities."

"Leia. Her name is Leia, and she's not your daughter."

Spencer shrugged. "She's had a much better life in the US than if the adoption had been completed. What were you doing in Toronto?"

"I'm a soloist with the National Ballet of Canada."

"Very good. One last question. How could you take on Kando's men before they took you down?"

David had to think for a second. "Anger." He didn't elaborate.

"I can appreciate that." Spencer turned to Nakamura. "His brain seems to be unaffected by the procedure."

David felt like shit, but he wouldn't let anyone in the room know. He fought against the urge to pass out by using his rage as a stimulant. Still, something about Spencer sounded off after this bonkers science experiment. In the short time he'd known him, the billionaire always seemed introverted and uncomfortable. A soft-spoken, doting father without even a trace of a real personality. The man in front of him mirrored every other testosterone-fueled silicon valley CEO who leaned in and measured his dick daily. Maybe the cancer therapy included a temperament upgrade at no extra charge. Or he was always this way and hid it well.

"Who came up with the treatment?" Maybe if he kept him talking, he might learn something that could be helpful.

Spencer frowned like a teacher being asked a dumb question. "A collaboration. Kando-san is a genius with DNA, and I'm a genius with software. I created an AI program that identified that most cancers would disappear if exposed to the right combination of blood proteins.

Frankly, I'm surprised the cancer industry hadn't already discovered it." Nakamura's assistant handed him an iced bottle of green tea, and he took a long swallow. "I wrote a software engine to sift through every public and private DNA database in the world to find what we wanted. We found Yumi first. Her newborn daughter was the second. You took the longest time. I'd almost given up until we got a hit from a hospital in Europe a year ago. It appears you were hospitalized briefly in Amsterdam. What happened?"

Spencer didn't know about the implant. "I ran into some problems." An understatement. He chose not to offer anything further. He looked over at Mass and saw the older man smiling. The spymaster knew what had happened and said nothing.

"Were you indulging in their famous recreational drugs and got a bad batch?" Spencer asked.

"Something like that."

Spencer sniffed the air and wrinkled his nose. "A side effect of my cancer was that I'd lost my sense of smell. Since the treatment, I can smell everything." He wrinkled his nose again. He leaned in and sniffed at David. "However, something in here stinks."

"No truer words have been spoken." He frowned at Spencer and said, "If you aren't sick anymore, why are we still here?"

"Because I cured my cancer. Erased it from view like it was never there."

"Unshackle me and allow me to congratulate you." He struggled against the bonds with no luck; he had the strength of his grandmother, and his side ached from the procedure. He wasn't sure what they took from him. All he wanted to do was lie back down and sleep for a hundred years.

The door to the room opened, and a pissed-off-looking Nicholas Moore entered with guards holding his arms as he struggled. Trailing behind him were Fitz and Razor. All three had their hands zip-tied.

"Nick, I'm so glad you could make it." Spencer stepped over to Moore with a big smile and, without warning, punched him hard in the face. Moore's head snapped back from the impact, and blood dripped from his lips. "I've been wanting to do that for years!" Spencer said.

Moore squinted and blinked his eyes. "That was a good shot. You must have grown a pair. Easy to hit a guy who can't defend himself. Unlock me and try again." His cuffed hands reached up and wiped his mouth. "You look like Nolan, but you sure don't sound like him."

"That's because I have a new lease on life."

Chapter Forty-Seven

Spencer nodded to the guards. They pushed Moore down in a chair and cut the zip tie on his wrists; they looked large enough to head off any problems. He left the room and returned dressed in a black T-shirt and jeans. A tiny bandage decorated just below his thin biceps on each arm where Nakamura had inserted dual IVs. Maybe he fancied himself as a reborn Steve Jobs who wished he was Japanese. All he needed was the round glasses.

"Mr. Knight. As the treatment worked, I'm sure you understand we can't just let you go. My esteemed colleague needs more testing to determine the effects the procedure had on the three of you."

"What worked? I flew here to bring you back. Not to hear more bullshit," Moore said.

"I'm glad to see the real you come out, Nick. I was tired of all your ass-kissing."

"You are such as asshole, Nolan. You need help."

"You don't want to help me. You just want me dead."

Moore said nothing and glared at him.

"Don't deny it. I barely made it out of my estate after you sent those mercenaries to kill me. I was lucky to be smarter than you and predicted your treachery."

"You told me you pumped knock-out gas into your house while you hid in the safe room," David said. Spencer had never struck him as the Dr. Evil type. More a middle-aged white man who'd never seen the inside of a gym. Of course, that was before he went all psycho-billionaire on him.

"I was in the safe room but didn't use knock-out gas." Spencer laughed. He found the whole thing funny.

"Why did you kill my men?" Moore asked.

A wry smile formed on Spencer's face.

"I sent those men there to protect you. I knew your regular detail had gone to the ballet with your daughter."

Spencer yelled, "She's *not* my daughter. I wouldn't have sired anyone with a *disability like that*. And those men were there to kill me. I saw the guns."

"No. You are delusional. Yoshi vetted them. They had permission to enter the house to check on you and patrol the property until security returned. They told me they found all the men dead."

Spencer stared at Moore until he went over and slapped his face. "You lying sack of shit. Do you expect me to believe that?"

"You killed the men hired to protect you. You are more fucked up than even I could imagine."

David had had enough of both assholes fighting. "Hey!" he yelled. "Which of you asshole rat bastards kidnapped and terrorized a twelve-year-old girl?"

Moore frowned. "Spencer engineered this whole thing and killed his security."

Spencer said, "You lying asshole. You grabbed Leia because I needed her for her blood. You moved up my timetable and almost fucked up the whole thing. I was lucky enough to have my friends find and bring her here."

Mass lit a cigarette, took a puff, and blew out the smoke. Spencer wrinkled his nose and coughed. "Gentlemen. Let me stop your schoolyard spat. Moore didn't grab Miss Leia in Seattle—I did. And spent a lot of money and effort to engineer the whole thing, including having this man," he pointed to the man with a smashed nose that bullied David's student, "plant some evidence to incriminate Spencer. I would have gotten him, too"—he pointed to David—"except we ran into a problem." He didn't elaborate. David figured Mass wanted to keep his secret for leverage.

Spencer said, "Masamoto-san, we had a deal. All you had to do was bring the mother to Seattle, and we could have done the whole procedure there. I've got a lab all set up for this. We wouldn't have been forced to use this,"—he looked up to the ceiling —"place."

Mass took another drag on his cigarette and then stamped it on the floor. "Spencer-san, your associates, and my clients have waited long enough for you to deliver on your promise and could wait no further. I took these steps to encourage your participation."

Moore's eyes widened. "What the fuck is he talking about? What associates?"

Spencer shook his head. "Moore, you are such an imbecile. Did you not figure out where the seed money for my company came from?"

"Japanese gangsters? That's bullshit. I saw the documents. We have a large Japanese investor that..." Moore stopped talking as he finally understood the company's financial situation.

"I've paid them back tenfold for their investment. However, to cure my cancer, I made another deal."

Mass walked over to Spencer. "Yes. You are cured. We held up our part. Give me what you owe us, and we'll leave you gaijins here to sort it out. All this American backstabbing is giving me a headache."

Spencer said nothing as if he was considering his options. He shrugged his shoulders, reached into his pocket, and pulled out a USB key. "Everything is there. Ten years' worth." Mass grabbed it from his hand.

"What did you give him?" David asked.

"The keys to his kingdom," Spencer said.

"I don't understand. You could have avoided Leia's abduction if you'd given him what's on the key a couple of weeks ago?" David asked. He struggled again against the straps on the wheelchair. He had started feeling stronger, but still not enough to do anything.

Fitz spoke this time. "Masamoto-san is associated with a rather exclusive group here in Tokyo. There are about fifty other clans in Japan. For several years, the government has restricted the clan's operations and enacted new laws that complicate their business. Most only have a fraction of their former influence. I'm guessing they wanted a way to get back into the game and turned to Masamoto-san for help." He looked back at Mass and Spencer. "Am I right, gentlemen?"

"Insightful as ever, Fitz-san," Mass said. He handed the USB key to a skinny guy in an ill-fitting suit. He pulled a laptop out of a bag, inserted the USB key, and scrolled through the contents.

"What the fuck did you give them?" Moore said.

Spencer held up his finger and said nothing. He watched the skinny guy reviewing the data. The man talked to Masamoto in low tones as he pointed to the screen. Mass laughed and had the guy keep scrolling. David heard "good" and "great" several times on whatever was on the screen.

"Leverage, I suspect. Tactful and strong leverage. They've been missing it in the last few years, and perhaps Mr. Spencer used his magic software to find the information helpful to the clan during negotiations," Fitz said.

David noticed Mass was nodding his head. "I see you haven't lost your skills, Fitz-san. You are correct. My associates grew tired of being shit on by the government. They wanted their life and culture back, and Spencer promised us he could help with that. Spencer's software discovered many connections and information about shady deals, illegal business practices, bribery, and many instances of infidelity with almost everyone in power."

"What's on the key should give you friends years of uninterrupted peace and prosperity. Your goal, however, is as we agreed. Use just a little at a time to help with business negotiations. Otherwise, the government might get wise. Using the information sparingly should give you enough leverage to raise your influence and reclaim your business success in Japan," Spencer said.

Moore looked like he was about ready to blow his top. He glanced at the guards with their Tasers trained on him, and David saw a more measured response. "You amaze me, Spencer. I thought you were just some kind of arrogant, snot-nosed nerd boy. Instead, you are a psychopath and a fucking piece of work. You are jeopardizing our entire company!"

"It's my company, not 'our' company. And I don't care. Security software was a dead man walking away. The first breach from a quantum computer and the business would be in the toilet. I plan to collapse my investment and go in a different direction."

"Which is?" Moore said.

"Biotech. Big biotech. Adding years to someone's life is worth a lot of money. And cancer was just the first disease we projected. Our research shows we can cure just about any problem: Cancer, Alzheimer's, diabetes, heart problems, and even aging."

"What are you talking about?" Moore said.

"We discovered certain combinations of proteins form a universal key that shuts down those diseases and rights what's wrong. The treatment will turn on the right cells and prevent the wrong ones from growing. Similar to how my anti-virus and security software works. All we needed was the correct initial combination—one from the human sitting opposite you in the wheelchair." He pointed to David. "The issue, however, is the solution is detrimental to the people that provide the key. Namely, the group of the three of them."

"Jesus Christ, man. You are Looney Tunes right now."

"I don't have to prove anything to you. My cancer melted away as my body interacted with the combination of their blood proteins. I feel like a new man." Spencer wore a huge smile and then squinted twice like he had something in his eye. "I'm a testament to technology and, humbly, to my genius."

David looked over at Spencer. Moore had it partially correct. He was a Looney Tunes character, except right now, that didn't matter. From the next room, he heard faint crying and realized it was Leia sobbing to herself. He had to do something.

Spencer noticed the noise too and yelled in Japanese. A man in a white coat disappeared behind the curtain. In another minute, Leia's crying stopped.

"How can you do this? She's only twelve. Even Hitler wouldn't kill his son, adopted or otherwise," David said.

Spencer scoffed. "She's not my flesh and blood, and I don't care. Her father was just a faceless gaijin."

Jonathan died a year ago, and he wasn't returning to claim fatherhood. He half-expected Mass to spill his secret, and he didn't. Maybe he had an angle David couldn't see. Instead, Mass said nothing.

Spencer turned to David. "I'm glad you are feeling better. We have one more treatment scheduled that might not go so well. Masamoto-san, do you want to do the honors?"

Mass looked at Spencer and sighed before nodding to two other men in dark suits. They rushed to open a double set of doors. An old man looking half-dead, clothed in a gray tracksuit, sat in a wheelchair as a younger man pushed it. A lit cigarette hung in the man's mouth, and a thin tube of oxygen ran under his nose to a tank hooked onto the back of the wheelchair.

A needle-shot of pain caught David in the temple. He recognized both men. The older one was the boss of a large yakuza clan, the oyabun. All the yakuza in the room faced the man and bowed. "Osewa ni narimasu," Mass said.

Like the Italian mafia, the yakuza viewed themselves as a family with parents, brothers, sisters, and children. The difference from a real family is that a yakuza *chatie* or "little brother" could rise to the big brother or lieutenant position like any other organization through hard work and doing what you were told. A memory told him Mass wasn't a yakuza member; he was more of a consultant.

Spencer bowed and said, "Irasshaimase. We have been expecting you." A smile crossed his face. David saw his right eye twitch.

The oyabun wore tinted sunglasses and trimmed short gray hair. His face looked sunken as he puffed on the cigarette. He waved the younger man close and whispered into his ear.

"I speak for my father. As you can see, he's taken a turn for the worse and has little time left. However, I do not favor this treatment."

Spencer leaned down and talked to the old man before his son stopped him. "My father prefers Japanese. Talk to me, and I will convey the information."

Spencer frowned and said, "There's no need. I'm fluent."

"No. You misunderstand. My father will not speak to a gaijin. I will speak for him."

Spencer stepped back, his eyes wide. David wondered if he'd ever been dismissed like that.

As David looked at the oyabun's son, a sharp pain stabbed his right temple. He shut his eyes for a second. A year ago, the pain meant that a memory had been triggered. He studied the son and the father again. He'd seen both men before separately. Not together. Something wasn't quite right.

Spencer bowed toward the old man and looked the son in the eye. "A few years ago, I made a bargain with Masamoto-san, and in return for some help, I'd provide information to your clan and a cure for the oyabun's cancer. I've now delivered. We can begin the treatment."

Moore yelled, "Don't believe this man. He's a liar and a cheat. Anything he does to you will kill you!"

Spencer walked to Moore and slapped him hard across the face. "I want to see you dead. Are there any of my friends that want to help me?" Spencer looked over at Masamoto, who stared back like a statue. "What do you say, Mass?"

Mass didn't smile. "There's no honor in killing another man's rival. Especially if the man has no honor."

"We had a deal. I deliver the information, and you do this last favor."

"We delivered on our commitment. You have the mother and the daughter. I suggest you kill him yourself."

Spencer went silent as if he was considering his options.

Moore said, "You aren't as much of a negotiator as you think, Nolan. Let me up, and you can have your shot. Or are you just a guy with a big mouth and a helicopter?"

Spencer ignored him. "I will pay you a million dollars to slit this man's throat. I just want to see it." He pointed at Moore.

A million dollars. All of Mass' men showed no response and no emotion.

"Two million. Three million." He repeated his request in Japanese. He stopped for a second and said, "I will give the man that kills this rat bastard ten million dollars right now."

Mass said, "We don't want your money. Leave Japan and never come back. The family doesn't like you. The men here don't like you. I don't like you. You are cured. If you cure the oyabun, you get to leave here alive."

Spencer's eyes grew red, and a cloud came over him. David could only hope Spencer might catch fire.

The oyabun coughed violently into a handkerchief and stopped the discussion. Mass bowed his head, and the son knelt before his father and whispered. The old man shook his head, and the son said, "My father is ready. He has no more lives left and wants one more chance. He expects you to honor the agreement."

Spencer's eyes glared at Mass who said nothing. Moore sat with a half-smile and kept quiet. David figured he didn't want to press his luck. However, Spencer might try to kill Moore himself.

"Your tainted blood makes me feel like shit. How many more times do you expect to do this?" David said.

"David, this might be the last time. But your sacrifice won't be in vain," Spencer said. "That's why we took cells and blood from all three of you in case the side effects are extreme. We'd planned to clone all the essential organs to create an anti-cancer factory, but that will take several months and, as you can see, the man in front of you doesn't have time. Cloned organs are much easier from a logistics point of view."

Nakamura grabbed David's wheelchair and wheeled him near the console that had connected him to Spencer before. Two assistants moved the unconscious forms of Yumi and Leia back to their original space.

The oyabun looked at David and Yumi before taking a long look at Leia. "If you continue, the three of us will die." David pointed to Yumi and Leia.

After a lengthy pause, the old man said, "Hai," and nodded to Nakamura.

Spencer smiled. "Get ready to regain your health, like when you were young."

Mass looked over at David and shook his head but never stepped in or backed off. He and the group of other gangsters hung back and waited.

The old man didn't look at Spencer, and the son sighed to himself as he pushed his father to the space beside Yumi.

David knew everything he needed to. This was the end of the line. Based on what the Hardy Boys had found, this would be the final test before Nakamura vivisected them like lab rats. They might not survive the procedure. They'd taken cells but couldn't take their organs until finished. Spencer couldn't generate a billion dollars with just three people. Organs need to be cloned and bone marrow grown—whatever it took to construct a working process to cure cancer. They wouldn't survive the ordeal, and nothing he could say would make this yakuza patriarch change his mind. And worse was that Razor and Fitz would also die to clean up loose ends.

He struggled against the straps on his legs and arms. Filtering Spencer's cancer-laden blood through his body had drained his strength. Both girls were still unconscious, thanks to Nakamura's device. He didn't want Leia or Yumi to know what would happen.

"I am changing the order. We will mix your blood and the mother's blood with our patient here before filtering it through the girl and back into the patient."

This would kill Leia. He was sure of it. "No. Filter the blood through me like the last time. It worked with Spencer. You don't want the procedure to fail and kill this man, do you?"

Nakamura nodded like David made sense.

"I'm willing to lessen your pain and put you to sleep so you will feel nothing," Nakamura said.

"No. I'm not a coward like the rest of you in this room." He repeated what he said in Japanese. Spencer didn't react, but Mass looked disgusted.

Nakamura's assistant wiped the oyabun's forearms and searched for a vein before driving a needle into each arm; one to drain the old blood and the other to receive the filtered blood. A port from Yumi's arm was connected into the central console. They followed with a tube into David's arms. He wasn't sure if Leia or Yumi would even survive another attempt. Their last few minutes would be to prolong an old man's life who probably didn't deserve it.

As the assistant was about to make the last connection from the oyabun to Leia and back, a tsunami of emotion smashed into David. Love, anger, rage, empathy, bitterness, and compassion filled up his entire body. Without warning, a deeper voice called out from inside him.

Jonathan's voice.

"I saved your son thirteen years ago, and this is how you repay me?"

The old man's eyes went wide, and his son gasped and said, "What did you say?"

David turned his head, the words coming out of his throat like flames. "You gave me your word. You owe me his life or yours." The words formed in his throat. Jonathan's accent. His choice of syllables. Different from his own voice. Older and mature.

The orderly tried to connect the tube to the port, and the old man pushed him away. *"Omae wa dare?"* the old man said.

The son said, "What is your name?"

Jonathan's voice continued, "You had set your son on an impossible task. To make peace with a rival clan. If he could do it, you would be confident he could take your position when you die." David took a breath in and struggled against his bonds. Stronger than before, yet still weak.

"You wanted an alliance, and they wanted you dead. You knew they wished to kill you and you sent your son to take your place."

The old man yelled in English, "No. No. That's not true." He looked at his son, who narrowed his eyes and tightened his lips.

"I saved your son. I demanded to know why he was there, and you told me." David gasped as he couldn't control the voice from coming out. He wasn't sure if he wanted to. "I am Jonathan Brooks. Or I was. I risked my life to save his. They killed two of your men that night. One was the son of this man." David pointed to Mass. "And he carries the pain of losing him every day."

The oyabun looked like he'd seen a ghost, and maybe he had. "The man before you carries my soul. Against his will, I might add." He took a deep and labored breath. He couldn't stop Jonathan's memory from talking and it seemed every cell in his body was being turned inside out. "You don't want to do this. You've lived a long life. You love your son and your family. Let go. Die with honor as a man. Don't take the woman I loved and my daughter to the grave with you." David's eyes looked toward Yumi and Leia.

Spencer's nostrils flared, as he ran up to David. "What the hell are you saying? Shut up!" and slapped him hard in the face. He said to Nakamura, "Get him under with one of your devices now!"

Looking flustered, Nakamura barked out an order in Japanese. His assistant left the room.

David shook, the sting of the slap sharpening his mind. The voice continued, "This gaijin has no honor. He drains the blood of an innocent child like a vampire."

"Shut up!" Spencer yelled. As he was about to slap David, the oyabun's son grabbed his hand. "Let him speak."

Spencer screamed and struggled with the son until a guard grabbed Spencer in a bear hug and pulled him away. The billionaire grabbed a scalpel on a metal tray and sliced the guard's hand, running towards the son, the scalpel raised, and his face contorted in a blind rage.

The son kicked Spencer hard in the chest. The scalpel dropped, and the billionaire fell to the floor, jerking up and down like he'd been bitten by an electric eel.

Then David saw it. Blood seeping from Spencer's eyes, nose, and ears as he shook. The blood poured out onto the floor until his body stopped convulsing, and he stopped moving. The blood wasn't from the kick.

Nakamura knelt and touched Spencer's neck with his finger. "His heart has stopped!" He yelled in Japanese for oxygen and adrenaline and pumped on his chest for several minutes as the blood seeped from his body. He jabbed a syringe into his chest and continued to pump.

Finally, after several minutes, Nakamura stopped, "He's dead."

"He can't be. A kick like that wouldn't have killed him."

Nakamura stood up and wiped the blood from his hands. "No. I don't think it was."

Fitz said, "David's blood killed him. A year ago, he underwent a terrible procedure that forever changed him and his DNA. I'm afraid your new treatment is worthless." Fitz said to Mass, "This is over. Let us take the mother and daughter away from here. They've been through enough."

Moore walked over to Spencer's body and kicked the dead body hard. "Asshole. This is all your doing."

Fitz held up his tied hands to Mass and said, "A little help here, please?"

Mass nodded. One of his men cut Razor's and Fitz's bonds. Razor undid the straps holding David in the wheelchair.

David felt the voice and memory of Jonathan ease out of his body and back to whatever corner of his memory it had come from. The oyabun slumped in his wheelchair. The son leaned in and listened to his father talk. "My father thanks you for stopping this gaijin from hurting the mother and daughter. I also thank the memory of the gaijin inside you for my life. The debt my father owed you is now paid." The son grabbed the wheelchair and pushed the old man through the door.

Fitz said, "Mr. Moore. It appears you got your wish. I helped you find David and Spencer, and now this has all ended. If you would be so kind as to help me arrange passage home for all of us, I might forget that you spirited me away from my hotel."

One of Mass' guards stopped Nakamura from leaving the room and brought him back to the machines. Nakamura's assistant sat in the corner, looking like a nervous mouse. Nakamura was about to unhook his devices from Yumi and Leia until Moore said, "Stop."

"Stop? What do you mean? We are getting out of here," David said.

Moore ignored David and said, "Nakamura-san, you said Spencer found Yumi and Leia's blood contained a particular enzyme in their blood?"

"Yes."

"And Spencer rather horrifically discovered the third enzyme from David here just would not work."

"Perhaps if we had done more testing," Nakamura said.

"As you've come so far, wouldn't it be prudent to do a little more analysis to verify if you can find the missing protein?"

"Well..." Nakamura said, "Spencer searched DNA databases worldwide and only found this man." He pointed at David.

"That's my point. Suppose we dedicate more of SCS's resources to finding the right DNA match. Wouldn't that make sense?"

"Yes, with more help from SCS..."

"Stop this now," David said, "Yumi, Leia, and I have been through a lot. We all just want this to end."

Moore nodded to his assistant, Jacob, who pulled a pistol from the back of his pants. The guards had missed it.

"We all just have to calm down and think about this logically. My assistant here will help with the negotiations."

Now unhooked from the wheelchair, David stood up. He wasn't back to full strength and wasn't sure he could do anything. Could he grab Moore fast enough to force his assistant to drop the gun? Or could he get the assistant to come closer and make a play for the gun?

"I need to make a phone call," David said. No one moved. "Does anyone have a fucking phone I can use? It's kind of urgent."

"No one will give you a phone, asshole. Why should they?" Moore said, a shit-eating grin plastered on his face.

Mass stood with his arms crossed and frowned at Moore but didn't do anything. David didn't know what the man was planning to do.

"If I don't make a phone call within the next couple of minutes, every piece of dirt we have on Spencer, you, and SCS will be published on every channel the internet has."

"You are bluffing," Jacob said. "There's no way you have anything other than rumors."

"A couple of days ago, I broke into that man's condo," he pointed to Nakamura, "and stole reams of data that implicates Spencer and how SCS accessed DNA data illegally from companies and government who paid for information protection. I also have evidence the CEO tried to kill me, his daughter, and her mother."

Jacob moved closer to David and pointed the gun at his head. "Hard to prove that if you are dead. And since your blood can't be used, you are expendable."

From the corner of his eye, David noticed Razor's face tensing up. Razor turned to Fitz and said, "I've had just about enough billionaire assholes trying to ruin the lives of my friends and me. And old man, this is all your fault!" He pointed a finger at Fitz, screamed at him, and continued to rant. "You bunch of sons of bitches," he yelled at Moore, Mass, and the guards, without getting too close. David had never seen Razor this animated. He got close to Nakamura and said, "And you are an asshole!"

Nakamura shrunk back before Razor launched left, landing close to

Jacob. As Moore's assistant realized his mistake and swung the gun at him too late, Razor tore the gun out of the man's hand before spinning backward and driving his elbow into Jacob's face. The assistant collapsed to the floor, out cold.

Razor threw the gun into the corner of the room. "That felt great!"

Moore grunted, came swinging at Razor, and threw quick jabs towards his head. Razor blocked the punches and nailed Moore with a headbutt to his nose, knocking him back. Moore came at him again, and Razor delivered a roundhouse kick to the COO's head, dropping him to the ground near his assistant.

"*Man,* that was good! I've wanted to do that to any entitled son of a bitch for a year."

Mass nodded to the two men that had brought David, Fitz, and Razor into the facility. They grabbed Nakamura, Moore, and Jacob and tied their hands behind their backs.

"Fitz-san, David-san, and Razor-san. I'm sorry we have brought you into this. My anger at my son's death had affected my thinking, and I hoped I would get some closure. Spencer was a bad influence on this clan and made big promises he couldn't keep. I might have killed him myself if he hadn't died after giving me the USB key. Jonathan's blood paid the debt by killing Spencer." Mass bowed to the three of them.

"What are you going to do with them?" David said.

"They have all broken Japanese and American law. We can deal with them here, or you can arrange for their trip back to the US."

Fitz nodded. "Give me a couple of hours. If you could be so kind as to hold on to them, I'm sure we can get an expedited decision."

Chapter Forty-Eight

MASS and his men kept Moore, Jacob, and Nakamura in the facility while Fitz made some calls. The yakuza clan had gotten what they'd wanted from Spencer—a USB key with information they could leverage, blackmail, and pressure the people in positions of power to help them regain their way of life.

From his hospital bed, a very much alive Arthur Westlake pulled long strings orchestrating everything between bouts of morphine to calm his pain. The doctors figured someone had injected him with a neurotoxin—probably puffer fish; Moore wasn't saying anything, and Spencer was dead. Maybe another one of Westlake's enemies had caught up to him. They'd never know for sure.

Westlake arranged for the Tokyo police to hold Moore and Nakamura in a cell long enough to extradite them to the US to face criminal conspiracy and money laundering charges. Nakamura would stand trial in Japan for several felonies. Practicing medicine without a license was the least of his problems.

The Tokyo papers ran stories for weeks about how an unknown entity had hacked a US-based software company, and data around the world was at risk. The English press picked up the story, and it went viral. None of the information on cancer cures or draining blood saw the light of day. Spencer's obituary read he'd died suddenly because of complications from his long cancer battle. None of the stories linked any yakuza clan with the reported security breaches.

Share prices in cyber security companies spiked as the shark-feeding frenzy began immediately because of the data breaches. SCS customers ripped out the compromised programs as fast as possible, and software sales reps in smart suits from rival firms all expected windfalls this year. Most raised their glasses to Moore and Spencer at company meetings.

SCS closed down, and all the talented SCS employees living in Seattle were let go. However, Google, Microsoft, and Amazon sucked them all up like a big HR vacuum.

Nolan Spencer's estate would be tied up for years as legal teams unraveled his extensive holdings, assets, and debts. SCS creditors would go after his money, and lawyers for both creditors and the estate would drain away as much cash as possible in legal fees. They would paint Spencer as a brilliant programmer that used his software to pressure customers into overpriced contracts and, at the same time, broke every privacy law in the books.

Leia was named the sole heir. His will hadn't been specific, and as he had no parents or siblings that the lawyers could find, the executor and the court decided to provide an admirable trust fund to draw from.

After David urged Westlake to intervene, Spencer's estate also provided a small transfer of funds to an older couple that had given Spencer first-aid services when he'd been shot.

Nicholas J. Moore, ex-Army, son of a Boston cop, would take the brunt of consequences for selling encryption software to anyone, anywhere, or any country, regardless of export violations. His lawyers managed to get the treason charge reduced, but just barely.

He would be in prison for a very long time.

After a few weeks in Tokyo recovering, courtesy of the US government, David arrived back in Seattle to collect some of his things from his company apartment. SCS had almost shut down, and the employees had all started new jobs.

It took a little digging, but he found what he needed. After taking an Uber to the wilds of Redmond, he walked into the lobby of Microsoft's Building 112, just off NE 36th Street.

After texting his appointment, a security guard brought him into a well-stocked cafe. He ordered an espresso and sat down at a booth.

"David-san, I'm so happy to see you!" Amai, his former student, wore a big smile as she ran towards him. She hugged him. "How did you find me?"

"I asked HR, and they told me Microsoft offered you a job the next day after the problems came to light," David said. "I'd heard you had offers from other firms, too."

Amai nodded and then frowned. "I understand you had some difficulties with your travel to Tokyo."

"That's why I wanted to see you. I want to thank you."

"For what, David-san?" She smiled this time.

"Your email. I found Nakamura, which made the rest of my travel successful." He lied, of course. He didn't expect Microsoft to record employee conversations while drinking coffee, but he didn't want to take a chance. Plus, they couldn't be all bad; they provided cream.

She smiled and nodded. "Arigato, David-san."

He'd figured the anonymous email that warned him about Nakamura had to come from someone within SCS that had access to confidential files. As Amai worked in information security, she had the keys to the kingdom, and he was glad she did.

She bowed and said, "I must get back to work. Thank you for teaching me, David-san. And thank you for helping me with my office problem."

"The pleasure was mine."

David's next stop was Canada, with a recovering Westlake, again erasing any evidence of David's involvement from the official record. Fitz and Westlake had made good on their financial agreements, and SCS receivers paid David a handsome severance package that allowed him a couple of years of buffer and living in a lovely suite a block from the Toronto beach.

At almost twenty-three, David was the prime age for a dancer. He wasn't dancing at the moment and had discovered, after several weeks of teaching dance to his SCS employees, that he liked being a teacher. No. Really liked it. He loved performing, but after what he'd just gone through, maybe a little less pressure and less spotlight might be the way to go. He'd take some time and feel it out and wasn't in a particular hurry for once.

Chapter Forty-Nine

Maitland Street, Toronto

THE REHEARSAL STUDIO sat in an old brownstone bought by the organization years ago. The facade of six row-houses stayed the same, with minor additions like a large main door, but unless you were familiar with the building, you'd never guess Canada's premier ballet school lived inside. A facility with classrooms, a cafeteria, dormitories on the higher floors, and of course, dance studios.

He'd talked to the registrar and the school's principal over the phone and explained the situation. He'd taught her privately and she'd shown lots of promise, but her family situation had gotten a little out of hand. The structured environment of the school and the dance training would benefit Leia. If she passed the audition, the estate would pay all the costs and deliver a sizeable donation to the organization.

David entered the old building and made his way to the studio, where he had first auditioned when he was the same age as Leia. He had arrived with a group of other boys and girls around the same age, all nervous and hoping to be chosen. Today, a wide Japanese man in a suit sat on a bench outside the large room. An extra-large sling the same colour as his suit supported his left arm as he recovered from the injury. Leia's trust included continuity of personal services for several years.

Yoshi. David hadn't seen him since the fight in Seattle. He'd been relieved the oversized bodyguard had wanted to continue his duties after surviving the shooting at the ballet.

"Nice to see you. I'm glad you are feeling better," David said.

"Hai. Me too," Yoshi said.

"How's the arm?"

Yoshi just nodded. "Getting better." He was the master of understatement. From what he'd been told, Yoshi took a bullet in the chest and one in his arm. He'd worn an almost invisible bulletproof vest under his shirt that had saved his life. His arm needed time to heal.

Yoshi looked around the hallway. "Looks like a dojo. You went to school here?"

"Yes. Five years."

The big man nodded and frowned. "No place in Seattle she could go to?"

"Not like this one."

He knew Yoshi wasn't asking, but if Leia and the school got along well, she'd be in Toronto for several years. She'd be the only student with a bodyguard.

Miss Julie gave Leia a big smile and invited her into the studio. Twenty-foot ceilings with wide spotlights and the afternoon sun flooded into the room. Yumi walked behind her with a smile as large as Leia. She'd been named guardian once the estate confirmed she was her mother.

However, mother and daughter were more like an older sister and younger sister. David could see on Leia's face she loved it.

"David has told us you want to become a dancer. Do you think you would like to be part of our school?"

Leia looked at David and at Yumi and nodded. "Yes. I love dancing."

"This isn't a test or an exam. I will take you through a class so you can show us how much you have learned so far. Please don't worry if there's a step that's unfamiliar."

Leia nodded, but a few stray tears ran down her face. "I'm really nervous." She said with a bit of a giggle and a gasp.

"That's okay, dear, I was nervous too when I stood in your spot about thirty years ago."

Leia's face brightened. "You went to this school, too?"

"Most of the teachers you will meet are former students that had a long career in ballet before moving to teach. We'd love to help you develop more as a dancer."

Leia rubbed her nose and smiled at Miss Julie and gave David a smile. The goth look had gone. David noticed once the bloodletting had stopped, and she started having a normal life, her natural beauty poured out of her, and she became a regular, almost-teenage girl.

Miss Julie nodded to the pianist, and the class began.

"Okay," Miss Julie said, "let's have fun with it."

END

I hope you enjoyed The Tokyo Diversion. I would be grateful if you took a moment right now to post a quick review wherever you bought your copy, and/or on Goodreads if you have an account there.

Also visit my website to learn more about my other books and to sign up for my newsletter at https://tonyollivier.com/.

Acknowledgments

No book is written in a vacuum and no writer comes fully formed out of a bottle.

While I've been writing for a number of years, I'd like to acknowledge my writing mentors, Jack Remick and Robert Ray, who taught me timed writing and the importance of strong verbs and a stronger story.

Benny Sims who read a later version and made some good suggestions to incorporate into the character and settings.

DC Palter who gently corrected my Tokyo setting mistakes and Google translated Japanese dialog into something passable from a gaijin from Canada.

My super woman editor Rachel Schoenbauer, who found all my missteps, errors, tiny plot holes and grammar hiccups that I missed through my multiple drafts of the manuscript.

And to the Pandamoon family, my first publisher, who supported my work from the beginning.

About the Author

Tony Ollivier is the author of the David Knight Series - a suspense thriller that features a memory-enhanced ballet dancer as the lead character. A veteran of the software industry, including working for Apple, Microsoft and IBM, Tony leads a corporate intelligence team at a leading software company and has been writing for twenty years. He resides with his wife in the fine city of Vancouver, British Columbia.